BE STILL THE WATER

"I loved the language, the vivid descriptions, the occasional bursts of wisdom, and the compelling characters. Karen Emilson has won my interest in her work and she skillfully establishes herself as an expert in the historical fiction genre."

—ARYA FOMONYUY, *Readers' Favorite*

"This is a book that everyone of Icelandic descent should read. They will find people like themselves and their friends in these pages . . . however, this is not a novel just for the Icelandic ethnic community. The characters come to life, their stories, while ethnic and Canadian, are universal. We follow Asta in her quest to find her sister but we also follow the lives of the many characters who make up the community as they search out both opportunity and love in a new land."

—W.D. VALGARDSON, author of *The Girl with the Botticelli Face*

"Karen Emilson's style is unique and the writing exquisite . . . characters like Asta are unforgettable and readers will so naturally feel drawn to her world. Apart from the beautiful prose and the absorbing plot, the author has a powerful gift for humor."

—DIVINE ZAPE, *Readers' Favorite*

"Emilson deals with that most mysterious of crossroads, life to death, with humour, and she allows mystery and the story itself to carry us there."

—MICHAEL KENYON, author of *The Beautiful Children*

"*Be Still the Water* is a simple but beautiful and intricate story about family, a reflection on love, life, tragedy, friendship and death. With its realistic storyline, it has the charm to make any reader wonder whether this is fiction at all, along with its unforgettable characters."

—LIT AMRI, *Readers' Favorite*

ALSO BY KAREN EMILSON

Narrative Non-Fiction

Where Children Run

When Memories Remain

My Every Breath

Fiction

Be Still the Water

BE STILL THE WATER

KAREN EMILSON

BE STILL THE WATER

Perpetual Books
Box 918
Grunthal, Manitoba
R0A 0R0 Canada

Cover and book design by Ninth and May Design Co.
Author photo by Kate Pentrelli.
Printed and bound in Canada by Friesens Printing.

LIBRARY AND ARCHIVES CANADA CATALOGUING IN PUBLICATION

Emilson, Karen, 1963-
Be Still the Water / Karen Emilson

For Laurie

PRONUNCIATION

Icelanders have traditionally used a patronymic naming system, whereby a child's last name is derived from his or her father's first name, together with an affixation of -són or -dóttir. Ella *Leifursdóttir* is therefore literally translated as Ella *Leifur's daughter.* Because of this system, blood members of an Icelandic family may have different surnames.

Most who immigrated to Canada during the 1900s, adopted the use of family names and eventually the spelling of many names were Canadianized. For ease of reading, the accents have been removed from names in this story, however, there is a peppering of Icelandic words. Accents and Icelandic characters are included in written correspondence and occasionally during introductions.

Here are a few pronunciation hints:

á as in *ow* in *owl*
é as the *ye* in *yet*
í as the *ee* in *seen*
ó as the *o* in *note*
ö as in *u* in *fur*
ú as the *oo* in *moon*
ý as in the *ee* in *seen*
æ as in the *i* in *wife*
ð as in *th* in *feather*
ei as in the *ay* in *way*
j as in *y* in *yes*

CHARACTERS AND THEIR RELATIONSHIP TO ASTA

Pjetur Gudmundsson, *father*

Ella Leifursdottir, *mother*

Astfridur 'Freda' Gudbjornsdottir, *grandmother, 'Amma'*

Leifur Gudmundsson, *older brother*

Signy Gudmundsson, *older sister*

Freyja Gudmundsson, *younger sister*

Solrun Gudmundsson, *youngest sister*

Lars Gudmundsson, *youngest brother*

RELATIONSHIP TO THE GUDMUNDSSON FAMILY

Jonas Kristjan 'J.K.' Kristjansson,
neighbor, husband to Gudrun

Gudrun Kristjansson, *close friend to Ella*

Finn Kristjansson,
friend to Asta, son to J.K. and Gudrun

Thora Kristjansson,
friend to Asta, daughter to J.K. and Gudrun

Langamma, *great-grandmother*

Stefan Frimann, *friend to Freyja/Leifur*

Asmundur 'Asi' Frimann,
family friend, Stefan's older brother

Bensi Solmundsson, *neighbor*

Pall Solmundsson, *classmate, son to Bensi*

Petra Solmundsson,
Freyja's friend, daughter to Bensi

Bjorn Magnusson, *friend to Asta, mill owner's son*

Magnus Magnusson, *mill owner*

Bergthora Magnusdottir
midwife, sister to Magnus, aunt to Bjorn

Siggi and Arn Magnusson,
younger brothers to Bjorn

Runa Magnusson, *friend to Asta, Siggi's wife*

Einar, *fisherman from Portage la Prairie*

Olafur Thorsteinsson, *husband to Signy*

Oli Thorsteinsson, *carpenter, father to Olafur*

CHAPTER ONE

Where good men go, that is God's way.
—TRYGGVI EMILSSON

PALLIATIVE CARE ROOM, LUNDI HOSPITAL
JUNE 10, 1980

I HAVE WATCHED OLD PEOPLE DIE, AND YOUNG ONES, TOO. MOST endings are the same so I'd be foolish to expect my passing will be much different.

They call me forgetful, eccentric. But never a fool. I am an old woman who has seen many things. Moving me to the palliative care room at the end of the hall underlines that I have little time left. When I stop taking in fluids it will take two days, maybe three.

Oh Freyja, where are you? Not knowing your fate has tormented me for nearly seventy years. Before I go, I will make good on my promise to find you.

How will I do that you ask? Quite simple. By travelling to the past.

Before you pooh-pooh the possibility—call me a crazy old loon—remember, I almost died once and it taught me something useful. Here, we will try it together: lie back, close your eyes, and let your mind soften. Focus on the blank space. Let yourself fall into it, that mysterious place between heaven and earth where all the answers lie to the questions hidden deep in your heart. Don't be afraid, your soul will return. As I said, I've done this before.

Time to relax and enjoy as a purposeful wind takes me now, back to 1906 and a place not far from here, nestled in the poplars under a giant oak, the place I still call home. *Eikheimar.*

* * *

"I HAD A SISTER ONCE."

These are the first words I remember Stefan Frimann saying to us. We were racing along the shoreline with you riding on his back, choking him as you hung on, spurring your heels into his thighs like he was a pony. Stefan was our first friend in our new home. We met him on the boat that brought our family from Chief's Point to the Kristjansson homestead a week earlier. One year younger than our brother Leifur, who would soon turn fifteen, Stefan was shorter but gave an impression of power. He twisted the brim of his cap to one side when he spoke and always seemed impulsively interested in everything that was going on. Father said Stefan must have a bit more Irish blood in him than the rest of us because of all the freckles and the hint of red in his wiry air. He was the first boy to cause my insides to stir in that exciting way that makes girls do silly things.

We all competed for his attention, including Leifur, who would rather be off with Stefan hunting partridge or following a deer trail through the bush, not wasting time with his giggling sisters.

As you slid off Stefan's back and started kicking sand against his legs, he grabbed your hands and began swinging you around. At first, you screamed, demanding that he let you go, but soon you were laughing as your long skirt swirled around and around as Stefan's heels dug into the sand.

"Asta," A voice called out to me.

I looked back toward the barn to see Finn running toward us. He'd just finished slopping the pigs and was anxious to join in the fun. Pale as the underbelly of a fish, Finn was all joints and bone. Do you remember

Finn Kristjansson? He lived here on this point of land with his parents, the people who were kind enough to take our family in that summer. We'd only known Finn for a week but already had overheard Mother whisper that he was brilliant. In the world we were born into—despite the Viking myths—intelligence is valued over brawn.

"I'm done," Finn said, lips parting to show a set of large, gleaming teeth. "Now what shall we do?"

Stefan and Leifur would have preferred Finn not be included, even though they didn't say it, but this was his home and he so desperately wanted to be their friend.

"There is a spot where we can dig." Finn pointed up the beach. "The Indians had a camp there and I found an arrowhead once."

Dizzy by then, Stefan's one foot crossed over the other and he landed on his back with you crashing onto his chest. He lay panting, gently holding you as you flung sand in his face. Then he squinted up at the rest of us.

"I know," he said. "Let's go to Ghost Island."

Hovering above them, my soul watches the scene play out again. Finn sat at the back of the twenty-foot skiff holding the tiller while Stefan hoisted the sail. Leifur and I couldn't see Ghost Island as we set out, but they assured us it wasn't far away. As the boat skimmed across the water, seagulls hung noisily overhead and, believing we were fishermen, dipped occasionally to probe us with hungry eyes, expecting us to lift a net.

"I despise them," Freyja shouted over the thrumming of wind and sail, "I saw them rip a baby rabbit in half once and gobble it up."

Had it been Signy, our older sister, sitting beside Stefan, I would have been cross-eyed with jealousy but it didn't bother me in the least that all his attention was on sweet little Freyja who sat possessively with her hip pressed up against his, admiring his every move.

"They are a nuisance all right," he said, searching the boat for something to throw at the birds.

I might as well admit the only reason I begged Leifur to go along that day was because of Stefan. We left without telling Signy, knowing she would have declared out loud that our father, or 'Pabbi' as we called him, would have forbidden it. Our parents had left by steamship a half hour earlier to go to the Lake Manitoba Narrows store, so the boys were in charge. For years afterwards I regretted going and to this day still believe that if it wasn't for boys, girls would seldom get themselves into trouble.

"Gulls are useful scavengers," Finn said as he adjusted the rudder, peering beyond the mast in the direction of the island. "They keep the shoreline clean of dead fish and the mice under control."

"Yes, but they still shit on our heads," Leifur said.

"Then wear a hat," Finn said, so seriously that it struck Freyja's funny bone and she started giggling with such infectious glee that we all, including Finn, laughed harder than the words deserved.

Eight-year-old Freyja looked nothing like the rest of us. One evening she'd carried the Eaton's catalogue to Mother's lap, and said: "Look. Me, Freyja." Her slender finger pointed excitedly across a page of porcelain dolls that looked much like her except that Freyja's hair could never be tamed. It grew wildly out in a fine mass of wild, white curls.

When someone met her for the first time, they would stop and stare, mesmerized. I would see their eyes soften as she danced around, telling stories that evolved from her make-believe world in such a clear, sweet, high-pitched voice.

Once you came to know her, you'd see her determination. She could coerce others into doing whatever she wanted and soon they'd believe her ideas were their own. Few could resist when Freyja reached out her delicate hand. They'd allow themselves to be dragged to see a nest of mewling kittens, and would pause to wait as she picked wildflowers.

As the boat skimmed across the water, Leifur and I dug our heels into the floorboards, leaning against the direction it was heeling, as Stefan had shown us, neither of us willing to admit we were afraid. We'd never been in a sailboat before.

"We're going to tip," Freyja cried, grabbing Stefan's arm.

"I have only put her over once, when I was first learning," Stefan chuckled. Leifur looked relieved and seeing that Finn was perfectly at ease helped calm my nerves.

"We set our nets here at freeze-up," Finn said, pointing to a narrow peninsula of rock and sand they named Gull Reef. A few naked trees angled up from the scrubby underbrush, every limb a perch for resting gulls. They, along with other water birds—cormorants and loons—nested here by the thousands.

We'd heard that Indians from the nearby reservation taught the first Icelandic settlers how to fish under the ice and, because of that, those pioneers survived their first harsh winter. Starvation and servitude were things our forebears understood. The desire for independence is why so many of us immigrated to America. We chose to live where we could farm and fish because that is what we knew and, like so many immigrants, chose the wilderness because it would afford us the opportunity someday to own property, a privilege denied us in our homeland.

When it came time to decide whether to settle on Lake Manitoba or in New Iceland (the larger settlement 100 miles east on Lake Winnipeg), Pabbi was ready to flip a coin, that is until he spent a day fishing on Lake Manitoba. He returned home from the frozen lake that night excited as we'd ever seen him—holding up a large pickerel in each hand—his mind set. Access to abundant fishing grounds meant we'd always have plenty to eat and a commodity to trade.

And now, June couldn't have offered us a gentler day to travel the lake. The sun was high, the occasional wispy cloud passed overhead. The southwest breeze, soft and warm, carrying the slight scent of water weeds and fish, was distinct and so pleasing. It has been said that once the essence of the lake is breathed in, it finds its way into a person's soul. That perfect June day it found its way inside me.

Ghost Island appeared from nowhere on the port side.

"There is a cabin at the north end," Stefan said, trimming the sail. "I will take you to the graves on the island, too, if you want."

I wasn't sure if we'd heard him correctly, given the wind and hum of the center board as it cut through the water.

"Drowned fishermen," he added. "The Indians believe there is a cavern beneath the lake where spirits live. If fishermen become too greedy, it angers the spirits, and a storm will suddenly come up, the ice will break, and the fish will jump back into the water."

Freyja's eyes grew wide. Leifur and I looked at each other but didn't say a word.

"Nonsense," Finn said, still holding the tiller steady. "You sound like my Langamma. She tried to scare us with the old stories until Mother told her to stop."

We had a grandmother too, but our Amma had other ways of making us behave.

Stefan twisted his cap and grinned, motioning for Finn to start steering toward the island.

"Father didn't believe it either, not until he was lost in a snowstorm after his best day of fishing ever," he said. "On the ice just north of the island he saw something, a half-man, half-beast, standing five yards in front of him. He blinked and it disappeared. Since then he always throws back a large fish from every net, just in case."

Shivers worked their way up my spine. We'd heard many old stories too, back in the communal home where Mother's family gathered in the baðstofa every evening. Huddled under wool blankets, we listened to old Uncle Ásgeir who stood bent under candlelight reciting from memory ancient myths that had been repeated for thousands of years. I'd assumed that we'd left the huldufólk, fylgjur and Gryla—those hidden people and frightful spirits—back in Iceland.

"There is no scientific proof," Finn said. "My father does not believe any of it and neither do I."

The island grew and soon loomed beside us. Towering trees ran in a wide strip down the center of it, surrounded by a wide belt of sand.

As Finn steered the boat to land, the bulk of the island stole our wind so the sail began flapping noisily. Stefan let the lines go and began pulling it down. Looking into the water, I saw the lake bottom rise up, and within minutes the keel scraped against mossy rocks. Stefan jumped out and pulled the bow up onto the sand so we could scramble out.

"The cabin is this way," he said, waving his arm for us to follow.

The boys ran ahead while Freyja and I struggled to keep up, following a trail that wound into the trees. Being in the bush was an unsettling experience for us. There was nothing like it in Iceland. There, we were accustomed to wide open spaces, rock, and ocean. And since arriving in Canada five years earlier, we'd only lived in the distant town of Lundi. I felt uncertain as the trees closed in around us. It was dark and the air cool. Birds chirped, insects buzzed, and leaves in the undergrowth rustled as voles and mice skittered underneath. There was a terrible stench of a carcass rotting somewhere.

"Asta, pick me up," Freyja said, tugging at my arm. She quickly wrapped her legs around my waist, tucking her face into my neck. "I don't like it here," she quivered. "There are trolls."

"No," I said to her. "They do not like it here in Manitoba. It is too cold."

I fought to keep the uncertainty out of my voice. I could still see old Uncle Ásgeir standing over us, eyes wild as he warned against creatures of the invisible world that hid in the trees and burrowed under rocks by the streams.

"Wait for us," I hollered, but the boys kept on so I ran to catch up.

The shanty was difficult to see as the weathered boards blended in with the oaks. Stefan pulled open the door and we followed him inside. I was surprised by how little there was. A stove, wooden table, and two chairs on a musty dirt floor, six beds built bunk-style along the walls, covered by worn feather ticks. There were no windows, so the only light that came in was through the door behind us.

"We were lost on the ice during a storm once," Stefan said. "Good thing this place was here. We made a fire and stayed the night."

Soon we were back on the beach at the foot of a lighthouse on the north end of the island facing The Narrows, the channel where the south and north basin of Lake Manitoba met. In the distance there was a small steamship but I couldn't tell what direction it was traveling. I hoped it was not our parents already on their way home.

Leifur picked up wide, flat stones as we traversed the beach and threw them sidearm into the lake, counting the number of times each bounced across the surface. Broad shouldered and capable, our brother seldom drew attention to himself and didn't seem to mind that our older sister often overshadowed him. Sometimes though, when I looked into those hazel eyes of his, I recognized a stirring. There was more going on inside Leifur than we girls ever realized.

Stefan tried showing Freyja how to skim stones, but each throw from her skinny little arm sent the stones either straight up or down and the rest of us shook our heads in laughter. We all joined in, flinging stones out over the water.

"You're no better than Asta," Leifur teased Finn, causing us all to turn and watch.

Finn tightened his lips and, squinting, side-armed a flat, black stone and this time it skipped three times. He brightened when he looked at me.

"That's nothing," Leifur said, easily shooting one out so fast it jumped seven times.

We all cheered.

"Time to quit while you're ahead," Stefan said and we started out toward the west side of the island. He stopped for a moment to pick up an eagle's feather then handed it to Freyja. She took it and ran the smooth edge against her hand and cheek. She held it up, twirling it, but soon grew bored with the feather, handing it back to him to put in his pocket.

Away from the shelter of the east side, the wind blew much harder, whipping our hair across our faces. Stefan stooped so Freyja could climb onto his back then boosted her up. We leaned in close to one another to hear what was being said as we kicked our way across the pebbly shore.

Finn paused to look up at the sky. "We should go back," he said, "the wind is picking up."

"We will, but first I want to show you the graves," Stefan said, leading us away from the shoreline toward the bush. He'd said earlier that his father grazed sheep on the island and we could see them at the edge of a small meadow. The ewes turned their heads sharply when they saw us, bleating for their lambs. Our eyes were drawn up to a nest at the top of a dead oak that looked like a giant basket in the sky.

"What a terrible place to build it," Leifur said. "There is no shelter here at all."

"Their wingspan is so wide they can't fly into the bush," Finn said, shading his eyes from the sun. "That's why they build at the top of a dead tree."

"Look." Freyja pointed over Stefan's shoulder.

Two bald eagles stood silently on the graves, golden eyes staring down their beaks at us. They bobbed across the ground then effortlessly took flight. Their strong wings moved slowly, lifting against the wind, and within seconds they were soaring over the water. They made a wide circle back overhead again, landing at the top of a tree not far away.

"Predators," Finn said. "They don't hide. They hunt."

I felt another shiver. It reminded me of the day we gathered to pray as Pabbi lowered our baby brother's body into a grave at the edge of the yard. I remembered what our Amma had said: "There is no need to fear dead people, it is the live ones you have to watch."

Stefan let Freyja down and took her hand. Two dead lambs lay at the foot of the graves, their eyeballs plucked out, bellies torn open. A ewe lay dead at the water's edge, feet sticking up, half buried in wet sand.

Freyja squealed, covering her eyes. "Did the eagles kill them?"

"Probably the mother died first and then her lambs." Stefan sighed. "This happens every year."

"The eagles killed them," she cried.

"No," Stefan said softly, but I heard in his tone that he would have told her that no matter what.

We leaned in to read the names on three crosses, but they were too weather-beaten. Stefan picked up a fallen grave marker and wiped the sand from it then carefully pushed it upright into the ground. He closed his eyes for a moment and, lips barely moving, silently recited the fishermen's prayer.

"Did you know them?" Leifur asked.

"No, they died long before father came here."

Finn was growing anxious so we started back toward the boat. As soon as we left the graves, the eagles began circling again.

"If I were your father I'd shoot them," Leifur said.

"You always want to shoot things." Freyja pouted, dragging her feet as she looked back at the dead lambs.

"The Indians believe the eagle offers protection," Stefan said, looking up at the treetops bending with the wind. "Best we leave them alone."

When the skiff came into view, there was a sense of relief. We all climbed in. Leifur pushed the boat away from shore as Stefan readied the sail, and we were all glad to leave Ghost Island.

The wind came in gusts now and the water churned, sending a light spray up over the bow as we chopped through it. We were more than three quarters of the way home and could see Finn's house when the wind shifted and began pushing us off course. Every time Finn pulled on the tiller to correct, the boom would swing back as the wind fell out of the sail.

"We should come about," Finn called. "We need to start tacking to catch the wind."

Stefan agreed and, crouching in the middle of the boat, held a line in each hand to pull the sail across. Finn turned the boat sharply and the sail began flapping furiously, creating a horrible racket overhead. Later I would learn this was the safest moment of the whole maneuver, but at the time, I closed my eyes and covered my ears, so I didn't see what happened the moment the wind caught the sail. I only heard Stefan call, "heads down." There was a thud, a surprised wail and, though I didn't hear the splash, I imagined it in nightmares for many years afterward. I didn't see Freyja in the water, not until the boat was past, but felt the jolt as Stefan sprang up and dove in after her.

Finn's head turned and in a split second he made a decision.

"Release the sail," he screamed as he steadied the rudder.

Leifur scrambled across to grab the line, jolting it as he'd seen Stefan do, and then the sail let go and began flapping again, the boom centering in the middle of the boat.

"Pull it down," Finn yelled.

Now we were at the mercy of the waves that pushed us toward shore, increasing the distance between us and the two heads that bobbed in the waves. Leifur picked up the buoy tied to a long rope.

"Not yet," Finn hollered, looking past Leifur. "We are too far. Use the paddles."

Each of us grabbed one and began cutting into the water. I kept my eyes glued to the spot where they were, and started praying. Thankfully, our mother had insisted that we all learn to swim. Blinking hard, I could see Stefan's hands holding Freyja's as they both tread water.

We were all screaming for them to hold on, that we were coming.

"She got scared and stood up," Finn said, the muscles on his lanky arms bulging. "I should have made her sit with me."

Freyja was struggling, her head tilted all the way back, chin pointing up to the sky. She bobbed as Stefan tried to calm her down. We heard some of it as we drew closer, the occasional steady word from him, her frantic cries that carried across the water. Then his voice rose, calling her name, as her head went under. He pulled her back up but she went under again. This time when she surfaced he pulled her close. Gasping like a drowning cat, she began clawing at him, trying to climb on top of his head.

I started screaming again.

Leifur kicked off his shoes, grabbed the buoy, slid it up to his shoulder and dove in.

Finn told me through clenched teeth to keep paddling. There was nothing more we could do as Leifur swam toward them. Freyja pushed Stefan under. Up he came, arms flailing, then he leaned onto his back and kicked her away with his feet. Freyja struggled for only a moment then sank below the surface.

Stefan paused to catch his breath then dove under. Right when we thought both were lost, he re-surfaced, left fist clutching the front of Freyja's shirt, lifting her head out of the water. He turned over onto his back and slid her up onto his chest and began paddling backwards with one arm toward Leifur, who was moving through the water at a surprising pace. We'd never considered our brother a strong swimmer but that afternoon his determination changed the way I viewed him for the rest of our lives.

I made a silent promise to God that if He let Freyja live, I would never let anything terrible happen to her again.

Leifur thrust the buoy at Stefan, who grabbed it with his free arm and rested for a moment, then began kicking as Leifur pulled them along.

"Keep paddling," Finn reminded me. He grabbed the line and began pulling them through the waves.

"She's not breathing," Stefan said, gasping as he grabbed the gunwale.

Finn was right there to pull Freyja out of the water. I thought she was dead. Her eyes were wide open but unmoving, lips the color of a bruise.

Finn immediately turned her upside down like a newborn lamb. Then he began shaking her. He could have easily killed her, I know that now, but by some miracle it worked. Freyja started coughing and soon she was whimpering and retching. She began crying for Mother as I took her in my arms and rocked her like a baby.

Stefan and Leifur pulled themselves into the boat, exhausted, and flopped on the deck. They lay on their backs, chests heaving, eyes closed.

Finn began to shake and kept muttering to himself that all this was his fault, then he leaned over the gunwale to throw up.

Stefan was still panting. He turned his head to look up at me. "I had to let her go otherwise she would have drowned us both."

I was so thankful he'd saved her I couldn't muster one word.

"Nykur tried to take me," Freyja rasped. "He grabbed my foot and pulled me down. I saw his face."

We all instantly knew Nykur. The malevolent water horse that was always trying to steal children who misbehaved had tried to take my sister.

It was a somber journey back to shore with the boys paddling through the rough waves with the sail at half-mast.

"We must keep this a secret," Leifur said, digging into the water. He glanced back at me to be sure I was listening, then at Freyja who stared vacantly out over the water. We all agreed that under no circumstances would we ever tell the adults what had transpired that afternoon on the lake.

Finn and I were the last to wamble off the boat. What I didn't see then because my back was to him, but I see clearly now, is Finn stopping for a moment to bend and pick something up. It was the soaked eagle's feather from Stefan's pocket. He stared at it for a moment in astonishment and wonder, then, as I turned to see if he was coming, he slipped it into his trouser pocket.

Years later, I would sometimes see Stefan staring at Freyja and sense that he was playing the events of that day over again in his mind. At the time I couldn't see it but now I do. There was something between the two of them even then.

Freyja nearly drowned twice that afternoon, first because of impulsiveness, and then when Stefan had no choice but to push her away to save them both.

CHAPTER TWO

Be kind to friend and kin and win for yourself thereby long enduring praise of men.

—VÖLSUNGA SAGA

FOOTSTEPS JOLT ME BACK TO THE PRESENT. I HEAR THE SQUEAK OF soft-soled shoes on the hospital room floor. It feels good to be back. Nobody wants to die before they are ready, and I plan to hold on for at least another week.

Books that I've kept hidden from everyone say that astral travel can be quite exhausting, but I always feel better afterwards. The excitement of it causes my heart to race wildly; it's as if I've just woken from an exhilarating dream.

What a thrill it is to know that events from my life played out exactly as I remember them. Watching it all again I feel all the same emotions, but I also see things I didn't the first time and even sense how everyone was feeling.

But now I smell lemon verbena perfume. The woman who stands beside my bed reaches up, separates the thick brown window drapes, and I hear little wheels whir across the metal tracks.

She is fiddling with the butterfly latch on the window. I've struggled with the same latch many times. Why hasn't that blasted maintenance man fixed it yet? She'll have to push the window in and turn at the same time.

There, she has it figured out.

I take in a deep breath. The air always smells freshest in June. Somewhere outside, likely in the shrubs under the window, white throated sparrows sing. Sunshine warms my face. Small gestures matter most to the dying.

Slowly I open my eyes and focus on her face, see that she is relieved I am still alive.

"Good morning, Asta, how are you feeling?" she asks. "Do you recognize me?"

"Of course," I say. "Thora."

Soft white curls frame her face, and her eyes are bright as ever, though she is thinner than I remember. We attended nursing school together. I am so glad she has come to sit with me.

"You are like a sister," I say.

She pats my hand and leaves a tender kiss on my forehead.

The old woman in the bed next to mine stirs.

"Who is she again?" I ask.

"Mary Strong from Dog Creek."

Thora slowly turns the bed crank until I am nearly upright. She slides her hand behind my shoulder blades and pulls me forward.

"Her family stayed with her all night," she says, adjusting the pillow. "I think they went to the café for breakfast."

I knew a Mary Strong once. Most people are terrible at remembering names, but I only have trouble with faces. She could be one of many Mary Strongs who live on the Reserve not far from here. Indians and Icelanders are the same in that we like to reuse names. It vexes the English who find it impossible to keep us straight.

"What day is it?" I ask. Without my spectacles, I cannot see the calendar on the far wall. I can see Jesus, though.

"Friday, the first day of the fair," Thora says.

I lift my hand slowly to point at the four-by-five-foot framed painting of Jesus hanging on the wall at the foot of Mary's bed. His palms are up, eyes turned toward heaven, and he is surrounded by a golden light.

"What if Mary wakes up and thinks she's dead?" I ask.

Thora glances back. Rolling her eyes, she covers her mouth, letting a giggle shiver through her shoulders.

Maudlin, I know. But as nurses, given all we've seen, we cannot help but view death as a natural part of life. It never is trivial though, watching someone die.

Thora lifts a glass to my lips, but I push it away. "I can't drink that shit."

She raises her eyebrows and tsks. The same way our mothers did every time one of the boys cursed. "Now you sound like Amma," she says.

I laugh. It's not the first time I've heard this.

"Town water . . . too much chlorine," I say.

"It's not so bad."

"For washing floors."

Through the open window I can hear the cars slowing at the stop sign, turning the corner away from the highway into town. "Is it busy today?" I ask.

"It will be soon," she says.

A nurse is coming down the hall carrying a tray. She places it on the table beside my bed. I haven't lost my sense of smell yet, so breakfast is an easy guess. Oatmeal and applesauce. Black tea. No salt. No sugar. No fat. No flavor.

No wonder I'm having a difficult time thinking straight. A brain needs fat and protein.

"Has she been turned?" the nurse whispers to Thora.

"An hour ago."

"Do you need anything else, Asta?" the nurse asks, loud and direct.

"You can go water my tomato plants," I say.

She cocks her head. "Asta Gudmundsson, you make me laugh."

Good. I hope my final words are witty, memorable.

"Ow-sta," I say. The English nurses can't wrap their tongue around my name. They call me "Ass-ta." Who wants to be called that?

The nurse adjusts my bed even though she doesn't need to and calls me Ass-ta again.

"Any pain?"

"Not much," I say.

Nothing exotic is killing me. I am an old woman and my body has simply given up. Even though my appetite is gone, my liver can't keep pace. I see by my swollen legs that my kidneys must be failing. My lungs are raspy and wet, but my heart is strong as ever. It will be the last to let go. How do I feel in my head? Like a teenager. I've always felt that way, even during the dark times.

The nurse checks on Mary who is still alive but unresponsive.

"Let me know if you need anything," she says to Thora before hurrying out the door.

I motion for Thora to sit on the chair. She pulls it close and places her hand over mine. Her eyes brim with love and it makes me tear up, but I know crying will steal my energy. I push back the emotion so I can talk.

"How old am I again?" I ask.

"You'll turn eighty-eight in a few days," she says.

I never imagined I would live this long.

"We were only fourteen," I say, remembering the day we met. "Everyone was amazed by how well our fathers got along," I say. "They had opposite personalities, clashing political views."

"Oh they disagreed, I remember that." Thora laughs. "But there was always respect."

"Like you and I."

When your days are numbered confessions come easy.

"I was selfish," I say. "There were years I was so preoccupied with everything that I couldn't think clearly. I am sorry for those times I pushed you away, didn't confide in you the way I should have."

She looks momentarily confused, then smiles softly. "Do not fret. You have always been so easy to love."

I cannot help but think of her brother Finn and the terrible misfortune that befell him. Our friendship was never the same after that.

"What is it?" she asks.

"Nothing," I say, and we relax as old friends do. I would challenge her to a game of chess but that would be cruel. Not once in all those years did she ever defeat me. I smile to myself. Only one person ever could.

Thora pours herself a mug of coffee from the thermos she brought from home. I am remembering the old days. We no longer cool our coffee in the saucer before drinking it, though some old-timers in the care home still do.

"Are you hungry?" she asks, leaning across to lift the tray lid. "You probably should eat something."

She is right, so I let her push the table to my chest, and she watches as I slowly lift the spoon. It is embarrassing how shaky I've become.

"Oatmeal without raisins, what would our mothers say?" I ask.

"About this food?" She claps her hands together and throws her head back with delight. "A disgrace. I imagine they'd roll in their graves at the thought of feeding this to anyone."

I inhale, joining her in laughter.

We didn't have much back then, but one ingredient our mothers put into every meal was pride. Even the simplest foods tasted wonderful. No one ever left the table hungry.

Now the tears come, now she is here, when I need her the most. Thora pulls a tissue from the box that sits on the window ledge and gently wipes my eyes, then her own. We stare at each other for a long time, until the warm sunshine lulls my mind. I am ready to travel again.

"Get some rest," she whispers, pulling the window drape closed just enough. "Everyone will want to visit with you later."

* * *

A WEEK BEFORE FREYJA NEARLY DROWNED, WE CROSSED THE LAKE on the steamship Lady Ellen. We'd lived in Canada for five years by then in the nearby town of Lundi with Mother's cousin and his family. By

1906 Pabbi had saved enough money that we were ready to farm on our own and he'd claimed a homestead.

I still remember Mother's cousin waving good-bye as we set out with everything we owned piled in the wagon, including a pregnant sow, three sheep, and a crate of chickens. Our brother Leifur led our shorthorn cow named Skalda the whole way. The oxen pulled our wagon overland through the Dog Creek Reservation and we boarded the Lady Ellen at Chief's Point for the short ride to Finn's parents' homestead. It was customary for immigrants already established to take in the new, and since they would be our closest neighbors, they were expecting us.

It was impossible to hide our awe as we stood on the beach staring at the Kristjansson house, a mansion compared to anything we'd ever seen in Iceland or in Lundi. It was a white, two-story frame home that had gables, shutters, and a covered verandah. The front door and windows faced the lake like a large, welcoming smile.

"My God," Mother said.

Pabbi didn't say a word. This was not unusual as Mother did most of the talking. You see, Pabbi had a lisp. He told us it had made him a target in school and had been a handicap during his teenaged years. A diminutive chin and prominent nose hadn't helped him win friends either. But Pabbi's strong belief in God and civility meant he never reacted in anger. Mother was the only girl who'd seen into his heart and he loved her dearly for it, and didn't mind her talking for him.

Finn's father, Jonas Kristjan Kristjansson, shook Pabbi's hand in greeting. If ever there was a man who inspired respect, it was J.K. He looked you square in the eye while speaking in a convincing, baritone voice. "Here along this beautiful lake, anything is possible." It was so convincing, we had no choice but to believe him. He dressed more like a shopkeeper than a farmer and his eyes gleamed at the prospect of a debate. Though he was two inches shorter than Pabbi, his reputation for measured argument lifted him above most men.

"I have named the place Vinðheimar," J.K. said, sweeping his arm from the lake across the land to show everything that was his. This was a wind-swept place, so it was suitably named.

Father liked him instantly, so Mother did too. One certain thing about Pabbi was his ability to read people. It was a hard-learned skill from childhood, to sense sincerity and kindness in others. Only once did his instincts fail him.

"I'd like to introduce my wife, Ella Leifursdóttir," Pabbi said.

"My pleasure," J.K. said as he appraised the two of them. Mother lowered her eyes and nodded in respect. She had warned us against presumptuousness. J.K. was welcoming, but it was an unspoken rule that usually the woman of the house would decide if visitors stayed and for how long. If the husband disagreed, he would not say a word until the travelers were well on their way.

Both Pabbi and Leifur stood with hands on hips. Father and son, they looked at each other and grinned. The two of them were, as they say, cut from the same piece of cloth. Our Amma Ástfriður—Pabbi's mother—stood the same way, but her bias ran in the opposite direction. Fortunately, we all had Mother, the seamstress who drew us together with her fine, optimistic hand.

When Pabbi introduced Amma, she stepped forward to shake J.K.'s hand, a most peculiar habit for a woman in those days, one that shocked more men than it pleased.

He looked amused. "Come with me," he said.

So like a band of gypsies we followed, leaving our possessions on the beach for the time being.

There was a tiny old woman sitting in a rocker on the verandah knitting socks. She looked up expressionless as we climbed the stairs.

"Mother," J.K. said, introducing us but allowing her to introduce herself. She didn't drop a stitch while stating her full name and where she was from in Iceland—"Sólveig Jónasdóttir frá Skagafjörður"—another custom my people brought across the ocean.

"I have a cousin there," Amma said and the words flew between them, in Icelandic of course, since none of us except J.K. and his wife spoke English.

What is that smell? I wondered.

The sound of cheerful music greeted us as J.K. pulled open the door. That is the first time I met Thora, playing the organ.

We came in between the front room and kitchen. Considering that six children lived there, two of them toddlers, the house was meticulous. Quilts hung neatly over the chesterfields and chairs and all the spines were perfectly edged in the bookcase that ran the full length of one wall. Footsteps raced across the floor above, then two children younger than us came bounding down the stairs, halting the moment they saw us. Both shyly looked away in search of their mother.

J.K.'s wife stood wearing her Sunday dress under a spotless apron in front of the most impressive stove we'd ever seen. J.K. beamed at the sight of her as she came around the length of a monstrous table.

"Gudrun," J.K. said with a flourish, "these are our new neighbors, Pjetur and Ella."

"Velkommin," Gudrun said. She wiped her hands on the apron then pulled each one of us into a warm hug, kissing us on both cheeks. The only thing sharp about Gudrun was her mind and, when necessary, her tongue. Everything else was rubenesque, hair neatly twisted into a bun, hands soft, hips full. Behind the small, round spectacles her gray eyes sparkled. When she spoke in her soft voice she seemed to consider every word carefully. I learned through the years that Gudrun was not a woman to be trifled with and only once did I see someone try.

"Ella," she said as she embraced Mother, kissing her, holding both Mother's hands, and staring deeply into her eyes as if reading her past and future all in an instant.

Mother and Gudrun were in many ways opposite. Short and thin, Mother did everything quickly. She frequently spoke without thinking until Pabbi calmed her down. Her optimism was infectious and it was quite unsettling for us on those occasional days when Mother's thoughts went inward and she did not speak.

"What are you baking?" Freyja asked, breaking the spell between the two women.

"Yeast-risen bread. You have never tasted it?" Gudrun asked.

Freyja shook her head.

"Well come sit down then," she said, leading Freyja gently by the shoulder around the end of the table bench. "It is time we all eat."

The food packed for us the day before was long eaten. Mother clasped her hands together and bowed her head slightly in gratitude. "We do not want to impose," she said.

"Nonsense," Gudrun said as she poured coffee into fine china cups.

It was a perfectly timed dance between the two of them and we knew better than to interrupt.

"When we came here there was no house so, by the grace of God, the neighbors took us in," Gudrun said.

"Very kind of them."

"And we would like to offer the same, that is if you find our home acceptable."

"My goodness yes," Mother said.

And that is how it was settled. We would live with them that summer.

Thora and I were equally excited to meet. We were both fourteen years old and our friendship was instant. She was a pretty, solemn, middle-child who, I was to learn, was easily crushed by words. She listened with her eyes so, if I wanted an opinion, I had to squeeze it out of her. She stood back allowing me to take the lead, quite a novelty since I too was accustomed to following.

Gudrun cut the bread into thick slices then placed it on the table. I couldn't pull my eyes away. None of us could. As we chatted, we kept going back to the bread, watching the steam rise up as we waited for Leifur and Finn who were bedding our livestock in the barn.

"Langamma," Gudrun called, "it is time to eat."

I looked over my shoulder at the old woman in the corner spinning fleece into wool—J.K.'s grandmother, a sinewy knot of ancientness, stoop-shouldered with a twist of gray hair at the back of her head.

"Nei," she said quietly.

"Are you sure?"

No answer, just the whir of the wheel and treadle.

The door opened and the boys came in, finding seats across from one another. Our family was on one side, theirs on the other.

"Langamma would rather spin than eat." Gudrun tsked as she sat down.

"Not our Amma," Leifur said. "She doesn't even know how to spin."

Amma stopped considering the bread long enough to stare at him.

"That is untrue," she said, lifting her chin. "I can spin and knit, but choose not to. I am afraid I would put the rest of you to shame."

Now would be a good time to tell you about our Amma Ástfriður, or "Freda" as the English like to say. Apparently, she was a handsome woman. Men said so all the time, but all I saw were the age spots on her wide, strong hands and the deep lines that creased her striking blue eyes set beneath straight, thick, dark brows. She often used those eyes to her advantage. She took Mother's suggestion that we leave Iceland and convinced Pabbi with the intensity of a hurricane that his past needed sweeping away and America was the place to do it. Once Amma was moving in a certain direction, there was no stopping her. Most people would shake their heads and say that they'd never met anyone quite like her.

I was named for her because I was cursed with those same eyes. Sometimes Mother said I was exactly like her, which left me wondering if that was a good thing or not.

J.K. held out his hands and we all joined together, bowing our heads. He gave thanks the way it should be done, thorough and ardent, his clear, deep voice so pleasing I imagined God must have liked it very much.

There were no disappointments that afternoon, certainly not in tasting the bread—which we gobbled down—nor in the conversation led by Gudrun who filled us in on what it was like living along the lake.

"Well," J.K. said as he finished his second cup of coffee. "Shall we see if your quarter section is acceptable?"

"Sections," Amma corrected, as we all stood up. "I have one as well."

CHAPTER THREE

Ill is the lot of him who has an ill name.

—GRETTIR'S SAGA

PABBI WAS IN A JOVIAL MOOD AS WE SET OUT. THERE WAS NO NEED to hitch the oxen to the wagon as our farm was so close.

"You must walk a piece of land to get a feel for it," J.K. said, leading the way across the sandy pasture where a line of freshly sheared sheep grazed, along a trail toward a thick line of bush.

"As beautiful as this place is, we cannot hope to succeed without a vision of the future," he said. "Men who come here with trifling ambitions leave disheartened, not realizing they defeated themselves."

If his intention was to create a wonderful first impression of our new home, then he was most successful. I remember every step of that walk and whenever I hear the words 'inspired beauty' my mind goes back to that day.

Picture it: a cloudless sky with a peaceful breeze, the delicious feel of warm sun on our skin, turning hot as the day wore on, the sweet smell of grass and fertile soil, still damp from light rain the night before.

Thora giggled as we joined hands. Killdeer chicks ran ahead on the path, veering off into the tall grass while their mothers squawked, trying to distract us, letting one wing flop down to the ground so that we'd chase after her instead. Of course we children knew better, having learned this trick while living in Lundi, and took off ahead of our parents, trying to catch the fluffy chicks.

Walking with Amma, Mother's head tilted to hear the conversation between Pabbi and J.K. but she still watched us, as mothers always seem able to do. Although I was too far away to hear their words, Amma's mouth was moving since, as usual, she was talking up a storm.

Freyja climbed onto my back and wrapped her arms around my neck. "I love you, Asta," she said into my ear.

The sound of the lake lapping sleepily against shore grew distant as we neared the bush and a whole new, dark and mysterious world appeared. Finn and Leifur rushed ahead until something in the grass startled them. Finn bent down to lift a garter snake by its tail high in the air, laughing as it wound itself in a circle trying to bite him, thrashing, until he tossed it, and both the boys watched it slither away. They each carried a buffalo bone and began jousting like Vikings exploring new lands.

Finn had wanted to bring his gun but Gudrun had forbidden it, to mother's relief. But as we stood there at the edge of the trees waiting for our parents, listening to the rustle of something unseen making its way through the forest, I wished he'd brought it along. The boys invaded the darkness without hesitation, stepping over deadfall, ducking their heads as they pushed away branches while we girls waited. There was, of course, nothing to fear.

As our parents neared I heard J.K. say, "We decided to leave this bush as the divider between my quarter section and yours. To their credit, the settlers before you cleared a fair bit."

We followed the path, wide as two wagons, through the bush then came out on the other side. J.K. pointed north, explaining that the trail ahead continued all the way to The Narrows and it separated the east and west quarters of the section.

"This is your land," J.K. said to Amma, pointing to the right.

Pabbi unfurled his map and we all craned our necks to see it. We were on a point of land surrounded by water on three sides. He looked up from the map and pointed. "And this is mine?"

Our eyes settled on a wide meadow, tall grass as far as we could see. The wind pushed it in waves, and the only interruption was a little shanty off to one side near the trail.

"One mile square," said J.K.

Pabbi's expression turned quickly to disappointment. "So many trees. How will we make hay?"

"Just beyond those trees is some of the best hay land you will ever find."

Into the trees we went, following a century-old buffalo path that led west to the hay land. Being in the bush with our parents made it less frightening and, in a way, more beautiful.

Finn ran ahead but Leifur hung back to pester Amma. She pretended not to notice him jabbing at her.

"Are you tired, Amma?" he teased. "Do you want me to fetch the wagon?"

"Bull feathers," she said. "The day I cannot walk is the day I would rather be dead."

"Then catch me," he said, poking her then jumping away. She ignored him as he darted back and forth until finally she grabbed his arm, pulling him into a headlock. They'd been doing this since Leifur was a child. We all knew he could easily wrestle free but never did.

"Say I am the smartest Amma in the world," she said, rubbing her knuckle on his head. When he refused, she pressed harder until he finally relented. Silly as it was, we laughed every time they did it.

A quarter mile is not a long distance and soon we were at the edge of another wide meadow, but unfortunately we'd attracted a cargo of mosquitoes along the way. There was no such insect in Iceland and Mother said she could not believe the terrible itch and swelling.

"If you plan to clear bush, I would suggest you start here then work your way back," J.K. said, swatting his face. "The sheep and cattle will keep it beaten down after that."

We were so preoccupied with the swarming pests that at first we didn't see the sheep grazing in the knee-high grass.

"How far does my land go?" Pabbi asked.

"To that knoll. Everything on the other side belongs to our neighbor."

It took a few moments for his words to sink in.

"So those are his sheep."

"Correct."

"On my hay field?"

"Correct again," he said.

"What sort of man allows his sheep to graze another man's land?" he asked.

J.K. sighed. "Bensi Solmundsson from Skógafoss. He came here the year before us."

Pabbi looked at Mother; a terrible realization passed between them. Amma was equally shocked.

"I was not aware he came here," Pabbi said, steadying his voice.

"Do you know him?"

Pabbi's face hardened. "If it is the same man."

My memory went back to the morning we left Iceland. As we stood for the last time in front of the sod house we shared with Mother's family, waiting as she bid good riddance to it, Pabbi had issued us a strict warning:

"Never speak of our difficulties here again," he said, looking at each of us children in turn. Hanging our heads, we quickly agreed. He needed a fresh start and had no choice but to entrust his secret to us. Then he'd looked at Amma and I'd seen his worry. Amma was known to speak impulsively.

"Mother?" he'd cautioned.

She cocked her head. "Yes?"

It was always like that between them. There would be an argument, an impasse, and then finally one of them, usually Pabbi, would give in. But not that time.

"Do you think I am an imbecile?" she finally said. "Mention what happened in Sleðbrjot? Never."

Pabbi startled me back to the present. "So this is how it will be?"

"I am afraid so," J.K. said, pointing at a wisp of smoke rising up from where Bensi's house lay hidden in the dense bush. "Bensi is the sort of man who will steal your hay then try to sell it back to you. There is no reasoning with a man like that. All you can do is outsmart him."

"Then that is what we will do," Amma said.

"The air at Lundi was the freshest I ever smelled," Father said, "but here—" He took in a deep breath, and we started walking back through the trees. Everyone opened up their lungs as far as they could to inhale. Breathing wasn't something I'd ever thought about until that day, but after that, no matter where I was, I could close my eyes and remember the song of the meadowlark, the breeze on my face, and the intoxicating air at the farm.

"Photosynthesis," Finn announced. "It is a chemical process that trees use to convert carbon dioxide into sugars using the sun. Oxygen is the waste product and that is what we need to breathe."

"And because of the abundant trees—" J.K. said.

"The air is full of oxygen," Finn added, looking pleased with himself. "So it is instinct to want to suck in as much as we can."

"Literature, science and mathematics," J.K. said. "Classes will resume in our kitchen when harvest is done, and your children are welcome to attend. I have applied to the province that our community build a school, but until then, I will ensure that the children who want an education shall receive one."

This pleased Mother and Pabbi, but Amma's mind was clearly still on Bensi's sheep.

"Should we graze that land," she asked, pointing back over her shoulder, "make hay on my meadow instead?"

"Even if you can spare one of the children to shepherd every day," J.K. said, "if the coyotes are hungry a child won't dissuade them."

I shuddered. Old Uncle Ásgeir had warned us about wild animals in the new world, the likes of which did not exist in Iceland.

"I will take the gun," Leifur said cheerfully as we emerged from the bush, tramping across knee-high grass. Our thoughts turned to the squared-off log house on Amma's quarter. The settlers who'd built it had left without closing the door and had taken the glass windows, so barn swallows were flying in and out.

As we stepped inside, the birds dove in an attempt to scare us away from their mud nests stuck near the ceiling.

"I hoped to never see this again," Mother sighed as she stared up at the sod roof then at the dirt floor. It reminded us all of the house we'd left in Iceland.

Amma was not pleased. She stood with her hands planted firmly on her hips.

"What happened to them?" she asked. "Freeze to death?"

J.K. explained that the two brothers who'd homesteaded here had decided more money could be made building roads.

"Bachelors," Amma muttered. "No wonder it's in such a state."

Mother peered out the front window. "Are those fruit trees?"

"The bachelors planted them," said J.K.

We waited as Mother paced the floor, assessing the place.

"There is no bush to the east so we will enjoy the morning sun," she finally said.

"And the breeze will be cool in the afternoon," Pabbi added.

J.K. stood in the middle of the floor. "New windows, fix the door, add a large stove and it will be quite comfortable."

"As a barn," Amma interrupted, shaking her head. "We cannot live here."

Pabbi cleared his throat. He did not want anyone to know that Amma had lived quite well in Reykjavík and the sale of her city home had paid for our passage here. She often told us that she had a sack full of money stashed somewhere and was prepared to spend it.

"First we will build Ella's house," Amma said. "Then in a few years we will build mine."

"Freda—" Mother began, but Amma was already shaking her head.

"All right, then I will build my house first and whoever wants can come live with me," she said.

We children began cheering, jumping up and down.

And that is how it was decided that Mother would get a new house.

We children stayed behind examining an old pot and utensils left by the bachelors and poking our heads through the window openings. Finn and Leifur found two long sticks and started jabbing at a nest. Within a few moments it somersaulted to the ground, spilling out four chicks. Dazed and half-dead from the fall they let out a few squawks then grew quiet. Morbid curiosity drew us all close and we stood staring at their rubbery transparent bodies, all blue-veined and bulgy-eyed. Every bit of energy went into their beating hearts, overly large and thumping hard in their chests.

By the time we realized what Finn was about to do it was too late.

A second later, Leifur raised his foot to stomp on the other chicks.

"Stop it," I screamed, but his foot came down again to make sure the birds were dead.

"If we don't kill them then they will come back to nest," Finn said. "You will be overrun in no time."

Freyja started crying. Finn picked up one of the limp birds and dangled it in front of her until she ran out the door. He turned to me, bringing the bird close to eye level and I stood there until I couldn't stand it any longer. Forgetting the first rule of playing with boys—never let them see your fear—I ran out, screaming for Mother.

Thinking something terrible must have happened, she reeled around.

"They are killing the baby birds," Freyja cried.

"I am tired of your hysterics," she scolded, waving an angry finger.

"But Mama—"

"Hush."

"But they—"

"There are too many birds."

"It is so cruel," I said coming to Freyja's defense.

"There is no point, Asta," Mother sighed. "Boys do what their friends do regardless of what we say."

"But you can make them stop."

"I cannot force empathy on them, they must learn that on their own," she said.

Father and J.K. were deep in conversation and Amma was leaning in so that she wouldn't miss a single word.

"The well is over there," J.K. said pointing to a dark patch of grass not too far from the shanty. "I have tasted the water and it is exceptional."

We walked across Amma's land until we came to the end of it, then started back in the direction of J.K.'s house, this time across the open prairie leading to the lake.

"How many sheep can we graze on Mother's quarter?" Father asked.

"At least 100."

Our parents beamed. 'Paradise' was one of the first English words we learned.

"How I wish *my* Freyja were here," Mother whispered, looking up at Pabbi. He wrapped his arm around her shoulder, squeezing her in close.

"Soon," he said. "We will send for your sister very soon."

A week later, on the morning Freyja nearly drowned, our parents stood on the dock waiting as the Lady Ellen blew its horn and turned into the bay. It would take them to The Narrows where J.K. and Gudrun would buy a few supplies and introduce them to others in this growing community.

"Do not eat anything," Mother said before they left.

"Do not touch the gun," Pabbi told Leifur.

"Do not go in the water," Amma warned.

They had not cautioned against going sailing, but as we sat there waiting for their return, I was overwhelmed with guilt.

"Remember," Leifur scowled as we watched the Lady Ellen chugging into view. "Don't say one word."

CHAPTER FOUR

For with law shall our land be built up and settled,
and with lawlessness wasted and spoiled.
—NJÁL'S SAGA

MARY STRONG'S FAMILY HAS RETURNED. I AM JARRED AWAKE BY the flop-drag-flop of a teenager's tennis shoes across the floor and the sweet, clear voice of the two-year-old girl holding her hand. A month ago these sounds were annoying, but now they serve as a reminder that the world will continue on long after I am gone.

"Shhhh," Mary's daughter says to them. Embarrassed, the teenager sees I have opened my eyes and looks away self-consciously. I would too, if my hair looked like hers. Permed like a poodle, it is ridiculous.

I chuckle to myself. More likely she is made uncomfortable by the sight of me. Crumpled old crone, legs bare, misshapen feet that have walked more miles than hers ever will. Better to look away than stare like the two-year-old who holds a homemade card to her chest.

Thora waves to the little one. She stares back wordlessly, her intense black eyes framed beautifully by raven straight hair clipped even with her chin.

The teenager startles when she sees the giant picture of Jesus. She pokes her mother in the arm and they both whisper and giggle. The two-year-old is too short to see Him. Thora coaxes a wave from the toddler before the teenager lifts her up, crushing the card.

"Why are they called tennis shoes?" I ask. "Nobody plays tennis."

Amused, Thora lays the newspaper on her lap.

"Running shoes," she says. "That's what the kids call them."

"She should lace them up," I say a little too loudly.

Thora opens her mouth to explain, but I wave it off.

I know, I know. It is the style. Tell me, when did the world become such a trivial place? Those new, acrylic-rimmed spectacles overpower Thora's face. I know they are called 'glasses' now but I can't get used to it. Life has changed so much my old brain resists. I despise that I have become intolerant, but cannot help myself.

"And they are 'children,'" I remind her. "Kids are baby goats."

Thora takes the glasses off, folds the arms. We watch as the two-year-old leans down to slap the card onto Mary's thigh.

More people come shuffling up the hallway. A skinny, pigeon-toed teenaged boy wearing a Dog Creek Chiefs baseball cap jams his hands into his pockets and waits for the heavy-set middle-aged man to lead the ancient one into the room. This is a painfully slow process. The old man focuses on each step, pushing a walker, glancing up to see how much farther. The teenager hesitates in the doorway, overwhelmed by all the age in the room. He pokes his head in and brightens when he sees the teenaged girl. Relief. Someone he can relate to.

I have watched people in hospitals most of my life.

The middle-aged man has no choice but to acknowledge us, while the old man only pauses to push up his spectacles then continues to Mary's bedside—and I see it: their whole life together reduced to a final few days.

"Bet?" I whisper to Thora.

She frowns and cocks her head, uncertain what I mean. How could she forget? I chuckle to myself. I have accepted the fact my memory is not what it used to be. So should they.

"The rally," I hint. "Will she or won't she?"

Thora shrugs, taking away all my fun.

It is an unexplained phenomenon that nurses and hospice workers see, how oftentimes the dying will inexplicably start to feel better, wake up, and sometimes get out of bed when they haven't done so in days. We call it the rally. It lasts for a few hours, days or sometimes even a week. There is no science behind predicting who will rally and who won't.

"She will," I say, feeling a tug of hope for her husband who's beside her now. The daughter quickly stands up, takes his arm, and encourages him to sit. He refuses in their mother tongue, Saulteaux. His words are high-pitched, faint. Seventy years of memories have grabbed him by the throat. The children respectfully step back, staring at their shoes. He shakes and tears trickle as he talks to Mary. He wipes his nose with his jacket cuff.

This reminds me that my days left on earth are limited. My dying wish is to know what happened to Freyja so I can tell my siblings.

"I need to sleep," I say to Thora and close my eyes.

* * *

LEIFUR TOOK THE LEAD AS WE FOLLOWED THE ADULTS TO THE house, asking questions about their day as if nothing had jolted ours. Our older sister Signy came out onto the verandah and frowned. If she knew we'd been in the boat, she would tell Mother. Older than Leifur by two years, Signy was the compass that kept us all navigating in the right direction. She was beautiful and direct, shockingly hot-tempered, and seldom it was that a boy didn't look at her twice. She ignored those glances and not one potential teenage suitor ever summoned the courage to pursue her, much to Pabbi's delight.

"Must you carry her everywhere?" Signy asked me.

Freyja annoyed Signy more than the rest of us. Normally Mother would have scolded her for harassing us, but she seemed unusually tired.

"That is a fine store at The Narrows," Mother said, handing Signy a bag of coffee, then she thanked her for making supper as the aroma of roasting meat wafted out the door.

Amma was gay as a schoolgirl, schottisching across the yard with a man half her age on her arm. She and Ásmundur, or 'Asi' as he was called, were still laughing at an earlier joke.

Asi was the ship's captain. Experienced. Confident. In control. He was rammy as a young ox, thirty-two years old and so full of energy he could barely contain it. He hammered his way into the kitchen, his presence filling every empty inch of the room.

"Come here, little brother," he said, pulling Stefan in close for a rough, playful exchange that shook them both. "So what sort of trouble did you get yourself into today?" he asked, eyes smiling. Then he tossed his cap on the floor and ran a thick, calloused hand through his hair.

"Not much," Stefan said. "Went in the bush, swam a bit, played on the beach."

All true.

Asi remembered each of us children by name, messing our hair as we walked past. We were delighted when he reached into his pocket then tossed a handful of horehound candies into the air, laughing as we all scrambled to catch them. It has been said that if you treat children with kindness they will think well of you no matter what else you might do. And they say that women are attracted to a certain type of man and there is no changing it. I see now how Amma's flirting embarrassed Pabbi.

Subdued, Finn sat down with a book while Leifur fidgeted by the window. Thora came down the stairs with her youngest siblings who wiped the sleep from their eyes.

The dead giveaway that something was wrong was Freyja's silence.

Lying was a terrible sin. A lie by omission made the devil grin. I peeked at Amma, but only for a moment. She sensed something was amiss but did not say a word.

Thankfully, Asi was distracting everyone. "Did you get all those books unpacked?" he asked Pabbi.

"They are in the barn."

Asi laughed as he shook his head. "If an Icelander ever came without a wagonload of books I'd ask to see his immigration papers," he said.

"Probably be an Irishman."

Then he looked at Amma. "So, where is that daughter you promised me?"

She laughed, eyes sparkling.

"You don't have one?" he said, feigning disappointment. "Too bad, I am looking for a wife. You might want to consider it."

Mother rolled her eyes. "There will be no living with her now," she said under her breath to Gudrun, who chuckled.

"Do you have any snuff?" Amma asked.

Pabbi squirmed as Asi quickly took a tin from his pocket, twisted it open and held it out. Amma took a pinch then inhaled it up her nose and he did the same.

"When will the lumber be ready?" Asi asked as he sat down.

"In a week," Pabbi said. "Magnus seems like a fair man to deal with."

"He is. And not a bad business partner."

Asi explained that the area was expanding. Their freighting contracts were increasing and so was the demand for lumber.

"Magnus has fifteen men hired at the mill, including his sons," he said.

Pabbi was impressed. "Sounds like a solid business."

Asi agreed. "I would buy it from him but he wants to give his sons a chance first. The oldest doesn't seem interested and of the three boys he is the only one with the brains to make a go of it."

Gudrun and Mother joined everyone around the table and began passing around food.

I loved the chatter of young and old, children playing on the floor, meat cooking on the stove, utensils on the hard table, the whir of the spinning wheel, the smell of coffee—those simple comforts that were the backdrop to our everyday lives.

"Where do you plan to build?" Asi asked, handing a plate of meat to Pabbi.

"On Mother's meadow, near the shanty," he said, forking a piece of mutton onto his plate. "I plan to turn it into a barn."

Asi thought carefully. "I don't like giving another man advice, but during the flood of 1882 that meadow was under water," he said. "The trail that leads overland to The Narrows divides your quarters and is the start of a ridge. You can barely see it, but your land is higher than Freda's. The water will never rise there."

Pabbi was listening hard. So was Amma.

"If it were me I would build straight north of here," he said, pointing his arm like an arrow toward Pabbi's quarter. "It was never leased until now. Everyone was discouraged by the trees."

"Then where do I build my house?" Amma asked.

"On the same ridge."

"The rules say there must be a house on every quarter."

"A foolish rule," Asi said, forking food into his mouth. "Made by people who don't understand the lake."

"I applied for that quarter and so did Bensi," J.K. said. "I outlined a plan to start clearing the bush but the government refused. If we are going to expand our farms, the homestead rule needs to change."

"Trees do not grow on wet land," Asi said. "Find yourself a hundred-year-old oak to build beside and you'll never be flooded out."

I think this last observation convinced Pabbi what he needed to do.

Gudrun lifted the coffee sock from the pot then filled everyone's cup. Each of them poured a bit onto their saucers and waited for it to cool. Gudrun must have noticed how I couldn't take my eyes off the hálfmánar cookies. They were made in the shape of a half moon and stuffed with sweet prune filling. She passed around the plate. We all took one, except Asi, who took two.

"You have a lot of work ahead of you," he said, eating an entire cookie in one bite.

Pabbi looked at Mother. "I cannot imagine attempting this without Leifur," he said, draining his saucer.

Signy's expression always reflected her thoughts. I saw her hurt and Gudrun, at the end of the table, must have as well.

J.K. glanced at Finn and his young sons who'd finished eating and were wrestling on the floor.

"While I cannot imagine what it would be like to have only boys," Gudrun said. "Not only do they get twice as dirty, but they eat three times as much."

"And no help in the kitchen," Mother added, bringing us children into the conversation.

Our parents sat back to enjoy the debate that followed as the girls raised their voices against the boys as each made a case in favor of who contributed more.

"I can work just as hard as Leifur," Signy said.

Leifur, who was at least an inch taller, scoffed.

Signy punched him in the arm and he shoved her back.

"Everyone is expected to work within their capabilities," Gudrun said, ending the debate. Mother agreed.

"We came to America for the girls," Amma announced. "Here they can achieve their heart's desire."

It would take many years before I understood why Amma said this.

In Iceland we'd heard stories about the Indians and wondered if what old Ásgeir had said was true. J.K. now broached the subject. Both Asi and J.K. had a solid respect for the people who'd lived here for thousands of years before we came.

"The buffalo calved here and grazed these meadows on the point, moving further inland during the rut," J.K. said. "In late harvest, when the Indians needed meat, they would chase the beasts back to where they felt safe, but once surrounded by water, they had no place to go."

"Very clever," Pabbi said.

"Indeed. The lies about Indians were intended to put fear in our hearts so we would not leave Iceland," J.K. said. "What we were never told is how they brought meat to the doors of starving settlers."

"Despite being cheated by greedy white men," Gudrun added.

"I know how that feels," Mother said, telling how she was still smarting over the fact she'd purchased first class tickets believing it would improve everyone's chances of surviving the trip. She was eight months pregnant when we left Iceland and her mother was in frail health. The added cost meant leaving her teenaged sister behind. What Mother had not known then was that there was good money to be made tricking emigrants. We ended up in the bottom deck of a cattle barge. Her mother died and was buried at sea, and Mother never forgave the agent for deceiving her.

"The Indians tell a similar story," J.K. said as he got up from the table. He opened the cupboard and took out a ceramic jug. "It is to their credit they treat us as well as they do."

Mother and Gudrun shared a glance. Neither woman touched alcohol, but allowed the men an occasional drink.

"Pjetur?" J.K. said to Pabbi, holding up the jug.

Pabbi nodded.

"Bring me a glass too," Amma said.

Mother tsked but Amma ignored her.

"We should look at ourselves before speaking ill of the Indians," Gudrun said. "Truth be told, many of us who came here were lice ridden as well."

"And I know of many an Icelander who cannot hold his drink," Asi said, taking a glass from J.K., raising it to his lips. "Fortunately I am not one of them."

"But our neighbor Bensi is," Finn chimed in from where he sat at the far end of the table. "I have seen him tight as a whistle."

"Yes, but you will never see him take a drink," J.K. said. "Claims to be God-fearing."

Asi snorted. "Thinks he is above all the Indians and most Icelanders as well."

"I take it you disagree?" Mother said.

"Unfortunately there are men who lie and cheat. The trick is learning who they are."

Pabbi opened his mouth to say something but Amma interrupted.

"Tell us more," she said, taking a sip from her glass.

The room fell quiet as Gudrun spoke silently to J.K. with her eyes, warning against too much gossip.

"I suppose we are all land hungry, but Bensi more than most," he said. "He will stop at nothing to get what he wants. He was cruel to the bachelors before you, and I question how he treats his own family."

More silence except for the creak as Asi shifted in his chair.

"He holds onto the old ways," J.K. said. "He follows the rigid strictures of the Norwegian Lutheran Church."

We understood what that meant. Our parents had tried to shield us from the reality that not all men indulged children as Pabbi did. The memory was still vivid of the time they left us alone with Uncle Ásgeir.

Amma had sold her house in Reykjavík in preparation for our journey so she was living with us, and Leifur had thrown a rock and broken a window. Uncle Ásgeir beat him with a rod and it was a terrible thing to see. The very act of beating seemed to make Ásgeir even angrier and, when he was done, he grabbed Leifur by the hair and forced him to kiss the rod, just as Amma came galloping into the yard. She jumped off her pony, picked up a stick and hit Uncle Ásgeir across the back. There was much cursing between them as they circled each other, Ásgeir calling Amma names as she threatened to hit him again. I am sure she would have if our aunt hadn't intervened.

"What is a 'whore'?" I'd asked Father that night. He became so outraged I didn't ask again.

Asi was a wonderful gossip so he picked up where J.K. left off.

"Bensi's two older girls disappeared," he said, sipping slowly from his glass.

"What happened to them?"

Asi shrugged. "Nobody knows."

Pabbi looked perplexed, almost relieved. He and Mother exchanged a quick glance and seemed to be thinking the same thing.

Gudrun stood to remove her apron. She hung it from a hook on the wall. "When we were living there I did witness Bensi beating the eldest girl for talking to a boy," she said as she sat back down.

"I heard one of the bachelors put a curse on his land before he left," Asi said.

Amma perked right up. There was nothing she loved more than a good curse. "Good for them, tell us more."

Asking a question about the invisible world was unheard of amongst those who considered themselves civilized in Iceland. But our Amma did it all the time. Also she was breaking the rule to never talk about curses, lest the misfortune happen to you.

With everyone listening, Asi replied carefully. "Hasn't gone well for him since. First the girls disappeared, then he was nearly killed when a tree fell on him."

Though Langamma was nearly blind, her hearing was sharp. She began to tsk and shake her head. She spoke in Icelandic and, with no direct translation, it has taken me this long to put into English what she said. It went something like this: When you do something wrong, it follows you around while fate waits for the chance to even the score.

"Langamma . . ." J.K. warned.

"Nei," she howled, her teeth rattling as she spoke. She concentrated on the wool strand, not allowing the foot pedal to break stride. "I have seen many truths."

Signy's eyes widened and we shared a sisterly moment, each of us knowing there would be much whispering later when we were alone.

"One thing I do give Bensi credit for," said J.K., "is how he treats his sheep. He is an excellent farmer who has a fine flock."

"His sheep are no better than ours," Finn said.

"He has put far more time and expense into his animals than I have," J.K. argued. "He has fine ewes and two purebred rams that were shipped all the way from Ontario."

"But you dislike him," Finn said.

"I do. But it is important to know that even the most disagreeable man is agreeable in some ways. Also he was kind to us initially and I cannot forget that. It is only fair to give credit when it is due."

Finn's cheeks flushed a bit. "He is a terrible man."

J.K. smiled. "His sheep would disagree."

"It troubles me that he always carries that gun," Gudrun said. "He says it is to kill wolves but I'm not convinced."

"The challenge with a wolf," J.K. said, lifting the jug to splash a bit more in everyone's glass, "is that you never see him, only evidence of where he's been. There is one that eludes me, has taken a few sheep—even killed Finn's dog—but I have not seen him once."

His words sent a shudder through all of us.

"Are you talking about Bensi or the wolf?" Leifur asked.

We all laughed at that, everyone except Finn, whose eyes went inward to a faraway place.

"Well he won't kill our dog," Freyja piped up, lifting the mood in the room. "We don't have one!"

Relaxing under the influence of J.K.'s brew, the adults let the subject of Bensi rest and began discussing the lake and the land.

Our family slept in the room at the back of the house. My parents never would have spoken so freely had they known I was still awake.

"He cannot be the same Bensi," Mother whispered into the dark.

"I believe you are correct," Pabbi whispered back. "The Bensi I knew had only sons."

The room was quiet for a moment. I was starting to doze when Pabbi spoke again.

"I pray to God they don't find out. What would they think of me then?"

"How will they?" Mother asked. "We did not come here as refugees. It is obvious you are an educated man."

"I know," he said, letting his thoughts trail off.

"Stop worrying," she said. "God is watching over us. You said so yourself."

Young men nowadays would shake their heads if they saw how Pabbi and Leifur set off the next morning, leading the oxen, carrying only two axes, a handsaw and steel bars. Mother and I stood on the verandah watching them leave.

"Your father decided to build on the ridge," she said, face tight with concern. "I hope he knows what he is doing."

All afternoon as we washed clothes and helped Gudrun bake and cook, Mother stole quick, worried glances out the window at the trail that led to our land.

With a dinner sack over my shoulder I ran along the bush trail with imaginary ghosts nipping at my heels. I arrived breathless and relieved to see their smiling faces as they wiped sweat from their brows.

Pabbi and Leifur had stepped out a blettur, the area they planned to clear. Young poplars surrounded a giant oak that towered 50 feet overhead. It was perfectly shaped, limbs growing out in all directions. Pabbi tried to wrap his arms around it but his hands did not touch.

"We will leave it until last," he said.

It was muggy and hot and the oxen stood grazing, their muscles shivering away the flies, tails swatting the mosquitoes that swarmed up from the damp grass.

Legs apart, Pabbi braced himself, swung the axe back taking out the first chunk of a mature poplar. Standing opposite, it was Leifur's turn. Then Pabbi, Leifur, Pabbi, and they continued like this until the tree toppled, and then we sat under the giant oak to eat dinner, enjoying the cool breeze.

"This will be a peaceful home when we are done," Pabbi said, relaxing only long enough to finish a sandwich and drink coffee directly from the jar I pulled out of the sack. Leifur took a deep breath and steeled himself as they went back to work while I ran back to Vinðheimar.

That evening darkness rolled in from the bush, drawing in around the house. Through the kitchen window we saw their shadows as they led the oxen home, and we hurried out to greet them.

"Supper is ready," Mother said. "Go inside, I'll put the oxen in the barn."

Pabbi protested but Mother already had the reins slipped from his tired hands.

"Thora and I picked a pail of Saskatoons," I said. The berries grew thick at the edge of the bush and already were our new, preferred fruit.

"Gudrun showed me how to make a pie," Signy said.

"Good girls," Pabbi said, slowly lifting a hand to rest it heavily on my shoulder.

"Did you eat it all?" Leifur asked.

"No, we were waiting for you," Signy said.

"Are you going to give me your piece?"

A quarrel brewed between them even in exhaustion.

"You can have mine," I offered, hoping to keep their banter from escalating into a full-blown fight.

Gudrun's family was already fed so they sat in the front room. J.K. looked up from his book as we came inside.

Pabbi shook his head. "To think we longed for trees in Iceland."

"I am sorry," J.K. said. "Finn and I cannot help you until we finish building the fence. It is the only way to keep Bensi's sheep out of my field."

Father waved it off, but Leifur shot Finn a jealous look. Building a split rail fence was far easier than felling trees.

Amma stood at the kitchen table holding a pot. "Come eat," she said, scooping food onto their plates. "I told Ella that dinner she packed for you today would never be enough."

Mother came in wiping her hands on her apron.

"Well now at least we have firewood," Pabbi said. "We would have chopped down more, but prying out those roots took most of the day."

Leifur said nothing as he dug into the stew. Pabbi explained again that if they didn't get the roots out the poplars would grow back.

"I don't see how," Leifur argued.

"They will find a way."

Leifur shook his head. "We are wasting our time. It isn't going to flood again."

"Asi would not have recommended it without reason," Pabbi said. "I trust that man. His family has lived here a long time."

"Easy for him to say," Leifur grumbled.

Mother scolded him, but Pabbi didn't say another word.

Leifur sighed as he reached for the pie. "I know one thing for certain. No matter how much they pay me, I will never work at the mill," he said, digging in his fork, sliding a piece onto his plate. "I am never cutting down trees again. Please, Pabbi, can't we just build by the barn?"

Pabbi answered with his silence.

Everyone saw how annoying Leifur's complaining had become.

"Being a ship's captain, that is what I'll do," he said. "It is easy work."

Amma snorted, having heard enough. She lifted his plate into the air. "You sound just like Soli. He had the same attitude. Never made anything of himself."

We all fell silent. You see none of us had ever heard our grandfather's name before. All we knew is that he was a drunken scoundrel.

"I never met a lazy man who wasn't a coward also," Amma said, digging her fork into the pie.

J.K. and Gudrun, who'd been pretending they weren't listening, looked up.

"I'm not a coward." Leifur sniffed, cheeks growing pink as he glanced at Finn whose eyes sparkled with delight. "And I'm not lazy."

Amma laughed and shook her head in a most sorrowful way. "I didn't think you were either," she said, finishing his pie.

CHAPTER FIVE

Every man must plough his own furrow.
—VÁPNFIRÐINGA SAGA

THE NEXT MORNING AMMA CAME INTO GUDRUN'S KITCHEN WEARING an old shirt and a pair of Pabbi's pants. She sat down humming to herself as if she wore his clothes every day.

J.K. raised his eyebrows while Gudrun stifled her laughter, turning her back as she reached for the coffee pot.

"Amma, why are you wearing pants?" Freyja asked.

Amma looked surprised. "What do you mean?"

"Those pants," she said. "They are Pabbi's."

"No, they are mine."

Freyja shrank a bit in her chair. "No they're not."

"Yes they are," she said, reaching for a piece of bread. She slathered butter on top as if nothing at all strange was going on.

"I gave those to you to mend," Pabbi said.

"I did," she said, pointing at a patch on the knee. "See?"

He leaned around the edge of the table to look. Taking a bite of bread, he chewed thoughtfully. "Is Ella behind in the laundry?"

"Probably."

"I am not," Mother chimed in. "Her dresses were washed yesterday."

"Then why is she wearing my pants?"

"She is your mother. Ask her."

Pabbi cocked his head in Amma's direction.

"Because I want to. I am an old woman and I will do what I want."

"You have always done what you wanted," Pabbi quipped.

"Yes, but I never enjoyed it before."

J.K. crossed his legs and leaned back in his chair as if watching a play.

"And you have always been old," Leifur said playfully, encouraging a reaction.

"Not so old that I can't outwork you," Amma said.

This elicited jeers and laughter from the rest of us.

"We will see about that," Leifur said, puffing out his chest.

Amma trotted out to the blettur with them. They told us that night that as soon as they chopped down a young tree, the moment it crashed down, she chased them away, picked up the bar and began working on the roots.

"Once I have it loose the oxen will help me," she'd said. Then she sang to herself as if she was all alone.

The next morning Signy put on a pair of pants and joined them. For another three weeks they labored. Each day I ran the trail, lunch sack slung over my shoulder, and on the final day when I arrived, they were standing facing the oak.

"I am not sure I can do it," Pabbi said as I laid our picnic on the ground.

Amma's feet were planted solidly as if she was bracing against a great wind. She always stood like this, face scrunched up in a scowl while allowing her gut to decide. Amma believed she was born with the gift of skyggni—or second sight—the ability to foresee what others couldn't. Pabbi would joke that if it were true, her gift was blind in one eye since she was only correct half the time.

"Then leave it," she said.

"What if a storm blows it onto the house?"

"It won't."

"How do you know?"

"I have a feeling about this tree."

"You are just tired of digging roots," he teased.

"So are you."

They looked at Leifur who had the habit of standing exactly like her, only now he seemed a bit taller. In a month of hard work, he'd grown noticeable muscles on his arms, chest, shoulders, and back. Signy stood taller too. Thank goodness it was me who caught him weeks later admiring himself in the mirror and not her.

"This tree is starting to feel like a friend," she said.

Amma agreed. "An old one who will still be here long after we are gone."

That night after supper, Pabbi announced that they were done and it was finally time to start building. I'd known the announcement was coming but cheered just the same. J.K. poured a celebratory drink and even slid a glass with two gulps in front of Leifur.

"A man's drink for a job well done," he said as they raised their glasses. "Cheers."

"Skál," Amma said clinking her glass hard against Leifur's.

He was so surprised he wasn't sure what to do. He smelled it first, then took a sip. He pulled a face and we all laughed, everyone except Finn, who looked so jealous I thought he might spit.

The moment I saw Bensi Solmundsson from Skógafoss, he inspired a sense of unease in me. Only a few years older than Pabbi, he came one day riding a roan horse through the bush trail across our land, head held high as if he owned the place. Bensi had a mouth that turned down like a crescent moon, giving his smile a mocking quality.

Decades later when I watched western movies, I always thought of him whenever the Sheriff rode up to the lawbreakers, back straight as a plank, rifle casually lying hip to hip. But despite his charming face and demeanor suggesting his word was law, Bensi was nothing like those honest, caring lawmen from the movies.

I see how Pabbi shrank during that first encounter.

We were all there, levelling the ground for the foundation, even Freyja whose job it was to help me clear away the sticks.

"Pjetur, I am surprised to see you," Bensi said, pulling back on the reins. The horse stopped, but instead of dismounting—the polite thing to do—Bensi stayed in the saddle and towered over us.

"Not as surprised as I," Pabbi said.

An arrogant man makes others feel small by ignoring them, an insecure man will hang on every word. Pabbi was trying hard to be neither.

"Ella," Bensi bowed. "Freda. I would have guessed you too old to make the journey."

Amma levelled her gaze at him. "My family would never leave me behind. Which makes me wonder, where are your sons?"

"I see you are building a house." He ignored her question, pointing his gun up at the cloudless sky. "You will never get the roof up in time. A week of rain is coming."

Pabbi laughed, wiping the sweat from his brow. "It never rains here in July."

"You are thinking of September," he smirked. "You should have waited until then. You will never finish before haying."

"We will see about that," Mother said.

Bensi seemed to enjoy how quickly she reacted, the annoyance in her voice. Normally, if they were prepared, Mother together with Pabbi were difficult to out-maneuver in an argument. Pabbi would think through the logic of the situation, then Mother would annihilate any opponent with her words. But Bensi had caught them off guard.

"That boy of yours looks like a good worker," he said. "What is your name, son?"

"Leifur," he said.

"You come work at my farm and I will make sure you get paid what you are worth."

Leifur looked flattered but irked at the same time.

"Not as long as I'm alive," Amma said. "I have a sack full of money to spend. Soon we will have more sheep than you."

Bragging was a sin almost as bad as lying. Whenever Amma talked about her money (none of us ever saw it), Pabbi shushed her while Mother rolled her eyes, but right now the three of them stood solid as a wall facing Bensi.

Bensi snorted. "We all know how you came by that money."

"And we know how you came by yours," she snapped back. "Don't think you are going to chase us off. We're here to stay."

"Not if your animals starve," he sneered. "You will never make a living on this quarter, it is the worst in the district."

"Asi Frimann disagrees," Pabbi said. "He has been here longer than you."

"Asi is a fool, though I am not surprised you are taking advice from him," Bensi said.

Pabbi flinched. By then his hands were furious, fingers pressed into his palms, knuckles white.

"Now the quarter over there," Bensi said, pointing to the shanty, "it is the better of the two. You should have chosen it."

"Time will tell," Pabbi said.

Bensi turned his horse, spurring with his heels while holding the reins back, lifting the horse's head. Then he clicked his tongue and jabbed his heels hard. The horse obediently took off in a full gallop back in the direction from where he'd come.

"Just wait until he hears we have both quarters," Leifur grinned.

The next morning, we awoke to pattering on the roof. Pabbi was already standing in front of the picture window, staring out at the grey sky. He did not answer when we spoke to him, preoccupied by the sight of the calm lake, its surface dimpled as far as we could see.

The mood around the kitchen table was cheerful nevertheless. The house smelled of pönnukökur—the Icelandic crepe we all loved so much, rolled with sugar and cinnamon; there was also warm bread and thick, sweet berry preserves. Coffee for the adults, fresh milk for the children.

A month had passed since the last rain so it came as a great relief. It replenished the pasture, prompted new growth and provided much needed moisture for the wild hay meadows that were only weeks away from being ready to cut. We would be busy then and everyone would work without a break from August through September. Years later when I'd hear someone quote the English proverb, 'make hay while the sun shines,' I found it amusing. Only a farmer truly understands the meaning behind those words.

"Pjetur, come have breakfast," Mother said quietly.

She wore an apron like Gudrun, and when we asked why she put on her best dress so often and why her hair smelled so sweet, her face brightened and she kept on with whatever she was doing. We didn't know at the time she was pregnant with our little sister, Solrun, who would be born during a fierce storm that coming winter.

"I think the children should do sums today," J.K. said.

We were unsure how serious he was so we took our cue from Finn and Thora who slumped like rag dolls in their chairs and groaned.

"That is a wonderful idea," Gudrun said as she sipped coffee. Mother agreed. It was obvious by the way she brought the delicate cup to her lips that she enjoyed living here very much.

Thora sighed. "For how long?"

"Until you get them all right. Afterwards, if you ask Freda nicely, she may read to you from the Sagas."

The table was cleared while Mother and Gudrun began knitting in the front room and Pabbi retrieved his ledger book to begin doing his own version of sums. He wrote comments, mostly about the weather, so he could reference it in the future.

Grouped by age, we sat at the table with J.K. as our teacher.

We were each given a slate and piece of chalk from the box packed away under the stairs. J.K. jotted a list of sums on three separate pages then placed them on the table. Thora and I shared one. Freyja and the little children read from another. Finn, Leifur and Signy began figuring quickly, blocking the slate with their free hand so the others couldn't see, since between them it was always a competition.

But I was the first to finish.

"Good for you, Asta," J.K. said, looking a bit surprised as he read over my slate. "All correct."

Leifur and Signy looked up, then Signy put her head down and began multiplying faster.

"You gave her the easy ones," Leifur complained.

Without a word, J.K. turned their page so I could see it. Their sums were more difficult, but I didn't want to disappoint him, so ignoring Thora and Freyja who stopped to watch, I sped through the figures and slammed my chalk down less than a minute after the older ones. Thora clapped with glee.

"Impressive," J.K. said. "Now you can either go play with the others or help Freyja."

I didn't see it as a choice. Freyja had no sense at all when it came to numbers so she needed me.

"Soon we will have our own teacher." J.K. winked at me.

Not wanting to appear conceited, I didn't react, but deep inside my heart swelled with pride.

He leaned down and with his hand resting on my back, in a confiding tone, whispered: "Learn as much as you can because no one can ever take that away from you."

When Freyja finally finished her sums correctly, we gathered on the floor around Amma who was seated on a wing back chair with a thick book waiting on her lap. For two hours she read to us from *Njál's Saga,* widening her eyes during the mysterious parts, whispering, before hollering out the frightening scenes, animating every word to regain our attention whenever we became distracted. Occasionally, Langamma, whose eyes were too weak to read, would mutter to herself while nodding in agreement, confirming that Amma was telling the story as she remembered it.

My earliest memories are of listening to the adults read. The Sagas contained medieval stories filled with lessons on how to live and die with honor. They gave strength, imagination and hope to all who believed it was circumstance, not genetics, that kept our forebears oppressed. Deep inside every Icelander was a belief that while life might not always be fair, our destiny was decided by our actions.

"It is said that he never lies," Amma said slowly of Njál, the hero. "He is wise, moral, and we understand from the story that his nemesis, Hrútr, tells lies to a woman who treated him with only kindness. His life was complicated by hardship ever after."

Amma's eyes locked onto mine. Why she singled me out I've never understood.

Then, as was her usual habit, she closed the book at a most suspenseful point. If we behaved, she would read to us again at bedtime.

The rain came down harder, water falling over the verandah roof.

Our parents moved to the kitchen table to play a game of Whist. Finn and Leifur, energized by the Saga's battle scenes, could not resist the temptation to wrestle. The girls followed our parents, leaving me alone with Amma.

"Tell me," she asked quietly. "What happened that day we went to The Narrows?"

I looked quickly at Leifur, dreading what would happen if I broke the promise.

"Nothing," I said, knowing that she would never ask again even though she didn't believe me.

Freyja returned from the kitchen and climbed onto Amma's knee.

"Will you show me your sack of money?" she whispered.

Amma hushed her and pulled her close. "Another time," she said, bringing a finger to her lips. Her eyes moved quickly to J.K. and Gudrun, Thora and Finn, so we knew she wanted to keep it a secret from them.

Poor Pabbi. The three-day rain felt like a week. His mood did not improve until we awoke the fourth morning to clear skies.

"Finn rode to see the neighbors," J.K. said, offering no reason, and Pabbi was too polite to ask. Pabbi thought it overly optimistic when J.K. suggested they take both wagons to the building site, each piled high with lumber that Asi had delivered the week before.

"We shouldn't take more than we'll need," Pabbi said. "It may rain again."

"It will be clear now for a few days," he said as he released the foot break and jolted out of the barn. "We will take the shingles tomorrow."

Pabbi raised his eyebrows but did not say a word. He did not want to offend J.K. so he placed a box of nails, a hammer and a saw on the seat, then he and Leifur climbed onto our wagon. Fortunately, the oxen, who could be stubborn at times, liked to follow. Pabbi easily coaxed them in behind J.K.'s wagon.

"Take Freyja with you," Mother said to me. "Mind she stays out of the way."

J.K. sang loudly the whole way. As we emerged from the bush trail at the place that would be our yard for the next fifty years, I did not understand what I was seeing. Pabbi didn't either.

Three wagons were parked and I saw Asi, along with men of varying ages milling around. Finn was sitting on his horse at the edge of it all, and another wagon was coming from the north bringing the area's well-respected carpenter, Oli Thorsteinsson. I understood then why Finn had slipped away that morning. Pabbi let out a whoop when he grasped what J.K. had arranged. He shook his hand vigorously for a long while, unable to say a word. J.K. looked delighted, patting him hard between the shoulders, then introduced him to the men.

I imagine Gudrun must have told Mother because they arrived at noon with enough food for that whole army of people. Mother cried as she handed out sandwiches, and she remained thankful until the day she died to those neighbors, many of whom became life-long friends.

It took only three days of persistent work and constant singing to raise the house. I have never forgotten the beauty of it, simple in its design but so much more than we could have ever hoped for. I'll always remember the echo of our naked feet on the floor and the tangy, live smell of new lumber.

Mother asked that her house have only two things: large windows facing southeast and a plank floor. Both would add warmth over the winter. There were two doors, one off the front room that faced the lake (even though we couldn't see it because of the trees) and one that we used every day from the kitchen to a lean-to that faced the barnyard. Amma's bedroom was in a nook off of the front room while Pabbi and Mother's opened into the kitchen.

Amma grabbed Mother's arm before she went inside. Superstition kept pregnant women from walking under newly raised rafters, lest they experience a difficult birth, but Mother thought it nonsense so she went in first anyway. We children followed and practised running up the stairs to the loft where we would sleep, boys in one room, girls in the other. We lay on the floor listening to the ringing of our voices against the walls.

"Shhhh," Signy said, sitting up. "What is that sound?"

At first I thought she meant the settling of timber and nails, but then, as our voices hushed to the rhythm of our own breath, we heard a soft patter on the roof.

Even today, whenever I think of rain, I remember lying in that room with a wool blanket pulled to my chin, reading to the comforting sound of heavy drops, safe from the wind and cold.

Probably what happened next is what solidified this memory. A loud whooping echoed throughout the house. We ran down the staircase to see the three most important adults in our lives had joined hands and were swinging in a circle. Amma was singing a song of thanks, Mother's head was thrown back in laughter and Pabbi beamed at them both.

Signy was the first to break in as the rest of us scrambled to grab a grown-up hand. We danced and spun, lifting Freyja's arms until her feet were off the ground. We jigged and sang until finally Amma said there was something we must do.

"It is good luck to move from one house to another in the rain," she said, breathless. "It will bring us wealth."

It was the happiest day we'd experienced up until then so not one of us flinched as the cool, fat drops fell on our heads, tickling their way down our cheeks onto our necks as we ran through the wet grass to Vinðheimar. Pabbi hitched the oxen and backed it up to the verandah.

Langamma turned an ear to the ceiling, clucking with approval, as we rushed around gathering everything that was ours. Gudrun and J.K. stood with their family waving good-bye as we rattled down the trail to our new home.

The last thing Mother unpacked was our only family photograph and we watched as she hung it in the front room over the sofa, standing back, adjusting a corner before turning with delight. Pabbi stood in the middle of the floor with his hands on his hips, looking like a man who'd achieved everything in life he'd set out to do.

"What shall we call our new home?" he asked.

He had the final word after considering everyone's suggestion.

"Eikheimar," Pabbi said. Our home in the oak trees.

Signy never let Leifur forget that it was she who named the farm.

I was not privy to the conversation that took place between Pabbi and Mother regarding the stove because we children were outside playing. But now I see Mother remove the lid from the tin can that she kept high on the cupboard behind the salt crock and carefully count out what they'd saved. When all the money was on the table in tidy piles, they stared at it as if it might double if they watched long enough.

"We have what we'll need until you start fishing—" she said.

"But if we send for your sister now, there is not enough to buy a stove," Pabbi said, finishing her sentence. We all knew how the decision to leave teenaged Freyja behind tormented Mother. Had she been a different sort of woman she would have cried or begged, and made promises impossible to keep. But that was not her way. She waited patiently for Pabbi to decide.

He took a deep breath, remembering the promise he too had made Freyja. He owed nothing to anyone except his mother—a life pattern he was unable to shake, but one he could live with.

"I will buy the stove on credit," he said. "We'll send for Freyja now."

A stove and her sister. More than she could ever wish for.

"Thank you Pjetur," she said, getting up to kiss his forehead. "I will never ask for anything that will indebt us ever again."

One afternoon a few days later we burst through the door to see Mother sitting at the kitchen table.

"What are you doing?" Signy asked.

It was a foolish question because the answer was obvious. There was an ink pot in front of Mother and she was bent over a tablet, pen in hand.

"Writing a letter to Freyja," she said, without looking up. She must have been working at it for hours as there were five tightly written, double-sided pages already filled. "She will read it to the others."

Now I know what her letter said.

She told them about the land and our house. The woodpile stacked taller than she stood. She described a lake teeming with fish and nobody except us to catch them. The only detail she neglected to include was how difficult she was finding the adjustment of having everything she ever wanted. It would take months before she stopped staring wordlessly out the kitchen window, reacting impatiently toward us when we interrupted her faraway thoughts. At the time we were confused, but now I understand why she wept for no reason.

There is an Icelandic saying that translates this way: 'If you live in misery long enough, you will start to welcome it.'

Now that Mother had a home, she missed the one she'd left. She didn't want to seem ungrateful, which she wasn't, but homesickness had a way of creeping in, even though the mind was content.

No, there would be no complaints in her letter. Everyone in Iceland already knew the downside of living here. The malcontent, those who regretted coming, and the naysayers who never left, were quick to point out America's shortcomings. Men like Uncle Ásgeir, who'd learned to live comfortably in discomfort, would rather stay in Iceland than risk improving his lot in life.

Mother read the letter over many times. She hid money in the folds for Aunt Freyja, then held it up to the light, placing it on the shelf above the table.

Then she fretted. The day Pabbi took it to The Narrows to post she began dithering that it would get lost in the mail or the money would be stolen.

I envisioned Aunt Freyja in Iceland pulling the creased pages out of her pocket at an opportune moment.

"I have a letter from Ella," she'd say and the room would grow quiet. There would be at least fifteen of them, young and old. Aunt Freyja would squint through the smoky haze, reading Mother's carefully chosen words. At the end, she would hold up the money. Except I have to re-imagine that part.

I knew old Ásgeir would scoff and his wife would find fault in every detail. In their hardheadedness they would call us cowards, weaklings, and traitors for leaving Iceland—the worst of all insults. I say this because that is exactly what happened to Mother when her cousin sent a letter to her.

Pabbi didn't have the heart to tell Mother what transpired the day he went to order the stove, so none of us ever knew. But I see it all happen now.

"How much for this one?" he asked the store owner, Helgi Einarsson, who'd finished negotiating a trade with a young Indian man on four tanned deer hides. Pabbi stood at the back of the store, eyes smiling at the stove he'd seen Mother admiring weeks earlier. She didn't know it yet, but he had already asked Magnus for a job at the mill.

"It is the finest stove I carry," Helgi said, hinting that it was more than Pabbi could afford.

"Might I set up an account?" Pabbi asked. "I have no debt and a job at the mill and will have it paid in full by the new year."

It was seldom that a person took an instant dislike to our father, but

I see immediately the suspicion in Helgi's eyes. Refusing credit in those days was a difficult thing to do.

"I expect to pay a reasonable rate of interest," Pabbi added quickly.

Helgi shook his head slowly. "I cannot extend credit to you for such an expensive item."

Pabbi wanted to ask why, but pride kept his lips tight. He felt foolish and wanted to leave the store and never return, but could not go home without ordering the stove. He would not ask his mother for yet another loan.

"May I borrow a pen?" he asked, taking Mother's letter out of his breast pocket.

Helgi watched as he opened the envelope and took out the money, then looked away as Pabbi carefully wrote, 'the money will follow soon.' Pabbi sealed the letter then handed it to Helgi along with enough coins to pay the postage.

"This was for my wife's nineteen year-old sister," he said, looking Helgi square in the eye as he gave him the money. "It seems I am left with no choice but to disappoint her again."

The day the stove arrived was one of great celebration. It was brought first by train from the Guelph Stove Company in Ontario to Portage la Prairie, then by boat to The Narrows, then by wagon from the dock at Vinðheimar. It took six men to unload. We danced as they grunted the black cast-iron beauty in through the door. Once it was in place and Pabbi had the stove pipe attached to the chimney, Mother stood in front of it with her hands clasped under her chin. She ran her fingers across the top and down the sides, gracefully opened the firebox, then the oven door, to peer inside. At first she would not allow anyone else to touch it, and many times over the years I'd catch her smiling for no reason at her Guelph stove.

CHAPTER SIX

Truth is the saying that no man shapes his own future.
—GRETTIR'S SAGA

I AM AWAKE AGAIN. NOW I FEAR THAT I MAY DIE BEFORE FINDING out what happened to Freyja.

This is irritating. The process is taking far longer than I expected. All the way back to childhood? What good is this?

A voice whispers in my ear, *Be patient. All will be revealed as it is meant to be.*

But I am tired of waiting for answers. I spent my whole life expecting things that never came.

This bed is starting to feel hard on my back. My heels and ass are sore. How long have I been asleep this time? It's still bright outside but that's no surprise since we are approaching the longest day of the year.

Thora went for something to eat. Someone has pulled closed the curtain that separates Mary and me. Only quiet, adult voices now, so the mood is subdued. They speak a mixture of English and Saulteaux, and it reminds me of how it was at home after we started school. Some English words, those that describe items foreign to Iceland crept into our everyday speech, but the Icelandic phrases and sayings, hymns and songs that have no English translation—they are what kept our language alive. Signy taught her children and their children as well. But the great-grandchildren have little knowledge of Icelandic. What a shame.

The door pushes open and Thora returns carrying a foam cup. I smell strong coffee.

"How do you feel?" she whispers.

"Stiff," I say, trying to push myself up. She sets her cup on the window ledge and helps me adjust. She looks tired and for the first time I see how hard this is for her. She is an old woman, too.

"Don't worry," I say. "I will be gone soon."

Her eyes widen. "Stop talking like that."

"It's true."

"That's not what Doctor Steen says. He thinks you are doing surprisingly well."

Her words are heartening, but I pretend not to care. I can't tell her that I am willing myself to stay alive, why I won't give in yet. Thora refuses to believe in anything she cannot see, despite all the things she *has* seen.

She begins reading out loud from the book I don't have the stamina to finish. The story is interesting, but I've lost focus because I am eavesdropping on the conversation going on behind the curtain. Their voices have risen, there is much excitement, but Thora keeps reading. It isn't until Mary's daughter hurries out of the room that she pauses. The daughter returns a few minutes later with rotund Doctor Steen. He is a homely man, docile and soft-spoken. A fine physician with a beautiful heart.

"Mary," he says, rounding the curtain, "how are you feeling?"

Mary muffles an answer I can't hear.

The daughter is elated, while the heavy man sitting on the chair starts pushing himself up.

The doctor is talking quietly to them now, listening to Mary's heart, shining the penlight in her eyes.

I smile at Thora, who looks surprised. "Told you," I say.

She shakes her head. "You should have been a doctor. You always were the clever one."

The thought never once occurred to me.

When he is finished examining Mary, Doctor Steen stops alongside my bed. His grit is legendary. He should have retired years ago, but has confessed to me that after giving his life to the profession, taking it back is no longer an option.

I understand. Older patients still expect house calls and he'd never refuse. The new graduates prefer the tidy structure of a hospital to trekking across the countryside.

"How are you, Nurse Gudmundsson?" he asks.

Norwegian, he is. Can pronounce my given name perfectly, but never calls me by it. He addresses me as I prefer.

"My back needs a good scratch," I say.

This amuses him.

Doctor Steen and I have often weighed the merits of dying in hospital versus at home but came up even every time.

He places the stethoscope on my chest. His mind is still incredibly sharp so I am certain he has never forgotten a patient, diagnosis or conversation. He has saved more people than he killed, though his hasty diagnostic skills sometimes raised eyebrows.

"I am not ready to die yet," I say.

He looks directly at me. "Then don't."

Doctor Steen believes the same as I do, that our soul lives on after the body dies. In fact, some of what I know about the ability to detach and then return, I learned from him. How to let go of the fear, relax the mind and fall into a trance.

"Now would be a good time to ask," he says. "How far do you want us to go?"

I shake my head. "No monitors, no feeding tube, no resuscitation."

"Fluids?" he asks.

"Yes," I say. "Continue with the morphine."

He writes this on my chart.

"Your family agrees?"

"Signy won't, so I will make her think it's her idea."

Doctor Steen pauses for a moment. "So you haven't seen her yet?"

I think hard. "Not for a while. I expect she will be in to visit soon."

* * *

THE SCHOOLTEACHER ARRIVED IN EARLY OCTOBER. PABBI WAS working at the mill six days a week, walking there early each morning, returning late at night. Mother asked us each day when we arrived home from school if there was any news.

Everything was worth repeating.

"Thora cut her hair but I liked it better long," Signy said as she placed an armful of wood on the pile by the stove.

"J.K. is going to butcher a pig tomorrow," I said, handing Mother the women's magazine that Gudrun had sent. We were fortunate there was an active literary community in Winnipeg that published papers in our native tongue, and Gudrun subscribed to them all.

"He thinks freeze-up will be early this year," Leifur added, making himself a quick sandwich before going out to do the evening chores.

What Mother wanted to know was if there was a letter from her sister tucked in a pocket that we'd forgotten. Logically, she knew not enough time had passed, but hoped anyway. If our aunt didn't make the crossing soon, we wouldn't see her until spring.

Little Freyja was the only one who understood Mother's lethargy as the months passed. She would climb onto her lap, wrap herself around the growing baby, and rest her head on Mother's chest.

Life at Eikheimar was increasingly difficult, but Christmas brought a bit of relief. The mill shut down for a week so the workers could travel home to their families. Though the weather was cold, the mood was festive as we trimmed the tree with handmade decorations on Christmas Eve. Mother prepared a traditional meal of hangikjöt (smoked meat) while Pabbi lit the candles and we sang carols.

"It is so beautiful," Freyja said, mesmerized by the glowing tree. She was the last one to open her gift, a tablet and pencil, and was delighted by it, while Signy and I hid our disappointment that we did not receive the customary new dress.

"Next year," Mother said softly as we each held up a pair of home-made socks and mittens.

Christmas day was spent with the Kristjanssons who exclaimed that for years they'd missed having neighbors to socialize with over the holidays. We played games and sang while Thora accompanied us on the organ. In coming years, we were quick to follow their lead by adopting the Canadian tradition of putting out a sock for Santa Claus and eating a turkey feast on Christmas day. On New Year's Eve, J.K. lit a giant bonfire to burn out 1906. As the calendar turned to January we began counting the days until spring.

"More snow than I've ever seen," J.K. said, shaking his head as one storm after another blew in across the lake.

How do I even try to describe what it was like? Frigid temperatures and bitter winds, so incredibly cold that our nose hairs froze instantly, throat catching with every breath. Pabbi did not return to the mill, so he and Leifur fished with J.K., but so few fish meant the nets were pulled up early.

Mother worried endlessly about the woodpile. She began limiting the logs put into the stove and, since we'd consumed all the meat, we were forced to eat fish every day for weeks on end. Amma said we should stop complaining, reminding us that as a girl she had starved to death more than once.

"Then why aren't you dead?" Signy teased, but Amma didn't think her funny at all.

"Because," she said, "a man was kind enough to give me a fish."

Stormy weather prevented us from seeing our neighbors who didn't dare venture too far from home. We children never fought so much as we did that winter, causing our parents to raise their voices more than they ever did when we lived in Iceland.

We eventually learned there was no point lamenting what could not be changed. All we could do was hunker down and look forward to spring. It arrived, reluctantly, in late March that year. A terrible storm came a month before the thaw and with it baby Solrun.

Father kept the trail to Vinðheimar packed hard most of the winter, but two feet of blowing and drifting snow made the trek on snowshoes particularly difficult the morning he set out to borrow J.K.'s horse. Then he rode along the frozen lake trail to the mill where the only midwife lived. Bergthora Magnusdottir was sister to the mill owner, a spinster who'd never had a baby herself but was quite skilled at bringing them safely into the world.

Although it was only a six-mile round trip, the journey was slowed considerably by the driving wind. Pabbi was distraught when he finally arrived home that evening with Bergthora riding beside him on her own horse, a heavy-legged mare who seemed accustomed to around-the-clock, weather-be-damned travel.

The door blew open and Bergthora came into the kitchen, shaking the snow off her giant beast of a buffalo coat. Her size was reduced by half when she removed it but still we stood in awe of her.

Mother started to cry. "The baby will not come," she whispered through clenched teeth.

Bergthora ushered all of us except Signy away from the bedroom.

"There now," she said, opening the black bag she carried. "You have done this before."

She handed the instruments to Signy, telling her to put them in a pot of boiling water.

Not knowing what else to do, Pabbi paced the floor. I hid around the corner to the front room, ducking back when Bergthora passed through the kitchen. She called out sternly, "Come here and make yourself useful."

So I did.

"I take it your brother can read to his little sister," she said, loud enough that Leifur must have heard her, because he picked up Freyja to take her upstairs.

"Come here," she said, handing me two rags. "Wipe your mama's forehead with the wet one and roll the other in case we need it."

I could not imagine what good a rolled up rag would do, but took it and went to stand by Mother's head.

"Four children and they all came easily?" she asked Pabbi over her shoulder.

"Five. We lost one."

"During birth?"

"No, later."

Bergthora moved to the end of the bed. She lifted the blanket and reached in. Mother cringed and cried out as she pressed down hard on her abdomen then reached inside.

"The baby is breech," she said quietly to Signy, then told her to retrieve the instruments from the stove.

"Ella, you must stop pushing," she said, repeating herself until Mother could focus. "Ella, look at me. I can feel one foot but the other leg must be brought down. Do you understand?"

Mother clenched through another contraction.

"Put the rag in her mouth," she said to me. "Now bite down," to Mother as she carefully reached inside again.

"Once I have both feet, you are going to have to push harder and faster than you have ever pushed before, do you understand?"

Mother's face was in a knot, teeth clamped down hard on the cloth. She nodded furiously.

Signy stood ghostlike at the end of the bed, trembling, as she held the instruments. Our eyes met. Sometimes women died during childbirth but, until that moment, we never understood why. Our mother's stifled, painful screams were something we'd both remember for the rest of our lives.

Then, finally, we heard a hint of victory in Bergthora's voice.

"Hand me the big one with the loops," she said to Signy, who fumbled, dropping the instrument on the floor. Embarrassed, she scooped it up and ran back to the stove, returning a few moments later.

"There, there," Bergthora whispered as her hands moved expertly under the blanket, her eyes never once leaving Mother's face.

"Ella, it is time . . . push."

Now that I am a nurse, I understand what she was doing. Normally, forceps are used on a baby's head, but they work just as well on the hips. I am glad I didn't know then how easily the baby's head could become stuck.

"Pjetur," Bergthora called.

Pabbi appeared at the door instantly.

"Asta isn't strong enough," she said, motioning for me to get out of the way. Pabbi understood what he needed to do once he saw Mother trying to push herself up on her elbows. He knelt down, wedging his arm and shoulder behind her back.

That is when Mother changed. She regained her focus as Pabbi's strength set her determination. She spat out the rag and began pushing. A short time later she gave one final scream and the baby came out in a swoosh.

The relief was unbelievable. Hearing our joy as Bergthora lifted the crying baby into the air, Amma emerged shakily from her room.

"I knew it would turn out fine," she blustered. "That is exactly how Pjetur came into the world. He's been nothing but trouble ever since."

We all laughed, including Leifur, who brought Freyja into the room a few minutes later.

"A girl baby?" she asked, scrunching up her face. We'd all been hoping for a boy.

"Now don't be jealous," Signy said, pulling Freyja into her arms. "You can still be my baby."

Freyja pushed her away so she could come over to pout by me, annoying Signy.

"You will see," I whispered in Freyja's ear, kissing her cheek. "Soon you will love the baby as much as I love you."

Bergthora washed and wrapped the child before handing her to Signy, then once again ushered us out of the room. When the afterbirth came minutes later, Mother asked to see it.

"I had a son born on the train crossing this country, his afterbirth, I don't know what happened to it," she said, looking into the pail. "Now he's gone. I've never been superstitious, but . . ."

Bergthora understood. Most women whose babies she'd helped deliver didn't dare tempt fate, choosing to dispose of the afterbirth the traditional way. She walked the pail discreetly by us, opened the stove's firebox and tipping the pail, let the shuddering mass slip into the flames.

"Now no harm will come to this child," Amma announced as she took baby Solrun in her arms. "Now that she has a lucky star."

Amma made supper that night while she visited with Bergthora as if they'd known each other for years.

"You have a choice," Amma said gaily at Mother's door. "Boiled fish with bread or bread with boiled fish. Which will it be?"

"I will take the boiled fish and bread," Mother said. "Can I have a little butter with that? A bit of salt?"

"Only if I am allowed to put more wood in the stove," she said. "We are freezing to death."

Once we were fed and tiny Solrun was nestled against Mother's breast, the difficult subject of how Bergthora would be paid was broached. She sensed that we were as hard-pressed as everyone else in the community.

"If one of the girls can come with me it would be a tremendous help," she said.

Mother and Father readily agreed.

Bergthora looked Signy and myself over, her eyes settling on me.

"You will need Signy here," she said wisely. "The young Asta needs to learn. I will bring her back in a month."

Parents and children today might find such an arrangement unsettling, but young girls working as domestics is how it was done back then, so to us it didn't feel strange at all.

I'd struggled with shyness my whole life, but didn't dare let on how nervous I felt. Amma must have sensed it though, because the moment we were alone she offered to go in my place. I knew my parents wouldn't think much of me if I agreed, so I shook my head no. A small duffel was packed containing a change of clothes, and I waited solemnly until the storm lifted.

The following morning at daybreak I followed Pabbi and Bergthora out the door without looking back. The sky was tinted pink and all was still except for a slight breeze that came from the west, bringing a hint of warmth with it. Bergthora needed no help mounting the horse, but Pabbi had to lift me up. I slid into the saddle directly behind her and grabbed onto her buffalo coat.

"It will be all right, Asta," Pabbi said softly. "Mind what Bergthora says, learn what she has to teach, and we will see you again soon."

As Bergthora turned the horse and we set out toward the lake, bells jingling, I looked back to see Pabbi standing in front of the house, surrounded by blue-tinged drifts, the sun's golden reflection bouncing off our kitchen window. The giant oak towered overhead, its branches heavy with snow.

Little did we know that it would be months before I would see Eikheimar and my family again.

CHAPTER SEVEN

Many hands make light work.
—GRETTIR'S SAGA

I SENSE THAT MY SISTER SOLRUN IS NEARBY.

I open my eyes and slowly focus on activity in the hallway. A nurse walks briskly from the station toward the care home, pushing open the heavy metal door. Behind it is where all the old people exist, sitting on well-worn chairs in tiny rooms, surrounded by the essentials: a wool blanket from the old country, tin of snuff, shoe horn, cane, thick socks, books, peppermints, and photographs that when thumbed through, jostle into view decades of memories.

The front door opens and in walks Solrun. I am not surprised. It always was like that between us. At first I ignored the serendipitous moments, but then, as we grew older, I realized that I always knew where she was, how she felt. I pointed this out to her once but she thought it all coincidence.

The day after Freyja disappeared, Solrun climbed onto my lap and whispered fearfully, "Asta, there is a pain in my heart." All of us were hurting terribly, but poor little Solrun thought she was getting sick again.

Today she carries a baking pan covered with a tea towel. She wears a new yellow cardigan. Good for her. She is a frugal and dutiful wife who has given her whole life to her family and the farm. She'd rather do without than live with debt. It was every farmer's dream, to find a woman like her.

I know even before the sweet smell of warm cinnamon wafts into the room what is hidden under the cloth. Every woman has a signature dish, one that took years to perfect. Solrun's cinnamon buns won first prize at the Lundi Fair so many years in a row, that she thought it boastful and stopped entering.

She is already smiling at me, looking the same as when she was a girl. Some women do have the remarkable ability of remaining young at heart and she is one of them.

She stops to offer encouragement to Mary's family and holds out the pan, lifting the cloth. They are already cut so it is easy to lift them out and she hands one to each of them. They are nodding in thanks, glad to lick the sweet goo from their fingers as they eat. It is obvious by the way they laugh that she knows them well.

Solrun leans over Mary's bed to say hello before coming over to kiss my cheek. Oh, and I should probably mention she still has a limp. I barely notice it anymore but I am certain others do.

"How are you today?" she asks.

"Nice sweater," I say.

"This old thing? I've had it for years. Would you like one?"

At first I think she means the sweater.

Thora sits up in the chair where she'd been dozing with a blanket on her lap, spectacles and paper on the window ledge. Solrun digs out a cinnamon bun, places it on a napkin to hand to her.

"Me too," I say.

They look surprised and watch as I slowly break pieces off then feed myself. I know it is incredibly good, even though my sense of taste has left me.

"Good news from our part of the world," Solrun says, pulling up a chair. "At the Fair we won Grand Aggregate, have the Grand Champion steer and one of our girls was just crowned Miss Interlake."

"Wonderful," Thora says, breaking off a piece of bun, popping it in her mouth. “Three champions from Siglunes. We are still a force to be reckoned with.”

That is what our community along the lake is called now, Siglunes, after Magnus Magnusson’s birthplace in Iceland. Funny she should mention it as I was just thinking about him.

Now they are watching me eat, surprised by how well I’m doing.

I point to the glass out of reach. Solrun holds it as I take a sip from the straw and clear my throat. I give her the same lecture about town water and she smirks, having heard this before.

A band of people come down the hallway, hesitate at the door. They are not sure they have the right room. A man carries the two-year-old we saw earlier. Her cheeks are stained pink from the stick of candy floss she holds. Solrun waves them in, pointing toward Mary’s bed.

The others stand, stretch, make quiet conversation and leave. The changing of guard I call it.

“Chief Strong,” Solrun whispers to us. “Mary is his grandmother.”

Then she encourages Thora to go home and get some rest. “I will stay with her,” she says.

Thora seems troubled as she gathers her glasses and thermos into her large purse. She stretches and stifles a yawn. “I will be back later,” she says, patting my hand.

We watch as she leaves, seeing her briefly through the window as she walks across the parking lot. Solrun opens the paper and starts reading out loud bits of local news.

“Pabbi didn’t send the money for Aunt Freyja,” I say, now that Thora has left. “At least not right away.”

Solrun looks up from the paper, confused, so I tell her again.

She shakes her head. “Of course he did.”

“It happened before you were born.”

Solrun shrugs. “Why would you bring this up now?”

We are distracted by the two-year-old who is getting bored. She starts hopping and dancing, her little shoes tapping the hard floor. She peeks around the curtain at us.

Solrun waves.

The little girl pulls the curtain in front of her face, then looks again. Her cheeks leave a stain on the curtain. She does it again. And again. Then, feeling brave, she holds up the candy floss stick, pretending it's a spear.

"I travelled back and saw what happened," I say. "You were just a baby, too young to remember their terrible fight."

Solrun looks at me the same way she does the child, as if I am sweet, misbehaving.

"Now, Asta," she says. "You know these are just dreams."

The little girl begins pulling at the curtain. The Chief tells her to stop and she looks at him for a moment, then her eyes go up to the ceiling. She gives it another tug and it moves. She starts swinging her arm back and forth, the curtain wheels roll in the metal track.

"Come here my baby," he says. "Stop it."

He picks her up and sits with her on his knee, but she stiffens and whines, sliding away from him, and goes back to the curtain. This time she grabs it and, watching the ceiling, starts running back and forth, opening and closing it.

They watch her and so do we. As it opens I see Mary propped upright on the bed. She is smiling. Then the curtain closes. Swoosh, it's open again. This time Mary is laughing. Her family looks at us, uncertain. Solrun tells them we don't mind. This is how children are supposed to be. The curtain closes.

I am starting to doze off.

The toddler is dizzy now. She staggers and lands on her diapered bum. The room erupts in full belly laughter. Mary says something quietly in Saulteaux and the Chief quickly gets up. He lifts the girl and places her in her great-great-grandmother's arms.

* * *

Pabbi had described the Magnusson's mill at Siglunes, but at only fourteen years old I was limited in what I could imagine. Despite this, there was no mistaking it for anything else when I saw the place towering up along the shoreline. There it stood - a magnificent house made from stone, visible for miles in all directions. For nearly a century travelers referred to it as 'the castle on the lake,' but only a few knew it was I who named it that.

Bergthora's mare knew exactly where to go. It trod up the snowy bank, past the house, into what looked like a little shanty town. There were boats of all sizes in dry dock and in the center of it all was the mill. Huge piles of logs ready for cutting and four-foot wide fish boxes stacked everywhere. As you can imagine, everything was covered in snow.

Bells on the bridle jingled our arrival and a few of the men—I counted ten in total—stopped piling fish boxes to wave. The horse seemed pleased to be home. She whinnied, trotting straight to the barn. We passed by a man chopping frozen fish from a mound that he fed to the sled dogs, each tethered to its own stake. As the man, who I later came to know as Einar, threw the fish, he seemed to enjoy watching the dogs fight. All the vicious biting was a terrible sight. The larger dogs forced the others onto their backs. I could only watch for a few moments before turning away.

"Has your mama taught you to make butter?" Bergthora asked over her shoulder as the horse stopped at the barn door.

"No ma'am, Signy does that," I said, "but I have helped Amma make skyr."

She swung her leg over and stepped down. For an old woman she was surprisingly agile and I felt childish needing her help.

"Our dog birthed a litter of pups," she said, reaching up with a strong hand. Icelanders are known for their big hands and thick wrists. "Finna is meek as a fawn. She's in the barn. Later you can pat her and handle the pups, but not until your work is done."

Just then, a young man came out of the barn carrying two pails of steaming milk. Bergthora took the milk, handing him the reins. As he led the horse inside, I tried to catch a glimpse of Finna and her babies.

"Bring your bag," Bergthora said as she strode up the well-worn trail that led from the barn to the house. She'd already explained that I would help make meals, clean, and mend. I'd soon find out that the hooks the fishermen used to untangle their catch from the nets were notoriously hard on their mittens.

Of course, men would be far more interested in the barn, the mill, and how many pounds of fish were caught daily, than in the house, but all I can tell you about is their home which, as a domestic, is where I spent most of my time.

We entered through a vestibule built on the back. It was a large room that smelled of fish. This is where those who lived and boarded there hung their coats and left their boots. Bergthora pushed open a heavy oak door and we stepped into the kitchen, the grandest I'd ever seen. A double cook stove, walls of cupboards and an indoor water pump. When her brother Magnus built the house, he'd had the good sense to build it over the well so Bergthora didn't have to fetch water like the rest of us.

Bergthora slipped off her buffalo coat and told me to hang mine alongside hers inside the door. "No need for us all to smell like fish," she said, marching into the kitchen carrying the milk. It was a terrible mess; dishes were piled everywhere.

"Welcome home," a voice said.

My eyes went immediately to the far end of the table, long enough to host the Last Supper. There sat a large-boned, older, weather-beaten man. His most distinct feature was a gray mop of hair and the wide, thick moustache that covered his upper lip. His nose was wide and cheekbones high, making his deep-set eyes appear smaller than they were. I remember how intimidated I felt as he looked up from his ledger book to stare over his spectacles at me. This was Magnus, the mill owner.

Back in Iceland, girls like me seldom had the opportunity to converse with the wealthy owner of the farm where our parents worked. Teenagers, especially the pretty ones, were discouraged from ever doing so, for fear the man might take a liking to her and use her for his own purposes.

"How was the birth?" Magnus asked.

"Mother and daughter are doing fine," Bergthora replied. "Pjetur is a generous man. He allowed Asta to come help with the work."

Magnus smiled softly at me. "Sons can be a curse at times, but daughters are always a blessing," he said. "How many children does Pjetur have now?"

"Four girls and one boy," she said.

"Já, a choice of who will care for him when he is old. And what about you, Asta, are you your father's favorite?"

My heart hurt ever so slightly at the mention of it, but the reality was no different than having brown hair instead of blonde. Some things could not be changed, only accepted.

"No, sir, Freyja is. She is everyone's favorite, including mine."

Magnus's eyes lit up when he laughed. He lifted a ceramic cup from the table and spit into it. Mother said that chewing snuff was a disgusting habit and didn't allow father to do it. Sometimes he snuck a bit when she wasn't around and we children kept his secret.

"Well, elskan, Freyja isn't here," he said. "And I have only sons, so you can be my favorite, já?"

My chest swelled a bit. To be called 'elskan' or 'dear one,' as the English like to say, was unusual for me.

"I have never been in a castle before," I said, marveling at the high ceilings and the polished staircase that led upstairs where later I counted twelve bedrooms.

"What do you miss most about Iceland?" he asked.

I thought about it for a moment. "Going to church. And seeing the nuns who ran the hospital."

Magnus looked surprised. "I did not realize your father is Catholic."

"We are Lutheran like everyone else, but my Amma says I can still be a nun if I want."

"Anyone who wants a devout life serving God will find a way," he said. "Do you like to read?"

"Of course. I read to Freyja but she doesn't like the *Passion Hymns* much. She prefers Amma's stories, the ones filled with adventure."

He patiently nodded. "Then you and I shall sit by the fire every night. I have a few new books that may interest you. Do you know how to open one properly the first time?"

"Yes, sir. My Pabbi taught me."

He reached back to the small table behind his chair then placed a book on the table. It was beautifully bound in leather, pages still compressed, never opened. He lifted his chin. "Show me."

Reaching out nervously I took the book in one hand, wiping crumbs from the table with the other. Balancing it on the spine I carefully splayed the front and back cover like wings on a bird, holding the pages tight. Then cautiously I opened the pages directly in the middle, split each section in half, then once again, slowly pressing them open, gently loosening the spine.

"Not bad," he said. "A smart girl. Do you play chess?"

"No sir, I don't know how."

"I am sure Bjorn would be glad to teach you. He is always looking for someone to play with. It takes more effort than many men here care to expend. The men would rather gamble or play cards."

"I won't be much of an opponent."

"Nei, you will do just fine." Magnus looked at me the same way Mother did the first time she held baby Solrun. "You are a clever girl, and pretty too."

Bergthora chortled as she went to the front room to place her birthing bag on a shelf.

"You say that to all the girls who come here," she said, clearing dishes from the table, nodding that I should help. I began gathering mugs, understanding fully what her words implied. Too many compliments and I might actually start believing them. Conceit was a loathsome trait.

"My head is throbbing," Magnus said, rubbing his temples.

Bergthora turned quickly to study him, eyebrows knit together.

He grinned. "Já, I have not had a decent cup of coffee since you left."

Disgusted, she shook her head. "Is no one here capable of cleaning up after themselves?"

"Consider yourself fortunate," he said, winking at me. "Otherwise we would not need you, dear sister. Will you make me a fresh pot?"

Bergthora pointed to a five pound can on the shelf over the window. I'd never made coffee before, but had seen it done many times.

"If they spent less time wrestling and more time seaming nets or splitting wood, I wouldn't mind the mess," she quipped. "Where is Runa hiding? Nose in a book again? She could have at least made dinner."

Magnus sighed. "She was sick again this morning. Siggi is worried she will lose the child if this continues."

"Pregnancy is no excuse."

"Sometimes it is. My Dísa was sick, too."

Bergthora shook her head. "Runa needs to toughen up. Siggi coddling her is no help. How will she manage once the child comes?"

The banter between the two reminded me so much of Leifur and Signy that a feeling of homesickness settled in my stomach. "How many scoops?" I asked. Mother and Amma always quibbled about the coffee. Mother liked three scoops, Amma five.

"Four," Bergthora said.

I filled the sock as I'd seen Mother do, twisted the end, then placed it in the pot, filled it with water, then put it on the stove to boil.

Bergthora assigned me my next task—skimming the milk using the cream separator at the far end of the kitchen. Magnus looked impressed that I already knew what to do, then he resumed writing in his ledger.

Bergthora quickly made dinner, then packed it in a fish box so that Magnus could take it with him onto the lake. When she was done, he closed the ledger book and placed it behind his chair on the shelf.

Bergthora relaxed the moment the door closed behind him. Mother was the same. And even Amma. There was something irritating about having men in the kitchen.

What amazed me were all their wonderful conveniences. Bergthora had an icebox, a black enamel bathing tub and a crank machine for washing clothes—all things Mother desperately wanted. There was plenty of furniture, some of it handmade, but most imported from Europe to Iceland and then brought here. Bureaus, sideboards, tables, and heavy chairs with padded brocade seats. One large chair that faced the massive stone fireplace was covered with fur. There were paintings, and photographs too, all from Iceland. One showed two men facing off in a wrestling match, while a thick crowd stood watching in the background.

I enjoyed being in the front room where I could stare out the big windows at the lake bank stretching into the distance. A distinct smell of soot lingered in the room and old books were lined up neatly on a shelf that spanned an entire wall. There was a solid roll-top desk with a mess of paper and ledger books stacked on it. I offered to tidy the desk, but Bergthora said if I did Magnus would never be able to find anything.

Here was my daily routine. In the morning I'd help make breakfast, clear the table, do dishes, skim the milk. Then I would help Bergthora make dinner, set the table if the men were in that day, or if they went on the lake, pack sandwiches into the box.

Afternoon was my favorite time, as those hours were spent mending in the front room. Each time I looked up from my lap, I had a full view of Magnus's library. My heart swooned, knowing that later I'd be allowed to take a book to bed. But those cherished afternoon hours were short. We also needed to bake bread, make butter, and skyr - a soft whey cheese that everyone loved. Then we prepared supper. Every second day we made a dessert, in pans larger than I'd ever seen before.

"There are no boarders right now, only workers," Bergthora explained that first afternoon as we stood at the counter making kleinur. "Some of the men eat with us, so I charge them a daily rate, while the others prepare their own meals in the bunkhouse."

I twisted the dough into little knots putting them on a tray.

"Of course there are the three of us and the boys."

I tried my best to keep it all straight.

"Bjorn, Siggi and Arn," she said. "You met Siggi earlier in the barn. He and Arn are not identical so you will have no trouble telling them apart."

She explained that after Magnus's wife died giving birth to the twins, they immigrated here and named the place Siglunes, which means 'a point to sail around.' Bergthora had worked as a nurse in Iceland, but retired to raise her nephews.

She moved past me to the stove where the pot of oil was heating. She slid one of the knots in and watched it sink to the bottom.

"The oil is not hot enough," she said.

"So how many do we cook for?" I asked.

"Eleven if you count Runa. She is Siggi's wife but spends most of her time alone in their house. I am sure you saw it, the little log one set off alone by the bush."

I had in fact. The red and white checked curtains that hung in the windows had caught my eye as we rode in.

"Before Runa became pregnant she would eat with us and even helped make meals, but that all stopped," she said. I could tell by Bergthora's tone she was miffed.

"Siggi still eats here and Magnus insists we take her a plate. But if it were up to me . . ."

She bustled past me carrying the tray. The oil crackled this time as she dropped each one in; they rose to the surface and the edges began bubbling. When they were brown on the bottom, I flipped them with a metal spoon.

"I say too young to marry in the first place," she said. "But there was no talking Siggi out of it."

I dusted the hot kleinur with sugar and cinnamon before arranging them on a plate. I wanted to ask more about Runa, but a noise outside caused her to squint at the clock. She began moving quickly. "They will be in soon."

CHAPTER EIGHT

The eyes of a maid tell true, to whom her love she has given.
—THE SAGA OF GUNNLAUG THE WORM-TONGUE

AS YOU BECOME AN OLD WOMAN, MANY MEMORIES BEGIN TO FADE like the colors on a well-washed shirt. But the day I met Bjorn Magnusson is one that is crisp as a bolt of new gingham, refreshing as a glass of lemonade on a hot summer day.

He came mushing the sled dogs in from Ghost Island as I was arranging the kleinur on the plate. I lifted it and turned when the door opened, expecting to see Magnus, but in came his firstborn son who looked nothing at all like him.

He was holding the dinner box, still wearing his coat, but his boots were off. He stood as I imagined Tyr—the God of law and heroic glory, son of Odin—might stand. His hair was the color of a brown hen's egg and he had the unusual habit of wearing it long, tucked behind his ears. His shoulders were square and his hands, when he stretched them out, were as large as dinner plates. I easily imagined what his mother must have looked like, beautiful and engaging, with the same square jaw, and blue eyes that sang.

I was too young then to fully appreciate how physical he was, to know the sort of pleasure a man like that could bring, but deep inside me there was an instinctive stirring. My heart raced as I inhaled, flushing pink with anticipation.

"Kleinur." He smiled as he came straight toward me, took one from the plate and popped it in his mouth. He chewed as he spoke, directly at me, something no other young man ever did. Always before it was Signy or Freyja who received the attention. Bjorn's eyes danced with praise as he looked me over without a hint of shyness. It was as if my soul recognized his instantly. I stood there mesmerized, turning to watch wherever he was, holding out the plate. It was impossible to stop looking at him.

"This is Asta," Bergthora said as he circled around me reaching for another kleinur. I would have given them all to him, but Bergthora interrupted by slapping his hand.

"You will spoil your appetite," she said.

"Never," he laughed, managing to grab another, dodging around her, dangling it out of reach. Bergthora feigned disgust, shaking her head, with hands planted firmly on her hips. There was a brightness in her eyes, though, and it became obvious in an instant that I wasn't the only one susceptible to Bjorn's charms.

"How was fishing?" she asked.

"Still slow," he said, splitting the kleinur in two, licking the sugar off his fingers as he started toward the door. "I think it is time we pull up."

"What does your father think?"

"That it usually gets better in March," he said, pulling the door closed and rolling his eyes.

Talk around the table that night was lively. I was soon to discover it would be like that every night. I sat at the far end from Magnus, on the side bench. Fortunately, the discussions didn't concern me, so I was able to keep my eyes focused on my plate, sneaking peeks at Bjorn when he added to the conversation, which happened often.

"I hear they plan to build a hall at The Narrows this summer," he said as he slid another piece of roasted mutton onto his plate and scooped potatoes from the bowl, smashing them with his fork. "Helgi is excited about it."

"With good reason," Magnus said. "The more people frequenting The Narrows, the more business for his store."

Everyone nodded in agreement.

"That new settler Halli Eyolfson is selling shares in it," Bjorn said, adding that Helgi recommended it since he was heading up the committee. Someone had to collect the money.

"But nobody around here knows Halli," Bergthora said. "We barely do and he is one of our closest neighbors."

The conversation paused while everyone thought, eyes on their plates. It was astonishing how much food eight men could eat. I understood why Bergthora was quick to suggest I come work for her.

"People know," Magnus said thoughtfully. "Halli is honest."

Everyone agreed, except for the four fishermen who were not from the community.

"Ehh, he could take everyone's money and run," the fisherman named Einar grunted. The other three laughed.

"Not likely with a wife and five children," Magnus said.

"All the more reason. The last thing I'd want, ehh, is a woman and a pack of snot-nosed kids weighing me down."

He didn't actually say 'snot-nosed' but there is a similar saying in Icelandic.

"With a face like yours no need to worry," Bjorn teased, smiling at his brothers who sat across from him. I soon learned it was the way of young men to constantly tease one another. Most of it was good-natured, but often the jibes held more than an ounce of truth.

Einar shook his head then caught me staring at his bulldog face.

"Ehh, who's this?" he asked pointing with his fork.

"I introduced her when you came in but you were too busy talking," Bergthora said. She could barely take her eyes off his dirty hands. "This is Asta. She is our new domestic."

The men turned to face me, chiming, "Hello, Asta," all at the same time. It was comical and I blushed. The three men from away seemed nice, especially the tall, beak-nosed man. Then Einar belched. Not a quiet, cover-your-mouth rumble that snuck up on a person, his was loud and purposeful. The men shook their heads.

"You are excused," Magnus said, eyeing Einar.

Fortunately for us, Einar left the table shortly after that. Fishermen who slept in the bunkhouse did not stay after supper unless invited.

Once he was out the door, Bergthora let out a heavy sigh. "I have told him more than once to wash those hands," she said. "Even after fishing all day they are still dirty."

Arn examined his own pruney fingers. "He doesn't pull his weight, that's why," he said.

"He hasn't taken a bath all winter," Bjorn said.

"Or changed his clothes," Siggi added.

"I noticed," Bergthora said as she cleared the dishes.

I was already filling the sink with hot water from the stove.

"Asni is not all bad," Siggi said.

I thought this hilarious. They'd nicknamed him donkey, but Bergthora did not find it humorous at all. "Magnus, you must talk to him."

The old man flung us a playful look, said that he would, then retired to his bear-hide chair by the fire where he spent the evening reading.

"We should make Einar wash dishes instead of Asta," Bjorn said. "So she could play chess with me."

Bergthora caught my eye. "She can. Once she is done."

My room was at the foot of the staircase, at the beginning of a hallway that led to the family bedrooms. Upstairs there were a dozen more. There was a door at the end of the hall, which opened onto a verandah that spread across the front of the house facing the lake. Except for quick trips to the outhouse at night, that door wasn't used much.

I imagined my room was the one Bergthora gave to women travelling alone. There was a braided rug beside the bed, a mirror above the cherry wood dresser and a lace curtain that blurred the view outside but did nothing to keep out the moonlight.

Curious, I opened every drawer and found a hairbrush (thankfully, since Signy hadn't let me take ours), a nightdress, and a stack of rags. I put my change of clothes in the top drawer then pushed it shut.

I didn't sleep much that first night. The bed was comfortable enough, in fact I've slept on one like it—wrought iron with a feather-stuffed mattress—most of my life. No, it wasn't the unfamiliar bed. This was the first night I'd slept without my sisters. Missing them, plus heart-twirling thoughts of Bjorn, kept me awake. I spent most of the night reliving how we'd sat in front of the fireplace, on either side of a small table, with a chessboard between us; how serious his expression had become as he bent over the board, explaining each chess piece. I remembered the names easily enough but the strategies confounded me, not because it was difficult, but because I could only concentrate a short time before my thoughts would drift back to him. I heard the compassion in his voice, hung on his every word; I noticed the shape of his fingernails, not where he moved each piece. And that hair. I'd never seen anything like it on a man before.

The next morning I twisted my braid into a tight knot, then pinched my cheeks to bring a little color into them like I'd seen Mother and Signy do. Using the sleeve on my dress, I rubbed my teeth until they shone. Up until that point in my life I'd barely even looked in the mirror so I was a bit surprised to see that the girl who stared back at me looked older than the last time I checked.

"Good morning, Asta," Magnus said, looking up from the newspaper. "How did you sleep?"

"Very well," I lied.

What a strange feeling it was to see Bjorn sitting there after dreaming about him all night. He offered a distracted "Morning," as did Arn, who was reading one of Winnipeg's Icelandic papers, over his shoulder.

"Sigurdur writes that the Education Bill will likely pass," Bjorn said.

"Pabbi reads *Lögberg,*" I said.

"Ha!" Bjorn said to his father, knowing Pabbi's Liberal leanings without me having to say another word. Then I turned to Magnus, "but Amma reads *Heimskringla.*"

"Smart woman." He winked, turning his paper so I could see its masthead. "What do you read?" They all paused awaiting my answer.

"The women's magazine, *Freyja.*"

Bergthora smiled triumphantly. "Good choice. What is your opinion of the editor?"

"Mama hopes to someday meet her."

"So do I. Equality for women and education for all."

"Já, well, on that issue we definitely agree," Magnus said. "The only way all children in Iceland will receive an education is if government legislates and pays for it."

"But parents don't want their children taught by those who don't share their religious views," Bjorn said. "Teachers must be independent from religion and politics."

Magnus raised his eyebrows. "Do you think the church will give up that control?"

"It may have to," Bjorn said.

"Are you certain?" Magnus asked. "Your paper says religion is the issue, but I disagree. It is the attitude of the peasant who promises to sit his children down every day to teach them; however, it is much easier, plus more profitable, to send them out to work. Sometimes people find an excuse."

"That is unfair," Bergthora said, putting bread, cheese, and meat on the table. "For the poorly educated it is a difficult task, and children do not make it easy. It was all I could do to force you boys to learn."

"That is the lesson," Magnus said. "There is always another side to every story."

I wondered if it was the same here as in Iceland. "How many for breakfast this morning?" I asked, opening the cupboard door. I felt harried being the last one up and vowed it wouldn't happen again.

"Just us. Einar and the others will not pay for breakfast, so they have coffee at Siggi's instead."

I circled the table, carrying plates and utensils, trying hard not to stare at Bjorn.

Bergthora's jaw was set as she squinted out the window over the wash-basin at Siggi and Runa's house.

"Einar just left with a loaf of bread," she said, turning away from the window to refill the coffee cups. "Siggi earns the same as he does, and who do you think makes that bread?"

"Já, well, Siggi might enjoy his company."

She paused, hurling him a look of disbelief. "He is taking advantage of the boy's softhearted nature."

Magnus sighed. "When Siggi grows tired of him, it will end. Men have ways of sorting out disagreements. You will see."

"But I don't trust him."

"Sister, you worry too much."

"Well one of us has to," she said, raising her eyebrows.

Bjorn and Arn stopped reading. The conversation had taken an abrupt turn, and everyone but I understood its direction.

"It makes no sense," Bjorn said. "We are losing money."

Bergthora finally settled on her chair and I was told to sit as well.

"Já, well, I promised these men work until the end of March. They are counting on it."

Bjorn sighed and his face softened toward his father. "Some are complaining they want to go home. Einar is inciting them. You should hear what they say behind your back."

Then I remembered the conversation the night before, that fishing was poor but Magnus was reluctant to pull up.

His disappointment gave way to resignation. "We will pull up mid-March and those who want to leave can," he said. "I will tell them after dinner."

"What about the rest?"

"They can work in the mill. We already have more orders than we can handle."

"Good," Bergthora said. "If Einar needs help packing I will gladly offer it."

CHAPTER NINE

Be warned by another's woe.

—NJÁL'S SAGA

I HAVE NEVER UNDERSTOOD WHY PEOPLE WANT TO DIE AT HOME.

They are attracted, I think, to the idea of spending their final days surrounded by family in the place where they experienced so much life. During the day this makes perfect sense. I wonder, though, what it is like for them at night if they awaken to the silence. Anyone who has lived alone or suffered from insomnia understands how sluggishly the hours pass, with only the frightening shadows in a moonlit bedroom for company.

But the hospital is not like that at all. It is quiet without the stillness. It is dark in the hallway, but soft light filters in from the nursing station, where everything they do is muted. Waking here in the night is like watching a pleasing dream unfold.

I like being alone. I like it especially here. Always have. I told Solrun that I wasn't going to die that night so she should go home. Since I cannot die in the place I spent most of my childhood, it makes sense to take my last breath in the place I've spent most of my life.

I hear Mary breathing heavily in the bed beside me. I am accustomed to the sound, even welcome it. She stirs, waking herself up. Her daughter is twisted like a pretzel on the chair beneath Jesus. Mary is fidgeting now, moaning a bit. She knows her daughter is there but doesn't want to wake her.

Now I remember Mary. Her grandfather was a fine horseman who bred, broke, and sold beautiful horses to supplement what they didn't have living on the Reserve. Pabbi bought his first team, a mare and gelding, from him. Mary's father and brother worked on J.K.'s fishing crew, so we became acquainted with the family and over the years would see them, usually at ball tournaments where the old man would always ask about the horses, concerned about them, had they turned out well?

"Cancer?" I whisper into the dark. So many people smoked before they understood it was killing the people around them.

Her head wavers.

"Lung?"

"All over."

Reaching back over my head I press the call button. I am still able to reach it—one last defiant gesture of independence.

The nurse comes down the hall to check on me and I point to Mary, who I already know won't ask for what she needs.

Idealistic young nurses hired straight from school were always further ahead of us in their knowledge of the newest treatment. It took them only minutes to learn a newfangled gadget that took the rest of us a week to understand. But it is the experienced ones who know what can never be learned from a textbook.

She asks Mary if she is in pain, but Mary does not want to be a bother.

"Take a bit more," I say. "It will help you sleep."

The nurse pokes Mary's hip with a needle.

"If you need anything else, just press the button," she whispers as she leaves. She returns a few minutes later carrying a blanket from the warmer. Unfolding it silently, she gently covers Mary's daughter.

That is something she learned from us.

Mary and I lie there for a while listening to each other breathe.

"It was you," she says, breaking the silence; her voice already sounds lighter. "You took care of my father."

I remember.

She gathers her thoughts. "I feel the angels around me."

It is a phenomenon nurses who work the night shift understand.

"They are always here," I say.

* * *

"DO YOU WANT TO SEE THE PUPS?" BJORN ASKED, STICKING HIS head into the kitchen. It took a few moments before I realized he was speaking to me. I looked at Bergthora, who waved toward the door, telling me as I pulled on my coat to bring back the milk.

Outside, the air was crisp but you could feel a hint of spring. Mornings would remain cold for the next month, but gradually, as the wind shifted and began blowing from the south, it would bring warmth during the day. You could already feel the sun regaining its power.

Dust swirled across the hard packed floor when Bjorn pulled open the barn door and we were greeted by the savory scent of cured hay and the sweet bite of manure. From overhead we heard whistling and footsteps in the loft.

"Siggi always does the barn chores," Bjorn said as a forkful of hay fell through an opening at the far end of the barn, landing on the floor. "Nobody likes milking cows more than he."

Morning light shone in over the horses' heads where they stood placidly waiting in their stalls. Four cows were tethered side by side at the end of the barn. Siggi monkeyed down the ladder and quietly called each cow by name, patting their rumps as he began forking hay into the stalls. The cows swung their heads, grunting softly, reaching their long tongues around the wispy strands.

Gentle whines from behind a closed stall caught my attention, but then the door opened behind us and Stefan Frimann came in, cheerfully shaking off the cold. I hadn't seen him much since he'd saved Freyja from drowning. It was obvious he was happy to be at the mill, even though there was plenty of work to do at home. I'd overheard Magnus chuckle that Stefan and his father were too much alike to get along, and it had been old man Frimann's idea that Stefan come work at Siglunes. This was greatly to Magnus's benefit, since Stefan had inherited from his father tremendous instincts when it came to animals. Even the orneriest cow or skittish horse was calm when he took its lead.

"It's nice and warm in here," Stefan said, rubbing his mittens together. He was right. A well-kept barn is a most comfortable place to be. He lifted a bit and bridle from a hook on the wall and rubbed the bit vigorously on his sleeve, then deliberately steamed it with his breath.

"What are you doing?" I asked.

"Ever stick your tongue on frozen metal?" he asked between breaths. "Horses don't like it much either." He went over to a tall brown mare in the first stall, softly patting her as he circled around, stroking her back and ribs. He spoke to her and she nickered as he positioned the bridle between her ears and across her nose.

"There we go, girl," he said, gently pushing the bit into her mouth. "It will be calmer on the lake today."

He grinned at us as he led the horse out, the dust swirling up again. Bjorn closed the door behind him. More whimpering, louder this time, reminding us why we came.

"Finna," Bjorn said as he lifted the stall latch. "How are you today? How are your pups?"

Her tail thumped hard on the dirt floor, eyes turned upwards. Finna had a long, thick, creamy coat, and ears that flopped down but lay flat when she listened. She was easily the biggest dog I'd ever seen; she came to my waist when she stood, sturdy and thick bodied. But for now, she lay on her side with six little black and white sausages grunting as they dug at her belly.

Everything inside me softened at the sight of them. Only the runt was solid black, the rest were noticeably bigger, with varied white markings, including two with saddle backs. The runt was by itself, head bobbing as it searched for a teat, but it couldn't fight its way past its brothers and sisters.

"Born two weeks ago," Bjorn said, pulling one saddle back off Finna to set the runt in its place, holding it steady until it latched on. "Everyone says you should put the runt out of its misery but I don't have the heart to do it. Probably won't amount to much, but someone might want her."

Bjorn explained that over Christmas a doctor migrating from the east coast, on his way to Swan River, had boarded with them.

"He had a huge dog with him," he said. "Came on the lake with us one day so we harnessed him to a sleigh. He could pull as much as three huskies."

"What was his name?"

"Doctor Bennett."

"I mean the dog."

"Samson," Bjorn said. "Usually huskies will attack a strange dog, but none of ours had the courage to try."

"What did Samson do?" I asked.

"He just stood there, tongue hanging out. Sure drooled a lot."

I laughed, thinking it served those huskies right. Likely Samson was a Newfoundland and Finna a Great Pyrenees, but at the time neither of us knew much about dogs.

"I asked Doctor Bennett if I could buy Samson, but he refused. He loved him so much he wanted to keep him in his room, but Bergthora said no, so he slept in the barn."

"The doctor?"

"No, the dog." He grinned. "But I think the doctor considered it."

Patting Finna lightly on the head, he moved over so I could reach in too.

"This is Asta," he said. "She won't hurt your pups."

Then he carefully picked up the biggest one, holding him so I could see the jagged white slash on his chest. "This is my favorite. He never cries. I think he is as brave as his father already."

"Looks like a lightning bolt," I said, gently stroking the white mark. "Are you going to keep him?"

"Yes, but my aunt doesn't need to know. At least not yet."

"What are you going to call him?"

"Thor," he said.

I thought it a clever name since Thor was the God of Thunder.

Bjorn held the pup up high over his head, and little Thor was not afraid at all, even though his eyes were barely open. Then he brought the pup to eye level. "My mama would have liked Thor."

I waited, sensing he wanted to say more.

"We had a dog in Iceland, his name was Smalé. After she was gone he kept running away looking for her. Father tied him up but Smalé hated that."

"So she died?" I asked, realizing my stupidity after I said it.

"I was two. I can't even remember what she looks like now," he said, handing me Thor.

I thought of the day Solrun was born, remembering Mother's screams. I didn't know what else to say, but could imagine how he must have felt.

Siggi came from the back of the barn carrying the milk.

"We will take those inside," Bjorn said over his shoulder.

Siggi put the pails down, smiled at me holding Thor. "Runa should come see them," he said. "It might make her more excited about the baby."

When the pups were finished feeding, Bjorn persuaded Finna to stand up. The pups yipped as they unlatched, rolling in the hay as she stepped over them. Bjorn had brought along two frozen fish and, knowing their morning routine, Finna's tail wagged as she followed him outside. I tried to hush the yelping pups by stroking them, but it was no use. They were too young to want anyone but their mother.

Voices outside the barn meant the hired men were getting ready to go onto the lake. By then Siggi had brought out two more milk pails so we carried them to the house. After that Bjorn jogged to where the men stood waiting. This became our morning routine and one I looked forward to—glad to see the pups and anxious for the chance to talk with Bjorn alone.

On my third day there, Bergthora handed me a covered plate to take to Siggi's wife Runa in the little cottage. We'd finished dinner and there was a stack of mending in the front room. It was the only job I despised but would willingly tackle it ten times over if it meant I didn't have to approach a stranger's door.

I obeyed silently, pulling on my coat, then trudged reluctantly across the yard.

When Runa opened the door the first thing that struck me was her extraordinary beauty. She had a heart-shaped face, wide set eyes, and slim nose. I saw immediately why Siggi had fallen in love with her. The second thing that delighted me was the cozy little house, and I easily pictured myself living there with Bjorn.

"Hello," she said, surprised. She stepped back while pulling the door wide to invite me in.

Despite her beauty, Runa looked pale and wispy as a ghost, quite gaunt beneath the long nightdress; a heavy knitted wool sweater hung open from her shoulders nearly to her knees. Noticing my eyes go to the bulge that was her baby, she self-consciously wrapped the sweater closed and folded her arms. Her eyes went to the floor, and in that moment Bergthora's words, "she is trying to starve herself so she will lose that baby," rang true.

"Put it over there," she said, motioning to the kitchen table. "Are you Bensi's daughter?"

This shocked me. I shook my head no.

"Oh?" she said. "He was here before the storm. I assumed he brought you."

"No, my father is Pjetur Gudmundsson," I said. "We live near J.K. and Gudrun. Bensi is our neighbor." I could think of nothing more to say and began feeling foolish. "I need to get back."

She shrugged. "I understand. There is always so much to do at the big house . . ." she said, words trailing off. The only other thing she said to me as I turned to leave was, "Please do not tell Bergthora I haven't dressed yet."

So I told her I wouldn't.

Weeks passed, and each day I took Runa dinner I dreaded it less and less. Soon I looked forward to seeing her and even enjoyed our conversations. We talked about the weather, then Bergthora, the men, and finally we began to reveal bits about our own lives.

"So you believe in God?" she asked one day as I sat across the table. Her face was drawn and her eyes and nose red and swollen.

"Why wouldn't I?"

"I am not so sure anymore." She sniffled. She blew her nose into a handkerchief then dabbed her eyes.

The next day I arrived with Thor under one arm. She must have seen me coming because she opened the door and was already smiling before I came in.

"His name is Thor," I said. "He is Bjorn's favorite."

"I can see why, he is so sweet," she said, taking him right away. Thor licked her face but then squirmed so much she put him down. He bravely trotted across the floor, smelling everything while we visited. When it came time to leave, she told me that she would take Thor back to the barn. I believe it was the first time in weeks she'd put on her coat to go outside.

The next day we were sitting at the table together drinking strong tea sweetened with sugar. I'd added logs to the stove so the house was warm. After staring a long time into her cup, her lip began quivering.

"What is wrong?" I asked.

"It's about the baby," she said, blinking hard. She wiped her eyes with the sleeve of her gown and then, like a river spilling over its banks, she told me her fears so quickly that I couldn't interrupt.

Bergthora would have understood and been able to piece together what Runa said and guess the parts she'd left out, but I was too young to understand why she might think the baby was not Siggi's.

She made me promise not to tell anyone her secret.

How could I tell anyone anything? With only an inkling of how babies were made, I was more confused after the confession than when I'd come into the cottage. But what I did understand was her shame.

Talking about it was such a relief to Runa that her mood lightened from that day forward. The next morning, she put on clothes and, with my help, started housecleaning. She even said that perhaps it would turn out for the best, that the baby would be born blonde-haired like Siggi. She quietly hoped for a girl that she would name Sigga, after her husband and her grandmother who'd died a few years before.

Siggi was delighted when he came in that afternoon. He squeezed her thin shoulders with a loving hand and gave her a kiss on the cheek.

He passed by me and whispered, "Now I understand why Father calls you our good luck charm. First you tamed Bergthora, now Runa is happy again."

It was incredibly heartening to hear this, but I felt a shiver of fear. While Siggi's words were meant as a compliment, everyone knew you should never say thoughts out loud, as fortunes were quick to reverse.

Later that evening, as I sat with Magnus in front of the fireplace, the *Passion Hymns* open and resting on his lap, he asked me a question I didn't expect.

"How well does your father know Bensi?"

I sat there for a moment, unsure how to answer.

"He asked if your father owed me money, said he couldn't be trusted," he said. "And that he is hiding something. Do you know why Bensi would say this to me?"

It was impossible to hide my shock. To refuse to answer was almost as rude as him asking.

"We were told never to mention it," I said softly.

Magnus nodded thoughtfully. "Then it is not your story to tell."

To sum up my time at the castle, I'd have to say each day ran into the next, punctuated by moments alone with Bjorn.

"Nearly four weeks," Bergthora said one afternoon while we dug through the pile of freshly washed fish mitts, discarding those damaged beyond repair, matching its mate to another. I learned that I would much rather knit a mitten from scratch than repair a torn one.

"When can I go home?" I asked. Not wanting to sound ungrateful, I said that I missed my family.

"And so you should." She handed me her wide-eyed needle to thread. She adjusted her spectacles as I easily slipped the yarn through then handed it back. "I will take you home on Sunday. Perhaps you will work here again?"

"I hope to," I said quickly. While I sat darning thumbs, I fantasized that I was married to Bjorn. I imagined myself in Bergthora's shoes with a handful of children running through the house. This was so delightful I barely noticed when Magnus brought Halli Eyolfson inside.

"How are Anna and the children?" Bergthora asked as they sat down.

Magnus lifted his ledger book from the small table. Like Pabbi, he kept track of everything in one book—daily entries in the front, financial calculations and monthly summaries in the back.

"Very well," Halli said excitedly. "The house is warmer than we expected and we have more fish than we can eat. What else could a man want?"

"How is the ice holding up at The Narrows?" Magnus asked.

"The current is really moving now," Halli said, sliding a folded paper across the table. "Helgi finished pulling up all his nets yesterday."

"Já, a worrisome thing," Magnus said, putting on his spectacles. "We are almost done, too."

He unfolded the page then began jotting down the details, calculating how much lumber was needed to construct the new hall. They made small talk for a while, then Magnus handed him the quote. "Let me know when you are ready to start building."

"There is one more thing I must ask," Halli said, clearing his throat as he stood up to shake Magnus's hand. "I brought along a young man who needs work. His parents were from Hofsós. His name is Arni Thordarson. He lives with his Amma, Afi and brother in Winnipeg. They have relatives at Big Point."

"I knew his father, God bless him," Magnus said.

"Arni worked for Helgi all winter and stayed with us," Halli said as he buttoned his coat. "A nice young lad."

Bergthora sighed as she cleared the table. "Another mouth to feed."

"Spring will be here soon and we will hire another girl," Magnus said, waving good-bye to Halli. "Until then, Asta, my favorite, will help, já?"

"Only until Sunday," she reminded him.

Thinking back on that moment and seeing the two of them standing there perplexes me. How is it that sometimes the best of intentions end with disastrous results?

CHAPTER TEN

Fear not death, for the hour of your doom is set and none may escape it.
—VÖLSUNGA SAGA

"HOW FAR IS THE NARROWS?" I ASKED ON MY LAST MORNING THERE as Bjorn and I scuffed through fresh snow.

"About six miles north of here," he said. "We lived there for a while. Father worked for Helgi and we lived on the island until he bought this place."

"Ghost Island?" I asked, turning back around to look past the house at the barren lake. "Where exactly is it?"

"Good question," Bjorn chuckled, shielding his eyes against the rising sun. "You can't always see it, but it is there. About four miles out."

I squinted at the horizon. The harder I focused the blurrier it became until my eyes stung. "Then your father built the mill?"

"Thirteen years ago," he said, as we continued to the barn. "Sometimes I wish he hadn't. Everyone thinks we are rich, that Father gives me everything, but I work as hard as everyone else."

I'd witnessed how the brothers were always first outside in the morning and the last ones in at night.

"When the hired men become jealous they go work for Helgi. They find out wages are the same everywhere," he said, pulling open the barn door. "They think I am lucky, but I believe a man makes his own luck."

"My Pabbi says fishing brings him luck," I said, stomping the snow off my boots. "He is working for J.K. until he has enough money to buy his own nets."

The pups were six weeks old by then and accustomed to our routine. All except the runt were wrestling. Finna was up and she hurried outside to where Bjorn had left her fish.

"J.K. is a good man," he said, kneeling down. "Not everyone trusts him, though. Father says people are suspicious of the successful."

I tried to persuade the runt to come to me, but she cowered into the corner. She yelped so loud when I picked her up that I immediately let her go.

"You should hear what some say about Helgi." Bjorn grinned. "The ones who cannot get used to the idea that he has half-breed children with an Indian woman."

He said it so casually that I didn't know what to think. Since I was young I waited to hear his opinion, but Bjorn said nothing more, allowing me to make up my own mind.

The barn door opened and light came streaming in. The tall, beak-nosed fisherman looked over the stall door. "Something is wrong with Arni," he said.

An hour later Bjorn had harnessed the dog team. With the skill of someone who'd done it a thousand times, he ran behind the sleigh until the dogs were up to speed, then jumped on, mushing them toward The Narrows.

It was the day Bergthora planned to take me home so, watching Bjorn leave, I knew there would be no opportunity to say good-bye. I went inside to pack my clothes into the duffel, then sat it by the door.

Magnus was sitting in his usual spot. He and Bergthora spoke in hushed tones. The door opened and in came the twins followed by all the hired men.

"Asta, will you prepare a coffee lunch," Bergthora said, pulling on her coat. "I will be outside."

I retrieved the cheese and meat from the icebox, sliced bread and spooned skyr from the crock.

The chairs scraped heavily against the floor as the men all sat down at once.

"What is this about, ehh?" Einar asked. "I hope you are finally going to pay us so we can leave."

Magnus took a piece of bread from the plate before passing it around.

"Nei, not yet," he said. "Today will be a day of rest."

"What a waste of time," Einar said, leading with his chin. He hadn't shaved in more than a week. "Won't make any money, ehh, sitting in the house."

A few others agreed as they helped themselves to the food.

"The agreement was you'd work until the end of March, já?" Magnus said, waiting for their nods. "Have I paid you every month?"

The men agreed that he had.

"Then why do you complain?"

"You are making all the money," Einar said, looking to the others for support, "I want to get out of here while the ice is still good."

Siggi and Arn eyeballed each other. I knew, because Bjorn had told me, that every year there was at least one who tried their father's patience.

"There is an issue that must be dealt with first," Magnus said. "Once that is done, you are free to go."

Not even Einar had the nerve to ask. Looking back, I can see that I was the only one without an inkling of what had transpired in the bunkhouse the night before. We ate in awkward silence until finally the tall, beak-nosed fisherman found the courage to speak.

"Does this have anything to do with Arni?" he asked.

Magnus nodded. "Bjorn will be back soon. In the meantime, you are welcome to play cards. Anyone who wants to read can join me by the fire." With that he stood up. "Start another pot of coffee," he said to me, and I saw his worry for the first time. "Elskan, will you bring me a cup please."

As the hours passed I wondered why Bergthora had not returned.

When the dogs started barking, I hurried to the window and saw Bjorn. I recognized the doctor by the surgical bag he carried. I thought something must be wrong with Runa, but instead of going to the cottage, they hurried to the bunkhouse. Bergthora met them at the door. It wasn't long until the three of them tramped heavily toward the house, expressions grim.

Magnus came into the kitchen. The doctor set his bag on a chair as he took off his coat. He was thin and tentative looking with a name we couldn't pronounce. Magnus had mentioned him once before, saying that he'd received his training on the front lines during the Boer War—his specialty was gunshot wounds. But to look at him inspired no confidence at all.

"What is it?" Magnus asked.

"As we thought," Bergthora said.

Magnus turned to the doctor. "Explain it to me and I will translate."

The grave-faced doctor stood in the doorway. Each fisherman had a different way of steeling himself against what we were about to hear. One fellow laid his cards down and stared at the table. Another kept playing as if nothing at all was wrong. Einar was the most dramatic, throwing his cards down, vaulting up, sending his chair crashing to the floor.

"I am no fool," he said. "I know what this means."

Expecting to see a fist fight, all the men's eyes rested on the doctor. We did not understand his words as he spoke only English.

We looked at Magnus whose explanation was swift. "Barnaveiki. There are cases of it now at Big Point. Arni visited family there not long ago."

There were gasps, then the house became uncomfortably quiet. The coffee pot hummed as the water boiled on the stove. The men stared dumbly at Magnus, who, if you chose to see it that way, appeared to be blocking the door.

"How can this be?" a man asked. Back then, foreigners like us believed that no disease, not even Diphtheria, could withstand the brutal Canadian winters. We also believed that because the weather hadn't killed us yet, nothing else could.

"I'm leaving," Einar said.

"No," the doctor said nervously. "Siglunes is now under quarantine."

This sent a wave of discontent through the room.

"For how long?" the beak-nosed fisherman asked.

"At least a month," the Doctor said as Magnus translated. "I won't lift it until all signs of sickness are gone."

"A month," Einar said clenching his fists. "You cannot keep me here for another month."

The men looked at him, then at Magnus, calculating who would win if it came down to a fight. If circumstances were jovial, they probably would have started placing bets.

"Já, we can and we will," Magnus said raising his voice.

Einar argued that the longer they stayed, the more likely it would be that they'd catch the disease. Magnus explained everything he understood about incubation periods, that it was already too late, but Einar was not listening. No wonder his nickname was donkey.

"I caught it when I was a boy," the beak-nosed fisherman said to Einar. "I would not wish it on anyone. Not even you."

A few nervous chuckles. The doctor began speaking again.

"Even those who have had it before might still carry the disease," Magnus translated. "Nobody can leave."

The beak-nosed fisherman agreed. "I don't want to take it home to my children."

A murmur rose up and Magnus raised his hands to quieten them.

Watching it all again, I see that most of the men barely understood a word despite Magnus's translation. Regardless of intelligence, there is only so much an uneducated man can absorb. All these men could do was trust. It became obvious as they resigned themselves who respected Magnus and who didn't.

Siggi brought in an armload of wood and stoked the fire while Arn retrieved his violin and began playing. When the men were settled,

Bergthora raised a finger to her lips. It was time for us to follow the doctor outside. We waited as he nailed a yellow quarantine sign on the vestibule door, then the three of us went to the cottage where Runa waited.

"How bad is it?" Runa asked, shuffling to the stove. She opened the door before adding two thick pieces of oak to the fire. All the windows were clamped tight so it was as hot as I imagined hell would be. It must have made sense to her to boil every bit of moisture out of the air.

"The bunkhouse is now an infirmary. All the men have moved upstairs," Bergthora said to her. "It is best you stay indoors for the next few weeks."

Runa's eyes softened. "Of course."

The doctor opened his bag and took out a needle and a tiny glass bottle. He explained that the anti-toxin was new but had been used with some success. Whoever received the injection might still become sick. Because Runa and I were so young, our chances of contracting the illness were high—more than fifty percent—but less if we'd had no direct contact with Arni.

Runa's eyes settled on me. Her smile was wistful, like an older sister who'd been handed a bouquet of flowers.

"What will it do to the baby?" she asked.

The doctor said there was no way of knowing how the anti-toxin might affect her pregnancy.

Runa looked at me. "How many times were you near him?"

"A few meals, and once in the barn," I said.

"I have not seen him except through the window," Runa said.

Thinking back on it I was brave, clenching back the tears as the doctor stuck the thick needle into my arm.

"Thor will not become sick, will he?" I cried, remembering how I'd handed him to Arni a few days before.

"No, elskan," Bergthora said. "Finna and her pups will be just fine."

It took three days for poor Arni Thordarson to die. I heard that his neck swelled up and turned black, slowly suffocating him to death. I watched through the window as Bjorn, Arn, and Magnus trudged to the bunkhouse then carried Arni out like a sack of flour. They laid him in a six-foot wooden box along the bush, where the snow was deep and the sun never shone. Bergthora came out a few minutes later carrying Arni's bed sheets and a blanket. She put a match to the bundle after dropping it in the fire pit.

I overheard them say later that the dilemma surrounding a spring death was that a warm spell could cause a body to start decomposing, before the ground was soft enough to dig a decent grave.

"He should freeze solid by morning," Bjorn said. "Then we will shovel snow on top to keep it that way until we can send him home."

Two men with sore throats went to the bunkhouse that afternoon. Bergthora stayed with them, slathering their necks with the same smelly concoction she'd used on Arni.

When I started to feel sick, I didn't dare tell anyone because I didn't want to die in the bunkhouse. So I snuck off to my room, closed the door to block out the golden hue of the oil lamps and thick smell of cigarette smoke and lay in bed listening to the men talking in serious tones. One or two sometimes laughed. Occasionally I heard Bjorn's voice, but mostly it was Einar and another man. Their voices grew louder the more they drank.

As I started to doze, I overheard Einar say my name.

"All because of her, ehh," he said. The room grew quiet as his voice rose up. "We were fine until Huldra came here."

Most laughed off his suggestion, but I knew there would be some who, the next time they saw me, would cast a suspicious eye. Growing up, we'd all heard stories about the dreaded Huldra—a beautiful seductress who appeared suddenly out of the storm—so enticing that no man could resist her charms. Eventually, he who gave into her would see his life start to go wrong. No girl wanted to be labelled a huldra. The mere suggestion had a way of sticking.

"You are ridiculous," Bjorn said. "Leave Asta out of this."

"The devil does not do his own work," Einar warned.

"Then maybe the sickness came because of you," Bjorn shot back.

There were jeers and laughter until Magnus silenced them.

As the realization sank in that Einar believed I was responsible, a heart-wrenching chain of thoughts occurred to me.

Pabbi's difficulties began the year I was born. It was me who begged to go sailing the day Freyja nearly drowned—now this. The tightness in my throat seemed to grow worse. I feared I would die.

"Please God," I prayed, begging forgiveness. "Don't let me suffer like Arni."

CHAPTER ELEVEN

When ill seed has been sown, so an ill crop will spring from it.
—NJÁL'S SAGA

Now, from this place between the worlds, I must watch one of the most painful events of my life unfold.

"Do I have to go to the bunkhouse?" I whispered. My symptoms had worsened so there was no hiding that I was sick.

"No," Bjorn said, putting the large pup on the bed by my feet. "I brought him to keep you company."

Thor's tail wagged as he crawled up onto my chest and began licking my face. He was nervous being on the bed but soon settled and began gnawing at the blanket.

I drifted in and out of restless sleep. I had no idea if it was night or day. I dreamed about Mother, Pabbi, and of Freyja's near drowning, and woke up crying fitfully after seeing Leifur and Signy lying in their beds with swollen, black necks.

Bergthora came running and forced me to drink a tincture that tasted like weeds.

One night I thought I would surely die, even wished for it. I surrendered to the pain until I felt an odd sensation of letting go. The relief was shocking. My mind detached from my body and began floating away. I saw my body lying limp on the bed and Thor's curious stare up at the corner of the room. A deliberate force pulled me without effort through the wall to the outdoors. The air was below freezing yet it felt warm as I whirred over the trees and was enveloped in the sense of home-coming. This should have frightened me but it didn't. I felt only calm. There was our house. Mother and Pabbi slept in their room facing each other with Solrun in between. Upstairs, Leifur snored peacefully on his side, Signy on her back with the blanket pulled up to her chin. Freyja was downstairs in Amma's bed, tucked neatly under her arm. Then, in an instant I was back at the castle slipping back into my body. With a jarring thump, I felt the pain of the sickness, but knowing it hadn't touched my family made the discomfort bearable.

By the fourth night I felt better. I lay propped up in bed with the door slightly ajar, too dazed to think about practical matters; and to this day I cannot remember who fed Thor, who put a fish box filled with straw in the corner of the room for him to sleep in, who cleaned up the straw when he spread it everywhere.

In quiet, wakeful moments I thought of what Einar had said about me.

"Thor," Bergthora scolded, late one evening. "Look at the mess you made."

He leapt from the bed, wagging his tail, jumping against her legs, his fat paws digging at her. She brushed bits of straw off his body, scolding him softly as he mouthed her wrist.

"How are you feeling?" she asked, her hand gentle on my forehead. The full moon shone brightly in through the window. Her face was tight with concern.

"Much better," I said, hoping to ease her worry.

"I think the worst of it is over now," she said, tucking the blanket tight under my arms.

"How is Runa?" I asked.

"Runa and the baby are just fine," she said. "Giving you the antitoxin was the correct choice."

I was relieved to hear this. "The others?"

"Don't concern yourself with them," she said, kissing my forehead. "Get some rest."

In the middle of the night the bedroom door opened again. My mind was still churning so I awoke easily. My initial thought was that Bergthora had returned to check on me, but the footsteps were different and I sensed it was a man.

"Bjorn?" I whispered, opening my eyes.

He didn't say anything as he stood beside my bed.

"Magnus?" I asked.

As my eyes adjusted to the moonlight shining in through the window, I saw it was Einar. He stank of sweat and alcohol.

"Huldra," he said, words slurred and mocking. "You have everyone fooled, but not me."

By the time I realized that I should scream it was too late. His disgusting hand clamped down hard on my mouth, pressing my head against the pillow. The moonlight on his face morphed it into a vile mask as he bent close.

"Why did you come here?" He grabbed my hair with his other hand. "To tempt me?"

My heart leapt in my chest. Deep in my gut there was an understanding of what he wanted and a fear like nothing I'd ever experienced. I started to cry.

I could hear Thor whining and growling in the corner.

"Girls and their tears," he taunted. "What did that bitch tell you, ehh?"

My mind whirled. I had no idea what he was talking about. I tried to shake my head no.

He laughed. His hand let go of my hair and pulled back the quilt.

"Please, no," I begged. He slapped me hard. A painful flash of light behind my eyes and then he grasped my throat. He began squeezing. I flailed at him, the breath trapped in my lungs.

When all the fight left me he released his hand and I choked in a gulp of air.

I dared not scream fearing he would strangle me again.

Then he called me a whore and all at once I understood how vile a word it was, what old Uncle Ásgeir had meant when he said it to Amma.

I whimpered as he climbed on top of me and forced my legs apart.

"You want it," he whispered, breath hot against my ear. "I see how you look at me. You and Runa both."

The pain was piercing, like a knife. He pressed his forearm across my mouth. My mind drifted far away. I listened to Thor and his puppy growls as Einar pounded me into the bed until he was spent. The anger left him. My insides throbbed and it took every ounce of control to quiet my sobs.

"Tell anyone and I will kill you," he rasped. "Don't think Bjorn can protect you from me, he is a coward. I will enjoy killing you and your dog."

I heard footsteps and a voice in the hallway. It was Bjorn. "Asta?"

Einar hissed. He pushed himself up from the bed and slunk out of the room as quietly as he'd come.

"Einar? What the—"

"Beat you to it," he hissed.

"You bastard," Bjorn said.

Harsh whispers, swearing, and then banging against my door. A struggle and grunts. Einar laughing. The front door swung open and slammed shut.

It is over, I told myself. *Over, and he's gone.*

"What's going on?" Bergthora called from her room at the end of the hall.

Bjorn hesitated. "Nothing," he said into the quiet darkness. "Einar had too much to drink that's all."

"Well hush, you'll wake the whole house."

He stood just inside my door for a long while. "Asta?" he whispered.

"Yes," I heard myself say.

"Are you all right?"

I found the quilt and pulled it up like a barricade.

"Are you all right?"

"I am sorry," was all I could say. The shame was unbearable. I must have been sobbing because he stood frozen in the moonlight, arms hanging uselessly by his side.

"It's not your fault," he said.

"It is," I said. I couldn't tell him how desperately I dreamed of marrying him, tried to look prettier and older than I was to gain his attention. I had attracted Einar instead. This most certainly was my fault. Everything Runa had told me that afternoon in the cottage made sense. Einar had even confirmed it.

"I should have known," he said through clenched teeth. "I should have done something before this—"

There is a story in the sagas about a man who bullied everyone around him, wreaking havoc wherever he went until finally a small man stood up to him, and even though the man lost his life by doing so, it roused everyone else and eventually the bully was killed. I remembered the look on Amma's face as she closed the book.

"He hurt Runa too," I whispered.

Bjorn's head tilted. He was unsure if he'd heard me correctly. "What did you say?"

I stared at the quilt pulled tight over my knees. It was hard to formulate the words.

"Tell me," he rasped.

"That is why she is sad all the time," I whispered. "And does not like the baby much."

It took a few moments for Bjorn to piece it all together. The shadow of his jaw tightened as my words began to make sense.

"You should have told me," he said.

"I didn't understand until tonight."

Bjorn growled. He stood shaking his head.

"Please don't tell anyone," I said.

He was no longer listening. He looked at me one last time, eyes the angriest I'd ever seen, and left the room, leaving the door ajar.

Fearing Einar might return, I lay awake most of the night. As daybreak began filtering in through the window, I rose on wobbly legs. My face felt swollen and tight. I pulled the sheet from the bed, determined to scrub away all evidence from the night before.

The sun was barely up. All was quiet in the house, but outside I heard the faint sound of voices so I went to the kitchen window. Two shadows were crossing the yard half-dragging something between them. As they neared I recognized Bjorn and Siggi pulling Einar across the frozen ground. Einar had one arm crossed protectively over his ribs. Bjorn shoved him hard. Einar fell forward onto the ground, his other hand protecting his head. Siggi kicked him hard in the gut. Bjorn grabbed him by the coat, pulled him to his feet, shoving him forward toward the lake. When he fell again, Siggi kicked him repeatedly in the head. The brothers dragged him the rest of the way to the lake bank.

This was a most horrific thing, and yet I needed to see. On tiptoes, I ran to the end of the hall and opened the front door just enough to peer out.

A frigid draft blew in, chilling my feet.

They dragged Einar to the sleigh that was already hitched to the dog team. They swung his body onto the sleigh. Bjorn mounted, cracked a whip overhead, and the dogs took off in the direction of Ghost Island. Siggi stood there watching until they were out of sight.

I closed the door, tiptoed back to my room, but continued watching out the window until Bjorn returned with an empty sleigh. He must have sensed me standing there, because he looked up. Our eyes locked together in a moment that would become the secret we'd share for the rest of our lives.

"How are you feeling, Elskan?" Bergthora asked an hour later as I stood at the sink washing the sheet. I'd been so preoccupied thinking about the night before and what I'd seen in the early morning, I hadn't heard her come into the kitchen.

I spun around, so rattled I could barely speak

"Much better," I said.

It was not a total lie. The fever still plagued me but seemed trivial compared to everything else. Nor could I look her in the eye. Never before had I experienced such shame.

"There are rags you can use in the bottom dresser drawer," she said. "Wash them out and take them when you leave. I have no use for them anymore." Her monthlies were long done and she assumed mine had started.

During breakfast, Magnus asked why Einar wasn't there. I looked immediately at Bjorn. He looked up from his plate, directly at his father, and shrugged innocently. The knuckles on his left hand were raw. Siggi said nothing as he kept his head down. The rest of the men, including Arn, kept eating.

"Probably started walking home," Bjorn said.

"Without getting paid?" Magnus said, looking up from his newspaper. "That seems unlikely."

"He had no intention of waiting out the quarantine," Arn said. "Snuck away when we weren't looking."

Magnus shook his head. "Já, well, I wish there was a way to warn his family. I hate to think of all the innocent people he might infect."

The rims of Bjorn's ears flushed. "I'm glad he's gone."

"I've never met a more brutish man," Bergthora said with a snort. "Well at least Runa will not have to make him coffee anymore."

Without a word Siggi stood up and took his plate to the sink. He threw it in, startling everyone, then stormed across the floor then out the door.

"I guess Siggi didn't like him after all," Arn chuckled, and everyone except Bjorn and I laughed.

"I agree, good riddance to him," the beak-nosed fisherman said. "I never did trust the look in his eye."

A murmur of agreement flowed around the table and the mood lightened. Einar was gone and nobody cared what happened to him.

I never discussed with Bjorn how much I'd seen that morning. He always quickly changed the subject the few times Einar's name came up.

Three weeks into the quarantine, Siggi burst into the house. "The baby is coming," he said, breathless.

"She seemed fine yesterday," said Bergthora, coming around the corner from the front room, grabbing her bag. She told Siggi to wait but waved at me to come with her.

The sun was warm and the air smelled of hot wood as we hurried by the men working in the mill. The shrill of the buzz saw shaving through oak logs filled our ears, blocking out all other sounds, until it halted and another log was slid forward. It was in those moments we heard hammering, the rhythmic sound of caskets being built.

Runa was sitting on the edge of the bed in a daze, massaging her stomach.

"It is too soon," she said, looking up at us.

"I know," Bergthora said. "Did your water break?"

Runa nodded.

"Pain?"

"It comes and goes. It started early this morning. I did not want to worry Siggi."

This time it was I who took the instruments from the bag to place in boiling water as Bergthora helped Runa lie on the bed. I shuddered as Bergthora skillfully lifted her knees and spread her legs, the image of Einar so vivid I had to excuse myself for a few moments, to sit down until the lightheaded feeling passed.

"There is not much we can do," Bergthora said softly.

"But why?"

Bergthora shook her head. "Sometimes this happens."

"Will the baby live?" Runa groaned, clenching, as a ripple that began along her spine crept up over both sides of her belly, tightening hard, causing her to cry out. When she could breathe again, she asked Bergthora a second time.

"It depends," she said. "Sometimes the date is wrong. If you are further along than we thought, there is a chance."

This seemed to lighten Runa's outlook. "Further along . . . that would be wonderful."

Runa labored for another four hours until it came time for her to push. The baby was tiny and came quickly with no need for instruments. Runa laughed and cried, her chest heaving with exhaustion, as Bergthora quietly snipped the cord.

"A boy or a girl?" she asked between breaths.

"Go get Siggi," Bergthora whispered to me.

I ran out of the cottage, my feet slipping almost immediately and I landed on the hard packed snow wet from the melt, banging my head on the ground. The sky overhead was a disorienting mash of sun and fluffy clouds. The squeal of the saw was relentless.

I shook it off, praying as I ran that everything was going to be all right, focusing on the yellow sign on the vestibule door. I knew that Runa had prayed, too, early on in the pregnancy that she would miscarry. Then later, that she'd rather be dead than give birth to Einar's child. But once the baby started to kick, she began prayers of hope.

I flung open the door, hollering for Siggi. Magnus and Bjorn threw on their coats and followed. Magnus had already sent for the doctor. We all came quietly in and stood watching as Siggi went over to the bed. Bergthora whispered something to him. He dropped to his knees.

Runa was crying, holding the naked baby to her heart. Born too early, he was a fair-skinned child with blonde hair. His muted cries and tiny clenched fists were weak and, after only a few minutes, he grew quiet as his tiny lungs began failing. His skinny legs pulled up to his chest and there was nothing any of us could do except watch his energy slip away.

I've never forgotten Runa's despair, how her hope dissolved. Bergthora didn't have to say the bleeding was heavy, as she swiftly removed the padding on the bed, replacing it many times over.

Placenta accreta. Now I understand. Massive bleeding during delivery due to a placenta embedded too deep in the uterus.

Magnus and Bjorn sat silently at the table by the window. Arn refused to come in. He sat on a bench outside the door, waiting. Hours passed and when the outcome was certain, Bjorn looked at me with such disbelief in his eyes, I turned away. He bent forward and placed his head in his hands. Magnus, in his soft, comforting voice began reciting the 23rd Psalm.

Siggi held Runa's hand, stroking her hair back, whispering that she was going to be all right, but Runa turned away. She was distracted by something going on elsewhere in the room.

"Please do something," Siggi whispered to us through clenched teeth.

Bergthora gently patted his back. She took the dead infant and wrapped it in a blanket. I have never forgotten either how peaceful Runa became as she focused on the wall, speaking to her dead grandmother, saying how glad she was to see her again, whispering that she needed to go. Her last words to Siggi before quietly slipping away: "We will see you soon."

For weeks afterwards, every time I closed my eyes, all I could see was the image of Siggi crying over his wife's body, their son lying at the foot of the bed like an afterthought.

CHAPTER TWELVE

Long shall a man be tried.
—GRETTIR'S SAGA

THE OLD WOMAN BESIDE ME HAS DIED.

I slept through her passing and so did her daughter. I know this because there were no wails or anguished cries, only muffled sobbing as the nurse led the daughter from the room, whispering reassurances that she'd died peacefully.

I expect her soul has joined the others that crowd the room, kind spirits who gather to let the dying know they are welcome on the other side. Or perhaps I am imagining it all.

Thora looks apologetic when the nurse returns to remove the body as if this death might cause me to lose heart. She does not comment, though, as she turns to unlatch the window for, what is it now, the eighth morning in a row? Her dedication is impressive. Some believe it's hard to sleep on a not-so-comfortable chair, drinking stale coffee, eating dinner from a paper bag. But old timers like us see no hardship in short-term inconvenience.

"Who was she again?" I ask once the nurse has wheeled the body out the door.

"Mary Swan," Thora says.

"Of course." I nod. "Do you remember?"

The word croaks out and I cough, trying to loosen the tangle in my throat. I feel better than I sound. Using my elbows, I push myself up.

Thora tilts her head. "Remember what?"

"Our years at Winnipeg General."

She hesitated then her mouth quirked upwards. "Those were good times."

"The hardest three years of our lives."

"Tell me what you remember most," she says, encouraging me to roll onto my side. She begins massaging my shoulders and back. Her hands are petite but effective, though I wish she'd thought to trim her fingernails first.

I see in my mind's eye a room full of young, tittering apprentices wearing dark blue starched uniforms, white aprons, and caps. Most were boy-crazy, others smoked whenever they found the chance, but we all shared the same goal—to become a nurse.

It sure wasn't easy. Some girls cried over nothing, and the occasional one defied the acerbic head nurse who pretended she hated us all. We lived with the pressure of on-the-job training, twelve-hour shifts. Rigid rules. Suspensions.

"They thought we were sisters," I say. "Except Dr. Bjornsson. He played along so we could trick the others into thinking we were."

"An Icelander—"

"So he was never fooled," I say. "What do you remember?"

Thora pauses and her hands relax for a moment. She dabs a rag with rubbing alcohol, begins massaging it into my skin.

"How exciting it was to be in Winnipeg," she says. "Riding on the streetcars. Going to the cafés. Hospitals were impressive."

"They certainly were."

"Mostly, though, I remember the maternity ward," she says, her voice breaking a bit. "Especially the unmarried girls who were forced to give up their babies."

"Dr. Bjornsson was kind," I say. "He arranged Icelandic homes for many, some right here in Lundi. And he did help us try to find Freyja."

Thora tenses and I know I've made a mistake, hurt her again. Our few disagreements were about Freyja. There is nothing to gain by saying more. Especially now.

"I want to go outside today," I say, rolling onto my back after she refastens the nightgown.

"We will," she says. "The fresh air will do you good."

* * *

"Good morning, elskan," Magnus said over his spectacles. He was sitting at the table with his journal open. "Good news. The doctor sent word that the quarantine is over. Bjorn can take you home today if you wish."

I'd been so preoccupied with my own awakening over how cruel men could be, and the deep need to hide my shame, I'd been sleeping in later and later. I had to think hard how many days had passed since Runa died.

"Yes, I would like that very much," I said. "Where is Bergthora?"

"She took Siggi something to eat."

"He hasn't come out yet?"

Magnus shook his head. When the door opened Bjorn and Arn stepped inside carrying the milk. Magnus closed his journal then unfolded a letter that sat with a stack of mail on the table.

"Arni's mother asked that he be buried at Big Point," he said. "He and the Jonsson brothers can be sent home on the Lady Ellen with the casket order. Their community was hit even harder than ours."

"And Halli?" Bjorn asked.

"He needs only one casket," Magnus said. "We will ask Stefan to take it on his way home."

Thor jumped against my legs as he followed me to my room, wanting me to play with him. All I could think about as I packed my duffel was the look of shock on Bjorn's face when he saw me at the bedroom window. We'd said very little to each other since, and had not mentioned Einar.

Tension hung between us, even the night before when we'd played chess.

"Soon I won't be able to beat you," he'd said quietly when I took his rook early in the game. Clearly he was preoccupied, while I'd discovered that concentrating hard helped push all the ugly memories away.

"How long until all the ice is gone?" Bjorn had asked Magnus as he set up the board for one last game.

"Not long, why do you ask?"

He shrugged. "I haven't been to the island in a while."

My insides turned at the mention of it and I felt my cheeks warm.

"Já, well, you know how the lake is this time of year," Magnus said. I'd looked over to where he sat, legs up, thick socks facing the fire. "She is like a lover, já, one whose predictability should never be taken for granted."

I placed my bag by the door then finished washing the dishes.

"Still working," Magnus said as he came from the front room holding a cloth envelope.

"I feel terrible leaving Bergthora with so much to do," I said, folding the dishrag on the counter.

"You have been a tremendous help, now we must discuss how much I owe you," he said, opening the envelope.

His words caught me by surprise. "Nothing sir. I came here to repay Father's debt."

Magnus lowered his chin so his eyes were level with mine. "Já, and that you did, but stayed on much longer, so now it is I who am indebted to you."

A girl like myself wasn't worth much, so the thought of taking money from him seemed wrong. "Father needs a dog to keep the coyotes and wolves away from the sheep." I could already see myself sitting in the boat with Thor on my lap, his little puppy face staring with curiosity in the direction of Eikheimar. My family would come running to the shore, throw their arms around me, and be thrilled to finally have me home.

Magnus's eyes twinkled and he nearly chuckled, but did not give me

Thor. He'd grown fond of having him in the house, a practice that was unheard of in those days. He went to the barn and returned with the runt, who was still smaller than her littermates but had grown considerably. "This one reminds me of you," he said, handing her to me.

I bit back my disappointment. There was a lesson for me in this, one I wouldn't fully understand until many years later.

"I don't think she will be much good against the coyotes," I whispered, blinking away tears. "She is a coward."

"A dog is like its master," he said. "How she turns out will be up to you." Then he grew serious as his thoughts shifted. "Stay away from Bensi," he said. "I do not trust that man. Remind your father that the only way to win against a bully is to stand up to him . . . and tell Pjetur to not let his secret destroy his life."

Following Magnus, Bergthora, and Bjorn to the dock, I tried coaxing the pup to come, but she ran back toward the barn. I chased her down and she whined when I picked her up.

"Good-bye, Asta," Magnus said, pressing a wad of folded bills into my hand. Then he cautioned Bjorn to watch for rocks hidden along shore as he climbed into the small rowboat.

Bergthora leaned in to hug me. "He is too old for you now, but time will change that," she whispered. "The day will arrive and you will know what to do."

"Say hello to your Amma for us." Magnus winked as he handed Bjorn my duffel, and I stepped into the boat and sat at the stern as Bjorn, facing me, took the oars. "Tell her to come for a visit some time."

I turned away from them so that Magnus and Bergthora wouldn't see my tears. When the boat was far enough away from the dock, I waved. The sight of them standing there watching me leave is etched in my memory.

The lake was calm along shore but still frozen less than a mile out. We both rowed in silence, unable to stop ourselves from sneaking quick peeks at Ghost Island. Bjorn didn't relax until we rounded a bend and could no longer see it. We could not meet each other's gaze, and then I covered my ears at the honk of wild geese gliding low overhead, much to his amusement.

"The snow is almost gone," he said hopefully, nudging the boat toward the shoreline.

It was true. The warm April sun had melted most of it. Rivulets lacerated the fields as the run-off muscled its way to the Siglunes creek, a meandering low spot that separated their land from Bensi's. I thought of Magnus's words as we rowed past the log house partially hidden in the trees.

"What will you tell your family?" Bjorn asked, voice low and serious.

Einar was never far from my thoughts so I knew without hesitation he was referring to that night.

"Best if you don't say anything to anyone," he said, "because they will ask questions."

I could see the dock at Vinðheimar in the distance.

"And you can forget about Einar," he said. "Siggi and me, we put the fear of God in him. He took off and won't be coming back."

It was then I realized he didn't know how much I'd seen.

"Will you promise?"

"Of course," I whispered.

Expecting my family to be waiting at the dock was unrealistic since nobody had known I was coming home that day. But seeing us approach the dock, J.K.'s family came running out to greet us, and all were thrilled to see me except for their youngest who, believing I was a ghost, hid behind Gudrun's skirt.

Word of the casualties at Siglunes had travelled here but somehow, in the telling of it, the young woman who'd died in the cottage was me. Gudrun persuaded her daughter to touch my arm; she reassured me that my family knew the truth.

"Your mama cried for days when she thought you were gone," Gudrun said, hugging me tight. "I am so glad you survived, Asta. You are such a delightful girl."

No one had ever called me delightful before.

"Would you like to come in?" she asked.

Bjorn said he needed to get back to the mill.

J.K. offered to take me home by horse but I said I would rather walk so I set out with my duffel over my arm and the pup at foot. And I see now that Thora accompanied me on that walk home, asking many questions that I answered in a rather dull fashion.

The pup began whimpering and refused to go any farther when we reached the bush so I was forced to carry her the rest of the way. She'd thrown up in the bottom of the boat so her breath smelled terrible.

Everyone was shocked when I came through the door.

"My Asta is home," Freyja yelled as she ran to greet me, nearly knocking me down. Pabbi lifted me up and hugged me hard, but I was unable to hug him back because I was still holding the large pup.

"I brought a dog to guard the sheep but I don't think she will be much good," I said.

Pabbi's brows raised and he laughed, eyes moist with tears. He handed the dog to Freyja who was jumping up and down, clapping her hands.

"Asta brought us a dog," she cheered.

Next to pull me into a warm embrace was Amma, who sang a short prayer of thanks for my safe return. Baby Solrun, who'd been asleep in a fish box on the floor, began to cry.

"Asta," Mother said as I hugged her. "You look so grown up."

Digging into my bag I pulled out the money Magnus had given me. Mother smiled, motioning for me to give it to Pabbi. The look on his face filled me with pride.

"Asta, my girl," he said. "I always knew you were an industrious one."

Within minutes it was as if I'd never left.

Freyja climbed onto my lap. She wrapped her skinny arms tightly around my neck. Amongst the noise and clatter, Leifur and Signy began arguing as we finished eating. Pabbi was curious to know how Magnus's fishing crew had made out that year and asked many questions that I tried my best to answer.

I must have mentioned Bjorn's name too many times because Signy began grilling me with questions. When I refused to answer, she started teasing.

"Asta has a sweetheart," she sang.

"Bjorn is too old for me," I said.

Signy raised her eyebrows. "Well, not too old for me."

The look on my face told her everything she needed to know.

"Ah-ha!" she said.

"Magnus told me to say hello to you, Amma," I said, changing the subject, "and that you should visit soon."

"Did he?" Amma cooed. "Awfully nice of him."

Mother slanted her eyes in Amma's direction. "Not your next victim, I hope."

"Are you going to wrestle him?" Freyja asked.

"I just might," Amma said, humming to herself.

"Freda," Mother scolded under her breath.

Freyja leaned in to whisper: "J.K. lied. He told us you were dead."

I shook my head. "He did not mean to, he believed it was true."

"Promise you will never go away again," she said.

"I promise."

Through it all, Leifur stared. I could not look at him for more than a few seconds without turning away. My heart lurched at the thought that he might know my secret, that I was as different on the outside as I felt inside.

"What did the dead men look like?" he asked.

"Hush," Mother said. "Asta will tell us when she is ready."

But I never was. I pushed it all away, pretending Arni's neck hadn't swollen up and that Runa didn't die. But most of all, I locked away memories of Einar. I concluded that God does have a way of answering our prayers, but not always as we expect. Arni's suffering was short. So was Runa's.

Mine would last a lifetime.

CHAPTER THIRTEEN

Fear is the mother of defeat.
—KING ÓLAF TRYGGVASON'S SAGA

LIFE FOR ME AT EIKHEIMAR WOULD NEVER BE THE SAME, EVEN though the daily routine returned to normal—so quickly, in fact, that I felt rather insignificant. A close bond had developed between Signy and Leifur that no longer included me. I sensed their hesitation. It was almost as if they regretted mourning me and didn't want to be tricked into it again.

Sleep did not come easily. I was plagued by nightmares and dreaded the nights the moon cast our bedroom in a blue shadow. Many times I did not fall asleep until the early morning hours, making it difficult to rise in time for school. Sometimes I'd jolt awake to Mother's alarm.

"Asta, it is just a dream," she'd say, hands gripping my shoulders.

On the nights sleep eluded me, I'd listen to the family undertones. Signy softly falling asleep on her back and barely moving. Freyja's constant mumbling. Leifur thrashing so violently that he'd wake himself up. Footsteps downstairs and the rub of the front door as Amma visited the outhouse.

A week later the ground thawed enough that a funeral date was set and the caskets were dug out of the shoveled pile of snow and ice. We gathered on a foggy, damp morning at the mill, in a small clearing not too far from the cottage, where Magnus performed Runa's service. I stifled back tears, hiding my face in a handkerchief the whole time. Everything Magnus said made me think of Einar. When he was done, I was convinced that God couldn't let what happened go unpunished.

"I will do it myself," Siggi said, jaw set as he picked up the spade. Bjorn protested but Siggi chased him away with angry eyes.

As we walked slowly to the dock, the only noise that echoed through the trees was the hollow thud of dirt on the casket top. It's a sound you never forget, even after hearing it only once.

We boarded the Lady Ellen again for the short trip to Halli's farm, which sat close to the lake on land that was low and wet. I was surprised by the number of boats pulled up to shore and how many people milled around, waiting for the funeral to begin.

We filed up from the beach in a straight line. I barely recognized Halli, who stood at the edge of it all, under a thick oak whose leaves hadn't yet started to bud. In later years, that tree would be a lasting reminder of that spring's devastating toll and the heartbreak that our community never forgot. The image of that single casket sitting on the ground settled forever in my soul.

When the door of their little log shanty opened, Halli's wife appeared with their oldest daughter, so close they appeared fused at the hip. They came to stand by Halli, whose most notable trait, exuberant cheer, had completely dissolved.

As we gathered around the grave Magnus began the service, reading four names from the paper he held. All but one of their children had died. Unable to separate them in death, Halli had placed their little bodies together in the casket.

Magnus's words were mercifully short. When he finished, Halli's wife stepped forward like a woman in a trance, her tears long dried up. Somehow she found the strength to kneel down to pray alongside the casket. It was Bergthora who helped her to her feet.

Asi cleared his throat and with a hand crushing his hat tight to his chest, began singing Góða Nótt, a hymn I hadn't heard since Amma sang it the day we laid my infant brother to rest.

We all joined in, our voices tight and wavering, until gradually we gained strength from the words. Stefan stared solemnly at the sky until his shoulders began heaving. When he looked at me, the moment bonded us forever in a mixture of grief and hope. Somehow I knew, without him ever having to say so, that this was how his older sister had died.

Everyone fell in love with the pup we named Setta, Freyja especially so. When Mother looked at our sister's pleading face, she softened to the idea that Setta be allowed to sleep in the lean-to.

Having spent the last three months with adults, I was now aware of how contrary children could be, but when it came to Setta we all agreed. We carried hay for her bed and not one of us ever complained when it was our turn to feed her. Even Leifur was quick to clean up her messes—fearing that if Mother noticed she'd be exiled to the barn.

The mere sight of us would send Setta into a wagging frenzy. So excited to see us, she'd lick our faces, but was never offended when we pushed her away. Morning and evening she trotted on Leifur's heels to the barn to watch him milk the cow. She went with Amma to the well, jumping back when the water swooshed out. Her cautiousness meant she stayed away from the oxen's feet and always followed a safe distance behind the wagon.

There was only one person who could give Setta a meaningful scolding and that was me. She always listened when I spoke, tilted her head questioningly, or cowered when I raised my voice, especially if I wagged my Signy finger at her. I think she knew deep down that I'd loved Thor and was desperate for my approval.

"We should have named her after Freyja," Signy said one afternoon while planting the garden. I looked up from covering the seed potatoes with my foot to see Setta rolling in the fresh dirt, tongue lolling out. A few feet away Freyja pranced in a circle, waving a stick like a fairy wand.

By mid-June the creeks were still high, and thick with pickerel spawn, but the ground was nearly dry. The fish flies were out of this world, buzzing in off the lake, sticking to everything before dying in heaps that stunk so badly under the windows we had to shovel them away.

Asi was in a particularly buoyant mood the day he brought a lumber order to the Vinðheimar dock where J.K. and Pabbi waited with their wagons.

"Our hay crop will be tremendous this year," Asi said as they unloaded the wood. "I bought a dozen Shorthorn heifers from Big Point. They have more for sale if you are interested."

"Cattle?" Pabbi asked.

Asi nodded. "We are not in Iceland anymore. There will always be a market here for cream and beef."

The community chose a spot on the same ridge as our house, two miles as a crow flies from the lake along the road to Siglunes, to build our first school. A work bee was organized and construction began. We were anxious to hear how the first day went when Pabbi and Leifur arrived home that evening.

"You should have heard Bensi," Leifur said as Signy put supper on the table. "He tried telling Oli the carpenter he was doing it all wrong."

Mother shook her head, glancing at Pabbi. "What did Oli say to that?"

"He listened. Nodded a few times, but we all kept right on building as he'd shown us in the first place," Leifur said.

I wished Amma was there to hear the story, but she'd left two days earlier to visit Bergthora.

"Then Bensi had the nerve to ask who is going to administer the school," Pabbi said. "J.K. told him it will be decided at a meeting."

"Does J.K. want to do it?"

"No. There is talk that we need to form a municipality and you know how J.K. loves politics," he said. "He and Magnus are on that committee."

Mother was quiet for a moment. She left Pabbi sitting at the table to fetch the coffee pot. "Someone has to do it. Why not you?"

Pabbi was clearly flattered but shook his head.

"You are more educated than most men around here," she coaxed. "Can you think of anyone better?"

"Oli, Asi, Halli—"

"Nonsense," she said.

We could see by his expression, the inward turn of his eye as he blew on his coffee, that he was considering the idea. Though none of us dared say it, we knew he hesitated because of what had happened in Iceland.

"The people here are kind," she reminded him.

"I think you should do it," Leifur said as he stood up to go to his room. "That would show Bensi a thing or two."

"That is not a good reason," Pabbi said, draining the saucer. "I will do it, but only if the community believes I am the best man for the job."

This reminded me of what Magnus said the day I left the mill. I'd forgotten about it until then but waited until Pabbi and I were alone that evening.

"Bensi went to see Magnus," I said. "He asked about you."

Pabbi raised his eyes from the book he was studying. He was teaching himself to read and write English so he practiced every night.

"He asked who paid for the lumber for our house."

The muscles in Pabbi's cheeks twitched and he found it hard to look at me.

"Magnus said that I should stay away from Bensi," I added.

"Did he say anything else?" he asked. I knew the answer was important to Pabbi so I repeated Magnus's words carefully.

"Bensi told him you have a secret. Magnus said to not let it ruin your life."

One afternoon at the beginning of August, Pabbi rode with J.K. to the Dog Creek Reservation, returning that evening leading a white mare and black gelding—two powerful, thick horses that were well matched in size. Pabbi named the female Strong and the male Hector, after the man who'd raised them from colts.

Haying began a few days later. Those first years we cut the hay by hand using a scythe but soon Pabbi bought a mower. The horses were a tremendous help as one pulled the mower and the other the sweep, a contraption that piled the dry hay. There was an art to making a good stack, which Pabbi had learned while we lived in Lundi. A well-built stack was like a mountain—solid throughout with a rounded peak, making it virtually impermeable to rain.

Everyone except Mother worked in the hayfield, and many days I stayed back to help her with Solrun. Fresh hay caused my eyes to water and my nose to plug so badly I could hardly breathe.

"They are late," Mother said one evening as she pushed the door open with her hip. August was always hot, so most days we ate outdoors. Steaming pot in hand, she paused to look in the direction of the west hay field, our land that bordered Bensi's. Usually they brought a stack home each evening so it was a surprise when they came, horses bumping across the trail, with everyone sitting on the empty hayrack. Most of their anger had worked away by then, but we saw immediately that something was wrong.

Amma's words came out fast and furious. She called Bensi the worst curse word I'd ever heard, throwing her hat to the ground.

"He stole yesterday's stack," she said. "Must have done it last night."

Leifur threw his hat down beside Amma's. Every inch of him except for his forehead was tanned and covered with hay dust.

Pabbi was so irate he didn't say a word. He took a plate then held it out as Mother began dividing up the mutton stew.

"Probably jealous you bought those cows," Amma said.

"And the horses," Signy said.

"I think tonight when it is dark we should go steal it back," Leifur said.

Signy snorted. "It's not stealing if it belongs to you."

Everyone agreed. Pabbi sat down in the grass to eat. They'd already debated this at length while in the field and there was little Pabbi resisted more than discussing something more than once.

"We have no proof," he finally said.

"Who else could have done it?" Amma howled.

"I know," Pabbi said, voice rising. "But I can't prove it."

I missed what was said after that since Mother sent me inside for the coffee pot.

Pabbi did not believe in an eye for an eye like most others. He'd already learned the hard way that ill intentions brought an ill reward. Because of this, he always prayed for guidance while encouraging us to do the same. I expect that is what he'd done all afternoon—despite Amma, Leifur, and Signy's outbursts.

"God will punish him," I said, thinking this would console Pabbi.

Amma held up her coffee cup since she was always first done.

Pabbi looked up from his plate. "There may be nothing I can do about Bensi stealing my hay," he finally said. "But I will do everything in my power to prevent a thief from running our school."

Mother agreed wholeheartedly. "Who shall we ask to nominate you?"

"Do not worry about that," Amma said quickly as she lifted the cup to her lips, wincing a bit since the coffee was even hotter than she was. "You let me take care of it."

CHAPTER FOURTEEN

No one is a total fool if he knows when to hold his tongue.
—GRETTIR'S SAGA

PABBI'S ANGER SETTLED INTO A QUIET RESOLVE AS HE WAITED FOR the meeting. Every evening, he and Mother sat together under Amma's oak (we named it that after she saved it from the axe), making notes. We were not allowed to listen as Pabbi stood alone facing an imaginary audience, looking up from the page, pausing occasionally to scratch out a word. He came in at night distracted, with his speech still rolling through his mind.

When the day finally came we put on our best clothes and clambered into the wagon, baby Solrun on Mother's knee, Freyja on mine. Amma sat in her usual spot on a chair leaning against the backboard. She immediately lit a cigarette.

"Who did you get that from?" Mother tsked as Pabbi turned the horses, clicked his tongue, slapped the reins and the wagon jolted forward.

"Magnus," she said.

Every time Amma lit a cigarette, Leifur asked if he could try it but she always refused, except this time she handed it to him. He hesitated, unsure what to do as he put it to his lips.

"Now take a deep breath," she said. "Take the smoke all the way into your lungs."

Leifur's eyes were bright. Concentrating, he did exactly as told.

"Freda," Mother scolded, turning all the way around in her seat.

Leifur's eyes widened. He coughed hard, and a stream of smoke burned out through his nose. He shook his head as he handed it back to her, wiping his mouth with the back of his hand. "That is horrible," he said, spitting twice over the side of the wagon.

Amma laughed. She took a deep drag, held the smoke in, then turned to the sky, blowing a straight line into the air. "Best you never get used to it," she said.

"Don't worry, Ella," Pabbi whispered, "she did the same thing to me."

We were a half mile from home before I realized that I'd forgotten to brush my hair. I began running my fingers through it. Signy noticed and asked what I was doing. I shrugged like it didn't matter.

"Excited to see Bjorn?" she teased, singing his name.

It was so difficult to hide anything from her.

"I know you are," she giggled.

The truth was I'd had only nightmares since finding out the meeting would be at the mill. In those horrible dreams, Bjorn turned his back on me as Einar chased me up the staircase, down the long hallway. The moment I was caught, his grinning face became Bensi's, and Pabbi was there but helpless to do anything. Night after night I relived it all, waking up screaming.

"I can hardly wait to meet him," Signy said, pulling my thoughts back to her. "He is closer to my age anyway."

My heart hurt but I kept my thoughts private.

"He will probably think you are an ugly cow," Leifur said to Signy, raising his arms up to protect himself as she punched him hard.

"Leifur," Mother scolded over her shoulder. "Stop talking to your sister like that."

"It is true." He laughed. She punched him again.

Amma always enjoyed it when those two fought, taking a different side each time.

“Consider yourself lucky to find a wife as pretty as Signy,” she said.

Surprised, Signy beamed, while Leifur pulled a face, pretending to vomit.

“I was pretty like that when I was her age,” Amma said, taking another drag from her cigarette. “Look at me now.”

Leifur threw back his head in glee. Signy’s eyes widened.

“We all need something to look forward to,” Mother quipped, patting Pabbi heartily on the knee, but his mind was elsewhere. At the time I didn’t see Pabbi’s nerves. He ignored our banter even as Leifur pointed excitedly at a full-grown buck standing in the school yard. Pabbi didn’t even react.

“It’s so beautiful,” Signy said.

Of course Leifur thought she meant the buck.

Our school looked as most did in those days—big enough for thirty students, with a teacher’s desk at the front. The door (which was never locked) opened into a vestibule where we hung our coats. A big stove inside the door on one side, shelves that eventually became our library on the other. But what I would remember most was the row of windows that let in the sunshine on beautiful spring days, and how the chalk dust danced in the rays that warmed my face. I often sat daydreaming. As the years passed, the shiplap siding would turn from creamy gold to a weathered gray. That school would stand there, the first in the region, for the next sixty years.

My fear fell away as the mill came into view, the house looking far less ominous than it did in my nightmares. My stomach churned knowing that soon I would see Bjorn.

The first person we all noticed was Bensi, who stood at the vestibule door, talking to everyone before they went in. Mother tried to pull Amma back, but she hopped off the wagon, determined to reach the door before the rest of us. Pabbi patted his breast pocket, double-checking that his speech was still tucked inside. As we hurried after Amma I wondered if Siggi was still holed-up in the cottage or if the memories had driven him out.

Amma stopped less than a foot from Bensi to look him square in the eye. "We are missing a haystack. Any idea where it went?"

"Hello, Freda," he replied with amusement. "Nice seeing you again."

"Bull feathers. I am the last person you want to see," she said, the edges of her mouth curling up the same way I imagined the devil's would.

Pabbi gave Bensi the same consideration he would a boulder on the path, by stepping around him. Bensi seemed to enjoy that Pabbi refused to shake his hand, and a wide grin spread across his face. "Good day, Ella," he said.

"Did you leave your wife and children home to do the chores again?" she asked.

Annoyance tightened Bensi's face and he even flinched a bit. Amma, who held open the door for us, looked from Bensi's shoes to the top of his head, then snorted as she followed us inside.

Like cream in a separator, the men went one direction, women in another. The atmosphere was light as the men discussed haying and speculated on how fishing might be that fall. The women told details of recent letters from Iceland, complimented Gudrun's new dress, expressed concern that the store was going to have to lower its prices.

"Have you heard from your sister?" Bergthora asked.

Mother sighed and shook her head.

Somewhere in the background I heard Bjorn's voice.

Bergthora's eyes lit up when I slid in beside her. It was such a natural thing for me to offer help. Signy looked envious as I moved deftly through the kitchen. I took the canister from the shelf and measured the grounds to start a fresh pot; put out the cups, saucers and opened the icebox as if I lived there.

Magnus placed an easy hand on my shoulder. "Good to see you again, elskan."

The conversations would have carried on all afternoon had he not tapped a wooden gavel on the table, calling everyone into the kitchen.

"Goodness," Bergthora exclaimed, realizing that the younger children were riding Thor like a horse down the hallway. "Asta, will you put him outside, please."

I took him out the front door then made a mad dash for the outhouse. Seeing it was occupied, I went into the thick bushes behind. That is when I caught a glimpse of Bensi talking to Asi and Stefan's father, who was clearly alarmed by what Bensi was saying. What surprised me more than his words was that he made no effort to lower his voice, not caring who heard his disgusting remarks about our Amma. Embarrassed, I snuck back inside without them seeing me.

Bjorn stood in the hallway holding a chair. "Hello, Asta," he said.

I barely acknowledged him, mind whirling as Bensi's words played over in my mind.

As Magnus outlined the meeting formalities set out by the Board of Education, I slid along the wall to stand with the rest of the children. Bensi came through the door then sat himself in Bergthora's usual spot at the end of table. Leifur came inside a few moments later, looking furious. He could not even look at Bensi, whose confidence was overflowing by then.

Magnus explained it was the ratepayers' responsibility to elect our first school board. The Secretary-Treasurer would arrange the purchase of furniture, hire the teacher, pay bills, arrange its general upkeep, and consult with two board members on important matters.

"Before we start, I would like to thank everyone, especially Oli for supervising the construction of the building," Magnus said.

There were murmurs in agreement and polite clapping. All eyes turned to Oli, who raised his skillful hand.

"Magnus donated the lumber," he said. "So I think in his honor we should name the school Siglunes."

"Here, here," Bergthora, Amma, and Gudrun cheered. They were sitting together at the front of the room.

Asi Frimann pounded the table-top while the children began cheering. We all stood—nineteen of us in total—leaning against the wall. This annoyed Bensi and he was the first to interrupt.

"Is it necessary to have them here?" he asked, inclining his head in our direction.

"They are the ones attending the school," Gudrun said. She folded her arms across her chest.

Bensi muttered, shaking his head.

Magnus tapped his gavel. "Já, these children are the future of our community. I see nothing wrong with it."

Neither did anyone else, so he continued.

"The province has entrusted us this responsibility so we must choose our Board wisely," he said. "The term shall last three years, then another election will be held."

Slight murmurs, then a voice rose from the crowd. "Would it not be wise to have J.K. stay on, at least for now?"

"Only if he agrees," Magnus said.

All eyes turned to J.K. who said that he would be willing, but only if Magnus would as well. "That way, if I am absent, the Secretary-Treasurer might consult with you."

It was quickly decided that the two of them would form the Board. J.K. made a quick note of it on the tablet in front of him and Magnus explained that in order to elect the Secretary-Treasurer he would ask for nominations.

"Once all nominations are final, we will allow the nominees to speak, then we will vote," he said, giving us a few moments to digest the rules.

Pabbi shifted in his seat, looking straight ahead. The room became deafeningly quiet.

"I nominate Pjetur Gudmundsson," Gudrun said, voice clear and strong. Bergthora nodded in approval. Amma did not move. She just stared down the table at Bensi with her devil eyes. Now we knew what she meant when she said she'd take care of it.

"Pjetur, do you accept?" Magnus asked.

As Pabbi opened his mouth to speak, Bensi interrupted.

"I challenge the chairman to explain how this is in order," he said.

"We are following procedures set out by the province, correct?"

"We are."

"To my knowledge, women are not allowed to vote, so they cannot nominate. Neither can any of the boys under the age of twenty-one."

Bergthora stood up. "Women should be allowed the vote," she said.

"I do not agree," Bensi argued. "Matters of importance should be left up to men to decide."

Gasps and outrage. The room erupted, leaving Magnus unsure how to proceed. We all knew this debate, if started, could run long into the night.

"Am I correct?" Bensi challenged.

It took Magnus a few moments to gather his bearings. He thought carefully before he spoke.

"Já, Bensi, you are half correct."

"Magnus," Bergthora hissed.

He raised his hands in surrender, apologizing to every woman in the room. "I do not make the rules," he said. "And can only imagine what they would think in Winnipeg."

"All the more reason to do it," Bergthora said while the women nodded.

We all looked to J.K. who was obviously thinking hard. "We cannot behave like a community of fools. To err in ignorance is one thing, to do so deliberately is another."

Gudrun did not take well to the stinging. Neither did Bergthora who stood up and went to stand by the sink, turning her back on everyone.

"Is now a bad time to ask for more coffee?" Asi asked innocently, holding his cup up at her. She picked up a dish towel then dropped it on his head. The room was in such an uproar after that, Magnus was forced to tap his gavel twice to call the meeting back to order.

"Only men may nominate and vote today," he said.

Bensi looked around the table. "I nominate Asi Frimann," he said.

Asi looked as if he'd just been dropped down from the moon. "Me?" he laughed. "I am not built for serious matters. Leave it to those who are.

I decline."

Before anyone else could speak, Bensi nominated Oli, who was equally surprised.

"Give me a saw and hammer," he said. "But books and schoolchildren? A shameful thing for an Icelander to admit, but I have no time to read. A half-wit would be a better choice than me."

"That is the direction we are headed," Bensi quipped. There were gasps and shocked expressions since everyone knew that Pabbi wanted the job. Mother looked ready to fly across the table at him. Pabbi sat stoically enduring what was quickly becoming a nightmare.

"For whatever my opinion is worth, I think that Pjetur would do an excellent job," Oli said.

"You barely know him," Bensi said quickly. "Why should you care? Your sons are already grown."

Magnus hammered the gavel and a hush fell over the room. He levelled his gaze at the end of the table. "Are you implying that Oli and I should not have an opinion on the future of this community because of our age?" he asked. "If so, I will gladly allow you to chair this meeting so that I might exercise my right to vote."

"No," Bensi stammered, looking for someone else to nominate. "Gudmundur did similar work in Iceland so he is qualified for the job."

Gudmundur shook his head no.

"How many men are you going to suggest?" Oli asked, bewildered. "Should I bring in my horse so you can nominate him too?"

Another burst of laughter followed by raucous clapping.

Gudrun, who was fuming by then, stood up and waited until the room fell to a hush.

Magnus signaled for her to proceed. She took her time, made eye contact with every man before she began.

"The fact women are denied the vote may be law, but it is an abomination that will soon change," she said, words fiery as a storm. "We Icelanders will see to it."

It was a bold statement that caused my heart to swell.

"Here, here," Bergthora said.

"In the meantime, give serious thought to how your wife would vote today. If you do not agree with her, then you should forfeit your vote as well."

Every woman in the room clapped with such vigor, that not even Asi had the courage to make jokes after that. Gudrun straightened her skirt as she sat down.

Magnus's eyes twinkled. When all was quiet he cleared his throat and thanked Gudrun for putting the situation into perspective. Bensi shrank ever so slightly as J.K. nominated Pabbi. Oli quickly seconded it. "I do not have a wife so I am safe," he whispered.

Magnus asked for the third and final call for nominations.

"I think someone should nominate Bensi," Amma called out. "That way he cannot complain later that we did not give him the chance."

Bensi quickly refused. "If you trust Pjetur with the school's finances, then good luck to you all."

Pabbi ignored him as he stood up. I hoped that no one noticed how his hand shook. Even though he'd carefully written his speech on a fresh sheet that morning, it looked dog-eared by now. Everyone listened carefully as he outlined everything he could think of regarding plans for the school, right down to how to obtain a winter's supply of wood for the stove.

"And I believe that our children should be taught in English," he concluded. "So my intention is to hire a teacher who speaks both languages fluently."

This final statement caused a few eyebrows to rise. Those who were unsure turned to J.K., who shifted in his seat.

"I have always employed teachers from our homeland because I believe it gives my children an advantage," J.K. said. "How will they learn if they do not understand the language in which they are being taught?"

Pabbi was prepared for this reaction. "There is no question you have done an excellent job. I have never met a boy as bright and well-educated as Finn. My children, well, it is obvious they have their Mother's wits."

"And her looks as well," Asi quipped and we all chuckled.

Pabbi explained that before emigrating he'd given serious thought to how his children would manage in Canada as foreigners. He did not want to personally benefit from the move at our expense.

"We may doom our sons to farming and fishing and daughters to work as domestics unless they receive an education, one that extends beyond what our little school can provide. How can—"

"What is wrong with farming?" Bensi interrupted.

"We have chosen this life, but it does not necessarily suit—" Pabbi began but was interrupted again.

"My son does not need to learn English any more than I do," Bensi said.

"Some might rather be doctors, craftsmen, shopkeepers," Pabbi implored, "but without English they are limited outside of the Icelandic community."

"You do not believe that farming and fishing is an honorable way to make a living?" Bensi challenged.

Pabbi sighed. "If you think that is what I've said, there is no reasoning with you. To everyone else—if we want our children to reach their full potential, we cannot limit them by a short-sighted decision. How can they attend university in Winnipeg if they speak only Icelandic?"

Eyebrows were raised, then everyone looked to J.K.

"Disagreements in New Iceland have split that community apart," J.K. warned. "We cannot have that happen here."

"Religion and politics are areas where we will disagree," Pabbi said. "Some teachings are best done at home. English is not one of them."

Everyone except Bensi seemed to agree by then.

"Any final words?" Magnus asked.

Pabbi read from his paper again. "I would like to establish a mentahvöt, a library that moves from home to home. I will start by donating some of my own books and ask that J.K. and Magnus do the same. I also believe we should—"

Bensi raised his hand. "What if our Secretary-Treasurer conducts himself in an unsatisfactory manner?" he asked.

"It wouldn't say much for us, now would it?" Asi laughed. "If the first person expelled from our school is Pjetur."

The room erupted again.

"My brother Stefan should have that honor," Asi said, grinning at the boys standing along the wall. Stefan blushed and shook his head as Finn gave him a playful push.

Pabbi quietened everyone with a raised hand, before continuing.

"We should begin church services on Sundays once a month. We will have dances, sporting events and picnics where we can speak Icelandic to our hearts' content. The school will enrich our children's minds and our community's spirit as well."

Then he sat down.

Magnus closed the debate then called for the vote. Every man raised his hand except Bensi. The women voted in defiance of the law so I jerked my hand up, too.

When the moment arrived that I felt ready to face Bjorn, it was too late. He'd slipped out the front door with the rest of the young men.

Magnus invited Bensi to enjoy a drink, but he said loudly that his lips never touched 'devil water' then hurried outside. Pabbi was able to relish his victory in peace.

"That was a fine speech," Asi said. "Even Ella couldn't have done a better job."

"Who do you think helped me write it?"

"It is not often that I change my mind," J.K. said, slapping Pabbi on the back. "But it was not entirely your doing. Seeing Bensi agreed with my argument, it became obvious I needed to re-think it."

A young woman stood beside Asi, smiling. He introduced her as his future bride.

"It's about time you found yourself a wife," Amma said, looking the young woman over. Her name was also Freda, which pleased Amma greatly.

"Do you smoke?" she asked.

"No," Asi interrupted. "And I've warned her to stay away from you."

"There is plenty I can teach her. Most of it you would like."

"Those aren't the things I'm worried about."

Amma kissed Freda then pulled Asi in for one of her famous bear hugs. "My instincts tell me you chose well."

"My instincts tell me everything that happened today was arranged," he whispered. "Bensi didn't stand a chance."

I could see Amma was anxious to mention the stolen hay but it would have to wait until another time.

Stefan came from the front room with Freyja riding on his back.

"Where is Leifur?" Mother frowned as we prepared to leave.

I looked out the kitchen window to see him sitting in the wagon, looking anxious to go home. It struck me that he was the one in the outhouse and had overheard Bensi's cutting words to Stefan's father.

"A little harlot," he'd said. "All those girls are. The same as old Freda. How do you think she made her living in Iceland? God will punish her, you will see. Tragedy follows these girls everywhere, so Stefan would be wise to stay away from them."

Stefan's father had been speechless with surprise.

Mother was on top of the world as we drove away. She restrained herself until we were out of earshot, then let out a wild cheer.

"Good for you, Pjetur," she said, grabbing him in a one-armed hug.

Pabbi laughed as he shook his head. "Now I'm not so sure."

"You were by far the best choice."

"A helluva lot better than Oli's horse," Amma called out.

"That may be so, but Bensi is outraged," Pabbi said.

"Who cares? He is a bully and now everyone knows it."

But none of us, not even Amma, could predict what Bensi would do next and certainly not how Leifur would react.

CHAPTER FIFTEEN

Trust not him whose father, brother or other kin you have slain no matter how young he be, for often grows the wolf in the child.
—VÖLSUNGA SAGA

LÖGBERG-HEIMSKRINGLA.

In the 'olden days,' as Solrun's grandchildren like to say, there were two Icelandic newspapers. *Lögberg* and *Heimskringla.* Hard to believe such an insignificant number of immigrants could support two Winnipeg-based papers, but we did. Now the two are combined and it is written mostly in English. That I don't like.

Thora was reading out loud from it as I drifted off. Now I'm awake again, she is lost in thought, staring at the painting of Jesus with faraway eyes.

"Do you have any regrets?" she asks.

I am caught off guard. I need to think before answering so I change the subject.

"You will make sure my obituary is printed in there," I say.

She looks down at the paper. "Certainly."

I ask her to glue it into the back of my scrapbook, a way to finish off my life.

"That old relic?" she laughs.

The book sits on the bottom shelf of my bedside table. I admit it is strange looking. Four joined scrapbooks the size of a child's dresser drawer, swollen up ten times its original thickness like some ancient volume from medieval times.

Keeping it bound together has been a constant chore. I took off the paper bindings then put it through the sewing machine, ten pages at a time. I punched holes down the long edge and tied it together with string, but it flopped all over. I tried stapling it, but that didn't hold. I inquired a few years back about having it professionally bound, with a hard cover, but the quote was exorbitant. Then one day Solrun's husband carried it away like a sick calf and returned it, completely healed, with fencing staples and a newfangled thing called duct tape. Marvelous stuff. The book isn't pretty, but it will outlive us all.

"Ready to go outside?" a nurse asks as she comes into the room. She has brought an orderly with her to help get me out of bed.

I sit up, swing my legs so they dangle at the side of the bed.

Thora holds the wheelchair steady as they lower me onto the seat.

"Where did you get this?" the nurse asks, admiring the cane back antique that is as uncomfortable as it looks.

I say it has been in my family for years.

* * *

"Who wants to go to The Narrows?" Pabbi asked one morning. He'd pushed hastily through the chores and now we understood why.

"On the Lady Ellen?" Freyja asked.

"It would take too long by wagon over that bumpy trail," he said.

She shook her head. "I will stay with Mama."

"Are you sure you don't want to come?" Pabbi asked the two of them as he pulled on his coat. Mother said she had plenty to do. She handed us a packed dinner and off we went, racing to the dock at Vinðheimar. The first to reach there would hoist the flag. Usually it was Leifur, but this time Signy beat him to it.

Asi blew the horn as he turned in, letting us know he'd spotted it.

J.K. and Gudrun waved from the verandah.

"Stop in for coffee when you get back," J.K. hollered through cupped hands as we ran to the end of the dock.

"On official business?" Asi asked loudly over the roar of the engine as we boarded. He took Amma's hand even though she needed no help.

"Benches, tables, and a teacher's desk," Pabbi said. "It all should be there by now."

"It is," he said, setting the engine to full steam. "I unloaded it two days ago."

"Why not just bring it here?" Pabbi asked.

"That isn't how it works. You pay Helgi, he pays me. Otherwise I get nothing for the freight."

Asi lit two cigarettes, handing one to Amma.

Stefan came up from below deck to sit beside us. Leifur reached for the sack, digging in for a sandwich.

"Hey—" Signy said.

"I'm hungry now," he said, handing the sack to Stefan.

It was a beautiful day to travel the lake. September had arrived and with it the killing frost, but summer was still up to her playful tricks, pulling back for days so that we thought she was gone, then surprising us with a week of shirt-sleeve temperatures. The sun hadn't given up today either, winking overhead, the wind whispering to us to enjoy every moment because soon winter would swoop in.

I sat on the shore side, not flinching at all as a light mist splashed up on my arm and face. The air was fresh, except for the occasional whiff of Amma's cigarette as unfortunately she was sitting upwind from me.

My stomach churned with excitement as the castle came into view. I strained to catch a glimpse of Bjorn, but all I could see were indistinguishable men working the mill, the shrill sound of the saw echoing through the trees, at least two decibels higher than the engine that rumbled below deck.

"You can let me off here," Amma yelled over the noise. "I want to talk to Magnus about my house. It needs to be built next spring."

Asi turned sharply toward the dock.

Pabbi was adamant another house was an expense we didn't need, but Amma had her mind set. This was one of those times when they came to an impasse and neither would budge.

"I will find my own way home," Amma said.

Asi laughed. "I'm sure you will."

He blew the horn to announce Amma's arrival and within minutes we were chugging through the water again. "Someday I will own that place," he said. "I feel it in my bones."

As The Narrows came into view we began craning our necks to finally see the place we'd heard so much about. The water ran fast and the ship moved with the current through the channel. On the far side were log houses, birch bark canoes pulled up on shore, and animal hides stretched on wooden frames drying in the sun. Brown-skinned children stopped playing to wave at Asi who pulled playfully on the horn as we passed. A whitewashed church stood high on a rocky ledge, reminding them that God was watching. I lost track counting the boats.

"That," Asi said, pointing over the ship's bow to a rocky island in the middle of the strait, "is Manitou-wapow. The Indians believe the great spirit Gitche Manitou can be heard speaking in the wind as it whistles through the trees. This is a sacred place for them."

Our forebears had centuries of experience dealing with the English so we sympathized with the Indians and understood how difficult it must have been for them. The missionaries trod across Iceland as well, admonishing us for our pagan beliefs. So even though we now considered ourselves Christians, we understood how deeply rooted ancestral beliefs are; and how difficult they are to unearth.

Horses and cattle grazed right up to the water's edge, where homes dotted the shoreline.

"There's the new hall," Stefan said, pointing to a long building at the edge of a huge, mown field. It was built near the store, a close walking distance from the dock.

"We need flour, sugar, lamp oil," Signy recited as we tramped up the dock behind Pabbi. A little bell tinkled as he pulled open the door, then again as it closed behind us.

We'd only been a few times to the store in Lundi. Helgi's shop was at least twice the size and far more interesting. The shelves were made from up-ended fish boxes, packed to the low-slung ceiling with everything a person might need—household staples on one side, animal pelts, guns, tools and fishing equipment on the other. Furniture and stoves were piled in the back. The scent of raw fur, tobacco and spices hung in the dusty air.

A young Indian woman eyed us shyly from behind the counter.

Pabbi's voice lowered when he asked if Helgi was there.

"Yes," she said, casting her eyes at the floor as she wove through the tightly packed shelves to the back door.

Leifur and Stefan went straight to the steel traps tethered by rope to the rafters. Signy and I were immediately drawn to the rack of factory-made dresses, coats, and shoes. Along the wall was a shelf filled with dressmaking materials, more than we could have ever imagined.

"It's been so long since I wore a new frock," Signy whispered, admiring a bolt of cornflower blue cloth. "Do you think Pabbi would buy this for us?"

"It is not thick enough for winter," I said.

She went to the cutting-table, running her hand across a bolt of deep red velvet. "Did you keep any of the money Magnus gave you?" she whispered, eyes flicking briefly over my shoulder at Pabbi.

"Signy—" I rasped. The idea never once occurred to me. She rolled her eyes, but then I saw her mind begin to work.

The doorbell tinkled again as an older woman came in who looked like she'd stepped out of the women's finery page of the Eaton's catalogue. She bowed politely at Pabbi then strode across the floor to the men's wear.

"That must be Helgi's wife," Signy whispered.

As I leaned in to correct her, Helgi appeared from the back of the store. He had the weathered face of a fisherman but wore moccasins and a tanned hide shirt like an Indian.

"Mrs. Sifton, how are you this fine day?" he asked.

"Mr. Einarsson," she said. "I am well. And you?"

"I've had better days," he said. "What can I help you with?"

It was hard to tell how long it had been since the gentlewoman had left Britain—that accent must have been hard to shake, though I expect she hadn't even tried.

"Butter, soft cheese, eggs," she said. "And mittens. By chance have you received any in yet?"

Helgi waved the clerk to the back of the store to bring the items from the icebox.

"No mittens yet," he said. "Next month."

Mrs. Sifton sighed. "Last year I came in too late so my husband had to make do with a pair from the year before. They are the finest mittens he has ever owned and I want to buy two pair exactly like it."

"I know the ones," he said.

"Indeed. Made by the Icelanders. Tightly knit, wool of course, with two thumbs."

Helgi understood. "Not all are made exactly like that—"

"Well those are the ones I want. I expect you will put at least two pair aside for me."

"I'll make a note of it."

"Because no others will do. Icelanders do make the finest mittens. I will pay extra, double even, if they are made from dark wool."

Helgi took the package from the clerk then handed it to Mrs. Sifton. "I will send word as soon as they come in."

"Thank you," she said, marching to the door. As she reached for the knob, she called back over her shoulder, "Remember, two thumbs." The doorbell tinkled behind her.

Helgi chuckled.

Signy and I looked at each other, thinking exactly the same thing. I gave her a shove, raising my eyebrows in Helgi's direction.

"Mr. Einarsson," Signy said. "We are Icelanders."

It was an absurd thing to say since the only person who hadn't realized that was Mrs. Sifton. "What I mean to say is that we know how to make mittens. With two thumbs."

Helgi eyed Pabbi first for approval. "How many pair can you make before freeze up?" he asked.

"How many do you need?"

"Every pair," he said. "But you heard her, no Doukhobor mittens."

We had no idea what that meant. "We make them from wool," I said.

"From our own sheep," Signy added.

"Já," Helgi said, amused. "Well, you bring them in. If they are good, I will pay top price for them."

Signy was incredibly pleased. She immediately began calculating how many yards we'd need as she turned back to the bolt of cloth.

Pabbi took Mother's letter from his pocket and handed it to Helgi.

"The others, with the money for my wife's sister," he whispered, "they were all sent?"

Helgi nodded as he placed a stamp on the corner then put it in the mail box. He seemed distracted by another matter.

Pabbi grimaced. "I thought by now we would have heard from her."

The back door closed with a bang. I looked back to see two men standing there. One raised his hand, motioning for Helgi to come.

"I will be there shortly," Helgi called out then turned back to Pabbi. "A body washed up on shore this morning."

"One of your men?"

"Not sure. They come and go. This one looks like he has been in the lake for a while."

Signy was chattering about a roll of lace, saying how nice it would look around the collar and sleeves of our new dresses, but I barely heard her. She wanted me to count out eight buttons that matched.

"Asta," she scolded. "What is wrong with you? You don't care about anything anymore."

"I'm listening," I shot back.

"No, you're not."

I was, just not to her. I feigned interest in the buttons, but my gut was wrenched up into my throat.

"Probably some fool who had too much to drink," Helgi said. "Or someone who tried to cross the lake late in the spring. It happens."

Convinced it was Einar, my first thought was of Bjorn.

Helgi opened a book, flipped through, adding Mrs. Sifton's purchases to the bottom of a long tally. "What can I help you with?" he asked.

"I am here to pick up the desks and supplies for the Siglunes school," Pabbi said.

Helgi seemed pleased as he turned to the back of the book. "Good. It is a sizeable order taking up space in my storage room. Cash?"

Pabbi was quiet for a moment. He glanced at the boys, who were standing behind him, each holding four traps. He lowered his voice as he leaned forward.

"J.K. Kristjansson said that you offered to extend our school credit until we have our finances in order. He will be collecting taxes after harvest so we will have the balance paid before Christmas."

Helgi sighed. "I agreed to extend credit to J.K., but given the circumstances—"

"He paid a deposit of half, correct?"

Helgi nodded.

"Then I do not understand," Pabbi said, the words catching in his throat. "Classes will start in a week. We need desks and slates."

Helgi reached under the counter for a piece of paper that he carefully placed in front of Pabbi. Both men studied it for a few moments, then their eyes met. Pabbi was in a state of disbelief. He read the document again then looked away.

"I paid for my stove in full. We purchase all our goods here. Why do you believe I intend to cheat you?"

Helgi's eyes softened but his words were firm. "I cannot afford to get caught in the middle."

Signy was still chattering about the buttons, completely unaware. Pabbi looked across the store at us, then at Leifur who had heard every word.

Helgi sighed. "I was told your community is divided about the school, with J.K. on one side, you on the other. Since he paid the deposit . . ."

"Not true," Pabbi said, hesitating as his thoughts wound back to the meeting.

"That is what I was told. How will I get paid if half refuse to support the school?" Helgi asked.

Pabbi looked at the paper again. "You are asking me to sign a personal guarantee for an entire community?"

"If you are confident there is consensus, then what difference does it make?"

"Pabbi," Leifur said. "J.K. would never go back on his word. He is not a two-face."

Pabbi reached for the pen, holding it for a long time while staring at the page. Finally, he wrote his name across the bottom in an enraged, almost unrecognizable, scrawl. He slammed the pen on the counter then stormed out the door.

Helgi shook his head firmly as he placed the paper under the counter. Then he turned to the boys.

Leifur clearly felt in a bit of a jam so he nudged Stefan. "Asi says that you will finance our traps if we sell the furs to you," he said.

Helgi's face softened. "Yes, I will."

"We would like to take four each."

He handed them each a form. "Fill this out. Name on top. Each time you bring in a pelt I will deduct it from the cost of the traps. In no time they will be paid off."

As Asi and the boys loaded the crates on the ship, Pabbi stood on the deck, opening each one. He counted every item, slowing down our departure, annoying the passengers destined for Westbourne. When Asi asked if we were ready to go, I nudged Signy.

"The flour—" she said.

"We will do without," Pabbi growled. "We are never going into that store again. Period."

And within minutes we were on our way.

All I could think about was Einar's body washing up on shore, and a foreboding settled in my stomach as we passed Ghost Island. Signy wondered out loud how difficult it would be to knit in the evening once we ran out of lamp oil.

"Amma isn't going to like this one bit," Signy said with a bit of a grin.

J.K. and Finn stood waiting for us on the dock. The moment I saw the look on J.K.'s face, I knew Leifur was right. Pabbi didn't say much until everything was loaded in the back of the wagons, taken to our farm, and safely stored in the renovated shanty which now served as our barn.

"I said no such thing," J.K. said as they stood talking at the corral gate. "You know I completely support the school."

Signy told Mother about the agreement we'd made with Helgi to knit mittens. She suggested we start spinning that night. I told her about Mrs. Sifton.

"What sort of woman does not have a cow and chickens?" she asked, but we already knew the answer. Wealthy ones. Her mind turned the same way Signy's did when presented with a money-making idea so she barely heard our calculation on the cost to make the dresses. Signy was a whiz when motivated and figured it down to the last penny.

"Do you think Mrs. Sifton buys bread?" Mother wondered out loud, placing a pot of venison stew on the table. Leifur had dragged home a young buck (Finn shot it but Leifur said he saw it first) the week before. He promised to shoot another one before freeze up.

None of us dared say a word about what happened in the store because it was Pabbi's story to tell.

"I will just have to borrow flour from Gudrun," Mother sighed as we sat down to supper. "Signy was too busy looking at fabric to remember what we needed."

Pabbi's eyes softened for the first time that afternoon. He looked at Signy. "It's not her fault," he said. "It is mine. She reminded me but I was so angry . . ."

It didn't take long to theorize who was trying to sabotage Pabbi's efforts before he'd even started, but it took more than an hour to discuss.

"J.K. is going to have a talk with Bensi tonight," Pabbi said. "I am very curious to hear what he will say for himself."

Amma returned the next day. That evening we sat in the front room, Mother spinning the wool we'd collected, cleaned, and carded that spring, while Freyja wrapped the wool around her hand into a loose ball.

My enthusiasm for knitting was never so great. Signy had seized all the dark wool so I was left with light brown, but that didn't matter. I barely heard the story Amma read as my mind filled with thoughts of riches. I so looked forward to seeing the shine on Helgi's face when he saw the mittens. I hadn't forgotten how satisfying it felt to have money I'd earned in my hand. I already had one mitt with two thumbs half done when Pabbi placed the book he was studying on his lap.

"Let me see," he said.

I came to stand beside him. He held up his hand, spreading his fingers so I could check the mitt for size.

"You've done a fine job, Asta," he said.

"Why is Setta barking?" Freyja asked, still rolling the ball in her hands. We barely heard her, each one of us lost in our own thoughts. Then she said it again, this time loudly.

"Stop interrupting Amma's story," Signy growled.

"But Setta never barks," she said.

Pabbi sent me to check. I stuck my head out the lean-to door into the darkness. Setta's barking came from the direction of the barn and when my eyes settled on it I saw a warm glow through the front window. At first I thought Leifur had left a lamp burning.

"Fire!" I screamed when the realization struck.

Everyone came running.

"Get the pails," Mother yelled.

Pabbi and Leifur bolted across the road, vaulting over the corral. Pabbi swung the door wide and ran through the flames. Leifur hesitated, but only for a moment, then he too leapt through the fire. Grabbing a horse blanket, he began furiously pounding while Pabbi, like a man possessed, began forking burning straw out the door.

Amma was the last one to the barn. She paused at the water pump, filled a pail, and, straining under the weight, carried it to the door then heaved it onto the flames.

Mother was screaming for Freyja to stay back as she hoisted her skirt to stomp on the burning hay as it came flying out the door.

Amma and I went back for another fill, but this time she threw the water directly at Pabbi, soaking his smoldering shirt sleeves and pant legs. I handed her my pail then she soaked Leifur. It seemed that we did this for a long time, but in fact the fire was out in less than five minutes.

Our eyes settled on the scorched lamp that lay half buried in the smoking hay.

"How could you be so careless," Pabbi hollered, cuffing Leifur across the back of the head.

"It wasn't me, Pabbi," Leifur said. "I didn't even bring the lamp."

"Well how did the fire start then? Magic?" Pabbi's eyes were wild as he threw his fork to the ground.

"I don't know," Leifur said as he bit back tears.

Pabbi never struck any of us so we were shocked. It would take days before Leifur would speak to him again.

Mother looked at the rest of us. One by one, we all shook our heads. Amma wiped her hands on her skirt then bent to examine the blackened lamp. "Not even ours," she said.

Enraged, Pabbi stomped forward and kicked it across the corral. "That son-of-the-devil," he swore. "He did this."

"Pjetur," Mother said, "Your hands, come here."

But Pabbi wasn't listening. His whole body shook as he went back into the barn to examine the damage. Fortunately, the furniture was shielded by the crates, so only the fronts of the boxes were scorched black.

“He knew I would have to sign it,” he said, storming back outside. “How can a man who professes to be God-fearing be so hateful?”

“Come,” Mother said, reaching for his arm. “It is over.”

“Over?” he screamed, wrenching his arm free. “This is not over. It will never be over, not until he drives us away from here.”

“But there is no proof he did this,” Mother said.

Pabbi laughed, looking up at the starless sky. “There never is. Never will be. He is so devious, so much better at this than I. Never in my life could I . . .”

Mother sighed, placing a hand lovingly on his back, but he wrenched away.

“We could have lost everything,” he hollered, levelling his gaze at her. “Again.”

CHAPTER SIXTEEN

Word carries though mouths stand still.
—VÁPNFIRÐINGA SAGA

PABBI WAS SO DETERMINED, MOTHER KNEW THERE WAS NO TALKING him out of it. She went to the house to get the butter, bandages, and a blanket, while Signy and I made a bed of hay for him on the barn floor.

"God help him if he comes back," he said as Mother carefully salved and wrapped his shaking hands.

The following afternoon J.K. and Finn came and, with Leifur's help, loaded everything into the wagons for transport to the school. Pabbi, hands still bandaged and tender, could do nothing except ride along.

"We should have brought everything here yesterday," J.K. said.

"Thank goodness we didn't," Pabbi growled. "Otherwise we might have lost the school too. All because of his vendetta against me."

"He denied it of course," J.K. said slowly. "Told me Helgi must have misunderstood. He will likely blame Leifur for the fire. I have never met a man who lied so well." He waited, perhaps thinking Pabbi might explain the animosity between the two.

Eyes far away, Pabbi shook his head. He was beyond caring by that point. "I ask this be kept between us," he said as he rolled his blanket out alongside the school stove. "I will not give him the satisfaction of knowing I am sleeping here on the floor."

J.K. agreed. "Half the taxes are collected already. The rest will come once everyone sells their lambs. Bensi has already said Pall and Petra will be taught at home so there will be no money coming from him."

"The best news I've heard in weeks," Pabbi said. "I will pay his share if that's what it takes to keep his children away from mine and him away from our school."

Steina Erlendsson was equally fluent in both languages, making her a logical choice as our first teacher. I've never forgotten that first day. I see us filing in, unsure what to do. Steina took charge of us immediately, seating Freyja near the front, Thora and I in the middle desks amongst the other children our age; Signy, Leifur, Stefan and Finn took the back rows. Our instruction was in English, as Pabbi said it would be, and fortunately Steina understood how difficult this was for us. If there were times she felt exasperated, it never once showed.

We girls loved Steina and worked hard to please her because she was so kind and beautiful. The boys—likely for the same reasons—fidgeted and looked down whenever she stood by their desks or called them by name.

Those first months went by quickly and I remember well our first community event— the school Christmas concert. Weeks ahead of time we began practicing, while Mother sewed long into the night so our new red velvet dresses, purchased with money earned from the mittens, would be ready. I wasn't the only one who barely slept the night before.

Steina thought it hilarious when we suggested that Signy play the role of Joseph and Finn dress like the Virgin Mary, but none of us summoned the courage to go through with it, so we stuck to our traditional roles. The younger ones were stable animals and all the mothers in the audience tittered when Freyja pranced out wrapped in a wool fleece.

Leifur played one of the wise men, but, thinking himself too old for play-acting, he rolled his eyes the entire performance. Thora and I, wrapped in flour sacks with our hair pulled back and hidden under a rag, were cast in the objectionable roles of the two other wise men. Steina drew charcoal beards and moustaches on our faces. We had no idea how we looked until the audience erupted at the sight of us bearing our gifts for baby Jesus, who bore a striking resemblance to ten-month-old Solrun. Little Jesus cried throughout most of the play, probably because she didn't like being wrapped in swaddling clothes. Asi said something hilarious that we didn't hear, but the laughter from the crowd rattled me so badly that I forgot my lines.

How quiet the room became when we began singing yuletide hymns, all in Icelandic. Mother and Gudrun dabbed their eyes as the candles were lit and passed through the audience. After the first verse of our final song, 'Silent Night,' J.K.'s voice rose up and everyone joined in. Baby Jesus stopped crying as we sang the song written especially for Him.

When the performance was over we all lined up so Magnus could give each child a peppermint stick. His kindness endeared everyone to him; for some of the children, it was all they received that year for Christmas.

Thora and I snuck outside before the dancing started to shake out our hair and wipe our faces, but discovered when we returned that all we'd done was make ourselves look worse.

Leifur teased us, and the boys with him laughed. I was glad that Bjorn wasn't there to see my embarrassment. He was at the other end of the room talking to Steina.

All heads turned when Bensi arrived with his family, bowing his head graciously as he slipped quietly inside. Pabbi stiffened. He leaned in to Mother's shoulder. "No wonder he keeps her hidden from us," he whispered.

It wasn't like Pabbi to comment on a woman's homeliness so I was surprised. Then he said: "That is not the same wife he had in Iceland."

Mother said that now it all made sense. The girls who disappeared must have been step-daughters. Amma reeled around when she overheard them.

"The scoundrel," she said, a little too loudly. "Unfortunately, my prediction was correct. Exactly like his father."

More heads turned, including Leifur's—he hadn't forgotten Pabbi's slap. He looked at Bensi with such contempt it surprised even me.

The two men eventually faced each other; they reached a silent impasse. Pabbi's confidence grew, having won this first battle. He'd slept on the school floor every night until J.K. had collected enough taxes. When Pabbi had all the money in hand he'd climbed on his horse, ridden defiantly to The Narrows and handed Helgi the money, watching silently as Helgi tore up the guarantee. Helgi had been allowed to make up his own mind about whose word to trust in future.

"How is the dog turning out?" Magnus asked Pabbi as they sipped coffee while eating cake. Setta hadn't come up in conversation before so this was Pabbi's first opportunity to thank him for giving her to us.

"Not bad," he said. "Setta can handle the sheep. My lead ewe is a bossy young thing that all the others follow, but Setta will face her down. Other dogs must be taught, but this one is teaching herself."

Magnus seemed pleased. "And how is fishing?"

"Not bad. Hopefully it doesn't slow down in January again."

Magnus said it was impossible to predict. "Fishing smart is as important as fishing hard," he said. "What do you think of J.K.'s men?"

"I am most surprised by the Indians who work on the crew. Beneath those silent stares and solemn eyes is a sense of humor and appreciation for irony. The bad stories I have heard must have been told by people who'd never met an Indian."

Magnus nodded in agreement.

"J.K. will speak to us in Icelandic, to them in Saulteaux, but we all curse in English," Pabbi said. "Especially when someone sets close to us."

Magnus laughed at that. "Competition in the bay is getting tighter every year," he said.

Pabbi agreed.

Every man in our community either owned nets or fished on a crew. There was a gentleman's understanding that you didn't set nets in front of someone else's land, but everywhere else on the lake was fair game.

Given their competitive nature, most believed that if a man wasn't ambitious enough to get his nets in early, he probably wouldn't lift them early either. Nets left too long meant spoiled fish, which took money out of everyone's pocket. So it was indeed every man for himself.

"Já, the lake is turning into a beggar's sandwich with too much bread and not enough meat." Magnus winked. "With J.K.'s crew to the south and Helgi's outfit to the north, my nets are stuck in between. But my boys will not give in that easy."

Amma came over right then to give him a warm hug. J.K. lifted his fiddle and everyone started dancing a reel.

The merriment lasted well into the early morning hours. When it came time for us to leave, I wiggled through the dancers, hoping to ask Bjorn if he'd heard anything more about the body washed up at The Narrows. Months had passed but I'd heard nothing.

Bjorn stood with his hands in his pockets, back against the wall, looking incredibly serious and grown up.

"Merry Christmas," I said, and he quietly returned the sentiment.

"The drowned man, last fall," I whispered, checking over each shoulder to be sure no one was listening, "was it Einar?"

He did not look at me and his expression didn't change. I followed his eyes to the middle of the floor where Steina and Freyja were laughing and dancing.

"The fool shouldn't have tried to cross on soft ice," he said. "Father sent his body back to Portage la Prairie."

I inhaled sharply and he shot me a fierce, questioning look. I expected him to ask how much I'd seen that night, but he didn't. Instead his eyes went back to the dance floor.

I waited in the doorway long enough to see him cross the floor to take Steina's hand.

I was fifteen years old. For the first time since that terrible night in the little room at the castle, I cried myself to sleep.

CHAPTER SEVENTEEN

Bare is his back who has no brother.
—GRETTIR'S SAGA

IT IS SURPRISING WHAT THE DYING WILL TELL THEIR NURSE.

I imagine that is why Thora asked about regrets, to give me the opportunity to unburden myself. If I don't answer she will not ask again. Not everyone wants to confess her life's failings on her deathbed.

I remember early in my career tending to the elderly, who back in those days convalesced at home. Some made startling admissions. One woman told me that a neighbor had fathered her youngest son. Before she died, she wondered if people in the community had suspected. A man whom no one came to visit wished that he'd been kinder, that he'd allowed himself more happiness; he told me that his worry and grim outlook had made his life miserable. Another woman said she'd been lazy all her life; since being confined to a wheelchair, she'd wished so badly she could get up and run.

"What are you thinking about now?" Thora asks.

I've never known her to be so inquisitive. I cannot tell her that I am wondering why some events from my life are being shown to me while others are left hidden.

"I am thinking you are different than I remember," I say.

"Really?" she says, eyes bright. "In what way?"

We are distracted by Solrun coming down the hallway. She looks pleased and surprised to see me out of bed.

"Where is your sweater?" she asks. "That sun may be hot, but the breeze is still cool."

I tell her to stop fussing.

She hands a blanket to Thora then wheels me around. "Shall we go?"

"Yes, please."

Likely this will be my last trip outdoors so I want it to be memorable.

* * *

One day that winter, as I stood looking out the bedroom window toward the barren, snow-crusted lake, a knowing settled inside me. Months had passed and I hadn't seen Bjorn except from a distance and I could no longer remember his face. Even when I closed my eyes in concentration, the edges were fuzzy.

Were his eyes blue or gray? All I felt was sadness. I couldn't even look at Steina, especially after she moved from J.K.'s house to board at the mill. Jealousy possessed me as I imagined her sleeping in the little room and playing chess with Bjorn in the evening.

I enjoyed the fact she sensed something was wrong, how she tried to mend the tear between us without even knowing what she'd done.

I resigned myself to Bergthora's words, that if I ever were to have a relationship with Bjorn, it wouldn't happen for years. That kept hope alive in me as I looked forward to the times I might see him. Her words helped soften the bite of disappointment when our brief encounters didn't play out like they did in my dreams.

"What happened when you were at the mill?" Amma asked one afternoon as we sat together knitting in the front room with baby Solrun asleep on a bed of blankets between us. Skalda's bull calf had escaped from its pen so everyone else was out looking for it. Later, I would understand that she had waited weeks for the chance to talk with me alone.

She held up a mitt, turning it to see if it was fit for sale. It was perplexing how the two of us could knit the same thing but the finished product look altogether different. Amma was a loose knitter, whereas all my stitches were tight.

"Asta?"

Working was easy but thinking took so much effort. Emotion was drowning me, I felt barely able to breathe.

"Hmmm?" I replied.

"I asked you a question."

I could hear the words, but it was like listening under water. All I could think about was how Signy had kicked up such a fuss when Mother insisted that Freyja knit as well. Reluctance toward any task had a way of spoiling the result and Signy worried that Freyja's slipshod workmanship would affect the price Helgi paid for all our mittens. We'd made our first delivery early that fall of twenty pair and had been paid handsomely at 25 cents a pair. He'd told us to keep knitting, he needed every mitten we could make.

"Did that wool come from Gronn?" I asked. Pabbi had given each of us a lamb two years before and Freyja had named hers Gronn. It was a skinny, bottle-fed orphan that we fed for months.

Amma sighed heavily. "You are not the same girl," she finally said, not looking up from her work. "The girl we sent to the mill was bright and inquisitive, willing to please. The girl who came home is solemn and short-tempered, who no longer cares about anything except work."

"I am not short-tempered," I said.

"Asta," she said again, this time gently. I heard in her tone that she was not going to let this go.

We sat in silence for a few minutes. I stared at the mitt in my lap, at the one loose stitch that stuck out. I scratched it with my fingernail, brought the mitt close to look. When we were finished we would shrink them in hot water so the stitches would tighten.

"I see the tension between you and Bjorn," she said quietly. "Did something happen when you were there?"

Nothing I thought about could stop the warmth from flooding my cheeks. Amma knew. I cursed her skyggni, her ability to see things, to foretell the future and understand the past.

"No," I said, pushing away Einar's greedy sneer, hoping she could not read minds as well.

"I don't believe it," she said. "I asked Bjorn and his reaction was the same. He could not even look at me."

"Amma, please tell me you did no such thing."

"I did."

"No . . . Amma, *no.*"

"Yes."

Lying was such an impossible thing for me. She stared with such intensity, such determination as she waited. A version of the truth poured out when I opened my mouth.

"I am in love with him," I whispered. "But he loves Steina. My humiliation and his pity, that is what you see."

It was impossible to fool her completely. She saw how hard this was for me. "Your Mama thought something might have happened between the two of you," she said. "Do you understand what I mean?"

My face was as hot as the oven door by then. "Amma, Bjorn would never— Besides I am too young for him."

"Some men only like the young ones," she said with a hint of disgust, watching me closely as she spoke. "When was the last time you washed, or ran a brush through your hair?"

I thought no one noticed when we took turns bathing that I made an excuse to hide upstairs.

"Please do not tell anyone," I begged. "I cannot bear it if Leifur teases me."

Amma understood. In that moment, as our eyes locked, I almost blurted out the truth, but shame lowered my eyes instead.

"I will tell only your Mama because she is worried, but you must make me a promise," she said. I looked into her old, thoughtful eyes. We'd never had a discussion like this before and she seemed wiser than she had the last time I looked.

"I know there is more you are not telling me," she began. "But so be it. Just remember it is the nature of men to want what they cannot have while taking for granted what comes easily."

She waited as I absorbed her words.

"You must promise me that you will never punish yourself over a man again," she said.

I agreed. But it would take many years before I understood her meaning and to realize it was a promise I didn't know how to keep.

We went to the kitchen when we heard voices. Everyone was back.

"Did you find the steer?" Amma asked.

"Someone must have taken it," Leifur said, echoing the thoughts no one else dared say.

Pabbi sighed. "We cannot blame everything on Bensi. That makes us no better than him."

Leifur said it would be easy for Bensi to sneak into the corral after dark.

"He is right," Amma said. "Bensi wants us to believe the farm is cursed."

"Our farm is not cursed," Mother said.

"But if it were, how long would you want to stay?"

"I am not going anywhere."

"Neither am I."

"Then we will put it out of our minds," Pabbi said. "The steer wandered off and was killed by wolves. I do not want to discuss it again."

The first time he came to our farm was that spring, travelling the Siglunes shoreline, leaving wide prints in the damp sand, sniffing everything in his path. Up over the bank he went onto thin grass, through the oak bluff past Bensi's, across the open pasture. He lifted his wide snout, nostrils flaring, then began picking up speed, intent on what he wanted.

Setta saw him first.

Since the near burning of the barn, we took Setta's warnings seriously, especially since she worked mostly in silence. She'd chase magpies off the calves' backs with a lunge and snap and herd an errant sheep or lamb back toward the flock by calmly circling around. She only barked at predators.

"Go see what is bothering her," Leifur told Freyja who was playing with a kitten while Signy and I milked. Now that we had five cows Leifur needed our help.

Freyja held the kitten to her shoulder and opened the barn door. She stood there for a moment, then hollered: "A bear!"

We all ran to the door to look.

Setta stood outside the corral, head down, hair on her neck straight up. A growl began deep in her throat as the massive, black body lumbered across the field toward us. We'd never seen a bear before and realized, the moment its head raised, we weren't seeing one then either.

I recognized immediately the white lightening bolt on his chest.

"That's just Thor." I laughed.

Signy shook her head at Freyja whose eyes were still wide.

"Well, he sure looks like a bear," she said.

Hearing me call his name, Thor wagged his tail. He and Setta started circling each other and it took only a few minutes to realize that Thor was here on instinct. We'd all witnessed livestock mating before, but seeing Thor behave so hungrily toward Setta raised the hackles in us. Setta wasn't livestock, she was family. Setta wanted no part of what he wanted to do and, with her tail down, growled as she swung around.

"This is a bad idea, Thor," Leifur said, looking a bit embarrassed as he stepped between the two dogs.

"Stop it," I scolded, slapping Thor on the head. "She doesn't want to have your pups."

He cowered for a moment then was right back at it.

"Pups?" Freyja said. "But I want pups."

"It's not right," Signy said. "She's his sister."

Leifur shuddered. "We have to chase him away."

I shook my head, knowing this would be difficult.

Signy tried first by coaxing him with a calf bone and when that didn't work Leifur tried scaring him by waving his arms wildly in the air. He yelled, even kicked at him, but Thor only skittered, tail down, a few steps in the direction of home, then stopped. The moment Freyja said his name again, his ears pricked and his head tilted. We laughed at how hopeful he looked and, sensing our anger was fake, he came running back to us with his tongue lolling out.

Leifur sighed. "We'll have to lock Setta in the barn."

"But she will hate that," Freyja said.

We spoke to Pabbi about it and he agreed we had no other choice. Poor Setta spent two days in the barn howling day and night, and the next three quietly resigned to her fate while Thor waited patiently by the barn door.

"How long will he wait there?" Mother asked one morning, looking out the window.

"As long as it takes," Pabbi grinned, giving her a quick pat on the backside that none of us was supposed to see.

When it was finally safe to let Setta out, she hesitated.

"It's not your fault," I coaxed, opening the barn door wide. Thor eagerly went in and the two sniffed one another. "Now you can be friends."

When the dilemma of what to do with Thor arose over dinner, I offered to take him back to the mill. He'd been with us for nearly a week by then.

"He would leave on his own if you stopped feeding him," Leifur said, taking a bite of his sandwich.

"No," Freyja said, sticking her little chin out at him. "He loves Setta because she is his sister and he misses her."

Leifur rolled his eyes.

Signy laughed. "Will it work if we stop feeding you?"

Leifur pretended not to hear her. "Thor will not starve. A dog that big can take care of himself."

But we all knew it was best if dogs didn't have to rely on instinct to find food. It could spell disaster if one acquired a taste for raw lamb.

When it came time to take Thor home, we went out to discover he and Setta were gone.

"She will come back," Mother said when we ran breathless into the kitchen.

Many nights we fell asleep to the sound of a coyote or wolf, imagining a nose pointed up to the moon, the baleful cry calling out to others who would answer in quick succession until an eerie choir filled the air.

I slept so lightly that I always heard the chorus and tried to imagine where the wolves or coyotes were. They could be miles away but their howls travelled so clearly through the crisp night air, it sounded as if they were right under the bedroom window. Coyotes, when they were close, were quiet as can be. They'd circle the sheep pen silently and strike quickly. Seeing two usually meant there were more we couldn't see.

That night we were startled awake by ferocious barking. Pabbi's feet hit the floor and we heard Mother's voice as their bedroom door swung open. Leifur was quick out of bed, down the stairs in an instant. Signy sat up straight and together we listened, ears pricked through the silence in our room, to the heart-bending squeals of a dog fight outside. It was hard to distinguish how many there were, but we knew by her tone that Setta was one of them.

We heard the slide of Pabbi's rifle as it was loaded, the bolt pulled back. We ran downstairs to see Mother quickly lighting the lamps. We followed her out the back door.

It was a new moon that night so the only light came from the lamps Mother and Amma carried. They held them high and the light scribbled across the sky as their feet pounded on the cold ground. As we came closer we saw a bit more. Pabbi and Leifur side by side. The sheep huddled in the corner of the pen nearest the barn. A mass of swirling black fur with a tinge of silver spinning outside the pen.

Pabbi and Leifur were hollering. They stopped ten feet from the frenzy. We watched in near disbelief. None of us had ever seen a fight like this before.

Wolves. Three against Setta and Thor.

Mother and Amma held the lamps steady. I am sure Signy's heart was thumping as heavily as mine. Pabbi aimed but could not get a clear shot. He lowered the gun for a second then quickly aimed again, holding, holding, holding, then down.

"Setta, Thor!" he called, but neither heard him. The dogs dared not stop—so closely matched, they couldn't—weakness would make them a target, so they just kept fighting.

Thor and Setta's strength must have surprised the wolves who likely had never met a pair like this before. Thor recognized his chance when the largest male turned its head, and instantly threw all his weight onto him, forcing him to the ground, jaws clamped to his throat, but this left Setta to fight the other two on her own.

Setta hated the sound of gunshot. She understood that it brought the stillness of death. Every time she went hunting, Leifur told us, he'd see her standing over the dead ducks and geese, studying them with a mixture of curiosity and sadness. She seemed to connect the dots in that dog brain of hers that the butt end of the gun was the correct place to be.

"Pabbi, do something," Leifur rasped, fingers running long furrows in his hair.

The wolves had Setta down, one had her by the throat, the other chewed hard on her underbelly. But Pabbi didn't need any coaxing. Aiming to kill would bring the barrel too close to Setta, so he quickly ran his aim across the wolf's back, toward its hip, then fired. A wild yelp as all the wolves jerked free, loping into the darkness. He would have aimed again but Thor was in heated pursuit, crashing through the bush behind them.

"Setta," Mother cooed as she dropped to her knees and crawled to where Setta lay, covered in blood, panting out a thin whine. As a child, Mother had spent years as a shepherd and knew more about sheep and dogs than most men.

"How bad is it?" Pabbi asked.

"It's not good," she said. "We have to get her to the house."

I was careful not to touch the deep gouges on Setta's face as I cautiously reached out to stroke the back of her neck.

"Careful," Amma warned.

"She would never bite me," I said, looking deep into Setta's eyes. "Would you, girl? We are here to help."

Pabbi stood facing the bush, listening, with gun ready, until Thor came crashing back, his own face torn and bloody. Leifur tried to pat him but Thor was not interested in praise, he pushed past us and stuck his head right up to Setta.

"Go back to the house for a blanket," Mother said to Signy.

When she returned with the one from our bed, Mother didn't say a word as she laid it out on the ground. She guided our actions until Setta was on the blanket. Pabbi grasped one end, Leifur the other, and they carried her home. Thor trotted behind with his head high, looking from Pabbi to Setta then back again.

The rest of us ran ahead to gather up as much hay as we could carry, piling it in the corner of the lean-to. We stood for a while watching Setta after they lowered her onto it, until finally Mother said there wasn't much more we could do. Reluctantly, one by one, we all went inside. It took a few minutes to settle down enough to go back to bed, but before I did, I peeked through the door at her one more time.

Setta hadn't moved. Thor was standing over her, licking her wounds. Surprised, I looked at Mother, who didn't say a word. She just hugged my shoulder, lips pressed into a thin line.

Mother checked on Setta many times that night. I know because I heard every time her feet padded across the floor to the lean-to. I expect none of us slept well, especially us girls who were without our blanket.

Two days Setta lay there, refusing food or water, as Thor and the rest of us hovered. By the third day, we'd learned a lot about the desire to live and a body's ability to heal itself. Setta began first by sitting up. Then she lapped water. By day four she was sniffing the scraps we gave her, and the next morning we came down to see her standing beside the empty water bucket.

"Can we have our blanket back?" Freyja asked.

We all laughed at that.

Setta still looked traumatized, though. Her ears were flat and she flinched whenever we came close. Mother kept reminding us to be gentle, to let her sleep. Within two weeks Setta would be back to her usual self. But I wondered if I was the only one who saw the difference in her. She seemed older, more mature.

"Now we will find out her true character," Mother said. "There is no middle ground with dogs. Either she will cower and run every time she sees a wolf or she will hate them so much she'll fight to the death."

Pabbi coaxed Thor into the wagon, then took him home. When he returned that evening he drew an envelope from his pocket. Mother let out a tiny gasp as her eyes grew wide.

"It's not from your sister," he warned before handing it to her.

She stared at it for a long while then looked into Pabbi's eyes and they read each other's thoughts.

"Open it," Signy said, pushing Freyja and me aside.

"I will," Mother said, biting her lip. "Later."

We groaned as she placed it on the shelf. When she wasn't in the room, we took turns climbing up to examine it, holding it to the window, returning it perfectly so Mother would never know. The address on the envelope was written in old uncle Ásgeir's scrawl. The following evening the letter was gone.

That night we lay in our attic rooms, listening in silence to our mother crying. In between the words that came harshly off her tongue were gasps punctuated by fits of tears. Pabbi's voice was quiet and calm. His tone was apologetic, but she kept interrupting, unable or unwilling to hear his words.

We'd never heard our parents fight before. I stared up at the beamed ceiling, cringing every time Mother shouted. No one had the courage to go downstairs, except Freyja who was pulled back to bed by Signy.

"You will only make it worse," she scolded, embarrassing Freyja, who buried her face in the blanket after turning to face the wall.

"Where is Amma?" I whispered. "She should do something."

There was a loud bang as the downstairs bedroom door flew open. Mother's voice grew louder as she stormed into the kitchen. "You cannot possibly understand how I feel."

Pabbi tried to hush her, encouraging her back into bed, but her mind had shifted to that place where a woman's will go when she has been deceived.

"He is lying! He does not want her to come," she said. The outside door flung open hard.

Signy and I jumped out of bed and I shoved her over so we both could see out the window. It was a beautiful spring night - no wind, singing frogs, and the warm air came in exquisitely fresh with the smell of new growth. Mother appeared below. She ran head down, away from the house toward the bay. She stopped at the edge of the bush and, lifting her face to the sky, started to wail. It was distressing to see her like this, twisted with frustration into someone we barely recognized.

The door downstairs opened again and I assumed that Pabbi was going after her, but it was Amma who came into view.

"This is all her fault," Signy said.

I wondered how that could be possible. It was not Amma who wrote the letter. Now, I understand that Amma knew everything because Mother had confided in her when the rest of us were not around. Also, she'd heard every word of the fight.

Mother spun around when she sensed Amma's approach. Leading with her chin, Mother began punching the air, hollering at Amma until her voice lost its power and her strength dissolved. Her shoulders slumped as she pulled her sweater tight, staring at the ground, hugging herself; it looked like that sweater was the only thing holding her up. When all her energy was spent, Mother fell sobbing into Amma's strong arms.

Amma began leading Mother farther from the house.

"Where are they going?" Signy whispered, but we both knew. To the lake. To breathe in the peaceful stillness that could only be found along the water.

The next morning Pabbi was silently eating breakfast when we came downstairs. Mother's eyes were red and her face swollen. She refused to look any of us in the eye. We tried hard to pretend that we hadn't heard the fight.

When breakfast was finished, Mother stood up from the table, took the letter from her apron pocket, stared at it for a few moments, then wordlessly opened the stove's firebox and dropped it inside.

Freyja gasped. "Why are you so angry at the letter?"

Mother was too defeated to reply. She poured herself a cup of coffee then went to stand at the window behind Pabbi, laying a hand on his shoulder.

"Please tell us," Signy said softly.

Finally, she turned to look squarely at us all.

Pabbi stiffened. Leifur braced himself and I feared the crying would start again, but then we saw a difference in her. The anger was still there, but it had turned inward.

"Your Aunt Freyja is not coming," she said.

"Why not?" Signy asked.

"It is complicated," she said. "I have no one to blame but myself. I made the wrong choice long ago. Please do not ask me to explain."

It wasn't until I became an adult that Mother revealed what was written in the letter, and after that she never spoke of it, nor did she offer to sponsor anyone to come to Canada ever again.

CHAPTER EIGHTEEN

A person should trust their own experience rather than hearsay.
—BANDAMANNA SAGA

HOW MANY PATIENTS HAVE I BROUGHT HERE TO THIS PATIO TO enjoy the morning sun?

Oh how relaxing it is to sit listening to the chickadees, while Solrun concentrates on the crossword puzzle page folded into a tidy rectangle on her lap and Thora stares off at the street traffic. A poodle is yapping endlessly down the street.

I have always loved the intensity of the sun. My sleeves are rolled up as far as they will go and this ugly hospital gown is hoisted thigh-high, showing off my bony knees and swollen ankles. Solrun is worried that I will sunburn, but I don't care.

"What time is it?" I ask.

Solrun lifts her wrist. "Ten-thirty."

"Bill isn't usually late," I say.

"Do you mean Brian?"

Maybe I do. A father and son who look so much alike, I'm not the first person to mix them up.

"Who are you talking about?" Thora asks.

"The undertaker," I say. "He will be here soon to pick up Mary."

In the distance we hear the thump thump thump of rock and roll at the Fair grounds, travelling with the wind across town as the midway opens.

"That will be a big funeral," Solrun says a few minutes later when the black sedan slides discreetly along the side street and turns into the back of the hospital. A man steps out, then pulls open the back door.

Mary was a respected elder, the Chief's grandmother. Everyone from the reserve will be there.

"Who is that with him?" I ask.

"Her name is Jennifer. She came here from Toronto the day after Phyllis died," Solrun says. She takes a deep breath, bracing herself. I see her regret immediately.

"Phyllis died?" I ask, looking for clues to see if this is something I knew but have forgotten.

Solrun hesitates. She doesn't want to upset me but sees it is already too late. "January."

"How?" I ask,

"Massive coronary while she slept."

Phyllis was a good friend of mine. There are so few of them left. "She is dead?"

Solrun sighs as she reaches into her purse for a tissue then gives it to me. "Oh, Asta, I am so sorry. Try not to let life bother you so."

* * *

SPIRITS WERE HIGH AS WE LOADED A PICNIC DINNER THEN CLIMBED aboard the wagon. Pabbi snapped the reigns, setting the horses down the road towards the school at a steady trot. Leifur was the only one who was subdued, likely due to nerves since he'd never been to a baseball tryout before.

Every wagon arriving brought at least one prospect for the team. The younger children immediately ran off to play in the bushes while the older boys began throwing around Finn's ball. Signy and I followed Mother to the back of the school where the women sat on blankets, watching J.K. pace out a ball diamond. He was holding a piece of wood in one hand (the pitcher's mound) and one of Gudrun's metal pie plates (home base) in the other.

"So you want to join the winning team," J.K. hollered over our heads. We turned to see Asi and Stefan ride up on their horses. They'd played for The Narrows team the year before.

"They cut me." Asi laughed.

"Me too." Stefan pointed comically at his brother. "But at least I am better than him."

It had been decided after church the Sunday before that if Siglunes was going to be a community, it needed to start behaving like one, so that meant forming a baseball team.

"Are the Magnusson boys coming?" J.K. asked.

"Hope so. They can run like hell. I know that Bjorn has a good arm. Saw him kill a squirrel once from twenty feet."

J.K. paused to wipe his brow. "Will you manage the team?"

"I'm not sure I want to belong to a team that will have me for its manager," Asi said.

"I'm not asking because I think you'll be good at it." J.K. chortled. "I just want to see the look on Helgi's face."

"Well, in that case I'll do it."

Through a break in the trees I saw a wagon coming from the west, recognizing Bjorn immediately. He drove it like a chariot, standing legs wide, calves braced against the seat. Steina sat on the seat beside him while the twins kneeled in the back. Everyone cheered as they pulled into the schoolyard then jumped from the wagon, each with a glove. Steina had a blanket under one arm, carried a dinner sack and wore the expression of a woman in love. My heart fell to my knees.

When it appeared everyone was there, J.K. clapped his hands then motioned for all the young men to spread out and toss the balls back and forth. J.K. and Asi whispered to each other, quietly pointing at each boy. Asi counted heads, not once but three times. The air was charged with excitement, but it was obvious that we didn't have enough players to field a team.

“What about you, Pjetur, can you play?” J.K. asked.

Pabbi shook his head with surprise. “I am too old.”

“You are younger than me.”

“Not by enough. Besides, Ella will not allow it.”

“Then she should play instead,” J.K. said. “Ella looks fast. I think she would make a good short stop.”

Mother looked up from her conversation with Gudrun. “Not this year,” she said, rubbing her hand across her abdomen. The women all began congratulating her.

“I already suspected that,” J.K. teased. “Just the other day Gudrun asked if I'd noticed that you were getting a little plump—”

“J.K Kristjansson, I said no such thing.”

“Yes, you did, dear wife. You said: ‘Ella must be lazing about since she is looking a bit rounder than usual. Normally she is so skinny and frail.’ I remember exactly what you said.”

Gudrun's eyes widened as she cocked her head, masking a smile. “Keep it up Jonas K and the only one who will be skinny and frail is you,” she teased, turning to Mother. “What I did say is that I thought you might be expecting, because you seem more tired than usual.”

J.K.'s eyes danced. “You know how Gudrun loves to gossip. I am constantly telling her to stop, but she will not listen to me.”

“You are the one,” Gudrun said. “Why don't you tell them what you really want to say?”

He laughed. “No, my dear, this is your news.”

Gudrun's cheeks flushed and she was almost giddy when she said: “I am expecting, too.”

Everyone cheered and clapped.

“So what about you, Freda?” Asi interrupted.

Amma turned her head quickly. “Pregnant? No, I am more careful than that.”

More laughter.

“We need a back-catcher,” he said, waving her toward home plate. “Help us get started.”

Amma brightened. She pushed herself up from the stump, flicked her cigarette to the ground then stepped on it. She strode across the grass, rolling up her sleeves. "Had I known this I would have worn my pants," she said.

J.K. asked if any of the boys wanted to pitch to Asi so he could hit fly balls to the outfield.

The twins egged Bjorn on. He wound his arm as he trotted to the pitcher's mound.

"A southpaw," J.K. said, tossing him the ball. "Exactly what we need."

"Go easy on me," Amma hollered from where she stood behind Asi.

He cocked his head as he looked back over his shoulder. "What do you mean go easy on you? I'm the one who's batting."

"Yes, but I have to catch that thing when you miss it."

Asi pointed at the bush beyond the fielders' heads. "It's going straight over those trees."

"That's what you told Helgi," she said, crouching down.

Asi braced himself, ignoring everyone's laughter. Bjorn wound up, sending the ball straight across home plate. Asi swung, but missed. Amma jumped out of the way and the ball bounced, then rolled across the ground toward the back of the school.

Amma huffed as she chased after it.

"Lob it in," J.K. said to Bjorn. "We can work on speed later."

Everyone cheered when Asi hit the next pitch, a grounder to third base. Then another. And another. Winded, Asi went to stand with J.K. on the third base line as the boys took turns at bat. Red-faced and nervous, Leifur swung hard. He missed the first two, causing Amma to curse as she ran after the ball. He connected on the third try, sending a neat line drive straight at the shortstop, hitting Finn in the hip.

J.K. flinched.

"Well at least he stopped it," Asi whispered.

With their heads bent together they assessed each player until it was time for dinner.

I'm not sure what felt worse, watching Bjorn sit down on the blanket with Steina or knowing that Signy felt so sorry for me that she'd stopped teasing.

"Finn keeps looking at you," she whispered.

The girls sitting with us tittered.

Thora blushed, nodding that it was true.

Then came the moment that changed everything.

Four horses came trotting into the schoolyard. There were gasps and cheers at the sight of Oli Thorsteinsson's four youngest boys—all in their 20s, born one right after the other. These were the most intimidating young men I'd ever seen; long-boned and broad-shouldered, each stood well over six feet. All had high cheekbones, full lips and distinct noses that turned up at the end—a feature they'd inherited from their father, one that would be passed down for generations to come. The three older boys were dark-haired, but the youngest was fair-skinned and heavier set, with hair that stuck out like fresh cut straw.

I knew nothing about baseball—few of us did—but in numbers we had a team, and, by the looks of it, now with some strength behind it.

"We heard there are baseball try-outs today," the youngest one said as the four came confidently across the yard. His name was Olafur and soon we'd see he was full of energy and talk. "I think we might be able to help your team."

J.K. met them halfway to offer a welcoming handshake. "We will see about that. Have you ever played before?"

Olafur shrugged. "How hard can it be?"

J.K. grinned at Asi. "I guess you will find out."

Amma hollered that they must be hungry, nudging Signy, who boldly held a plate out to them while Thora and I shrank, stealing quick glimpses when we thought they weren't looking, giggling to the point we embarrassed ourselves without even knowing.

Few in those days could afford the luxury of owning a baseball glove, so most came empty-handed. Finn handed his glove to Leifur so that he could back-catch instead of Amma, and the team trotted back to the field.

"Which one of you wants to bat first?" J.K. asked the Thorsteinsson brothers. Olafur was quick to offer.

"Batting is as much about good technique as it is strength," J.K. explained, showing him how to stand, hold the bat and swing. "It is important to focus on the pitcher and not take your eyes off the ball."

Had J.K. been instructing a girl, she would have listened closely. But apparently Olafur already knew everything about batting, and was anxious to get started. He took the bat and examined it. Standing loosely at home plate, he let it rest on his shoulder.

"If I hit it over the trees, the prettiest girl in the community has to marry me," he said.

Everyone laughed, but the girls shrieked, captivated by this forward young man.

"And who might that be?" Asi hollered.

"She is sitting right over there in the blue dress," he said, pointing over his shoulder at Signy. "Someday she will be my wife."

Everyone gasped at his boldness. Bjorn looked unimpressed as he wrapped his fingers tight around the ball.

"Her father might have something to say about that," Asi hollered.

"He might not have a choice," Olafur quipped.

Everyone laughed again, steeling quick glances at Pabbi, whose cheeks were flaming by then.

"All right, Bjorn, let him have it," J.K. said.

Bjorn nodded, his mouth quirking upward ever so slightly. Focusing hard, he wound up, firing a fastball straight across home plate.

Olafur swung hard but missed.

Pabbi looked delighted as the ball thwapped neatly into Leifur's glove.

Undeterred, Olafur swung again. Then again. It wasn't that he swung far too soon that caused everyone to chuckle, but his loud grunt.

I jabbed Signy in the side with my elbow to annoy her. Without taking her eyes off Olafur, she punched me back.

"I was hoping you might be our clean-up batter," J.K. said, eyeing Olafur's brothers who were all smiling. "But perhaps I was wrong."

Olafur let the bat fall as he shook out his shoulders.

"How do you hold this goddamned thing again?" he asked.

Mother tsked, but Amma liked his spunk. I could tell by the way she clapped her hands and cheered, "Come on Olafur, show'em what you've got."

J.K. seemed pleased. He spoke quietly, lifting Olafur's right shoulder back, left elbow up. He coached, and Olafur's head bobbed as he listened, then he dug his heels into the grass and turned to face Bjorn. His smirk was gone, but not the gleam in his eye. He focused with such intensity, we all grew silent. A hiss escaped Bjorn's lips when he threw the ball again.

Anyone who has watched hardball knows instantly the crisp sound of a home run. We cheered wildly as the ball screamed over the trees, landing far in the bush. Olafur tossed the bat on the ground then sloped around the bases, the team patting him on the back as he went.

Signy blushed, but she did not giggle or change expression even when we teased her. She focused her soft smile on Olafur and did not look away when their eyes met. He touched the brim of his hat at her as he stamped his foot, crushing Gudrun's pie plate, then trotted to the outfield.

The morning of The Narrows ball tournament and picnic everyone gathered at the Siglunes dock dressed in their finest clothes. Gudrun and Thora were admiring the summer frocks Mother had made for us with the remainder earned from our knitting venture when Bensi and his family came up the dock. He went over to where Pabbi was talking to J.K. to announce in a loud voice that Setta had killed one of his sheep.

"I saw her carry it away," Bensi said, his tone more boastful than angry.

Pabbi was, of course, taken aback. It took him a few moments to deny the allegation. Then Bensi asked J.K. what *he* would do if the neighbor's dog began killing his sheep. The question stopped conversation on the dock. Everyone turned to hear the answer.

"Well, I am not sure," he said carefully. "My neighbor's dog does not kill sheep."

"But let's assume for a moment that it did," he said. "Would you expect to be paid restitution?"

"You have no proof," Pabbi interrupted before J.K. could answer. His voice trembled with anger. "Under no circumstances am I going to pay for a sheep that the wolves have killed."

Bensi held up his hands in surrender, pretending he meant no offence, but the glint in his eye told us he was pleased to have gotten under Pabbi's skin.

The rest of us looked at Mother, whose expression did not change. The day before, Leifur had come running inside with alarming news. Mother followed him out to where Setta lay at the edge of the yard. On the ground in front of her was a dead ewe. She was gently licking blood from its hindquarters. When Mother called to her, Setta looked up and her tail began to thump.

"Good girl," Mother said quietly then pulled the sheep away by its front legs, telling Leifur to take it and bury it.

"Probably a female hunting to feed her pups," she said. "The time of year is about right. Soon she will be teaching them to hunt for themselves."

Then she explained that dogs never kill the animals they have an instinct to protect and, if they find one injured, will try to nurse it back to health.

"Unlike people, dogs do not know how to hide their sins," Mother had said. "I see no guilt in her at all."

So there was no question in our minds that the ewe must have already been dead. That it happened to belong to Bensi was a stroke of luck, good or bad, depending how you saw it.

"Setta does not kill sheep," Mother said directly to Bensi.

"A less tolerant neighbor would have shot her on the spot," he replied.

CHAPTER NINETEEN

There is more in the heart of man than money can buy.
—GRETTIR'S SAGA

Nearly a year had passed since Einar's body washed up at The Narrows, but nothing had come of it. Bjorn appeared to have completely forgotten about that terrible night. He sat directly across from me on the Lady Ellen, engaged in lively conversation with Steina, whose leg touched his. She listened carefully to everything he said, laughing in all the right places as the ship chugged along. She even strained to see the shanty as we passed Ghost Island.

"Will you take me there sometime?" she asked playfully.

"If you'd like," he said, not flinching at all.

I glanced at Siggi who was watching the two of them. Shaking his head, he turned away.

Bensi's daughter Petra was between myself and Freyja in age. Life must have been awfully lonely for her living in Bensi's bush. I tried to ignore the little waif as she stared, seeking eye contact that invited conversation. It turned out Petra had more substance than I allowed myself to see that day and became someone I genuinely liked later in life. At the time I despised her father so intensely that friendship with her seemed impossible. Freyja on the other hand was so trusting she could be friends with anyone.

Watching Freyja and Petra again, and knowing what transpired between our families in the coming years, it tugs at my heart to see their first steps on the path toward friendship. Freyja, the indulged sweetheart desperate for a playmate nearer her age, is standing on the deck telling Petra about the nest of baby mice she found under the hay. Would Petra like to come see them sometime? Would Petra like to hold her kitten, a ginger tom that she believes will never dream of eating the mice? Freyja sits down beside her and grabs her hand. They both beamed. Each has a friend at last.

As we neared the hall at The Narrows, Asi throttled down the engine, swung the Lady Ellen around, then slipped up to the dock. J.K. began rallying everyone. With only a few practice games since the first tryout, the team needed reminding of the rules.

This was a much larger event than I had imagined. People were scattered all around the grassy area that surrounded the hall. Children were chasing one another. Teenagers stood in groups. Men were everywhere, talking and laughing, while the women sat on blankets under the trees. The crack of the bat announced a flurry of activity in the open grass beside the hall and players sprinted across the field, around the bases.

We paraded up the dock as if going into battle, with enough gloves for half the team and only one bat.

Having seen the Lady Ellen's approach, Helgi was already on his way to meet us. He brought a few men with him. Fortunately, we had Asi, who knew everyone.

"I've brought the Siglunes ball team with me," he said.

I didn't realize it at the time but now I see clearly the apprehension etched across every player's face. A clan of Icelandic boys showing uncertainty? That wasn't something you saw often. Helgi looked amused.

"I hope you are ready," Olafur said loudly. "We are here to win."

His words carried far and the men with Helgi laughed. This didn't sit well with Bjorn who was the first to cross his arms defiantly. The Thorsteinsson brothers scowled.

"Já, well you are late," Helgi said, pulling a watch from his pocket. "We have started already. We beat Big Point by five runs and are thrashing Kinosota."

J.K. beamed as he extended his hand. "I am confident you can fit us in," he said, patting Helgi on the back. They started towards the hall. "Give your team a rest. We can play back-to-back against the others and you will be right on schedule before afternoon coffee."

As the men veered off toward the ball diamond, our mothers took charge, choosing a vacant spot under a large tree overlooking the fast-moving water. In subsequent years we would know what to expect—speeches and political presentations, foot races, Icelandic and Indian wrestling matches, tug-o-war, and a dance that went on all night—but for now it was all new.

Mostly everyone there spoke Icelandic, except for the Indians of course, who were there in numbers greater than I'd expected. They set up their picnics close along shore where they roasted deer meat and fish on spits over a communal fire. Their children ran about with naked chests, throwing fish guts up in the air, laughing with delight as the gulls circled overhead, swooping down to fight. The teenaged girls were content to lounge about giggling, while the boys chased one another, wrestled, and competed to see who could throw beach stones the farthest. They were as curious about us as we were about them.

Helgi's woman was easy to spot since she dressed more like we did. Her blanket was spread out in the sea of white faces—and she looked as out of place as Helgi did when he was among her people. It didn't appear to bother her, though, which inspired Mother, who spent her day observing the Indians. For weeks afterwards she mulled over her conclusions, many of which were discussed as we worked in the garden or debated at the dinner table. Her opinions might not have been so strong had Bensi's disagreeable wife not laid her blanket within earshot of ours.

She was a fair-skinned, blue-eyed Icelander who thought herself better than everyone else. The first thing she did was tell Pall and Petra to stay away from the Indians. She scowled and her words sharpened every time she looked in their direction.

"I am glad those dirty savages are keeping to themselves," she said, pulling an apron from her bag. It was so incredibly filthy that Mother said later it should have been put directly in the fire. She also said that she and Bensi were a perfect match. Neither one would ever be forced to examine any error in their beliefs so long as the other was cheering from the same corner.

"What I know of the Indians is what I have seen with my own eyes," Mother said loudly. "It has been only good."

Gudrun added, "I would sooner have them at my table than a few Icelanders I know."

Steina was forced to lay her blanket next to Bensi's wife's and I thought it served her right. What I didn't realize at the time is that it was Steina who talked Bensi's wife into allowing Pall and Petra to attend our school that fall.

"They are such bright children," she said. "I would love the opportunity to teach them."

Bensi's wife relished the praise. She turned her back to mother, lowering her voice as she prepared their lunch. "We are concerned about the school's finances," she said, lifting from the box a loaf of bread, a jar of milk, a knife, and a piece of meat wrapped in cheesecloth. "Pjetur does not have a good reputation in that regard. Have you been paid?"

Steina was surprised. "Yes, of course."

"That is good to know," the wife said. "If he tries to cheat you, be sure to talk to my husband. J.K. and the rest are unaware of Pjetur's past. We do not want to make trouble for our neighbor, but . . ."

Steina frowned over at us sitting on the blanket.

So now I know. How many other lies did they tell about Pabbi?

We were a large contingent of Icelanders, the immigrants that settled from Peonan Point in the north to the town of Lundi in the south. More of us were situated around the lake than people realized, overshadowed in population, of course, by those who lived in New Iceland on Lake Winnipeg. Gudrun said it was high time the politicians travelled here to solicit our support. She took off her apron, tucked in her blouse and smoothed her hair, before marching toward the outdoor platform by the hall with Mother, Bergthora and the rest of us girls in tow.

"That is Margrét Benedictsson," Gudrun said as we joined the crowd gathered to listen to the politician on stage. He introduced Margrét as President of the newly formed Icelandic Women's Suffrage Society of Winnipeg and publisher of the women's magazine. Margrét had travelled here with the editor of *Lögberg*. He stood off to the side, holding a large camera and notepad. He waved to the crowd, then snapped a photograph of Margrét as she spoke. She preached temperance and equality.

"An honor to meet you," Gudrun said afterward as she introduced herself, Bergthora and Mother.

The rest of us were in awe that Gudrun had the courage to approach these heavyweights in the Icelandic community. Both Margrét and *Logberg's* editor were revered in our home.

Margrét asked if we'd be willing to sign her petition concerning a woman's right to vote, which would be presented to the Manitoba Legislature.

"Most definitely," Gudrun said, taking the pen and paper from her, signing it then handing it to Mother who did the same then passed it down the line. "I would like to renew my subscription to your magazine as well."

"Who do we have here?" Margrét asked, her eyes settling on us girls.

"I would like to sign if it is allowed," I said. It wasn't often that I spoke up, so Mother always smiled when I did.

"Of course," she said, handing me the paper. "Your future depends on it."

"Our Amma will want to sign, but right now she is helping our team," Freyja said, balancing the paper on her knee as she carefully wrote her name. The editor crouched and the click of the camera caused us all to look up.

"Our husbands will be by to sign it later," Mother said.

"Now can you point me to Helgi Einarsson's wife?" she asked.

Gudrun pointed as she cleared her throat. "That woman standing there, the beautiful one with the long, black hair."

Margrét's gaze rested on the woman for a few moments. When she turned back to Gudrun, her eyes shone. "Ah, to commiserate with a woman who is even more disenfranchised than us," she said as she strode off, "a pleasure indeed."

Taking Freyja's hand, we went to watch the team play.

"They look nervous," Pabbi said casually as we slid in beside him. "I hope we didn't enter the team too soon."

None of the boys spoke as they threw the balls back and forth. I searched for Bjorn, who stood on the periphery, shaking his hands, loosening his shoulders, staring off into the distance. Then he swung his arms in wide circles, first as if he was swimming forward, then backward.

When the whistle blew J.K. waved the team over.

"This is exciting." Freyja giggled.

And it was. Looking back, this was a historic event for us. The Siglunes ball team's first game, a team that would compete for nearly a century after that against some of the toughest amateur hardball teams in the province. But thoughts about Bjorn and Einar kept rolling through my mind, spoiling it for me. I remember little of what happened after that, except that the nightmares changed. They came more often, and always Freyja was with me. It was always Freyja's screams when he caught her that jolted me awake.

So imagine how I feel now watching that game again, feeling the electricity in the air. I see Bjorn, sense his nervousness. His father is watching and wants to make him proud, determined to show everyone that he is his own man. He raises his chin and stares at home plate. He knows the only way they are going to win is if he believes he's the best pitcher the area has ever seen.

But Big Point scores easily in the first four innings. As happens so often in baseball, they think they have us beat. But quickly our boys find their stride and, by the seventh inning, it is Big Point fumbling the ball, resulting in errors we turn to our advantage.

Bjorn's fire-power causes The Narrows pitcher—the team we will play last if we win the next game—to watch intently from the sidelines. Leifur catches an in-field fly ball. Siggi steals home. Finn chases down a runner between second and third. We all cheer wildly.

By the bottom of the last inning J.K. is pacing the foul line, wiping sweat from his brow. We manage to hold them to only six runs, because Bjorn strikes out all their best batters.

Finn outsmarts their pitcher by waiting until the count is full then bunts, surprising everyone, including the back-catcher who fumbles the ball then throws it into the grass by the first baseman's feet and Finn is safe. J.K. is so pleased he wallops Finn between the shoulder blades, nearly knocking him off his feet.

"Come on, Stefan, you can do it," Freyja hollers through cupped hands.

Stefan is too focused to hear a thing as he digs his toes into the ground. Holding the bat high, he hits a grounder past the short stop on his second swing. Two of our weakest batters manage to get on base. We are all crazed by then, cheering and clapping.

Olafur's confidence makes him the perfect lead-off batter. He saunters to the plate, looks directly at the pitcher then points at the bush. The center-fielder backs up.

"Make him pitch to you," J.K. hollers, clapping his hands.

Olafur watches the first two pitches go by then swings on the third, pulling the bat so the ball blasts over the third baseman's head. Finn scores on Olafur's double while Stefan holds up on third base. Two Thorsteinsson brothers pop out, but the last hits a single. With two out and the bases loaded, it's Leifur's turn to bat.

J.K. calls a quick time-out. He jogs across from first base to where Asi is coaching third. Asi nods, then hurries over to Leifur who looks relieved as he hands Asi the bat.

"What are they doing?" Freyja asks.

We find out later this is called a pinch hit.

J.K. claps loudly as he stands on the sidelines at third base, leaning forward, ready to wave Stefan home.

Asi digs in and what happens next teaches our team a lasting lesson. Our rally has the Big Point pitcher so rattled that he throws two wild pitches, putting them down in the count. Now, what the Big Point coach should have done was call a time out the moment Asi readied himself at home plate. He should have gone to the mound to talk with the pitcher, calm him down, use up their full three minutes to take a bit of wind out of our sails. But he didn't.

Asi hits a line drive and Stefan scores to win the game.

J.K. was known to say, "It isn't so much that I want to win, it's that I hate to lose."

That day our team learned how to ruthlessly expose another team's weakness and capitalize on it. J.K.'s optimism and competitive spirit set the tone and our team's cocksure attitude always drove the competition wild. We won more games by coming from behind than any other team.

Years later, when the men gathered to reminisce, someone would say: "The sweat stains on J.K.'s shirt went all the way down to his waist."

"And his hair," someone else would add, "stood straight up on his head."

Then they would all laugh.

"It was the top of the ninth, one out, and we were down by three. The bases were loaded and Stefan comes up to bat—pops out. You should have seen J.K."

"Then on the first pitch, Olafur hits a home run. J.K. pounded him so hard it left a bruise."

"Bruise Olafur?" another would say, and the whole room would erupt again.

"Then, to top it off, Olafur broke the bat so we had to borrow one from The Narrows team so we could finish the game!"

Oh, those were wonderful times.

We did not win the tournament that day, though in the telling of it you'd assume we had. Arrogance became our greatest asset. That determination to succeed brought our little community together in a way that nothing else ever would.

In the weeks that followed we waited patiently for our copy of *Lögberg* to arrive by mail. We gathered around Pabbi as he read the article out loud to us. When he was finished he laid the paper open on the table and we scanned the photographs for familiar faces. There we were, heads bent, all watching Freyja, whose hair blew wildly in the wind, the tip of her tongue sticking out in concentration. Margrét's expression told all who saw the photograph that she'd accomplished what she came to do.

CHAPTER TWENTY

Better to die with honor than live with shame.
—THE SAGA OF JÓMSVÍKINGS

I FELL ASLEEP AGAIN. I HATE WHEN THAT HAPPENS, ESPECIALLY mid-sentence. Alas, it cannot be helped. Decades of working the night shift winds a person's clock around. I'm too damn old to try and turn it back now.

"Is there a ball tournament this weekend?" I ask.

"There always is," Solrun says, studying her crossword.

"Take me," I say.

Now she looks up. "Pardon me?"

"I want to go. It's only a few blocks." That I remember. Never missed the Lundi Fair ball tournament in all the years I've lived here. Not about to start now. "What time does Siglunes play?" I ask.

"I'm not sure."

"Phone your husband. He'll know."

Thora jumps up from her lawn chair. "I think it's a splendid idea—let's go."

It's a bit of an ordeal getting me ready but, as I learned during nurse training, a person can achieve anything if she focuses. The hardest part is sliding on my pants. But once that is done, it is, as they say, smooth sailing.

"If we hurry, we'll make the start of the game," Thora says, glancing at her watch. She trundles me over the threshold at the front door.

"Well let's get moving," I say over my shoulder.

"Want to run?"

"You're the one doing the pu—" but before I finish, she takes off across the parking lot.

I'm surprised by how well she makes the turn onto the sidewalk.

"Not bad for an old woman," I holler, exhilarated. There hasn't been much speed in my life of late, so this takes my breath away. A car passes, arms stuck out the windows to wave. A celebratory honk as we wave back. I can hear Solrun's hysterics as she, with her limp, tries to keep up.

"That was fun," Thora pants as she slows to a brisk walk.

It sure was. We ran everywhere as girls and I miss it.

We turn onto the fairgrounds. The red and white jerseys are warming up. We are there in time for the first pitch. Solrun wheels my chair to the edge of the grandstand. Spectators shuffle over so Solrun and Thora can sit on the bottom row beside me. Everyone who passes says hello.

Just like the old days.

"Make him pitch to you," the coach hollers.

Printed on the back of each jersey is a surname—a few unfamiliar recruits, but most are the great-grandsons of our early team.

"Fetch me some pie," I say. "Saskatoon. Tell them to put a scoop of vanilla on top."

Solrun jaunts to the hall kitchen returning with three pieces, one for each of us.

Now this is real food. It used to be that fresh food was served at the hospital, but now most of it comes from a box or bag. The worst is margarine.

"I would like some butter," I say, looking up at the sun. I've never thought about it before, but the sun and butter are the same hue.

"Now?" Solrun asks.

"Later," I say.

"They only allow low fat foods in the hospital," she warns.

"Then sneak it in. Your purse is big enough."

A loud crack of the bat. Everyone cheers. Halldorson has hit a double. I like him. He reminds me of Olafur.

"They say it is unhealthy," Solrun says over the noise.

"Who are 'they'?"

"The experts."

"I promise I won't tell them."

She laughs. We've had this discussion before. Everyone knows the brain needs fat to function properly. That I can still string words into a sentence after all those years eating hospital food is an accomplishment.

A Siglunes boy steals second. I always like it when they steal. I can only eat three bites of the pie so I give the rest to the teenager sitting on the grandstand behind me. He looks surprised but takes it.

"Why hasn't Lars come to visit?" I ask, clapping as the team scores a run. It isn't much of a clap, just two crooked old hands sluggishly grasping air.

"He will be here soon," Thora says.

Lars. The youngest in the family, named after our brother who was born on the train but died that first winter in Lundi. That Mother and Pabbi gave their last-born son the same name as their deceased child mortified our English friends. They didn't say it, but we knew they thought it bad luck.

I remember what Freyja said the day he was born: "Lars came back down from heaven to be with us again. It is Lars, the same one."

So I looked to Amma for advice. She didn't say anything right away, but observed the baby for two weeks, then one day whispered: "Now Lars has a strong heart. You will see. It is stronger than most."

* * *

"SIGNY WILL COME AROUND," MOTHER SAID TO PABBI AS THEY DUG potatoes in the garden.

It was early September and already Mother Nature was up to her usual tricks, warm weather one day, cool the next. Today the air carried the scent of a storm brewing in the distance.

"It has already been a week and she hasn't spoken one word to me," Pabbi said. He stood his full weight on the shovel, digging deep before lifting then turning over a solid clump of dirt. He bent over to sift with his hands, tossing the potatoes that surfaced onto the row. They would be left to dry then put into bags. By the look of the first few plants, we'd have enough to last well into spring.

"I am her father. I know what is best," he said.

Mother walked ahead of him, pulling the withered plant tops, pitching them into a pile.

"Signy loves him," she said, breathless.

"How can she? They barely know one another," he grunted, jamming the shovel into the ground again.

"Don't you remember?" she said, pausing to stretch her back. The baby inside was due in less than a month.

Pabbi continued with the shovel and when Mother had pulled the last of the plants, she came back to where he was and began crawling opposite him, rubbing the damp soil from each potato as it came out of the ground.

"I am disappointed that she has no plans to further her education," Mother said. "But we've always known she might prefer marriage over school. It is not a bad thing, not for Signy."

Since the ball tournament, Signy and Olafur had been inseparable. It had started with him coming by on weekends. He and Signy would walk hand-in-hand to the lake with the rest of us tagging along. Many nights we sat under Amma's tree listening to Olafur's dreamy optimism. He wasn't afraid to share all his ideas, the plans he'd made for the farm and for him and Signy.

"This is the finest place on earth and a man can make something of himself here," he said one late summer afternoon, the sweat glistening on his forehead. Signy stared lovingly as he pulled a folded piece of paper from his pocket, smoothing it out in the grass, showing us the pencil drawing of the house he would build for her, a two-storey frame home that would rival the castle at Siglunes.

“Someday we will be rich. All we have to do is work hard.”

Even Leifur, who was prone to skepticism, believed in him.

“One thing for sure is that we will never go hungry,” Olafur said, repeating what his father had told him when he moved the family here.

“What about all these mosquitoes?” Freyja asked, hoping Olafur with all his wisdom had a solution. We were constantly slapping or scratching our arms and legs.

He laughed. “They have to eat too.”

Soon, he began visiting weeknights. He and Signy would talk so late into the night Pabbi had no choice but to ask him to leave. Olafur would wave as he galloped away, then return at the same time the next day.

Pabbi was the only one who hadn't seen it coming. It pained the rest of us to watch Signy and Olafur standing nervously in the kitchen, talking about nothing, until finally Olafur summoned the courage to ask permission. When Pabbi shook his head, our hero shrank like a whipped pup.

“Two years?” Signy had said. “We have to wait *two* years?”

“Until you are twenty-one,” Pabbi said. “If you still want to get married then, you will have my blessing.”

Signy was outraged. Olafur calmed her down, saying that he understood how Pabbi felt, that he didn't mind waiting. Signy thundered out the door with Olafur on her heels. Amma didn't say a word, but her expression changed, seeing a glimpse of the future she wasn't willing to share.

Pabbi saw her grin. “What?”

“Nothing,” Amma said quickly.

A week passed. Signy was too proud to ask again so she stopped talking to Pabbi altogether. Digging potatoes was a way for him to work out his frustration.

“Why Olafur?” he asked. “Why him?”

Mother's voice was soft. “Pjetur, don't you know your daughter yet?” She paused for a moment to rest. “I understand Olafur is not the sort of man you would choose for her, but you have seen how he looks at her. No other man will ever love her like that. She is bossy just like your mother. Olafur needs that. She can tame him."

"Why should she have to?" Pabbi asked.

"Because she wants to. Signy always needs to be right and with Olafur she can win sometimes. He admires her intelligence and respects her. That is what makes Signy happy."

Mother stood up, then wrapped her arms across his shoulders. "He is kind and honest. Sound familiar?"

Pabbi cocked his head. "Olafur is not good enough for her."

She smiled. "He will spend his entire life working to prove you wrong."

They dug in silence until all of the potatoes were unearthed, until the sky grew dark to the west.

"Put Signy out of your mind," Mother said as they walked toward the house. "It is Asta we need to worry about."

Leifur and I were on our way back from the barn after bottle-feeding the orphaned lambs. We met them on the road. Pabbi was listening with a most serious expression as Mother spoke, but her words trailed off when she saw us.

"Look at me," Freyja called out and we all turned to see her sitting on Setta's back.

"Come Setta," Leifur called, slapping his knees.

Setta broke into a trot, causing Freyja to lose her grip and slide off into the dirt. Amma stuck her head out the door right then, hollering that coffee was ready. Then a noise down the road caught all our attention. We turned to see a team of horses pulling a wagon toward us and knew something was terribly wrong. Bjorn was standing, jaw set, eyes focused on the lake. He slowed when he passed us, enough that we could see Bergthora and one of the hired men kneeling in the wagon. Stefan was lying on a bed of hay, his mouth open in pain and shock, Bergthora leaning over him, her expression grim.

Leifur began running before Pabbi could stop him. He caught up to the wagon then leapt onto the back. Pabbi hollered out, but it was too late. As soon as Leifur scrambled in, Bjorn slapped the reins, and once again the horses were at a full gallop.

By the time Pabbi had run to the bay, they'd already set sail. Gudrun and Finn were standing on shore watching the boat under full sail move swiftly through the water.

"Leifur went?" Pabbi asked.

"I offered to go, but he could only take one of us," Finn said, kicking at the sand.

Gudrun sighed, shaking her head. "They missed Asi by only a few minutes. Bergthora said the hospital in Portage is his only chance."

Pabbi looked up at the churning sky. "What in God's named happened?"

"Hunting grouse," she said. "The doctor removed most of the shot. He said if there is any chance of saving the arm, he needed to get to the hospital."

"Where is J.K.?"

"He will be home later today," she said, also squinting at the sky. "He's spent the last few days in meetings with government."

Pabbi ran his hands through his hair.

"Bjorn knows the lake, he's been sailing it his whole life," Gudrun said patting Pabbi's arm. "God will watch over them."

We met Pabbi at the door.

"What happened?" Mother asked.

Pabbi took off his jacket and hung it on the hook. "Shot himself." Then he told us everything Gudrun had told him.

Freyja began crying uncontrollably. "Is he going to die?"

"They have taken a terrible risk sailing in this weather," Pabbi said.

"Oh, Leifur," Mother cried.

"Is Stefan going to die?" Freyja asked again.

"I don't know," Pabbi said raising his voice.

A hush fell over us as Pabbi and Mother paced.

"Stefan can't die," Freyja cried.

Signy became instantly enraged. "Is he all you think about?" she said. "What about Leifur? What if he drowns? He's your *brother.*"

"Enough," Mother said through clenched teeth. "No more talk like that from either of you. Freyja, go upstairs. Signy, in the front room."

Freyja opened her mouth to protest, but Mother slapped her hand down on the table. Freyja sucked in her tears, turned, and ran. Signy spun on her heel, storming out the front door. The wind slammed it behind her.

I took little Solrun upstairs where Freyja was lying face-down on the bed.

"It is not fair," she cried as I pulled her into my arms.

Solrun sat on the bed wide-eyed, sucking her thumb.

"I know," I said.

"If it was Olafur who went . . ."

"Shhhh," I whispered, understanding exactly how she felt. I stroked Freyja's hair as she wailed, silently reciting the Lord's Prayer. Two hours passed and when both were asleep, I slid silently off the bed to tiptoe downstairs.

Mother was at the window watching Pabbi who stood on the road staring defiantly at the lake. His hair was pushed back from his face, shirt sleeves flapping like flags in the wind. Signy stood beside him.

"Where is Amma?" I whispered.

"In the front room," she said as she went to the door. Lifting Pabbi and Signy's coats from the hook, she went out to stand with them in the wind and rain.

"Amma?" I said.

She was sitting on Pabbi's chair with her eyes closed, hands resting easily on her lap. Her expression was serene, but her eyes twitched as if experiencing a dream.

There was so much I wanted to ask.

They hadn't meant for anyone to see. After the ball tournament,

Bjorn and Steina snuck off together behind the hall. It had been eviscerating to watch as he pressed her up against the wall, gently brushed back her hair then cradled the nape of her neck, pressed his lips against hers. I'd turned away, the pain so excruciating that I vowed to stop loving him.

In the months between then and now, I'd played out many scenarios in my head. I imagined them getting married. Making love. I saw her standing by his grave crying. I observed each drama like a bystander, forcing anger to overtake the sadness. If I could not be happy, why should they? Just that morning I'd been able to imagine Bjorn dead and feel nothing at all.

But to do such a thing was a sin. Wouldn't it serve me right if my hateful imaginings came true? Leifur and Stefan were with him.

It was the first time since moving here that Amma had allowed herself to slip away to that magical place she went to find answers. I knew about her ability, but had never witnessed a trance before. She was always quick to predict an outcome, so we mostly ignored her, especially since she wasn't always correct. This time it felt different.

I sat on the chair opposite her to wait, and it was a long time before she spoke.

"Your parents worry for no reason," she said, eyes still closed. "Leifur will be back tomorrow afternoon."

"But how do you know?"

Amma slowly opened her eyes. "It is like dreaming while awake. I ask for an answer, relax my mind, and trust whatever image comes."

I waited for her to say more.

"Your brother will have a long life," she said, as if sensing my apprehension, let her eyes close again. "I see his face as an old man. But I cannot see Stefan."

"And Bjorn?" I asked.

She slowly opened her eyes. "Be patient, my little namesake. Your chance will come."

CHAPTER TWENTY-ONE

Who dares, wins.
—THE SAGA OF HRAFNKELS FREYSGOÐA

NONE OF US EXCEPT AMMA SLEPT MUCH THOSE TWO NIGHTS. Freyja muttered beside me and each time Pabbi or Mother went outside to check the weather, to stare off toward the lake. Signy stirred in the other room. It made sense to her to sleep in Leifur's bed as a way to will him home. He would have cringed at the thought of it.

Amma did not flinch one bit when Leifur did not appear the next afternoon as predicted; in fact, she behaved as if nothing was wrong at all. The morning after that she was up early, whistling her way to the barn to do his chores.

By the second day, Pabbi couldn't stand the waiting so he rode to the mill to see if Magnus had heard any news. He returned optimistic, saying that no one had seen or heard from Asi either. Hopefully that meant they were all at the hospital in Portage la Prairie.

Hours later there was a commotion outside. I ran to the window in time to see Leifur jump down off Bjorn's wagon seat. Mother hugged him. Pabbi was so relieved that he couldn't manage a word. He shook Bjorn's hand. All Pabbi's emotions were tied up in that handshake and it took most of Bjorn's strength to keep his arm from being wrenched out of place.

I see them now, in the boat just south of Ghost Island. Everyone is soaked to the skin. Bjorn is working the sails as the boat chops through the waves. The hired man gripping the tiller has shrunk to the size of a child and is sobbing.

"I said hold her tight to the wind," Bjorn hollered over his shoulder at him. "I thought you said you'd sailed before."

"Let me off on the island," the man pleaded.

Bjorn shook his head. "We have to keep going."

"He is going to die anyway."

"No, he's not," Bjorn said through clenched teeth. "I won't allow it."

"You are a fool who will drown us all," the man cried.

Bjorn wasn't listening. Stefan was lying at the bottom of the boat, face to the sky. Leifur was baling in the bow.

"You steer," Bjorn told him.

Leifur quickly crawled past Stefan. The hired man willingly traded places but was too rattled to do anything but curl into a ball. He cried out every time the bow crashed down.

"Please God I don't want to die."

"Shut up or I will throw you overboard," Bjorn said.

Bergthora inched to the bow, picked up the bucket and started baling.

"Stefan, wake up," Leifur said, eyes on the horizon, one foot pressing hard against the side of the boat. "We are almost there."

Then Bjorn started singing into the wind:

Fifteen years, too young to die

The saint he fell within the last battle cry

Bergthora and Leifur joined in:

But the time has come for you not yet

Escape from the battle of Stiklestad . . .

Stefan began silently mouthing the words to the song they all knew well.

"Your father is going to be mighty pleased when we bring you home," Bjorn hollered. "Now Asi owes me for saving your life."

"I want at least two cows for risking mine," Leifur said.

"Plus their best team," Bjorn added.

Stefan grimaced as he squinted up at them, then he fell unconscious.

I ran out the door and met them coming toward the house.

"You saved Stefan?" Pabbi asked.

Leifur looked at Bjorn. "We did."

Pabbi's pride erupted as a wide grin. He blinked back tears. "Heroes," he said, reaching out to grab Leifur's shoulder.

"Hello Asta," Bjorn said.

Every speck of anger I'd felt toward him fell away at the sight of him smiling at me.

"Well?" Signy asked. "Tell us what happened."

Freyja was over the moon with happiness.

"Give them a moment to sit," Mother said as we flooded the kitchen. "They will tell us when they are ready."

Signy helped Amma fill the table with all Leifur's best-loved foods prepared earlier that day. By a strange coincidence, Bjorn took my usual spot at the table. Realizing this, he shifted over so that I could wedge in beside him.

Pabbi said Grace, finishing off by thanking God for bringing them safely home. Mother wiped away a tear and Amma broke the awkward silence that followed.

"Where is Stefan now?" she asked.

As we began passing around food, they relayed the story in tandem, Bjorn telling most of it, Leifur filling in the blanks.

"The surgeon says he will recover," Bjorn said. "He said the doctor from The Narrows saved Stefan's life by digging out the lead so it wouldn't poison his blood."

Leifur explained that they'd caught up to Asi at the Kinosota dock. They moved Stefan onto the Lady Ellen then sped to Westbourne, but arrived fifteen minutes too late. The train to Portage la Prairie had already left and the next one wouldn't come by until morning.

"Asi talked the station manager into letting us take the handcar," Leifur said. "A telegraph was sent ahead to let them know we were coming."

Two fishermen that Asi knew happened to be at the station and they volunteered to come along, spelling off Leifur and Bjorn. It took them nearly three hours.

"Asi pumped the whole way," Bjorn said, folding a piece of bread in half then taking a bite. "By the time we got there, an ambulance car was waiting."

"What happened to the hired man?" Pabbi asked.

Bjorn laughed. "Ran off." He forked a piece of meat into his mouth.

Word of their heroics spread quickly. They spent the first night at the hospital then in the morning a buggy took them from the hospital to a private home where they were fed and stayed the night, enjoying spirits with their host, an Icelander who owned a business in town.

"Stefan's arm?" Pabbi asked.

Leifur ran the heel of his hand down his left shoulder joint to show where it had been amputated.

We saw him a month later when we went to visit. There he was, sitting in a chair, smiling that crooked grin of his, using his right hand to eat as if nothing in his life was amiss. His mother had removed the left sleeve on his shirt and sewed the hole shut at the shoulder as if all shirts were made that way. It was shocking that first time. We could barely stop staring at his lopsidedness, but it was obvious that he hated all the fuss.

I see now that the only person he accepted sympathy from was Freyja. She hung back when we were at the door saying our good-byes. When no one was looking, she gently kissed him on the forehead.

Stefan became the subject of much discussion. How would he manage on the farm? Leifur tried working with his right arm tied behind his back to see what it was like.

We were outside the house and Pabbi was teaching Signy and me how to seam nets. Signy took to it immediately, leaning over the cord strung between two poles, fastening the mesh to it. She chatted cheerfully as she used a thick needle to slip the twine through six mesh, tied it, then slipped it through six more.

It was my job to add the loops then tie the floats and sinkers on.

"This would be impossible with only one hand," I said.

"I wouldn't want to live if I couldn't fish," Leifur said. He was hoping for an early freeze up because fishing was always better when the lake froze while the fish were still moving. "Have you told J.K. that we have our own nets?" He spread out the net for him and Pabbi to work on.

Pabbi frowned, saying he planned to that evening.

Right at coffee time, we looked up to see J.K.'s team coming up the bush trail. He pushed the wagon brake and everyone piled out. Gudrun took the children to the house, but Finn and Thora came to see us.

"We finished seaming yesterday," Finn said. "Fishing is going to be great this year."

I felt so embarrassed for him. That morning I'd overheard Pabbi and Leifur saying what a terrible fisherman Finn was, that his hands were always cold so the fish often wiggled from his grasp back into the hole. He ripped the nets with the hook and they tangled when it was his turn to pull them back under the ice—the complete opposite to Leifur who took to it so naturally.

"So I see you bought yourself some nets," J.K. said, crossing his arms.

Pabbi's cheeks flushed. "I've been meaning to tell you."

J.K. sighed. "Wish I had known yesterday. I turned down a man from Dog Creek looking for work. I was counting on you and Leifur to get my nets lifted."

Pabbi finished tying on a lead and let the bottom of the net drop to the ground. He told us to take Finn and Thora inside.

Feeling the tension between them, we obeyed immediately.

Mother and Gudrun were making plans to butcher the pigs and fattened sheep. That is why they'd come, for coffee and to see if it was a job our families should do together.

"The children need to learn how to butcher," Gudrun said. "Otherwise who will make the svið when we are too old?"

Svið, or boiled sheep's head, was a delicacy that we couldn't live without.

"Well, I'm not counting on Freyja in that regard," Mother said.

"Hmmmm?" Freyja asked, looking up from the table where she was sketching in her tablet.

"Nothing, dear," Mother said.

I went over to the window to watch Pabbi and J.K.'s conversation. Their heads bobbed seriously, each listening to what the other said. Mother called me away, reminding me that I hadn't yet swept the floor.

When the men came in, both were smiling. Outside in the October wind they'd reached an agreement that would see them continue fishing together. They would share the expense of the hired men; J.K. would arrange to sell and transport all Pabbi's catch to the buyer at Big Point while Pabbi would supply a sleigh, the team and his own fish boxes.

"To be honest," J.K. said, eyes twinkling, "I would respect you less if you didn't want your own outfit."

Then he took his coffee and told us about the time they were on the lake in late February. A six-week deep freeze had ended and there was a sudden warm spell that drove temperatures well above freezing. They were lifting south of Ghost Island when suddenly a thunderous roar caused the ice to shake violently. They fell to their knees, helpless, as the lake erupted like an earthquake. Monstrous slabs of five-foot-thick ice heaved up less than 200 yards away, creating a ten-foot-high wall that extended as far as they could see.

"It was unbelievable," J.K. said.

Finn listened thoughtfully. "A pressure ridge," he said. "Caused by fissures that fill with water then freeze causing the surface of the ice to expand. When ice expands, it presses against the lake banks and, with nowhere to go, it heaves upward."

J.K. was as surprised as the rest of us.

"It is the conclusion I drew after reading one of the scientific books Magnus donated to the library," Finn said. At seventeen years old he had already completed grade twelve by correspondence.

"And you want to spend your life fishing?" Gudrun asked.

"Miss Erlendsson said Finn should be a doctor," I blurted out. It was every Icelandic family's dream to produce at least one.

"A doctor?" J.K. said. "Now that is an idea I can get behind."

Until that point, all Finn had wanted was to be like Leifur—to spend his life working alongside his father. But I think he saw for the first time the gleam in his father's eye, and a way to make him proud.

"The thought has crossed my mind," Finn said, looking across the table at me. "Practicing medicine is an honorable way to make a living."

Our eyes locked and my cheeks grew warm.

"Stefan should come with me to the University," he said. "I don't think he will be much good to his father now."

"That is a splendid idea," Gudrun said. "Law school would be a fine place for him. He is smart as a whip and certainly charming enough."

Freyja put down her pencil to listen, excited.

"I am not sure his father would encourage it," J.K. said, "or Asi for that matter. All Stefan talks about is fishing again and playing ball."

Everyone raised their eyebrows at that.

"If he does not give up, that arm will become strong," J.K. said, focussing on Finn. "It is amazing what a young man can do when he puts his mind to it."

Within a week the lake froze over. Leifur was so excited that he barely slept. The night before they started setting, he anxiously asked if I would help Signy milk the cows, so he and Pabbi could get an early start.

Mother met them at the door with dinner wrapped in a flour sack while the rest of us watched from the window as they set out at first light, pulling the pile of nets behind them on a homemade sleigh. The ice wouldn't be strong enough to hold the horses for at least a month.

That fall, the catch was incredibly good. Steady, cold temperatures meant the ice didn't break up as it often did, so no nets were lost. J.K. said it was the best freeze-up he'd ever seen.

They fished every day except when the wind blew with such force they could barely stay upright. Pabbi and Leifur came home dog tired, nearly overcome with gnawing hunger, but satiated at the same time.

Men who remembered the patterns and could read the ice were the most successful fishermen. Leifur had caught on quickly. He'd learned from J.K. that perch school out by the islands where the lake bottom is soft, while pickerel preferred the hard bottom closer to shore. Tullibees would suddenly appear in the nets by the thousands at the coldest time of year.

Though Pabbi didn't say it, and none of us ever spoke of it, we all knew he hoped that Signy would change her mind. Olafur had transplanted himself into our family like a long lost cousin. We had an unspoken family commandment, Thou Shalt Not Say Things Out Loud. We didn't even realize the power of this rule until Olafur came along and started breaking it. His family commandment must have been Thou Shalt Say Everything.

Having Olafur eat at the table with us, talking happily while we all listened; seeing Pabbi's strained expression, Mother's patience and Signy's satisfied grin, I have to say I realized that Signy was far more resourceful than I had given her credit for.

She reassured Olafur that our parents didn't mind one bit that he ate with us, so every evening, after his chores were done, he'd jump on his horse and ride in at supper time. He stayed until well past dark, then rode home. Olafur believed everything he heard; he brought a new story with him every night.

"Good news," he said to Signy one evening in late November. "We are going to move our nets to the bay here."

The next morning the brothers arrived right after breakfast. They set their nets south of J.K. and Pabbi's and, since it made no sense to Olafur to go all the way home, he helped with our evening chores then came in on Pabbi's heels, hanging his jacket on the hook next to his. When a storm blew in, Amma suggested that Olafur should sleep on the sofa.

He'd talk all through breakfast the next morning.

"Is he ever going to go home?" Pabbi asked Mother when they were alone.

Mother shrugged, hiding the hint of a smile. "He is going to be our son-in-law."

"Will I get my house back then?" he asked.

"That all depends," Mother said. "The little house is ready for them now. If one of Olafur's brothers decide to move into it, he and Signy may have nowhere else to live but here."

One evening in late February, Freyja and I made a cake to celebrate Solrun's second birthday. Freyja watched anxiously at the window for the men to come in off the lake. "You should see what I did," she said, meeting Leifur at the door. "I made a cake for Solrun."

We immediately knew by Leifur's expression that something was wrong. His jaw was tight and his muscles were tense as he tore off his mitts and hat, throwing them on the floor by the stove.

Mother gave him a questioning look. He brushed her off as he sat down at the table.

Amma came from the front room, followed by Signy carrying our baby brother, Lars, who had been born in November.

The door opened again. Pabbi and Olafur came inside. All Pabbi could do was shake his head.

"What is wrong?" Mother asked.

"That Bensi needs a good talking-to," Olafur said, gritting his teeth.

"What did he do now?" Signy asked, but before he could answer, Leifur startled us all by slamming his fist on the table.

"He shot Thor," he said.

CHAPTER TWENTY-TWO

Sorrow is lightened by being brought out openly.
—THE SAGA OF SIGURD THE CRUSADER
AND HIS BROTHERS EYSTEIN AND OLAF

"Asta, you look tired," Thora says. "Would you like to go back now?"

I am, I would, but there is such a finality to leaving. I will put it off for as long as possible. Besides the game is only half over.

"There you are," a voice calls out. "The nurse said you'd be here."

We turn to see our brother Lars coming toward us. Lars is carrying a sealer jar in each hand. He holds them up, beaming at me.

My dying request was to taste water from the farm once again. At least two extra days. That's how long I estimate the water will keep me alive. I am not sure if they believe me or not.

Solrun hugs Lars as if she hasn't seen him in years. She is like that, always hugging people.

"How was the flight?" she asks.

"Not bad," he says, glancing at me, but speaking to her. "How is she?"

"Better today."

"You went on a trip?" I ask.

"To B.C.," he says, leaning in to give me a hug. "We have a house there now."

“Who’s taking care of the farm?”

“Don’t worry, everything is fine.”

Thora and Solrun slide over to let Lars sit beside me. “Enjoying the game?” he asks.

Lars is so full of life. Shorter and heavier than Leifur and twice as charming. Everyone always loved Lars.

He claps as the pitcher winds his arm the same way Bjorn used to. This boy is taller but his hair is the same and he pitches as well as my Bjorn. Southpaw. He fires it across the plate.

I try my best to follow the conversation going on around me. They talk about the weather. The crops. And of course the roads.

Everyone cheers as the batter strikes out.

“I hear the number of trucks travelling north has doubled,” Lars says. “The highway is suffering because of it.”

I know where this is going. “Please, let’s not talk about the government.”

They all laugh.

“Tell me how your children are doing,” I say, not taking my eyes off the game. “Start from oldest to youngest.”

He begins rattling off where his children live, their occupations, which granddaughter is expecting. It is a lot for an old woman to take in.

I try clapping again.

A klatch of people come from the hall toward us. Solrun and Thora are pleased. I should recognize the young woman wearing a blue party dress and jeweled crown. A sash runs over her shoulder proclaiming, ‘Miss Interlake.’ She is elated to see me. I pretend to understand what this is about.

“Elskan,” I say, struggling to remember her. “How are you?”

It has been like this for a few years now. My memory of the past is remarkably clear but yesterday sits in my brain like a fog. One thing I have learned is that I must not embarrass the young people with my forgetfulness. It is the vacant stare and the complaining that causes them to stop visiting.

So I pretend. If I wait, Solrun will give me clues.

"How are you Nurse Gudmundsson?" the girl asks. It is always awkward hugging someone in a wheelchair but she is better at it than most.

"Dying," I say, hearing that my voice sounds weak. "But I am not complaining. I will wait until the game is over."

She looks amused. "Glad to see you haven't lost your sense of humor."

"Is it heavy?" I ask, pointing up at her crown.

"No, but it feels weird."

She looks like a princess. Freyja would have loved a crown like that.

The coach pulls the pitcher, saving his arm for the next game. An older, heavyset young man approaches the mound for the last few innings. His knuckle ball fools them every time.

"Have I told you about the day my sister Freyja disappeared?" I ask.

I see in her expression that I have, many times. Young people also lose patience during the retelling of the same story.

"I knew your Amma and Afi," I say quickly. The perfect segue. Old people say this sort of thing all the time.

"Everyone knew J.J.," Solrun adds.

Now I remember her family. "A good man. And your Amma, a beautiful woman. I remember the day they moved to Siglunes."

"Elaine does volunteer work at the hospital," Solrun says to Thora. "Another Siglunes girl who plans to be a nurse."

"We play chess," I say. A safe assumption.

"She wins every time," Elaine adds.

"Wish now I'd paid attention when she tried to teach me." Lars laughs. "She beats everyone."

I think back. "That's not entirely true," I say. "There was one person I could never defeat."

* * *

Pabbi refused to let us see Thor's body. After breakfast Leifur buried it under a pile of rocks so the coyotes couldn't tear it apart.

They'd all heard the shot, but it wasn't until they passed Gull Reef that they'd seen the black mass on the ice near shore.

"Still alive?" I'd asked, choking out the words. The thought chilled me as if someone had opened the door letting in a cold wind.

Freyja was eleven years old but still innocent as ever. "Does Setta know?" she asked.

"I am sure she does," I said.

"Finn ran home to get the gun," Pabbi said quietly. "Someday Bensi will get his just desserts."

I was in a sour mood as Thora, Freyja and I trudged through the snow into the school yard. I kept imagining Pabbi taking the gun from Finn, placing it on Thor's forehead, closing his eyes before pulling the trigger.

Wouldn't you know it, the first thing we saw was Bensi's son, Pall, teasing a younger boy. He held the boy's hat in the air, taunting him.

As we walked by, I grabbed the hat to give back to the little boy.

Pall sneered at me. He was handsome to look at but his constant scowl and churlish attitude made him ugly. "So where is your dog?" he teased.

"I'm not sure," I said.

When he looked at Freyja she started to cry then ran over to where Petra stood sadly with her arms wrapped around herself.

I told the girls to go inside but neither moved.

"Boo hoo," Pall said, rubbing his eye with a fist. "I heard J.K. shot her."

Thora's eyes widened. She looked at me, then back at Pall.

"You are a liar," she said.

"Am not."

"Are so."

"Prove it."

Thora crossed her arms in front of her and I heard the anger in her voice. "Father was on the lake. He heard the shot. So did Olafur. My father would never do such a thing. He is not cruel like your papa."

Pall was two years younger than us, but almost as big. He slammed his palms onto Thora's chest, knocking her backward into the snow.

Blind with anger, I hit him. It was a full body tackle that caught him by surprise. He slipped, one foot crossed over the other and went down hard. His neck snapped back and his head hit the ground. He grunted when I landed on top of him. Our classmates began chanting, "Fight! Fight!" He grabbed my hair, triggering a memory, and a bold fury I'd never felt before.

It was Petra who ran to the school to get the teacher and Steina pulled us apart. "Asta, what in God's name are you doing?"

It was most shocking to see Pall stagger to his feet. I'd felt nothing while hitting him, but now the heel of my hand burned, and my arm throbbed.

"He hit Thora first."

"What business is that of yours?"

"His father shot Thor."

Steina was taken by surprise. I imagined her at the castle patting Thor, stepping over him as he lay on the kitchen floor, feeding him bits of fat under the table.

"Bjorn's dog, not ours," I said.

The color drained from Pall's face. "Well at least my papa is not a thief," he said. "Asta's father stole money from the church."

"That is enough," Steina said. "Everyone into the school."

She called Pall and me to the front of the room once we were inside.

"Now, apologize," she said.

Pall and I faced each other but neither was ready to back down. Everyone was watching solemnly from their desks.

"If you do not apologize to one another right now, I will speak to your parents about this."

Immediately I thought of Pabbi's reputation as Secretary-Treasurer.

"I am sorry," I said.

Pall smirked.

Steina saw it and pointed to the corner of the room. "You can stand there all day and think about what your father will say. Asta, you will sit at the back of the room and study alone."

Without a word I slid into a desk and opened my text book. I didn't feel one bit sorry about what I'd done. In fact, I decided to never apologize again unless I meant it.

When it came time to leave school that day, Pall came up behind us and began reciting a rhyme about Pabbi. Since he wasn't clever enough to make it up, I guessed that Bensi must have.

"If anyone hurts Setta," I said, "Leifur will come looking for *you.*"

Outside the lean-to door I swore Freyja to secrecy. Under no circumstances was she to tell Pabbi what had happened.

We went in to find everyone preoccupied with the latest catastrophe. Skalda had labored all day giving birth to a large bull calf that was coming into the world backwards. Pabbi and Leifur had spent hours trying to get the calf out alive, but their efforts had been fruitless and Skalda began hemorrhaging. Pabbi was forced, for the second time in only a few days, to end the suffering of an animal whose eyes he'd looked into many times.

"If Pabbi thinks I am going to wait another year . . ." Signy said.

It was a week later and we were upstairs, about to go to bed. She ran the brush through her waist-long hair, quietly counting the strokes.

"Here," she said handing me the brush. "Your hair is starting to embarrass me."

"Where do you suppose Pabbi went?" I asked.

She climbed into bed beside Freyja. "To the lake. Probably wants to talk with J.K."

"Why did Olafur have to say that to Pabbi?" I asked.

Signy shrugged. "If he wants to know something he asks."

It had begun after supper. Mother asked Freyja what she'd learned in school, but of course Freyja had been too busy daydreaming to answer, then Olafur asked if Pall was back at school yet.

He looked directly at me. "I hear you gave him a thrashing," he said. "My pa had a visitor last night. Bensi's on the warpath. Says you shouldn't be allowed back at school. Plans to write a letter so you will not be accepted into teachers' college."

Pabbi was staring at me but I was too ashamed to meet his gaze.

"What is this about?" Mother asked.

"I say good for Asta," Olafur said, leaning back in his chair. "About time someone put his little nuts in place."

"Olafur," Mother hissed under her breath.

"Oh, Ella," Amma said. "He's right."

"Asta?" Pabbi asked.

Everyone turned to look at me.

"Freyja, you tell them," I said.

She looked up from the table and her eyes widened. She stood up, actually stood up on the bench so everyone could see her, and began acting the whole thing out. When she got to the part where I tackled Pall, she jumped down and ran to the middle of the kitchen to flatten an imaginary Pall to the floor. I winced a bit when she began screeching like a wild animal, pounding her imaginary Pall with her fist.

Amma cheered. Leifur turned and I am certain there was admiration in his eyes.

Then Freyja, imitating Steina, said: "Asta, Pall, what in the world? Asta you should be ashamed of yourself."

Freyja placed her hands on her hips pretending to be me. "His father shot Thor so I am going to teach him a lesson." Then she kicked.

"I didn't kick him," I said over all the noise.

"All right," Mother said. "Freyja settle down."

"I can hardly wait to tell Magnus." Amma beamed.

Mother scolded her and reminded everyone about the letter Bensi planned to write.

Pabbi suggested that I apologize to the teacher to regain her respect.

There was an English word that I'd learned from the eighth grade matriculation exam—grovel—and knew this was something I'd never do.

"I have already made up my mind," I said. "I have decided I don't want to be a teacher after all."

Too bad it hadn't ended right there, but before anyone had time to react to my statement, Olafur finished what he'd intended to say.

"Bensi is spreading a rumor about you," he said to Pabbi. "He says that you stole money from a church in Iceland."

Pabbi stiffened. A dreadful silence filled the room. Not even Amma knew what to say.

"A lie," Pabbi said.

"I figured as much. But it would be nice to know the truth so that when the gossiping starts, I can set them all straight."

Pabbi pushed back his chair. He stood up. He looked Olafur direct in the eye before slapping his hand down on the table, rattling the plates and cutlery. "I will not have some young buck fighting my battles," he said. "None of this is any of your business. If you speak of it again, I will forbid you to marry my daughter."

There was nothing any of us could do but watch him storm across the floor then out the door.

Olafur's ears blazed and that was one of the few times in all the years I knew him that he was rendered speechless.

So we cleaned up the kitchen in silence.

Hard as that evening was, I've always credited Olafur for the change we saw in Pabbi after that night. Signy was right. While she and I were upstairs brushing our hair, Pabbi was conversing with J.K. on his verandah. My heart aches for him even now as I watch the two of them.

"I have lived with shame my whole life," Pabbi says into the still night. The moon shines through a mist of clouds and all else is silent except for the sound of their breathing. "Mother kicked Father out when I was a young lad so I barely have a recollection of him."

J.K. pulls a box of matches from his pocket then strikes one on the banister. He raises it to his pipe, quickly drawing in a breath, puffing on it until it starts to smoke.

"She changed my surname, sent me to a fine school," he continued.

"I've wondered about that."

"By the time I was a teenager, I realized that she earned a living by questionable means. But she was my mother and she treated me like a prince. They all teased me about her . . . and my lisp."

"Go on," J.K. says calmly.

"I did not take any money from her when I left home. Ella and I worked hard, acquired everything we had on our own. We were proud of that. Ella was proud of me." He takes in a deep breath, and laughs. "That smells so good I almost wish I smoked."

J.K. holds out the pipe but Pabbi refuses.

"We bought a small farm at Sleðbrjot and were getting by. During the ten years we were there, I made improvements to the land. I owed some money but nothing I couldn't handle as my credit was good."

"You are telling me this because of Bensi," J.K. says.

Pabbi lets his breath out slowly. "I was chosen as district administrator and there were decisions to make. I bought lumber from Norway to build a church in the belief that the money was available from the government. I signed for it. You can imagine the cost."

J.K. whistles. "A lot."

"Fishing was poor and the crops failed that year and the next. I was able to sell the lumber but it was to a scoundrel who knew how desperate I was. I was forced to declare bankruptcy the following year. I lost the farm."

"That is when you moved in with Ella's family?"

Pabbi leans hard against the railing. "They thought even less of me after that. Here . . . at least I'd hoped . . ." Pabbi chuckles. "All my life she's been nothing but good to me."

"I take it you left behind the debt?"

"I don't expect you to defend me to the neighbors. Judge my actions as you see fit. I just wanted you to know the truth. It would have taken me a lifetime to repay. I could not do that to Ella. Mother offered to help, but only if we made a fresh start—in America. I did not steal from anyone," he says, turning to face J.K. "It was Bensi who stole from me."

CHAPTER TWENTY-THREE

It is good to have two mouths for the two kinds of speech.
—THE SAGA OF THORSTEIN, VIKING'S SON

SPRING CAME EARLY THAT YEAR. THE WEATHER WAS MILD SO THE ewes lambed with ease and were on pasture by mid-May. The ice house was packed full and the door shut tight. Last summer's vegetables were long eaten except for a few wrinkly potatoes, but the garden was already showing signs of new life. The days were long, the air sweet, and the breeze blew calm; and because it was the month between the two busiest times on the farm—birthing and haying—that same calmness settled over us.

Leifur came home from the lake one morning with a full fish box. The commercial season was long over but the fish inspector allowed each family to set one net year round for the house. It was an unwritten rule that in the spring, fishermen would throw back the large, fat pickerel as they were usually the females filled with roe.

"Their flesh is too soft anyway," Leifur said. "These ones taste much better."

He called into the house for me so I took the knives out and together we started cleaning. It was an enjoyable job and I was proficient at filleting, so he always asked me instead of Signy. I looked forward to those mornings. There was something about handling fish that brought out the joy in my brother and it was pleasant to watch.

Setta and the cats (where those cats came from was a mystery) would wait, some more patiently than others, to sneak under the table, grab the entrails, then carry them away.

I only saw Setta kill a cat once. It was a large, confident tom that bullied all the others. The females scattered respectfully when Setta stuck her big head under the table, but the tomcat decided to swipe at her nose. A quick turn and she snapped his neck so fast he didn't feel a thing.

"You should see the creeks," Leifur said, grabbing a fish then deftly cutting off its head, sliding the knife under the gills, then spinning it around to chop off the tail. "Full of spawning fish. In a few years, you watch Asta, it will be tremendous."

He sliced down the belly, scraped out the entrails, then slid it over to me to remove the bones.

In those days we ate fish daily, sometimes morning and night. Mother boiled, fried, baked, and canned it. We'd leave the tails and skin on the last few dozen so Mother could soak them in salt brine then hang them to dry. They would turn into harðfiskur, a staple from our homeland that we all loved.

"This is as good as anything we ever had in Iceland," Leifur said as he stacked the splayed fish. We all missed the strong taste of cod, but in the years since coming here some of us even grew to prefer the milder taste of pickerel.

Pabbi went early one fine morning to meet with Steina. Classes had let out the week before so they had a few details to finalize before sending the school report to Winnipeg.

"Watch that your sister doesn't fall in," Mother called out as Freyja took Solrun's hand. They trotted off, each carrying a jam pail to catch frogs.

Leifur and I joined Mother to weed the garden. Earlier I'd overheard Signy whispering to Amma, and now we all watched them go east across the meadow and I saw puzzlement in Mother's expression.

When Pabbi returned, he drove straight to the barn, unhitched the team, then led them to water, the school ledger tucked under his arm.

Freyja saw him and hurried back, water sloshing out of the pails as she pulled Solrun along.

"Look what we caught," Freyja said, meeting him at the road, holding up the pails.

He exclaimed, peering inside, then lifted Solrun to carry her the rest of the way.

We all stood up to stretch. We knew by the slant of the sun that it was time for dinner. Pabbi said little until we'd all made ourselves a quick sandwich and were sitting under Amma's tree. We ate thoughtfully, watching Amma and Signy cross the field toward us with their heads bent together.

"Bensi has asked for an audit of the school's finances," Pabbi said.

Mother thought for a few moments. "Good. They will find everything in order and Bensi will look like a fool. Again."

"There is more," he said, finishing the last of his sandwich. "Steina has decided to accept a position in Swan River at a larger school, so I will have to find another teacher."

"After only two years?" Mother asked.

"Steina is leaving?" Freyja asked.

"I'm afraid so," he said.

"When?"

"Tomorrow. That is why she needed to meet with me today."

"But she will miss the picnic," Freyja said. "I won't be able to say good-bye."

"That is alright," I said. "I'm sure you will like the next teacher just as well."

"No, I won't," she pouted, but I was thrilled. Steina leaving was the best news I'd heard in months.

One day soon after, Asi brought the land inspector to our yard. Inspectors were thick-skinned men hired to keep farmers and fishermen abiding by the laws set out by the government. This particular land inspector wore a suit and carried a thin leather valise. We could see he was not accustomed to walking any distance since he had to pause to catch his breath, take a drink from the jar Asi carried, and wipe his brow with a handkerchief—all before shaking Pabbi's hand.

"This is Mr. Phillips," Asi said in Icelandic. "Picked him up at Westbourne. He is from the Land Titles Office. Asked if I knew a translator."

"Is he paying you?" Pabbi asked.

Mr. Phillips stood looking between the two of them, completely unaware of what was being said.

"Yes."

"Good."

"Where is the Lady Ellen?"

"Stefan and a hired man are finishing my deliveries."

"Coffee?"

"Of course."

Mother tugged on Signy's arm to get her to follow her to the house. It was considered rude to not invite a visitor inside. Bread was in the oven and I am sure Mr. Phillips with all his girth could smell it baking.

"J.K. offered his democrat but I made him walk," Asi said to Amma.

She reached into her skirt pocket for a pack of cigarettes. "This one is on me."

As the rest of us came close, Mr. Phillips turned.

We were so shy, not one of us said a word.

"Did you hear about Bjorn?" Asi asked, again in Icelandic. He seemed pleased about the news he was about to share.

Pabbi cocked his head.

"Two weeks ago. Moved to Swan River."

His words hit me like a punch to the stomach.

"Remember Sifton from The Narrows?" he said. "He's opening a store in Swan River. Likes Bjorn's ambition. Hired him to manage it."

"I am surprised Bjorn would leave Magnus," Pabbi said.

"Siggi and Arn are still at the mill. Between you and me, responsibility is exactly what those two need. Might toughen them up a bit."

"Bjorn is going to quit fishing?" Leifur asked. Clearly he thought this was the most unbelievable part of the story. Asi said he didn't think so, since he'd delivered a bale of nets to Sifton a few weeks ago. He thought it more likely that Bjorn would be put in charge of a crew.

"Who is going to set by Ghost Island?" Leifur asked.

"Slow down." Asi laughed. "Magnus will not give up his territory yet."

"How does this affect your plans to buy the mill?" Pabbi asked.

The Inspector cleared his throat, letting them know he was still standing there. Normally Pabbi would never leave a visitor out of the conversation, but this man was with the government. Clearly, he was nervous.

Amma stuck out her hand to introduce herself. "Ástfriður Guðbjornsdóttir."

Mr. Phillips leaned in, raising his eyebrows. She repeated herself. He appeared somewhat surprised by her grip.

"What does he want?" Pabbi asked. "Have we done something to anger the government?"

Asi shrugged. "He told me nothing."

"Pjetur Guðmundsson," Pabbi said at last, holding out his hand, then pointing to each one of us, "Leifur, Ástfriður, Freyja, Sólrún, Lars, Signý." He turned as Mother approached, "Ella Sigurveig Leifursdóttir."

Mother greets him sweetly, "Góðan daginn."

Mr. Phillips nodded, then cleared his throat again.

"Tell them I am here to discuss their land," he said, reaching into his valise for a piece of paper. "The parcels registered to "Pe-tur Gud-munds-son and As-frider Good-bjorns-daughter, respectively."

"He has questions," Asi said.

"What does he want to know?"

"Under the Land Titles Agreement that you signed," Mr. Phillips said, squinting at the paper, "on April 20, 1906, you took possession of these two quarter sections of land and agreed to build a home and make improvements to each parcel."

Then he pulled out another sheet.

"According to a letter of complaint received in our office dated March 7 of this year, you have not made the necessary improvements to one of the parcels, nor have you built a house. I am here to investigate to see if the allegations are correct."

Asi translated while Pabbi listened carefully, understanding more than he let on.

"This," he said, pointing to Amma's quarter, "is our pasture land." Then, turning, he pointed beyond the bush, "and over there is our hay land. We need both to have a viable farm. As you can see, this quarter is filled with trees and we have cleared as much as we can. For now."

Mother handed cups to both Asi and the Inspector.

"He wants to know why you haven't built another house," Asi said.

"There was a complaint?" Mother asked.

Asi nodded.

"From who?"

Asi shrugged. "Didn't say."

Mother looked at Pabbi who looked at Amma who placed her hands firmly on her hips.

"Pjetur wants to see the letter," Asi said.

The Inspector handed it to Pabbi who examined it carefully.

"This is Bensi's handwriting," he said. "Tell him our neighbor sent it, a man who wants this land for himself."

The Inspector listened, then shook his head. "I do not care about your petty squabbles. Your neighbor had every right to complain if you have not followed the rules."

"Tell him that Bensi has more land than us and only one house, he should go there to see for himself. Tell him to accept if Bensi offers a roast beef dinner. It will be very tasty."

Amma interrupted. "Pjetur, stop being foolish. He stole that calf last year. It will be long eaten by now."

Asi raised his eyebrows.

"This neighbor," Asi said, handing the inspector the letter, "has made trouble for this family since they arrived. He owns two quarters himself and has only one house."

The Inspector sipped his coffee.

"When they came here," Asi said, taking it upon himself, "a very wise man told them to build here, on this ridge. This land is registered to Pjetur, but since he and his mother are farming together they built only one house. They plan to build one for her soon."

Asi took a few steps, pointing northeast. "Now they know how high the water comes…"

Mr. Phillips followed Asi, shielding his eyes from the sun.

"They plan to build in that oak bluff," Asi said.

The inspector spoke.

"He wants to know why you haven't built it yet," Asi said.

"No time," Amma said, shooting Pabbi an 'I told you this would happen' look. I am not sure who Pabbi feared more, the land inspector or Amma.

Mr. Phillips dug into his case for another sheet. He read rapidly. Asi translated.

"Under the Dominion Lands Act, it clearly states that every tract of 160 acres must have 40 acres cultivated and improved within three years. You have not fulfilled that obligation on this quarter. He does not believe that you intend to build, since you look quite comfortable here. He says he has been sent out to revoke the title and issue it to someone more worthy." Then Asi added, "Whatever you say next, make it good."

"Ásmundur Frimann," Amma said. "I will handle this now."

"The old woman wants to talk to you."

This shocked the Inspector. He had no clue that Amma had dealt with men like him before.

She began by taking the coffee cup out of Pabbi's hand and throwing it to the ground. She lowered her chin, raised up her hand and began wagging her finger at Pabbi and Mother.

"Our country's God, our God's country, our life is a feeble and quivering reed, we perish, deprived of thy spirit and light, to redeem and uphold in our need," she preached.

We all—including Asi—reacted with such surprise to her gibberish, the Inspector believed, as she'd intended, that she was scolding Pabbi for getting the family into such a mess. She shook her head in frustration and such a sorrowful look came across her face that, if you didn't know her well, you would think she was about to start crying.

"Come," she said, grabbing the Inspector by the jacket sleeve, pulling him across the yard. She paused briefly for a moment to glare at us (for effect), then with Asi and the Inspector double stepping to keep up, she crossed the road into the east meadow.

For years afterwards we begged Amma to tell us what she'd told him but she never did. And Asi kept quiet about it, too. When I asked her once, she just smiled and said: "It is best to keep me on your good side."

It thrills me to see my Amma again, to watch it all unfold, to cross the yard with the three of them.

"That daughter-in-law of mine is conspiring to get rid of me," Amma says, "so I must keep my plans secret."

Asi quickly translates, adding that the Inspector must have seen cases like this before, where an old woman is tricked into paying the family's way then is cast aside.

Mr. Phillips thinks for a moment.

"The lumber is ready and waiting at the Siglunes mill," she says. "Ask Magnus Magnusson if you don't believe me, he will show you the receipt."

He listens.

"If you take this land away from me, I will be forced to live with them for the rest of my life. I can hardly stand that woman. And all those children? The noise? Terrible."

"But how do you intend to improve the land?" the Inspector asks. "That still must be done."

Amma's eyebrows shoot up. "I am not as old as you think. I can still do a man's work. Not long ago I filled in as back-catcher with the Siglunes ball team."

The Inspector looks skeptical.

Asi shrugs. "I have seen her play ball."

"I have another trick up my sleeve but you must promise to keep my secret. The older boy and I have an agreement. I will give him half my sheep in exchange for his help. Ella thinks that everything I own will belong to her when I die, but the land and the sheep will go to the boy."

"So he will help you develop the land? How will you pay for these improvements?"

Amma waits for Asi to finish translating.

"Tell him I have a sack of money that no one knows about," she says.

Asi's eyes widen.

"If we lose this land," she tells him, "we will be forced to leave here."

"She says she will build this year," Asi says. "All you need to do is report that the house is started. They will finish improving the land this year."

"You are asking me to file a false report?"

Amma and Asi wait, trying to read the Inspector's thoughts. When he starts shaking his head, saying that it is a highly irregular thing to do, Amma uses those powerful eyes of hers to stare at him until he's forced to look away. Then she turns to Asi. "Listen carefully and repeat word for word what I am about to tell you." When she is finished, Amma calmly closes her eyes. Asi takes a noticeable step away from her—again for effect.

"Are you sure you want me to say that?"

"What do we have to lose?"

Turning to face the inspector, Asi raises his hands in surrender. "This is something that I do not want on my head."

"What in God's name are you talking about?" the Inspector asks.

"Well . . . " Asi hesitates, taking a deep breath. "She tells me that if you take the land away from her, she will bring harm to herself, but before doing so will put a curse on you and this land, lasting one hundred years. She told me not to tell you, but I feel you should know."

"That is ridiculous. I do not believe in curses."

A wicked grin turns Asi's lips. It is shocking to see him like this, so serious it's almost as if Amma has put a spell on him.

"You don't have to," he calmly says, "because we do. No one will lease this land. They will fear the sheep will die from grazing the grass, and the children will become sick from drinking the cow's milk. There will be rain and fire. This land will either sit unoccupied or misfortune will come to all who lease it for a century. Word will spread. You will be known as 'Mr. Phillips the man who caused Ástfriður Guðbjornsdóttir to take her own life.' You will be blamed for every misfortune in the district."

"Nonsense," he says.

"Trust me. I have seen it. They will turn their backs on you from here all the way to New Iceland. We are determined people. If the curse sticks to you, in all likelihood you will lose your job. Terrible things happen to people who ignore a curse."

There we were, all anxiously waiting under the tree, watching Asi and Mr. Phillips hurry down the road, then disappear into the bush trail leading to the lake, as Amma strode toward us, intensely pleased with herself.

"Well?" Pabbi asked. "Did he take the land away?"

"Of course not," Amma said. "But I should warn you, Mr. Phillips believes Ella is a troll and that I am a witch."

Pabbi chuckled. "Half correct, then?"

CHAPTER TWENTY-FOUR

Sweet to the eye is that which is seen.
—VÖLSUNGA SAGA

"We should go back now," Solrun says, turning my wheelchair.

I fell asleep again. I cannot remember the final two innings.

"Did we win?" I ask.

"Of course," Lars says.

He is watching me now with such a pained expression it is embarrassing. He stands quickly. Brothers are never sure what to do when emotions are involved. I want to tell him that I am fine, but suddenly am too exhausted to utter a word.

Thora tries to lighten the mood by linking her arm in his, leading him to the sidewalk while Solrun and I follow. She says something that I can't hear and he does a little dance, causing her to laugh.

It takes the three of them to lift me onto the bed.

Solrun offers to take everyone home for a bite to eat. Lars says he will stay behind to sit with me. I tell him to go, but his mind is set. Once they leave we share a few uncomfortable moments. Like I said, brothers are not good at this.

"I will be fine," I say, reaching for his hand, and I see for the first time how much like Mother's it is—short and strong, nails almost square. My hands are more like Father's, long and thin. I've seen Solrun's so many times, but do you think I can picture them now? I will have to look again.

"Solrun tells me you are experiencing dreams," he says.

"Not dreams," I say. "Travel. Like the Ghost of Christmas Past. You know, *Dickens.*"

He hasn't pooh-poohed me yet, so I continue.

"That place between heaven and earth," I say, feeling incredibly weak. He sees I am exhausted, but is curious; he leans in closer so I don't have to strain.

"Do you know what caused the fire?" he asks.

I have to say that despite our age difference, he and I have always understood each other, but I am uncertain which fire he means since there were two. "No, but I will soon, and about Freyja, too."

He opens his mouth to say something but thinks twice. I wait, hoping he will continue but he doesn't.

"Do you believe me?"

He smiles in that affable way I remember from our youth.

"I have always believed in you," he says. "Even when others didn't."

* * *

It was Amma who said to Pabbi that it would be prudent to allow Signy and Olafur to marry soon, otherwise, if Olafur decided to change his mind, it would leave Signy in a bit of a predicament.

It took Pabbi and Mother an hour or so to puzzle it together. Nothing was said, at least not to us. They simply gathered everyone together to announce that Pabbi had reconsidered. In other words, as Olafur had predicted the day he met Signy, Pabbi didn't have much choice.

"At least he is Icelandic," was all Pabbi said.

Plans were already underway to build a huge house on the Thorsteinsson homestead where all the sons would live with their families, but in the meantime Signy and Olafur moved into the original log home that was there when his father bought the land. It later became the shed where Olafur hung his nets over the summer months.

It was obvious by the way Oli Thorsteinsson looked at us with unwavering respect, especially when Pabbi spoke, that he was proud that one of his boys had married into our family, that now we were a part of their clan.

Seeing they'd built the largest farm in the district, you'd think those Thorsteinsson boys had enough to do, but all four of them turned up, along with Oli, when the lumber for Amma's house arrived. They set aside three days to get it done and by golly that's how long it took. Pabbi and Leifur looked almost insulted that Amma hadn't needed their help.

When Oli finished hanging the door, Olafur joked that the house wasn't much bigger than the double-seated outhouse they'd built at their farm the year before. Amma was quick to reply.

"I need one of those too," she said. "One hole will do. When can you get started?"

Oli laughed, saying it served Olafur right. His eyes danced at everything Amma said and he enjoyed her wit so much, he started coming by for regular visits. His wife had died a few years before so he was in need of female companionship.

"Nine children we had," he said of his late wife. "All I did was look at her sideways and the next thing I knew she was in a family way."

He and Amma spent all those summer visits outside, sitting under a tree if it was hot, in the sun if it was cool. Every time Magnus came for a visit, however, she always invited him in, then closed the door.

Eventually Oli put two-and-two together, realizing that Amma, despite his many hints, had no desire to marry him. This didn't offend him in the least, but he came around less often.

He used to say that Amma "helped him through a rough patch," that it was she who gave him the courage to find what became the second love of his life—a widow from The Narrows who was thrilled to move into the big house.

"Have you looked at her sideways yet?" Amma asked, the first time she saw them together at a dance.

He winked. "Still working up the courage."

"Well you aren't getting any younger."

"That's what she keeps telling me."

They both laughed. They always danced together at least twice at every community function and for a while, his second wife didn't know what to make of their friendship. She must have figured it out, though, seeing Amma's face light up like a schoolgirl when she was with Magnus, because soon after that she and Amma started a friendship that would last the rest of their lives.

Once Amma's house was built, Setta began splitting her time among three places. From dusk until dawn she was like a black island among a sea of sheep, returning home to sleep in the shade until early afternoon, and then plodding over to Amma's where she was allowed indoors to continue her nap.

"What a lazy dog you are," Amma would say.

Setta would stare up at her, ears drooping submissively, tail hammering against the floor, waiting for a scrap of meat. Which of course she always got.

I visited there often.

"Where did you get that new stove?" I asked one afternoon in early August. It stood in the middle of the house, facing into the kitchen, the back of it along the front room wall.

"So nosy," she said. "No wonder I moved into my own house. Can't a woman do anything without a thousand questions?"

"What am I supposed to do, pretend I don't see it?"

Amma smirked. She preferred banter to regular conversation and I was getting the hang of it.

"If you must know, Bergthora gave it to me."

"How did you get it in here?"

"Magnus and the twins."

"It looks new."

"Too small for her kitchen. It was moved out to the barn years ago. Didn't you see it?"

"No," I said. "But mostly I played with the pups."

"Well there you have it. Often we only see what we are looking for."

The sun shone in nicely through the kitchen window. Her table pushed up underneath it reminded me of Siggi and Runa's cottage. Amma always knew when something was bothering me. She poured me a cup of coffee then asked what had me so preoccupied. She sat down across from me, placing a sugar lump between her teeth, just like Pabbi did.

"Finn came for a visit last night. We spent the evening playing chess."

"And?" she asked, taking a sip.

"It was fine," I said. "Has Magnus said anything about Bjorn?"

"Some. He seems to like working in the store. He lives in the back. Sifton is a task master, but Magnus warned him of that before he left. Fishing is good."

"And Steina?"

"Magnus expects they will marry."

"I thought as much," I said, the words barely squeaking out.

I was long past the point of feeling bitter toward him for leaving without saying good-bye. I wished, though, that he'd been at Signy's wedding to see how Finn kept asking me to dance. It was obvious to everyone that Finn was smitten with me.

Amma fetched the pot from the stove to add a bit more to our cups.

"Life has a way of working out the way God intended," she said. "Look at your Pabbi. He moved thousands of miles across the ocean only to end up living next to his worst enemy."

I shook my head. "Why would God arrange such a thing?"

"Your father is a better man now because of it," she said. "We cannot run away from our demons, Asta. We heal by facing them head on. You must remember that."

In the months since his talk with J.K., Pabbi did seem happier. With his secret no longer hiding like Gryla waiting to pounce, he was more relaxed, and while he never said, I think his shame had dissolved.

It did not change how I felt about Bensi, though.

"The nerve of him, bringing his family to Signy's wedding like that."

"It certainly was a surprise."

"Why didn't Pabbi send him away?"

Amma sighed. "Because that would make him worse than Bensi. Someone has to take the first step if they are ever going to get along. How do we know that was not Bensi's way of trying to make amends?"

Amma was clearly in a conciliatory mood while I was not. It was time I let go of Bjorn once and for all, but it was such a difficult thing to do. She saw my angst and softened, her large hand reaching across the table to gently cover mine.

"Your heart is broken and it is impossible to understand right now," she said. "Someday you will look back on your life and the answer will be there."

"But your vision," I said. "Bergthora thought we'd be together, too."

Amma, who usually had an answer for everything, was quiet. I stared silently out the window. She got up to start supper. Lifting the crawlspace door, she crouched down to pull up a cloth bag.

"How do you feel about Finn?" she asked, reaching into the bag.

By the way she said it I presumed she was hoping, along with everyone else, that a spark might ignite a fire between him and me. Since the wedding he'd visited regularly, usually bringing along his chessboard.

"I am not sure," I said.

"He is handsome and kind," she said, placing a handful of potatoes on the counter. "Surely you have noticed."

"I have, it's just that..."

"You are afraid," she said. "Giving your heart to someone only to be disappointed makes it hard to do again."

I agreed but deep inside I believed it was more complicated than that. Allowing myself to fall in love with Finn was something I wanted, but there was an invisible barrier between us, one I didn't know how to penetrate.

"Can a man truly love a woman who is inferior?"

"Asta, you can't possibly believe that," she said.

"But I am not like the other girls," I said, letting my words trail off.

Amma stopped peeling potatoes to examine me.

That is exactly how it felt, like those eyes of hers were boring into my soul. There was a hint of understanding between us and now I see that she knew.

"I understand exactly how you feel," she said. "But I didn't let my past destroy me. I am stronger because of it. Someday a man will come along who loves you for who you are."

I thought back to the night before, when Finn and I were playing chess.

"But how will I know?"

"You won't," she said. "Not unless you give him the chance."

Everyone began counting on their fingers the day Signy's baby was born. She made excuses: the child was so big he came early; she must have conceived the same month as their marriage in July. But the neighbor ladies knew better since this was a trick a few of them had used themselves. Gudrun quietly reminded them of that fact, putting an end to the gossip.

"Isn't he the most beautiful baby in the world?" Signy gushed, still overwhelmed by what she and Olafur had created.

Mother agreed, saying he looked exactly like his father—questioning eyes, ruddy cheeks, pug nose, and a robust cry that could be heard clear across the yard—and when she held little Petur that first time, I saw the bond strengthen between mother and daughter as Signy watched her kiss the top of his head. But I also overheard Mother confess to Gudrun that with Lars barely over one year old, she was having a difficult time accepting she was now an Amma.

Gudrun was so wise, oh what a gift she was in Mother's life.

"Children keep us young," she said, patting Mother's hand. "Remember, this little one is not your responsibility. You can indulge him, then send him home."

Pabbi didn't say much after the baby was born, but he did admit that he liked the change he saw in Olafur. Becoming a father slowed him down a bit, made him stop to think.

One flawless Sunday that June, everyone milled outside the school after the church service chatting while admiring the pink cascade of wild roses that were in full bloom along the edge of the bush.

Finn took me aside to ask if I might like to spend the afternoon sailing in the bay. It was an invitation I was expecting since he'd hinted at it for months. All through Magnus's church service I could hardly think of anything else, knowing that he'd brought his father's democrat for that reason, so that we might spend time alone.

Up until then I'd unfairly compared him to Bjorn, but now he was a man, the same age as Bjorn when I'd met him, I allowed myself to see how attractive he was; tall, slim and muscular with a face that, after studying it, I realized was beautifully symmetrical. Perfectly spaced eyes, tidy ears, a nose that was neither too big nor too small. He'd even grown into his teeth. No wonder the younger girls always tittered when he was near. All at once the fog lifted in my brain and the realization struck that in the three years I'd been pining for Bjorn, Finn had been doing the same for me.

"Mother made us dinner so we will have to stop at the house," he said, climbing into the democrat, reaching out to take my hand. We'd never touched like that before and the tingle was electric. I was surprised by the strength in his grip as he easily pulled me up onto the seat beside him.

The world looked brighter that afternoon as the horses trotted along—the bush, the wildflowers, even our house seemed fresh and new. It was like seeing it all for the first time.

"Did you hear the news?" he asked, squinting into the sun that shone through the trees lighting up his face as the horse clomped down the trail to the lake. "They hired Bensi as the new fish inspector."

"No—" I said. We'd heard rumors that the inspector from Big Point had been transferred south, that Magnus had filed a formal complaint against him.

"Bensi told the fish inspector Stefan wouldn't be able to fish and he should take away his license," Finn said. "Didn't even give him a chance."

"But why would they hire Bensi?"

"In the government's mind, anyone who will rat out a neighbor will make a good inspector."

Terrible as it was, part of me was glad that Bensi was targeting someone other than Pabbi.

"If Bensi continues like this he is going to run out of pawns, then you know what will happen," Finn said. We grinned as our eyes met. Checkmate.

The telltale sign of a good sailor is someone who knows, by memory and instinct, what lies hidden below the surface. Finn was as careful on the lake as he was in life. I felt safe with him.

"Have you been to Gull Reef?" he asked, pointing ahead to a thin jut of land close to shore. Seeing my interest, he pulled expertly on the tiller, veering us slightly to the right. He navigated around all the rocks I couldn't see, through a channel of boulders that barely broke the surface. Our approach sent the hoards of nesting seagulls frantically into the air in a great, circling squawk. The cormorants were much braver. They opened their mouths, toddling along the shoreline, one icy-blue eye on their nests, the other watchful of us as our boat slid effortlessly up onto the sand.

Finn was quick to jump out and for the second time that day I felt a jolt when he took my hand. I shielded my eyes from the sun, looking up at the gulls then along the full length of the reef. What surprised me most was the sand. It was bleached almost white.

"The reef is limestone," he explained. "The cliffs north at Steep Rock are spectacular. I will take you there someday."

Not much survived on a reef and the fact there was life here at all was amazing. A few tired-looking trees jutted up, their limbs plucked clean. The gulls began landing cautiously at the far end, except those whose nests were buried amongst the scrub, and they hovered, swooping down, trying to scare us away.

At first we didn't notice the eggs, monotone gray with speckles, bigger than a hen's but smaller than a wild turkey's egg. Seeing a few shells split open, we began searching for chicks. We pulled back the wild potentilla, awash in yellow flowers, and were startled when a handful of soft brown chicks popped up, their little heads oscillating as they ran across the sand toward the safety of water.

We trudged through the scratchy underbrush toward a smooth granite rock big as a dinner table situated in the center of the island.

"Too bad everything is covered in bird shit," Finn said, carrying the dinner sack.

"That's why you wear a hat, remember?"

Chicks skittered away from our feet; the anxious mother birds screeched.

"How did this rock get here?" I asked, "And look at these smaller ones around it, they look like chairs."

"The ice pushed them," he said, laying out the lunch. It was difficult to estimate how much the rock weighed, hard to fathom that ice, so fragile and easily destroyed, could have so much power.

"How nice it would be if we could chase away all the birds, scrub the rocks clean and keep this place for ourselves," I said, brushing away the sand.

At home the sandwich would have tasted common, everyday, but out here in the bay, surrounded by sunshine and a soft breeze, it was wonderful.

"Unfortunately nature does not work that way," Fin said, taking a bite, chewing, examining the meat between the bread. "It is the wildness of this place that makes it exciting. Remove that aspect and we would probably find it dull."

I tore a bit of crust from the bread, tossing it into the air. The birds swooped and the greediest gull gobbled it down.

"Now that you have a table and chairs I expect you would want a house." He grinned. "Then you'd need firewood, food—"

"And a stove," I said.

"Once you had all that, you would need pots, dishes and more furniture."

"And a dog."

"Then you would want to bring Freyja."

"Imagine, trying to get both Setta and Freyja into a boat." I laughed, brushing away a spider that came up over the edge of the table top.

"Did you tell anyone about that day?" he asked.

"No, but Freyja has been afraid of water ever since," I said. "Did you?"

"Father would have throttled me. I should have known better," he said, thinking back. "It is a miracle they survived."

We finished our sandwiches in silence facing each other. I had my back to Ghost Island.

"I think when I build a house for someone, it should be on land like everyone else's," he said. "I cannot imagine ever living anywhere but along the lake. You?"

I pretended not to notice how he was weaving me into his future plans. "Definitely by the water," I said.

When we finished eating, he tucked the sack in his back pocket and we continued to the far end of the reef. We walked so close that my shoulder bumped into his arm. He gingerly reached out to take my hand. I did not pull away, though I could tell he thought I might.

"What do you like most about the farm?" I asked.

He thought for a moment. "The horses. I am amazed by their power. Father and I plan to build a new barn for them. I am looking forward to that. I like building things."

"Hunting?"

"It is an instinct men have," he said. "But I find the more we are able to raise our own meat, the less desire I have to hunt. Not because I am awful at it; in fact, it is one of the things I am good at."

He held out his left arm, closed one eye and tilted his head as if looking down the barrel of a gun. He deliberately brought up his right hand, held it mid-air and stood like that, finger on an invisible trigger. At first it struck me as odd, until I realized he was showing me how long he could stand perfectly still. It was the first time I took notice of the strength in his arms, the absence of even the slightest tremor in his hands.

"You see, I do not care to hunt," he said, still staring into the imaginary sight. "Leifur, on the other hand, is so keen that when a deer comes into view, he fumbles out of excitement. He misses for that reason."

I came around to stand in front of him, spreading my fingers like antlers, placing them on top of my head. I batted my eyes like a doe, stuck my tongue out, but he didn't even blink. So I started prancing around. An inkling of recognition of what I was trying to do caused his eyes to dart up, but the rest of him did not move.

"I believe the best hunters are those who don't want to kill," he said.

I continued prancing, stuck out my tongue, then started snorting, all in an attempt to make him laugh. Finally, I snuck around behind him and began poking him in the sides. I felt the muscles in his back stiffen, and it wasn't until my fingers crept up and began furiously tickling under his arms, that he relented. He grabbed me, lifted me, my feet off the ground, spinning me around. It was a most exhilarating feeling. He pulled me close for a kiss and for the second time that afternoon I did not pull away.

"Oh, Asta," he whispered, brushing my hair back. It was only then that his hand shook.

We slowly strolled to the north end of the reef.

"Should we go to Ghost Island?" he asked, watching my reaction carefully.

"I would rather not if it means nothing to you. That is not a peaceful place."

Despite Amma's belief that we must face our demons, I did not want to go to Ghost Island to exorcise it from my mind. Everything was still so vivid, all I needed to do was close my eyes and pretend I was standing at the foot of the lighthouse to imagine Einar lying on the ice, to wonder whether or not Bjorn had killed him, whether he'd frozen to death or got up and started walking home only to fall through the ice and drown. There was no reason for me to go, to dredge up all the old hurt. No, standing here in the sunshine with Finn holding my hand, I was ready to shut the door to the little room off the kitchen and never look into it again.

Neither of us wanted to go back yet, so we went to sit again, this time on top of the table rock with our feet resting on the stone chairs.

"Thora plans to attend the training school for nurses when she is twenty-two," he said. "They do not accept girls younger. The schooling is rigorous. But I suppose you already know that."

I told him I did.

"Have you ever thought of going?" he asked, reaching for my hand.

Everyone knew I'd lost the desire to teach. Nursing was an option, but I'd been so preoccupied with the past, I had given little consideration to the future.

"That is why I brought you here, because there is something important we need to discuss."

I knew how badly J.K. and Gudrun wanted him to enroll at the University. He told me an acceptance letter had arrived in the mail and now it was time to decide.

"I am seriously considering it," he said, staring at our entwined fingers. He sounded disappointed, as if it was a punishment, not a choice. "Father does not need me. He can easily hire someone to take my place."

"Not true," I said.

"It is." He chuckled in resignation. "I fish the same way Leifur hunts."

"But you are exceptional at so many things," I said.

"Like chess?" he said, raising one eyebrow.

"I've had more practice than you," I said.

The truth was, Finn belonged at the University and everyone knew it. I asked what he planned to study. He said he wasn't sure but regardless would be away for four years.

We sat in silence for a long time.

I felt as if my chance for happiness was once again slipping away. Another young man leaving me for something better, and here I sat with no dreams of my own. But when I looked into his eyes I saw that he wasn't looking beyond me, but inside, trying to read my thoughts.

"Asta, I love you. I have since the first day you came here. I want to go, but if it mcans losing you . . . I enjoy farm work well enough and this is a good life."

Elbows resting on his knees, he looked out over the water.

"Mother wants me to become a doctor, but Father thinks I should study engineering."

"What do you want?"

"I want to make my Father proud."

I thought about how every choice Signy made was for herself and because of that she'd found a man whose dreams matched hers exactly. And then there was Leifur. He would never leave the farm and, if he married, it would be to someone who devoted herself completely to him.

"The decision is not about attending university," he said softly. "It is what comes after that. There will be no work for me here. I will be forced to live in Winnipeg."

He let the words sink in and waited.

I understood what he was asking. Until then, I'd never considered leaving Siglunes. But I dreaded the thought of a life alone. I believed by the tenderness in his eyes that Finn would never hurt me the way Einar had.

"I will go too," I said. "Four years from now, with Thora. We can become nurses together."

He was delighted. "So if I leave now you will wait, and then join me?"

I promised I would.

CHAPTER TWENTY-FIVE

He's a wise man who knows himself.
—THE SAGA OF HRAFNKELS FREYSGOÐA

"She is asking for him again," Lars says.

He has been sitting at my bedside for a few hours and now the others come breezing in. Solrun takes charge, landing her purse on the window ledge, quickly slipping off her sweater.

"It is far too warm in here," she says.

Thora begins fighting with the window latch. Lars stands up quickly to get out of their way.

"Asta, can you hear me?" Solrun asks, pouring water from the sealer jar into a glass. "We shouldn't have taken her out today."

"Bull feathers," I whisper.

"Here, drink this."

I take a few sips. It still tastes the same. It is God's blessing, that water. It came up from the ground without us having to dig for it and, for a reason none of us understood, lacked the iron and sulphur found in most neighboring wells. The only thing that compares to it is lake water in wintertime. Fishermen still chop holes in the ice and dip their cups before pulling up a net. It is indescribably fresh and invigorating. For me, it was the best part about accompanying Pabbi and Leifur on the lake.

Solrun complains that I sat in the sun too long.

"You can't get . . . too much sun," I say. "Or butter."

I see her smile, but then she points out that a patient in my state should never become dehydrated. Now she thinks she's a nurse. She holds the straw to my lips. As I raise my hand, she tsks. "How papery your skin looks, Asta." I remind her my hands have always looked like this.

"I'm sorry, I didn't realize." Lars says, words trailing off as he jams his hands in his pockets.

She waves him off, slipping her hand behind my head to help straighten my neck. "She is stubborn, so she probably would have refused anyway."

I want to say how unusual it is to have the youngest sister bossing everyone around, but sucking a straw is hard work.

"Where is . . . Signy?" I am finally able to ask.

The room grows silent. They seem embarrassed. Why has the one person I expect to be present at such a critical time made no effort to appear? I wonder if we've had a falling out I can't remember.

"She has the flu and doesn't want you to catch it," Solrun says.

This makes me feel better. Signy and I had a disagreement years ago over Freyja so we didn't see each other much after that. There were always reasons; she was busy raising the boys, I worked nights. But still I've always wondered if my love for Freyja ruined our sisterhood.

"She will come as soon as she can," Thora says.

"Such a . . . good day," I say. "Memorable."

Lars looks out the window and I see he is troubled. I can always tell when something weighs heavily on his mind.

* * *

Telling Mother and Pabbi that Finn was my beau delighted them beyond belief. They had dared not say it aloud for fear of cursing it, but they had hoped that someday Finn might become my husband—cementing the bond already formed with the Kristjanssons. It was, as you say, too good to be true.

Still, Mother was guarded. Having learned a lesson with Signy, she sent Freyja along everywhere Finn and I went. He didn't mind at first, but soon tired of this and found ways to sneak me off without Freyja knowing. On those few times he succeeded, he'd press his body up against mine and kiss me with such intensity that sometimes I couldn't breath. When the smothering became too much of a reminder, that little room door would creak open and I'd push him away. He thought I was being coy, but I was scared to death and didn't mind one bit when Freyja cheerfully interrupted us, completely oblivious to what was going on.

One summer evening he walked me home along the bush trail. It was a bright, warm night and the air was filled with the sound of crickets. A beautiful ending to a Sunday spent combing the shoreline for pretty stones and buffalo bones.

"Do you know how they are able to chirp?" he asked, turning his ear to listen. Then he explained how the males run the top of one wing along the teeth at the bottom of the other wing and, holding it open, the sound is carried to the females.

"Crickets stridulate during all stages of the mating cycle, quietly when the female is near and aggressively if another male is around," he said. "The most satisfying sound, I imagine, is the gentle tremble after a successful mating."

We stopped at the edge of the bush where no one could see us and he kissed me passionately, backing me into an oak trunk, pressing hard. His hand came up to my breast and touched so lightly it sent a shiver through me. Deep inside I was throbbing.

"Can we?" he whispered through short, halting breaths. "Before I go?"

My mind swirled so much that for a moment I considered it, but knew I was nowhere near ready.

"We can't," I whispered back. "Not until we marry."

I felt his annoyance as he sighed.

"Signy confided in me it happened to her their first time," I lied, pulling away from him. "What would we do if that were us?"

He was frustrated, but agreed. The most effective way to get through to Finn was by appealing to his ever-present sense of logic.

All too soon autumn arrived and the long hot days gave way to brisk frosty mornings and the instinct to begin piling stores against the oncoming winter. Finn would be leaving soon so his parents thought it appropriate to throw a going away party.

Everyone in the community was there, including Bensi, who arrived wearing a new suit. Already he'd experienced the consternation in our community that had come with his new position as the fish inspector, but he seemed to enjoy it. He spent the entire afternoon moving from guest to guest, straightening his tie, promising that the rules on the lake would be less strict, at least here in Siglunes.

"Entertaining the king, are we?" Asi whispered in his best British accent, sounding as silly as the English when they tried to imitate us.

It was uncharacteristic for J.K. to be rude, but his reaction toward Bensi bordered on that all afternoon. Finn and I were standing hip-to-hip talking when the door opened and Bjorn stepped inside with Steina on his arm. Everyone greeted them with cheer—hugs from the women and handshakes, backslapping from the men.

"Miss Erlendsson," Freyja squealed, skipping across the room with arms open. "I miss you so much."

Steina gave Freyja a one-armed hug as she slipped off her jacket.

"I miss seeing you too," she said smoothing her hair as she looked around the room, clutching a handbag as she watched Bjorn smiling widely at the people he'd known most of his life. He pulled her along, working his way over to us.

"It appears this party is for you," Finn laughed, extending his hand.

Bjorn was caught off guard by Finn's comment and he glanced at Steina. There was an awkward pause that likely had to do with Magnus's prediction there might be a wedding.

"Congratulations," Bjorn said, recovering quickly as he shook Finn's hand. "Not everyone who applies to the faculty of engineering gets in on his first try."

Finn blushed. "Your father's recommendation letter certainly helped."

"He does have a few friends at the University, but he says you were accepted on your own merit."

"A score of ninety-seven percent on his provincial exams certainly helped," Steina beamed at him. Then she turned to me. "Hello Asta, how are you?"

"Very well, thank you," I said, squeezing Finn's hand. I'd fantasized many times how I would react the first time I saw Bjorn and her together, but since falling in love with Finn, I'd forgotten every spiteful word.

"What is new around here?" Bjorn asked.

"A wolf is killing our sheep," Finn said. "Lost another again this morning."

Bensi stood within earshot and his head turned ever so slightly in our direction.

"Are you sure it wasn't Thor?" Bjorn asked, glancing back over his shoulder. "Oh yes, I forgot, someone shot him. Now the wolves can do as they please."

We had never heard Magnus's reaction to losing Thor. But now I see it. I see how everything played out: Bensi pushing his horse hard down the road to the mill, fabricating a lie. Pall had told him that he'd killed the wrong dog. I hear the possibilities rolling through his mind. He rejected the option of blaming Pabbi, knowing that Magnus would never take his word over Father's.

Bensi thinks up the story by saying he, too, heard the shot so he went to investigate and saw Pabbi and Leifur take the dog's body off the ice, but had no idea who'd fired the gun, assumed it must be Indians who were known to hide in the bushes and shoot coyotes for their pelts when they came onto the ice to eat the rough fish left behind by fishermen.

What Bensi doesn't realize is that Magnus knows about the conversation with the fish inspector.

Bensi and Magnus are standing under the sawmill roof. Magnus says: "Any man who would do such a thing but not own up to it—not apologize—has no honor."

"Well that does not surprise me, the Indians . . ." Bensi's words trail off. He cannot look at Magnus.

"A man with no honor is not much of a man; and even less an Icelander," Magnus says. Then he starts the sawmill engine and turns his back on Bensi.

"How do you like your school?" I asked Steina. It took a few moments to pull everyone back into the fold, especially Bjorn who was eavesdropping on Bensi's conversation.

Steina brightened. "Very much, although I must say few children are brighter than those I taught at here at Siglunes. How are Pall and Petra?"

"Pall quit to farm with his father," I said.

"I am still friends with Petra," Freyja said. "She is truly a good person even though nobody gives her a chance. Our new teacher is nice, except he is a man."

Stefan chuckled. "What is wrong with that?"

I expected that she might say that he was old or strict, but then her eyebrows went up when the idea occurred to her. "You should become a teacher." She beamed.

Stefan laughed, shaking his head.

"But you would be good at it," she said.

"Have you seen his handwriting?" Bjorn teased. "It's terrible."

Freyja brushed him off, shaking Stefan's good arm. "It is what you should do."

"Bjorn is right," Stefan said. "Even worse than before."

Frustrated, Freyja rolled her eyes and her shoulders slumped.

"No need to worry about me," Stefan said, patting her shoulder. "I'd make a lousy school teacher."

"He would," Bjorn agreed, grinning at us. "Too many fights to break up. How would he do that with only one arm, and his weak one at that?"

"I can still break up fights," Stefan said.

"Not with one arm you can't."

"Of course I could. They are just children."

"What about Signy's son? Just wait until he goes to school. Half Thorsteinsson, half Aunt Asta," Bjorn teased, shooting me a sideways glance that I ignored. "Good luck, my friend."

"You aren't my friend," Stefan shot back.

"Yes I am, I saved your life."

"No. Actually, I don't even recall you being there."

"You are such an ass."

"Arm wrestle?"

Bjorn hesitated, but only for a moment. Stefan's face lit up. Two years had passed since the accident and he'd been practicing. We wound through the adults to the table. Bjorn sat at one corner and Stefan took the seat across from him. The room fell into an excited hush. Everyone stopped to watch.

"Two lefties in a right-armed match," Asi said. "This should be interesting."

Both Bjorn and Stefan turned serious as they placed their elbows on the table with their thumbs entwined. Asi stepped forward to cup his hands over theirs.

"When I let go—"

"Come on, Stefan," Freyja said, her hands clenched up to her chin.

The room grew silent as Asi counted to three.

As competitive as Bjorn was, he got off to a weak start. His brief look of surprise quickly dissolved; in a few seconds their fists were even again. They stayed like this for at least half a minute, muscles bulging.

"Getting soft working in a store." Stefan grimaced.

"Ha," Bjorn grunted as he pushed harder, his face scrunched up.

It was an incredibly even match until Bjorn started ever so slowly to gain. We all cheered when it was over, not for Bjorn, but because we all saw how Stefan hadn't given up, even when he knew he was beat.

"Next time," Stefan said.

"There will be no next time." Bjorn laughed, catching his breath.

It wasn't until later that night, long after the party was over, when I was lying in bed, that I realized my yearning for Bjorn was over. The realization came with both sadness and relief but also joy that my life was beginning anew.

How did I come to such an understanding? It was so silly. I found myself concerned more about Steina's handbag than him. I had barely kept from staring at the lovely jeweled case and I wondered where I might find one, how much it would cost and what items I should carry inside.

CHAPTER TWENTY-SIX

None outlives the night when the Norns have spoken.
—HAMTHESMAL

FINN KEPT TRUE TO HIS PROMISE TO WRITE WEEKLY AND I BEGAN anxiously awaiting his letters, thick envelopes that contained pages of description about life at the University. When I unfolded the latest, coins dropped onto the floor. Everyone gathered around as I read the letter out loud.

February 19, 1911
Dearest Ásta,

Today while sitting in this stuffy lecture hall I could not help but think about the lake and how much I miss it. I feel tired though I have used nothing but my brain for weeks. The snow here is packed hard and so dirty it is hard to look out the windows at the gray sky and stay optimistic. It is dreaming of our future together that keeps me going.

I have a roommate; his name is Stanley Burroughs. His father came from England and works at one of the legal firms in the city. Their house is along the river. By the looks of it they are wealthy. They invited me last Sunday for dinner. Here in the city they call supper 'dinner,' dinner 'lunch' and lunch 'snack.'

Stanley's father fought in the Boer War (he knows the Doctor who saved Stefán) so he has many interesting stories. They seemed fascinated when I described fishing. Can you make them each a pair of mittens? The expensive gloves they have do nothing to keep their hands warm. They offered to pay, but I said that we do not accept payment for gifts. I can tell by how they watch me speak they find Icelanders interesting and introduced me to their friends as 'the Icelander from the north.' Having never ventured outside the city, they believe I am from New Iceland. I keep reminding them I am from Siglunes on Lake Manitoba. They say, 'Sig-loons' which sounds ridiculous, but I have not yet corrected them. I imagine my English pronunciation causes them to snicker as well.

I hope you don't think it conceited when I say that I am at the top of my class. The professor said that I will easily find a job when I am done since Winnipeg is booming. Engineers earn an impressive wage so I am hopeful to someday afford one of the homes along the river. For now, what motivates me is knowing that someday you will be here with me.

Lovingly yours, Finn.

P.S. The Burroughs insisted on paying the postage for the mitts.

I opened another page folded in half again, a signal to me that these words were not meant for anyone else to hear.

I caught Mother and Pabbi smiling as they watched me sitting at the table penning a reply. As I addressed the envelope, I wondered if Finn might change his mind about being my beau after reading about my boring life.

March 7, 1911

Dearest Finn,

Without knowing the size of their hands, it is difficult to make a pair that fit perfectly. I know Pabbi likes the ends to touch the tips of his fingers, because it makes it so much easier to work. But I imagine Stanley and his father will be walking, so I hope it suits them to have the mitts long. As you know, too short is even worse, so I have extended the cuffs as well. I hope they like them. It was nice they invited you for supper.

Despite his promises, the power has already gone to Bensi's head. Yesterday he condemned a whole box of Leifur's fish because of two spoiled ones. To think Bensi was given that job even though he has never fished a day in his life!

Leifur is beside himself. Pabbi says the only thing we can do is a better job. He is sure that there will be so many complaints that Bensi will lose the position, likely by the end of this season. Fishing was good this year, much to Bensi's disappointment. He does not want anyone to make more money than him.

Signý is expecting again. I think it is going to be a girl this time, but Amma says she will have another boy.

Stefan was here yesterday. He and Leifur had another arm wrestle, but this time Leifur beat him. I think arm wrestling Asi every day is too much, he should rest his arm.

Amma and Freyja send their greetings. Ási predicts we will have an early thaw and that the Lady Ellen should be back in the water by mid-April. That is all for now. I can barely stand the wait until summer.

All my love, Ástfriður.

Another uneventful year passed. In April of 1912, while Finn finished his second year at the University, his Langamma died in her sleep. She'd been in her late 90s when we came here and six years had passed since then. We watched J.K. and Gudrun drive past with her casket in the back of the wagon, along the trail to the newly built road that extended from Siglunes to Lundi where Langamma had asked to be buried.

"Three quarters done," Pabbi said, encouraged that lambing season was nearly over. This would be the morning of May 1st. He and Leifur had come in for breakfast after matching up the ewes with lambs born in the night. By then Pabbi's herd had grown to a considerable size. Sheep are a frustrating animal to raise but they were what we understood; they have brains about the size of a walnut and their survival instincts are worse than pathetic. Once an ewe has willed herself to die, she is nearly impossible to save. So every spring was a test of who could be more stubborn—us or the sheep.

The skies clouded over and it began snowing soon after dinner. We hadn't picked up the mail at the new post office at Siglunes in over a week, so I decided to go. I tucked a letter to Finn in my pocket, saddled Hector, then set out down the road, facing the bitter wind that came from the north.

"C'mon boy," I said, spurring him along, adjusting my scarf to cover all but my eyes. He seemed reluctant to go, but I persisted, expecting that a letter from Finn was waiting.

The squeal of the mill saw could be heard long before it came into view. As the horse trotted up the long, winding lane I saw a half dozen men hammering together fish boxes while the rest sawed and stacked wood under the huge pole shed built to keep it dry. Each man looked up to see who was coming, a few waved before turning back to their work.

I'd been practicing my English, knowing that I'd need it if accepted to Nurses' College. So that is what I was doing as I rode along—speaking English out loud. Hector's ears twitched every time I said a word he didn't understand.

The Lady Ellen was docked and two men, hats pulled down with collars up to their ears, were quickly unloading crates. As I approached the barn Stefan came from the house with a satchel containing outgoing mail slung over his shoulder. He carried it twice a week from The Narrows to Siglunes then back again, over land by horse until the lake froze, then by dogsled.

"Hello," I said in English. "How are you today?"

He looked at me a bit perplexed.

"A new colt was born yesterday," he said in Icelandic. "Do you want to see him?"

I thought for a moment. "Horse. Are good for work," I said. My reading skills were passable, having learned that in school, but speaking was still difficult.

"My horse name Hector," I said as I dismounted. "See him there?"

Stefan chuckled, motioning for me to follow him into the barn, which was exactly as I remembered it, calm and bathed in muted light. A pleasant wave washed over me as I remembered being there with Bjorn, playing with the pups.

"He is back here," Stefan said, and I followed him to the stall at the far end of the barn. The mare turned as we neared, whinnying a bit, then shook her head. The colt, a brown male with white boots and a star on his forehead wobbled beside her.

"I think Magnus is going to give me this colt," he said.

"Magnus doesn't want him?"

"I am not sure." He picked up a brush then ran it in long strokes across the mare's back. "I had a dream I was riding a horse exactly like this and now here he is."

I was thinking how to translate his sentence when he asked a question that caught me by surprise.

"Does Freyja love me?" He was standing directly under a window so I could easily see him though the light was dim. It wasn't often that Stefan looked so serious.

"Freyja is only fourteen," I said.

His expression grew solemn and I waited, knowing he had something important to say.

"Father does not like that I spend so much time with her," he said, waiting for my reaction.

"He shouldn't listen to Bensi. Bensi always says spiteful things," I said.

"I know, but since my accident Father worries more."

"About what?"

"Did Bjorn tell you that I died?" he asked. He said it so matter-of-factly, he may just as well been asking what I'd eaten for dinner.

"But you are not dead," I said.

"I was. I stopped breathing." His words had a dreamlike quality that prickled my scalp. He said that while the surgeon was removing his arm, he floated up, away from his body, and hovered, watching everything that was going on. He'd felt no pain until his soul returned to his body.

"I saw the nurse start my heart again."

"You are sure?" I asked.

"My older sister was there. I did not see her, but felt her presence, heard her voice and knew it was her. She told me to go back, that it wasn't my time to die."

Up until that point I'd been able to convince myself that what had happened to me during the fever had been a hallucination.

"You think I've lost my mind," he said.

"No," I replied quickly. "I've heard of this before."

He was encouraged and began talking fast, his eyes drawn inward as if remembering something important.

"I saw my future. It came in quick pictures, so fast there was no time to make sense of it. I was playing ball, fishing, carrying the mail into the kitchen . . ."

"But there was no post office here then," I said.

He agreed. "I saw Freyja, standing in a little house looking unhappy, but I was out on the lake, thrilled, mushing the dogs, bringing the mail home. It was the last thing I saw before being sucked back into my body."

"Have you told anyone else this?"

"Only Asi and Bjorn," he said, stroking the colt's neck.

It would take many years for me to piece it all together, to understand what was predetermined versus how much of our future is altered by choice.

"Sometimes I think Freyja and I are not supposed to be together," he said. "She does nothing but worry now. She doesn't want me to fish or carry the mail, but how will I make a living otherwise?"

"You could go to school."

"I don't belong there," he said. "I told her that."

So had Pabbi. I'd seen the two of them standing in the kitchen, Freyja pouting because Pabbi did not agree with her. He warned against forcing her opinion on Stefan as his decisions were not hers to make.

Stefan gave the colt one final rub. "Asi says it was all a dream, but I know it was more than that."

The kitchen smelled of bread fresh out of the oven and coffee boiling on the stove. Bergthora stood at the counter looking out the window at the blowing snow. She was concerned about the storm so it took a few moments for her to acknowledge I was there.

An official from Canada Post had come all the way from Winnipeg to train her in the proper procedures required to handle mail. They'd chosen the little room off the kitchen as the new post office and the transformation—which included the addition of a table and a shelf that was divided into boxes for each family—erased all evidence that it had ever been a bedroom.

Bergthora went into the office, returning with a thin bundle of mail.

"Papers for your Pabbi and Amma," she said, "and a letter from Finn."

She went directly to the stove, poured two cups of coffee, then motioned for me to sit across from her.

"Have you heard the news?" she asked. "Bjorn is opening a store. They are out there right now unloading the dry goods."

He'd been away for three years by then and I hadn't seen him since Finn's going away party. "Here?" I asked.

"Yes, in the cottage," she said.

"I thought Bjorn liked living in Swan River."

"He did," she began. "But you will have to ask him about that yourself."

She looked up at the clock then rose to rinse out the coffee pot and start it brewing again. "How are you?" she asked over her shoulder. "How is Finn?"

"Never been happier," I said.

She observed me so carefully I couldn't help but wonder. I shook off the feeling that she didn't believe me, took a deep breath, and smiled. Bjorn had made his choice, so I had made mine.

"Thora and I are going to study nursing. Finn will graduate in two years and I will go to the city then. He is already talking about buying a house in Winnipeg along the river."

"Has he asked you to marry him?" she asked.

"No," I said. "But he will."

Bergthora's words were strained. "Regardless, I am glad that you have decided to become a nurse."

It felt wonderful sitting with her discussing our lives woman-to-woman and we visited for the better part of an hour. When I stood up to leave, I tucked the mail in my pocket. When I stepped outside, the force of the wind whipped my dress against my legs nearly knocking me over. I turned away from it pulling up my collar. The shoes, light stockings, and cotton frock I'd put on that morning when the sun shone brightly, seemed a foolishly optimistic choice now.

As I hurried toward the barn, the conversation with Bergthora was running through my mind, how impressed she'd been that I'd pulled Runa out of her malaise and did not flinch when she was dying. I don't remember comforting Siggi afterwards, but apparently I had. Honestly, all I remembered was how inadequate I'd felt.

Asi and Bjorn were lugging wooden crates to the bunkhouse. I hurried ahead, surprising them, swinging the door against the wind to hold it open for them.

"Asta." Asi grinned. "Never been happier to see you."

Bjorn gave me a sideways glance as he and Asi shouldered the crate through the door. Their boots echoed across the floor as I poked my head into the dark building to see the boxes stacked against the back wall all the way to the ceiling.

"We need the moisture," Asi said. "It didn't rain much last fall so the lake is low."

"Not much in Swan either," Bjorn said, glancing at me as they stopped briefly at the door. "This storm will help."

We all looked up at the sky then down the road at the near solid white wall of cloud.

"I'd better go," I said, waving as I hurried to the barn. Hector was standing with his head down, an inch of snow on his back. I quickly brushed it off then swung my leg up over the saddle. When I turned the horse around, I looked back toward the house to see Bjorn watching me. He raised his arm up so I waved back, then put my head down and began galloping home.

Fortunately, Hector knew where to go since I couldn't see more than fifteen feet in front of us. Everything was covered in a deep blanket, and the snow was blowing so hard from behind that the oak bluffs that I knew so well looked frighteningly unfamiliar. We'd all heard stories about people getting lost in a blizzard, how some died only a short distance from home. Until now I'd always found it hard to believe.

It wasn't until we plodded past the school that I was able to get my bearings again. I considered stopping there to wait out the storm, but knew Pabbi would worry and might come looking for me. Glancing back, I saw how quickly our tracks were filling in and decided to press on. Hector seemed to understand as I patted his neck, whispering encouragement into the wind and, as our house came into view, I understood why men fall so in love with their horses.

I made him take me straight to the house so I could let everyone know I was home, but had to dig through the snow first to get the door open. The warmth from the stove was comforting as I stomped the snow off my shoes.

All was quiet. The pot of venison stew Mother made earlier sat untouched. Solrun was sitting with Lars on the kitchen floor.

"Where is everyone?" I asked.

"Finding the sheep," she said. "They ran away when the storm came."

I have lived a great many years now, but still cannot articulate the tumble of emotions farmers feel when things begin to go wrong.

I pulled a pair of Leifur's pants over my stockings, then, opening the firebox, threw in a piece of wood. "Stay away from the stove," I reminded them.

When snow comes in the winter, it can be dry as chaff, but spring blizzards are always wet. Squinting into the wind, I rode Hector across the road to the barn. It wasn't until I came closer that I saw two figures in the pen at the far side. Pabbi and Leifur walked delicately through the snow, holding each leg high then lowering it slowly, testing to see what was buried beneath before allowing their foot to bear weight. They were checking the inside perimeters of the fence, holding the top rail to keep their balance. Setta was not so delicate. She ploughed through, head down. She stopped, stuck her nose deep, then began digging furiously. Leifur waded over, dropped to his knees, hand shoveling beside her.

I jumped down and Hector went behind the barn where Strong stood out of the wind. I trudged through the corral to the fence corner as Leifur pulled up a lamb and began brushing its face. Setta stuck her head in further, digging. Leifur, buried to his chest, pulled out another lamb. He carried two over to me.

"Take them to the barn," he panted. He turned back to where Setta was still digging.

I quickly unbuttoned my coat and brought their limp bodies against mine, wrapping the coat tight.

The barn door was open a crack. Mother looked up from where she and Freyja were kneeling in the hay, each rubbing a mewling lamb.

"Asta, thank goodness," she said as I let my jacket fall open and handed her the lambs. Mother began rubbing their bodies with a sack, laying her ear against each chest to see if they were still breathing. She'd made a fire in the middle of the dirt floor and had the ewes cornered tightly in a pen. In between massaging the chilled lambs, she milked the ewes and Freyja fed the little ones with a bottle.

Halfway back to the fence I met Leifur carrying the ewe. Pabbi wasn't far behind cradling two bigger lambs, with Setta behind him, head high, carrying a lamb the same way she would a pup.

"Gronn," Freyja cried when Leifur pushed into the barn and laid the limp ewe in front of the fire. "That is my Gronn," she sobbed.

"Who knows how long she was buried," Leifur panted, rubbing his snow caked mitt across his nose.

Mother scrambled on her knees, looking into the ewe's eyes. She pressed Gronn's chest then rotated her legs to get her blood circulating.

"I think she is too far gone, but I will try."

"Good girl," I said, taking the limp lamb from Setta, and began rubbing it vigorously.

The longer it took, the less chance we'd have of finding animals that could be saved, but we continued checking the pen until every foot of snow was stamped down. It was so unpredictable. Some of the lambs that were buried revived quickly, while others—those brought to the barn first, the ones that we thought for sure would live—inexplicably died.

I pieced together what had happened from their solemn conversation. The scent of lambing had brought a pack of starving coyotes to the barn, scattering the pen of yearlings in all directions. A good six inches of snow had fallen by then, so Pabbi and Leifur were on their way from the house to check the new lambs when they heard Setta's bark. Leifur ran back to get the gun. Pabbi arrived in time to see Setta chase down the leader. A furious fight ensued. The sheep were so frightened they'd pushed down the gate, clambered over one another, then run toward the bush with two coyotes on their tails. More were yipping out of sight.

Setta followed the sounds of bleating death cries into the bush with Pabbi and Leifur not far behind. She bowled over two young coyotes trying to drag away a dead ewe, easily overpowering the bigger of the two. Leifur took careful aim, killing the female that stood watching. Setta, her hatred strong, used her powerful jaws to squeeze the life out of the male she had pinned to the ground.

This had all happened around the time I was sitting in Bergthora's kitchen. They'd spent the next hour trying to herd the young females out of the bush, a difficult task since the traumatized animals had no one to follow—their young leader, a tall graceful long-legged animal that Pabbi counted on in times like this, had been an early casualty.

"Of all the ones to kill," he said.

By then, the blizzard was in full force. Pabbi and Leifur gave up on the sheep in the bush, turning their attention to the ewes with newborn lambs in the maternity pen. They were quickly being buried as they hunkered down over their lambs.

Amma always said it was easy to keep livestock alive if they were housed dry and out of the wind. On her suggestion, Pabbi had stacked hay to block the snow and wind that came from the west, creating a large cove, the perfect place to winter the ewes. Amma was there watching over the ones close to lambing.

"Two sets of twins and triplets. All are doing fine. A few more will lamb tonight," she said. "Tell your father I will take care of it."

Thinking Solrun and Lars would be growing restless, I went in before everyone else to re-heat supper. The two of them were asleep on the sofa.

The storm continued for another day and night.

When the skies finally cleared, three feet of snow had fallen. On the first full, clear day afterwards, the sun was downright hot, causing the snow to melt so fast on the rooftop it created a shower along the eaves. We put milk pails over our heads before running in and out of the door.

That week, the temperatures stayed above freezing and as the snow shrank it began revealing the extent of the storm's destruction. All but two of the newborn piglets had died, but fortunately the sow was fine. The chickens all survived, but the stress of the storm set their egg production back by weeks. The heifer calf born right in the middle of it all ended up with badly frozen ears. She turned into a pretty good cow, but seeing her in the pasture in years to come, ears burned off all the way to the cartilage, was a constant reminder of that early May storm that killed more than half our sheep.

"Your Mama does not need reminding of the ones she could not save," Pabbi said, explaining why, after Mother had done all that she could, she refused to go back to the barn. He told Leifur this as they loaded the stiff bodies piled outside the door onto the stone boat. I expected Freyja to start crying when she saw Gronn but she didn't. She stood there with a blank expression, soaking up the scene in such a way that it occurred to me years later that the storm may have damaged more than our flock.

Leifur stayed behind with his gun after they'd unloaded the carcasses at the west end of the farm. He waited until well past dark, but was only able to shoot one coyote when a pack came to scavenge the remains.

Pabbi's depression didn't set in until a week later when the snow was almost completely melted and it seemed we couldn't walk anywhere without finding another dead sheep. He didn't speak for two days after discovering the ram where it had suffocated after wedging itself between two trees in the bush.

If I could pick the day that our lives took a nasty turn that lasted nearly a decade, it began with that storm.

CHAPTER TWENTY-SEVEN

Youth is hasty.
—THE SAGA OF HARALD HARDRADA

THE MONTH OF MAY, I ALWAYS THINK, IS A GREAT TRICKSTER. A half dozen heart-soaring days early on always leading us to believe that summer has arrived. The buds on the trees open, the south-facing wild chokecherries blossoming along the edge of the marsh where the frogs bubble to the surface and begin singing.

But then without fail, the skies cloud over and we smell the rain coming. There's no wind at first as the fat drops splatter against the ground, then the downpour comes, eventually easing off into a drizzle. Ten degrees on the thermometer in May is bone-chilling; colder than ten degrees any other time of year.

Often this weather lasts two weeks, saturating everything it touches, and our world droops under the weight of it. But then finally the clouds dissipate, and the sky turns a shade by which all things blue are measured as everything comes to life.

It is still like that now, living along the lake.

May 20, 1912
Dearest Ásta,

Life here in the city can be lonely but it pleases me to say that I have discovered that Icelanders are quite well thought of here. I've been told that we are respected immigrants because we are quiet, polite, hardworking, appreciative, and seek knowledge. High praise indeed. We have professors at the University and doctors in the hospitals.

Remember how Father celebrated when T.H. Jónsson was elected as a member of the Legislative Assembly? He had supper with the Burroughs last week. Even the English know of Margrét Benedictsson and I hear in their tone how well-respected she is. I have no reservations about working here in the future.

Stanley is now like a brother to me. It is shocking that they have such a stately house with only one child. His mother is so fond of him she said: "After we created the perfect son we decided to end it there," but I see sadness in her eyes, so there is more to it than that. She is a lovely woman and I am confident you will like her.

Stanley's father (I shall refer to him as Kent from now on) fears Great Britain is on the verge of war. Russia is re-building its army making Germany nervous. Stanley's mother believes if there is a war in Europe it will be large scale. Her brother is a Colonel in the British Army, so they are privy to more than they can say.

Father would enjoy these discussions so I am trying once again to persuade the Burroughs to come visit the farm. Hopefully our own war doesn't break out as their views and Father's differ greatly. It would be interesting to see which side your father and Magnús take. Their opinions mean a great deal to me.

The Burroughs invited me to join them at their cottage in Kenora, Ontario. The family will drive out in their motorcar the day after exams so I would be delayed by a week coming home. They say the fishing is tremendous and have friends they want me to meet. I would like to see Kenora, but am also anxious to see you.

Tell me what I should do—

Love, Finn

This time he'd written on the double-folded sheet a poem that described a love as wide as the sky and deep as the ocean.

My little nephew Petur ran to me and I lifted him up. He'd grown since the last time I'd seen him so I could barely lift him above my head.

"Where is Finn?" Signy asked, handing baby Oli to Freyja so she could cool her feet at the water pump. We were outside the kitchen door of the new hall built at Hayland the year before. The ball team was warming up and we all hoped Finn would arrive home that day.

"He promised he'd be home today," I said. "He spent the week in Kenora with Stanley."

"But he has not seen you since Christmas." Signy tucked the wisps of hair that had escaped her braid behind an ear, resting her other hand on her bulging tummy. She was expecting her third child in November.

"He will be here soon," I said.

Freyja shifted the squirming baby to her other arm. "Do you think you will have a girl this time?" she asked.

"I hope so." Signy sighed.

"What time will they auction our lunches?" I asked, swiping the mosquitoes away from little Petur's head. I quietly hoped that Finn would be there in time to bid on mine.

"Right after the game," Signy said. "But it will serve him right if he is late."

Petur started to squeal when he saw Amma, so I let him down and he ran to her. She picked him up, swung him overhead, then rested him on her hip. Holding up her thumb, she said: "Who is this?"

"Temmeltott," he said.

"And this?" Amma said, extending her index finger.

"Sleikipott."

"And?"

"Langimann."

Amma finished the rhyme by holding up each remaining finger, "Íli-brann, og litli putti spilamann."

We found a spot along the third baseline to watch the game. So much had changed in just a few years. The Siglunes team now wore uniforms, had two bats, and the number of players had doubled—so now it took more than owning a glove to earn a spot on the team.

"It's Asta's birthday," Solrun sang as she came up behind us. She loved birthdays, likely because the re-telling of her birth during the storm had become one of Amma's special stories.

There were murmurs and a few gasps from The Narrows fans when the game started and Stefan came up to bat. He'd sat out the previous years, practicing his batting at home. It was a calculated move on J.K.'s part to have Stefan lead off - and it worked. The Narrows pitcher looked rattled.

"Have an eye," J.K. hollered out.

Stefan watched the first pitch go by then swung at the second, hitting a grounder to the short stop who was so surprised he fumbled the ball. We all stood up and cheered when the first baseman, seeing a one-armed locomotive barreling toward him, misjudged—the ball tipped off the end of his glove, rolling into the bushes as Stefan rounded first base to second.

I watched the game but saw little of it. I was jolted from my daydreams when our team jumped up from the bench, thrusting their arms in the air as they ran to the pitcher's mound to congratulate Bjorn. J.K. was first in line to shake hands with The Narrows team with Stefan right behind him.

Asi stood at the front of the hall cupping his hands around his mouth, announcing it was time for the box lunch auction. He invited all the unmarried girls to line up on one side, the bachelors on the other.

I was too late to sneak the lunch I'd prepared off the table so I grabbed Leifur by the arm as he and Bjorn walked by.

"Bid on my lunch," I whispered.

Leifur scowled. "I don't want to eat with you."

"Please—"

He cringed, shaking his head.

Asi began the auction by choosing the plainest pail, holding it up for all to see, asking for a bid. "Not fancy," he said, "but I can tell by the weight of it, this girl knows how to feed a man."

A tall, skinny ballplayer from The Narrows raised his hand.

"You sure you can eat all this?" Asi asked.

The boy shrugged.

"Do I have another bid?"

The player beside him raised his hand.

"Not getting enough to eat at The Narrows I see. Anyone else?"

The tall, skinny one raised a hand. Asi pointed to the second bidder who shook his head. "You will starve today if you didn't bring more money than that." Asi waited for the laughter to die down. "Sold!"

Olafur's cousin, who'd moved to the area with her parents, stepped forward. Asi handed her the pail.

"Smart choice, those Thorsteinsson girls know how to cook," he said, winking at the bidder as everyone started clapping.

"This is so much fun," Freyja whispered. "I hope Stefan knows which pail is mine."

I kept looking at the door, hoping Finn would appear.

Asi picked up another jam pail. "Very nice," he said, pointing at the lace ribbon tied to the handle. "I have a feeling the girl who made this looks just as pretty."

Thora blushed and started to fidget, giving herself away. Asi shot her a sly look. The boys were peeking around one another's heads to see who the pail belonged to.

"Am I right?" he asked.

A hand went up.

"Three cents," Asi said. "Who will give me four?"

Another hand went up. "Five?" And then another.

The girls all started giggling. "Six?"

The first boy raised his hand again, and when Asi couldn't coax another bid, sold the lunch. "Those boys from The Narrows are hungry," he said, holding out the pail to Thora. As she reached for it, he pulled it back. "Is there Pönnukökur in here?"

Thora giggled nervously. He laughed, handed her the pail, and she hurried away with the boy ambling behind her.

"Any chance those players will defect to our team?" Asi asked.

A few cheers from us, boos from them. It continued like this until half the lunches were sold. I tried to get Leifur's attention, but he avoided looking at me; he bid on the Sveistrup girl's lunch. Lars, who thought this was Lena Kristjansson's lunch, bid against Leifur, causing the room to erupt in laughter.

Gudrun caught Asi's attention then discreetly pointed to the back of the table.

"Alright, Lars," Asi said holding up the smallest pail. "Let's try again."

Everyone cheered when he paid two cents for Lena's lunch.

"Now look what we have here," Asi said, holding up Freyja's pail in one hand, mine in the other. He waited for a few moments until everyone had taken a good look at the pails.

"Both have lovely ribbons." He cajoled: "My bet is these belong to sisters."

He held Freyja's up higher. "Who is going to give me a three cent bid for this one?"

Freyja looked as if she might burst. She glowed at Stefan when their eyes met. His hand went up immediately.

Asi chuckled. "Anyone have four?"

Another hand. Then another. And another.

"I see we have a bidding war," he said. "If my brother is going to get this one, he's going to have to spend more than that."

Stefan held his hand up and did not bring it down.

"We have a bid of eight cents. Do we have nine?"

The Narrows back catcher raised his hand.

Asi looked at Stefan. "Ten?"

Stefan's head bobbed.

"Eleven?"

The back catcher nodded.

"Are you going to let him tag you out?" Asi asked.

Stefan shook his head. "No goddamned way."

"I hope not." To the back catcher. "Thirteen?"

He took a deep breath and said: "Twelve is all I have."

"Well, that's fine," Asi said. "We will get it from you soon."

Freyja didn't even try to hide her excitement as she skipped across the floor to take the pail from Asi.

Stefan dug into his pocket, handed Asi the money, then they went to sit outside in the grass.

"And now, the box with the blue ribbon," he said. "Almost as pretty as the eyes of the young lady who owns it."

I did my best not to react.

"Who is going to give me three cents?"

Two hands went up.

"Five?"

The Narrows pitcher looked at the back catcher then raised his hand.

"Six? … Seven?"

They bid back and forth up to eleven cents.

I was mortified. I didn't want to spend the afternoon making small talk with a strange young man.

"I know you have only twelve cents," Asi said to the back catcher. "Is that your final bid?"

His shoulders fell.

Asi pointed to the pitcher. "Can you beat that?"

The fellow smiled. He was a handsome young man who made all the girls swoon.

"Then it is sold for thirteen cents, to this young man right here."

Over the sound of everyone clapping and laughing, a voice called out: "I bid fourteen cents."

Asi raised his hands to quieten the crowd. "Did I hear another bid?" All the young men turned to look. I could not stop myself from blushing. I was so incredibly relieved.

“We have a late bidder,” Asi said.

The pitcher called out, “Fifteen.”

“Sixteen … Seventeen … Eighteen.”

Asi cocked his head at The Narrows pitcher, then pretended to take him into his confidence. “I know that fellow. He will not stop until he wins.”

A few titters from the crowd, neighbors from Hayland who did not realize how serious Finn and I were. The girls on either side of me, the ones whose lunches were still up for auction, giggled uncontrollably.

“Sold, for twenty cents.”

“But I only bid eighteen—” said Bjorn.

“You’re lucky I let you off that easy,” Asi said, holding out his hand for the coins. Then he whispered: “You owe me for this.”

Amma and Bergthora, sitting at the table nearest the door, looked up at us, and for a moment I sensed something strange in their expressions. It wouldn’t be until later, when the evening was over and I was lying at home in bed, that I understood why they were quite satisfied by the turn of events.

“Thank you for saving me,” I said the moment we stepped outside. “I can’t imagine what Finn would think if he heard I had lunch with one of those two.”

Bjorn smiled. “I can.”

Shielding my eyes from the sun, I looked out over the grass to where Stefan and Freyja sat together in the shade. They weren’t sitting side by side like you’d expect; he was sitting with his back against a tree, legs stretched out, while Freyja sat facing him, her legs folded under her dress, one hand resting on his knee. The lunch box was between them and they were laughing as they shared a sandwich.

Growing up does not happen overnight, it only feels that way to the people around. Freyja was already past the gawky stage. I admired her for capturing the heart of the only boy she’d ever loved.

“We are here to keep an eye on you two,” Bjorn said.

Freyja looked up, surprised.

"Be my guest," Stefan said. "But there is no way you are getting my lunch."

"I have my own," he said as we sat down. "I saved Asta from having to spend an hour with that boor from The Narrows."

"The pitcher?" Stefan asked. "Pitchers are all the same. Show-offs and conceits."

Bjorn gave him a shove and he laughed as he caught his balance. Freyja scowled, annoyed that we'd joined them.

I opened up the pail then handed Bjorn a sandwich. It tugged at me to watch him bite into it—the sandwich I'd made for Finn.

"Did you see the look on his face when you came up to bat?" Bjorn said.

"No, I was watching the ball."

"Lot of good it did you."

"Well at least I hit it," he said.

"He felt sorry for you."

"Bullshit," Stefan said. "You struck out."

Bjorn was forced to agree. "He knows I hate inside pitches. Threw one every time. At the Narrows tournament I'm going to surprise him. Been practicing my switch hit."

Stefan looked impressed. Few could bat from both sides.

"It was an exciting game to watch," Freyja said. "Did you see when little Petur tried to run to Leifur at third base? I barely caught him. He is so sweet. Someday I would like to have a baby exactly like him." A mosquito landed on her forehead and Stefan reached out to pinch it.

"If that is the case then you will have to marry Olafur," Bjorn said.

"Bjorn," I said. He braced himself as I slapped his arm.

"He is right," Stefan agreed. "You did say 'exactly like him.'"

"That is not what I meant," she stammered.

Stefan's eyes danced as she tried to explain.

"Can we come sit with the rich boys?" Leifur was blocking the sun. He had with him other members of the team and a gaggle of girls all carrying pails.

"They are not rich anymore," I said, handing Bjorn another sandwich. We all moved over, Freyja and Stefan closer together, Bjorn and I farther apart, as the circle widened.

"You were supposed to bid on my lunch," I said.

"That would be cheating," Leifur said. "Besides, her lunch is better."

Bjorn raised his eyebrows. "I find that hard to believe."

"Brothers never appreciate their sisters," Freyja said.

All of us, including the Sveistrup girl, jeered, then she nudged Leifur in the side with her elbow. He laughed, poking her back.

The banter continued all afternoon. Teasing, telling jokes, having a great time together—none of us realizing that these were the times we would remember—the carefree days when life seemed complicated, but was really quite simple; a time when friendships meant more than anything else in the world.

"I wish Finn were here," I whispered to Thora after she came to sit beside me.

At dusk we sauntered back to the hall with our arms around each other's waists. She giggled when I asked if she liked the boy from The Narrows, saying he was nicer than she'd expected. The boys were still horsing around. Some of the men stood at the back of the hall, laughing at Asi's jokes as they passed around a bottle of home-brew. The door and windows were propped open to let in the cool evening air and the room glowed under golden lamplight. The music started as soon as J.K. came in with his fiddle and the dance floor filled up with folk of all ages twirling and sashaying around the children who chased each other from one end of the hall to the other.

Thora and I jigged for nearly two hours straight. We sat down breathless when J.K. slowed the tempo so the boys could start asking the girls to dance.

Solrun spun Lars and Petur around. Freyja and Stefan sat holding hands under the table while Pabbi twirled Mother around the dance floor. Gudrun made coffee in the kitchen and set out the lunch. Seeing her alone, a few women from Hayland danced their way across the floor to give her a hand.

Signy was fanning herself by the door. Leifur, Bjorn and the rest of our team were at a table behind us, directly across from The Narrows boys. The Thorsteinsson brothers sat across the table from one another, leaning in with one ear to listen, their big hands adding emphasis to their words, then throwing back their heads in laughter.

With The Narrows team still there and most of the young men drinking, there was a chance that a fight might break out, adding uncertainty to the evening, but the music was loud enough that it kept each team from hearing what the other said.

Stefan and Freyja were the first to get up. Leifur came over to our table, having finally mustered enough courage to ask the Sveistrup girl to dance. It was well past midnight when two players from The Narrows invited Thora and me onto the floor. Of course we said yes because it was rude to refuse, and besides, we loved dancing.

"I am Sigmar," the pitcher said. "You are?"

"Asta."

He seemed nervous as we moved across the floor. "This is a nice hall, I have never been here before," he said.

Sigmar was a good conversationalist so I concluded, when the song ended, that having lunch with him wouldn't have been so bad.

"Your fiancé does not dance?" he asked.

I must have looked surprised because he tilted his head in Bjorn's direction.

"He is not my fiancé. We are just friends," I said. "You know how it is."

He did. Small communities were all the same. I told him my beau was in Winnipeg studying at the University. There was a glint of hope in his smile. The third song was half over when Bjorn came up behind us.

"May I?" he asked, cutting in for a waltz. Sigmar was reluctant but then stepped back. Bjorn took my hand, turning me away.

"You don't like him, do you," I said as he pulled me across the floor.

Bjorn shrugged. "Sigmar is full of himself."

"He's not so bad."

"All the more reason for me to intervene. Imagine what Finn would think?"

I cocked my head. "What would Finn say if he saw me dancing with you?"

"You tell me."

I honestly didn't know. We danced in silence after that until I asked him about the store, telling him the community was anxiously waiting for it to open.

"Finished stocking the shelves yesterday," he said. "Will be open Monday."

"What made you decide to leave Swan River?"

His eyebrows narrowed. "Father needs my help," he said.

"But he has Siggi and Arn . . ."

"Yes, but I knew when I left that I didn't want to work for someone for the rest of my life, and with Bergthora not well—"

He saw my surprise. "A cough. It began this winter."

I thought back to our visit that spring. I hadn't noticed anything out of the ordinary.

"Besides, I like it here," he said. "Siglunes is my home."

"Then why did you leave?"

"I needed to get away for a while," he said quietly. He pressed his lips together and the look in his eyes took me back to that terrible night. It had been a year since I'd experienced fleeting thoughts of Einar, but I saw in Bjorn's expression that the remembrance was still with him; the guilt returning, maybe, even though he tried to hide it, shake it away?

"How is Siggi?" I asked.

"Still not over it."

We slipped across the dance floor in silence and then he brought his lips close to my ear. "There is one thing I need to ask," he whispered. "I didn't have the courage to look at the baby. Could you tell, I mean by how he looked, who . . . the father was?"

There was no way of knowing which answer might make bring him peace, so I told the truth.

"He was fair like Siggi."

I felt his breath on my ear as he exhaled. He seemed to relax after that. We swayed to the music through another song.

When he spoke again, his voice seemed lighter. "I was surprised when I saw you the day of the storm. You look so different now."

I took it as a compliment, thanking him.

"You did not answer my question before," he said seriously. "About Finn. What he would think if he saw us dancing."

"What would you think if you saw him dancing with Steina?" I teased.

His eyes softened. This reminded me of the Bjorn I'd fallen in love with years ago.

"I'd think that he was trying to steal her away from me," he said.

The rest of the night was like walking through a dream. All the conversations and laughter, the music and cigarette smoke, became too much. I went to stand by the door, desperate for air. Thora came bounding over, cheeks flushed. I strained to smile back. She'd spent most of the night dancing with the young man who'd bought her lunch.

"Do you like him?" I asked.

She rolled her eyes, giggling. "He asked if I am going to The Narrows picnic next week. Now I can hardly wait."

I truly was happy for her, but was having a hard time showing it. She tilted her head in sympathy. "I am sorry," she said. "Don't worry, Finn will be home soon."

We stepped away from the door to make room for a family that was leaving.

"I saw you dancing with Bjorn," she said. "Did he tell you?"

"About the store?"

She looked from side to side, hoping no one would hear her gossiping. "No, Steina left him," she whispered. "She ran off with another man."

CHAPTER TWENTY-EIGHT

The more folk stand in the way of two hearts that yearn for each other, the hotter the flame of love waxes.

—THE STORY OF VÍGLUND THE FAIR

"HAPPY BIRTHDAY." SOLRUN BEAMS AS SHE HURRIES IN THE ROOM, carrying a bouquet of yellow lady slippers in a short, fat Mason jar.

"I know, I know," she says, placing it on the table by my bed. "I didn't pick them, I used scissors, so no harm done."

She goes on for a bit how the municipality 'fixed' the road out by their place. She'd marked each lady slipper mound with a red flag, even showed them to the bulldozer operator before he began widening the ditch, but still he'd flattened the flags, leaving nothing but clay behind.

"Can you believe it? A protected flower," she says. "It seems nobody cares about anything anymore."

Then as quickly as her anger flared up it vanishes. Just like Mother.

She pulls the chair close to my bed. Her hands are soft. Short, square nails. I feel the cool smoothness of her wedding band on the back of my hand.

"Remember when we were girls?" she asks, eyes bright. "Every year on my birthday you'd tell me about the day I was born. You were always such a good storyteller. I liked it so much when you'd call me, 'Solrun my favorite.'"

It is my birthday. I'd forgotten.

And then as if she can read my mind, she picks up the glass from the little table and puts the straw to my lips.

* * *

"STAY AWAY FROM BENSI."

Though I hadn't consciously thought about Magnus's warning for a long time, the sight of Bensi riding into our yard vaulted those words to the most immediate part of my brain.

I saw him before he saw me. I was outside in the garden picking weeds but wasn't making much progress. I'd stop to stare off at nothing, pick a few more. All I could think about was Finn and Bjorn. As I knelt there, the hard soil pressing divots into my knees, I wondered if it was possible to be in love with two people at the same time.

Bjorn's comment had been so innocent at the picnic. "Is this what I think it is?" His eyes lighting up as he unfolded the cloth. "Nobody makes kleinur better than you."

All the years had rewound in an instant. Then when I heard that Steina had left him, it explained the contented remarks between Amma and Bergthora when we'd left the hall together.

The next day with Finn had been sweet. We'd kissed passionately. I was sincerely glad to see him. But as The Narrows picnic approached, I grew uncertain. I pretended my throat was sore.

"I will stay," Finn had said.

"The team needs you. I will be fine."

What a coward I was, afraid to be near both of them, fearing one might see the cracks of uncertainty in the veneer I hid behind. I should have gone anyway because it would have made no difference in the outcome of what eventually happened between Finn, Bjorn, and me.

Bensi came without warning into our yard. What caused me to look up I'm not sure, but there he was on his horse, gun across his knees, scanning our yard for what I don't know. I stayed, like a meadowlark chick, hunched down in the potatoes, waiting until he was behind the house, then ran as fast as I could to the back door, latching it behind me.

By the time I was in the kitchen, Bensi was on the road rounding the corner of our house. I flattened myself against the wall and stole fleeting looks out the window. He continued on towards the barn. When he came to the corral, he dismounted, then went inside carrying his gun.

I couldn't think straight. I spoke out loud, trying to calm my thoughts. Likely Setta is with the sheep. If I call her now, he will hear me and know that I'm home alone. That horrible, familiar feeling twisted my gut.

I waited by the window, watching. He wasn't in the barn long before he came out, closing the door. He walked all the way around it then mounted his horse, turning its head, gently spurring it toward the house.

If I were Leifur, full of suspicion and anger, I would load the gun and meet him outside. If I were Freyja, unaware that men were something to fear, I'd probably invite him in. But I was neither of them. My instinct was to hide.

One more quick glance out the window, seeing him closer, sensing his intention to come inside, I opened the cellar door then silently lowered myself into the darkness. Normally I resisted whenever Mother asked me to fetch something from the dank room, but as I crouched in the corner, listening to the rattle of him pulling at the door, I was thankful for the stillness that surrounded me.

Moments later, I heard the creak of footsteps overhead at the far end of house as he came in through the front door. I could only imagine what he was doing in our house, but now I see clearly the look of curiosity on his face as he steps into the front room. At first he simply stands there, looking around and then scans Pabbi's books, leans over the little table by Pabbi's chair to pick up the novel *Lord Jim* by Joseph Conrad. Pabbi had struggled through that book in English. He'd said: "If a Polish man can write a book in English then certainly an Icelander can teach himself to read it."

Bensi carefully opens the book. He cannot read any of it, so the meaning of that story, so important to Pabbi, is completely lost on him.

He puts the book down and looks at our family portrait on the wall for an unsettling length of time, then makes his way into the kitchen.

Below his footfalls I was shaking, eyes staring up at the wooden floor.

There's not much in the kitchen that interests him. He moves to the doorway of Pabbi and Mother's bedroom but does not go in. He slowly climbs the stairs to our bedrooms, ducking his head because the ceiling is low. He barely looks in Leifur's room, but spends a long time staring at the few things we girls own—a hairbrush, books, ribbons, undergarments in a heap on the floor. Freyja's stuffed doll. He touches nothing but I feel his frustration.

I waited in the cellar, eyes wide open to keep away thoughts of Einar, for a long time after he rode away.

The following night, when we were alone in our room, I warned Freyja to stay away from Bensi. She was examining herself in the mirror, her mind on Stefan. I could tell by the way she was admiring herself, puckering her lips, then smoothing her eyebrows with her fingers, she was not listening to me.

"Which side am I prettiest?" she said, watching me in the mirror, turning this way and that. All she thought about was herself and Stefan. She was so boy-crazy. We called it that even then.

"Did you hear me?" I said, still looking at her in the mirror.

"What?"

"Stay away from him," I said.

"Bensi wasn't even at the picnic," she said. "Neither was Petra. Her father doesn't want her to go to a dance because he's afraid she will meet a boy." She rolled her eyes when she said it.

"You are too trusting. Men can be cruel sometimes."

Her expression grew serious and, satisfied that she heard me, I went to the bed and opened a book.

I'd thought hard about whether or not to tell anyone that Bensi had been in our house. I liked Leifur better without the hint of vengeance in his eyes, which reminded me too much of Bjorn on the day Einar was beaten. I didn't want to be the reason once again that someone I loved reacted in haste.

Two weeks before Finn was to leave for Winnipeg, Amma called me outside to help bag carrots. I'd been sitting in the front room studying English, saying words and phrases to Freyja and Solrun who were quickly becoming proficient at the language. In fact, they were helping me. Their new teacher was an English marvel.

Amma was standing in the garden holding three large sacks. She loved carrots so she planted double what we could eat.

I began pulling them from the ground, breaking off the tops. Amma was alongside me. I could tell by how she chattered about nothing she was working her way toward what she really wanted to say, and it had nothing to do with carrots.

"I take it you plan to marry someday?" she finally said.

"Of course."

"Then you'd better start paying attention," she said, easily handling three carrots at a time, snapping off the greens. "They don't always say what is on their minds."

I thought about Pabbi and how distant he became whenever my sisters or I pressed him for an opinion.

"They don't talk for a handful of reasons," she said, vaulting upright but still straddling the row. She held one fist in the air, opening her thumb first.

"One, because they have nothing to say. A man's brain does not fill up with every detail as ours do. Sometimes their minds are completely blank."

I giggled.

"Two, they are thinking of an answer. Most men are slow-witted beasts and they expect we will argue so they want to be prepared."

She pulled a carrot from the ground, rolled most of the dirt off on her pant leg then took a bite. "The exception is Olafur. He says the first thing that comes to his mind," she said, chewing. "And we all know how that turns out."

I giggled again.

"Three, they can't stand being wrong. How often do you see a man change his mind?"

I raised my eyebrows.

"Exactly," she said. "And four, they don't want to upset us. There is nothing a man hates more than seeing a woman he loves cry."

Amma paused to take another bite, letting the weight of her words sink in.

"The last reason?" I asked.

She looked at her hand. "I can't remember," she said. "My point is this—you cannot assume to know what a man thinks or how he feels. You must ask then wait for the answer."

Her words made sense but I felt confident I didn't need the advice. I crawled back, scooping the carrots from my row into a bag. "Finn talks to me all the time," I said. "I always know what he thinks, not like—"

"Bjorn?" she asked.

I'd meant to say Pabbi.

"Have you spoken to Bjorn about your feelings for him?" she asked.

I immediately grew frustrated. I'd spent the last few months weighing the merits of staying with a man who I knew loved me against chasing a dream that had brought me only pain and uncertainty. I didn't want to feel that heartbreak again.

"Are you still planning to become a nurse?" she pressed.

"Yes."

"Why?"

"I promised Finn and Thora I would," I said. "Because it is the right thing to do."

"Are you sure? How do you know that God would not prefer you stay in Siglunes, that your destiny lies right here?"

"Pabbi wants me to go, so does Mama. They like Finn and hope I marry him."

"What do you want?"

"The same."

She lowered her chin, studied me, while I scrambled for something to say. Why did Amma always push me so? How could anyone ever know for certain what they should do?

"Sharing a bed with a man you do not love makes for a long life indeed," she said.

"How would you know?" I rifled back.

"There is a good man right here who loves you," she said, eyes fierce. "My mistakes followed me across the ocean. I don't want you to look back and wish you'd chosen differently."

As we finished bagging the carrots in silence I decided that, while men and women's brains might fire differently, the reasons we stopped talking were pretty much the same.

That encounter in the garden was the closest we ever came to discussing sex. Even Amma had difficulty broaching the subject and for Mother it was impossible. Conversations stopped at husbands and children.

"You are too young," is all Mother would say.

She said this again one afternoon, not to me but to Freyja. We were in the kitchen wearing our Sunday best, on our way to Signy's house for supper. What prompted Mother to start the discussion was seeing Freyja waiting by the window for Stefan.

"Take this to the wagon," Mother said, thrusting a covered pot at Leifur.

"I thought Signy was cooking," he said.

"It is good manners to bring something."

"It is just Signy."

". . . who is expecting in a few months. Now go."

Pabbi picked up Lars, gave Mother a sympathetic look, then followed Leifur outside.

"Asta, you stay." Mother stood in the middle of the kitchen with her arms crossed. "Freyja come away from the window."

Freyja turned and in the flagrant sullenness that mimicked every teenage girl who'd ever lived, let out a tremendous sigh, annoying even me.

"You are too young to be spending so much time with one boy," Mother said.

"But I love him," she whined.

"Stefan is five years older than you—"

"Six."

Mother looked so old to us, it was impossible to believe that she understood love.

"This nonsense has to stop," she said. "You must start spending time with girls your own age otherwise Pabbi will forbid you to see Stefan altogether, understand?"

Freyja's lips pressed tight as her eyes rolled to the ceiling.

Mother was exasperated by the time she turned to me. Already shame had attached itself to the desire I felt when Finn and I were close, and it was beginning to seem that my life would be much simpler with no love at all. Red-faced, I hurried out the door.

It was uncomfortable sitting next to Finn in the wagon after sharing such an awkward moment with Mother, and put a damper on our farewell dinner.

Amma was in a particularly buoyant mood. She was not bothered at all that I'd stuck to my original plan. She'd given her opinion and that was all that mattered. She sang the whole way to Signy's house, forcing us to join in, and by the time we turned off the road down Thorsteinsson's lane, everyone felt better. I am sure Signy heard us long before we came into view.

Olafur met us outside. He looked proud that we'd come and shook Pabbi's hand. His eyes lit up when Amma stuck out her fist. His big hand met hers and together they hammered their fists down, counting out loud to three. This was a game they always played, so we left them out in the sunshine to howl accusations of cheating at each other, even though everyone knew there was no way to cheat when playing rock-paper-scissors.

We filled up Signy's little house and it became fuller still when Magnus, Bergthora, Oli and his wife arrived.

"Freda, you are quite the woman," Oli said, slapping his knee.

Amma grinned slyly, pretending she had no idea what he was talking about. We all knew of course, since it was the highlight of the picnic when she won the old Amma race.

"I thought for sure that skinny one from Big Point was going to win," Oli winked, "until you tripped her."

"Nonsense," Amma said. "She was nowhere near as fast as me. Only a fool races wearing a dress."

"Apparently," Mother said, rolling her eyes.

Everyone began chuckling at the memory, how Amma had lined up with the other women then held up her hand for them to wait until she took off her skirt.

"I always ran like that in Reykjavík," she said, "and never lost."

"No wonder," Oli said. "Barreling toward the finish line in your bloomers. Asi and J.K. were laughing so hard they couldn't even judge who won."

"I did, fair and square!"

Oli's eyes danced as we all began jeering, teasing Amma that maybe she hadn't won after all. Five year-old Lars began poking at her, jumping back, exactly as Leifur used to do.

"Come on Amma," he said, "I bet you can't catch me."

Amma watched from the corner of her eye then grabbed his arm, pulling him into a headlock. "Who is the fastest Amma in the world?"

"Langamma," Lars said.

"Langamma is dead," Amma growled, knuckling his head until he howled.

Oli nearly doubled over with glee. Amma sized him up with squinty eyes.

"Careful or you'll be next," Magnus warned.

As we gathered around the table, Bergthora asked when I planned to take my training.

"Next fall."

"I do take some credit for that," Bergthora said. "Asta is a born nurse, I knew it the moment I saw her."

Everyone heard the strain in her voice, the cough that punctuated her sentences, and the kitchen grew quiet. I suspect that they were thinking the same as me, how ironic it was that the nurse in the room was the one who needed care. Mother spooned food onto little Petur's plate, and the rest of us began passing the dishes around. It was the first time I'd sat beside Magnus in a long while.

"Come now," he said, breaking the silence. "How could you possibly have known?"

"You saw how she mothered poor Runa," Bergthora said, then turned to Mother. "She made me explain how every instrument in my bag was used. She was absolutely heroic during the epidemic."

There was a hint of admiration in Signy's eyes when she looked across the table.

"I predict she will finish top of her class," Bergthora said, embarrassing me something terrible.

"Now, now, dear sister," Magnus said, winking. "You don't want the girl to become full of herself."

When we finished our meal, Signy brought two pies to the table. Mother cut them and Signy slid a piece onto each of our plates. Magnus turned his attention to Freyja.

"And what about you," he asked. "Would you like to become a nurse too?"

Signy snorted. Mother turned her head quickly but resisted scolding Signy since we were in her house. Neither Magnus nor Freyja seemed to notice.

"I might like to study theatre," Freyja said, "Or paint. Maybe take photographs like the editor of *Lögberg*."

"Very nice," Magnus said, eyes twinkling. "Be sure to consider *Heim-*

skringla. It is a far superior paper."

Amma, sitting beside Pabbi, slapped his leg. "Ha, I told you."

"Whichever," Freyja said, raising her hands. "It makes no difference to me."

"Spoken like a true Liberal." Magnus laughed. "Já, I should know, I raised one myself."

"By accident?" Pabbi teased.

"Of course."

"Bjorn is a Liberal?" Finn asked. Up until that point he'd sat silently beside me.

"He is," Magnus said. "I take it there are plenty of young men at the University who enjoy discussing politics?"

Finn beamed, straightening himself in his chair. He leaned across me. "I am one of them. I am a Conservative like you and my father."

Magnus opened his mouth to say something, but Freyja interrupted.

"But I'm unsure how to start," Freyja said, pulling the conversation back to herself. "I am going to live with Asta in Winnipeg. She will take me to the University to find out."

Pabbi's eyebrows narrowed. I hadn't meant to keep this a secret from him, in fact I was so wrapped up with my own concerns, that I'd barely listened as Freyja prattled on about her future.

"A very good idea," Pabbi said. "We came here so that our daughters might have a better life." And while he didn't say it, I knew he was thinking if that meant leaving a beau behind, all the better.

CHAPTER TWENTY-NINE

All things happen in threes.
—GRETTIR'S SAGA

FINN RODE THE STEAMSHIP TO WESTBOURNE, CAUGHT THE TRAIN to Portage la Prairie then on to Winnipeg. He'd tried to persuade Stefan into going with him, to spend a few weeks in the city, but Stefan had refused.

"Brave in so many ways," was the last thing Finn said about Stefan before kissing me good-bye. I stood on the dock with Thora until the ship was out of sight. She walked home with me and we talked about what an adventure it would be to live in Winnipeg.

"Where is Setta?" Lars asked no one in particular.

"She never goes far," Mother said. She was preoccupied as usual, this time canning wild plums. The kitchen was filled with boiling pots, empty jars, and full ones cooling on the table. Pabbi and Leifur were busy ploughing five acres of ground that bordered Bensi's, land they'd spent the last two years clearing.

"Maybe she is with the sheep," Solrun said.

Thora came with me to check the east meadow, but we saw no sign of Setta.

"She is probably with Amma." I led the way through a shortcut in the bush towards her house. The plums were ripe in the bluff so I expected we'd find her there. As we neared, I put a hand to my ear. Usually if Amma was close by we heard her banging and stomping, hollering out for someone to come help her, or at the very least humming or whistling. Mother always said she never feared berry picking with Amma because the bears were warier of her than she was of them.

"She must be inside," I said, veering in the direction of her little house.

"Amma," I called out, pulling open the door, but there was no answer.

Setta was sitting in front of the stove.

"There you are," I said. "Where is Amma?"

Setta's ears drooped and she whined a bit. She stood up.

"Maybe she is picking somewhere else," Thora said, nearly walking into me as I'd stopped suddenly. Amma was lying next to her table, plums scattered across the floor. She was on her side with one arm up over her head, the pail still attached to the cord around her neck.

"Go get Mama," I said.

Dropping to my knees I reached out to touch her. Her body jerked ever so slightly and she made a faint gurgling sound. Carefully, I pulled her arm down to her side then rolled her onto her back, lifting the pail cord from her neck, tossing it aside. Her eyes were half open and she was staring straight ahead. Her mouth hung, drooping to one side. She tried to speak, but her tongue was thick and slack.

"Amma, can you hear me?" I whispered, biting back the tears. "Thora went for Mother. It is going to be all right."

Amma flinched and jerked. All that came out were half-words. I used my shirt sleeve to wipe her spittle, the same way she'd wiped Leifur's face after he threw up on the ship during the crossing.

Taking her stiff hand, I closed my eyes, heart pounding in my ears.

"Our Father who is in heaven . . ." I was halfway through the prayer a third time when the house door swung open with a bang.

I scrambled backwards as Mother rushed in and pushed past me, kneeling down.

"Ástfriður, mínn," she said, carefully stroking Amma's forehead. "What has happened to you?"

Amma struggled to speak, her left hand wavering up, clasping Mother's arm, the other limp at her side. Her eyes were wider now and she struggled to speak.

"Shhhh, it is going to be fine, sweet woman," Mother said as she gently pushed her hair back. "Calm your thoughts. Pjetur is coming and the doctor, too. We will find out what is wrong and make you better."

I began pacing, wiping back the tears. It seemed to take forever until Pabbi arrived. I was standing in the kitchen with Setta when the door flew open again. When our eyes met, the look on Pabbi's face cut deep into my heart. Pabbi. The one expected to make everything right. He stood there for a few moments with his arms hanging helplessly.

"Pjetur, finally," Mother said. "I was afraid we might drop her."

Without a word, Pabbi crouched down, slipped his arms under Amma's shoulders and knees, and lifted her like a baby, carrying her to the bed.

"Mama?" he whispered after laying her down. "Can you hear me? Leifur went for the doctor. He will be back soon."

The thought occurred to me that it might be easier for her to breathe if she was lying on her side, the same as when I found her. Pabbi agreed, slowly turning her, supporting her head with a pillow.

My knees were so weak by then I had to sit. Setta slumped down beside my chair, groaning as her chin rested on the floor.

Freyja appeared in the doorway with Solrun on one side, Lars on the other.

"How is Amma?" she asked, lip quivering.

I motioned for them to come stand by me, taking their hands solemnly in mine.

"She is sick so you must be quiet."

"But Amma doesn't want us to be quiet," Solrun said.

"She likes it when we make noise." Lars grinned.

Freyja turned away. She started to sob. "What happened?"

I shook my head. "I am not sure."

Freyja went cautiously to the bedroom door.

"Come on, Setta," I said.

I couldn't stand being in the house any longer so I took Solrun and Lars outside. Sitting on Amma's stump chair, I picked up a stick to poke at her long-dead fire, mentally calculating how long the doctor would take. Leifur would follow the lakeshore on the way there because it was shorter, but they would return by road, past Signy's house and stop to tell her.

Four hours. If the doctor was home.

That afternoon I kept the younger ones from going back inside. We talked, told stories, and played little games. All the while, my mind kept drifting back to my last conversation with Amma.

The relief I felt when J.K. and Gudrun rode into Amma's yard was indescribable. Though medically speaking they provided no help, their big hearts had a calming affect on us all.

Sure enough, it was right around suppertime that Leifur came galloping home. He'd pushed Hector hard so both were sweating, eyes wild with uncertainty. The Doctor's black democrat was not far behind.

"Did I make it in time?" Leifur asked, pulling the horse to a stop. "Is she alive?"

I told him she was.

He jumped down, walked in circles for a few moments, breathing deep as he ploughed his fingers through his hair. I took the reigns from him.

"I did not want to let Amma down," he said, voice breaking.

"You never have," I whispered.

The doctor arrived and Leifur followed him to the door. He hesitated for a moment on the stoop—took a deep breath—then went inside.

Twenty minutes later, the time it must have taken to find Olafur and hitch the team, I heard a rumble. Olafur turned up Amma's narrow lane. Before he had the wagon fully stopped, Signy jumped off and came running toward me, cradling her belly with one arm.

"How is she?"

Olafur came marching up the trail with Petur in one arm, Oli in the other. His expression was stern, muscles tense and ready. If we needed anything done that required physical strength, by God, he was prepared to do it. Seeing me melt at the sight of him must have rattled his nerves because his bottom lip started quivering, those massive legs of his slowing when he realized there wasn't anything he *could* do. Of us all, I felt most sorry for Olafur. He'd never looked so helpless before.

"I think I will stay out here for a while," he said, sitting down on a stump away from us. I took little Oli from his arm and began pacing, glad for the distraction.

Solrun and Lars were pleased to have someone other than themselves to play with. Setta walked circles around them, her big mouth open, tongue hanging out. Petur picked up a stick and began hitting her on the head. Setta squinted as she turned away.

"Petur," Olafur rasped, but the scolding trailed off with his voice.

A half hour later the door opened and Signy waved us in. We stood in a semi-circle listening to the Doctor speak. Though it was the first time he'd been summoned to our farm, Pabbi held the Doctor in high esteem for saving Stefan's life.

I understand the diagnosis now. Amma had suffered an Apoplexy, resulting in aphasia and some paralysis. How much mobility she would regain, he couldn't say. There was much to learn about the treatment of stroke victims; back then there was little that could be done—at least where we lived.

After the doctor left, Olafur sprang to life. He went to get the wagon, backing it close to the door. Amma seemed to understand as the men grabbed the edges of her feather mattress to carry her out. Everyone walked behind Olafur as he drove slowly home. We moved Amma back into her little room.

Word traveled throughout the community and it seemed that every day for weeks afterwards someone came to our door leaving a gift of food after a brief visit.

Magnus and Bergthora arrived two days after it happened. I stood in the doorway of Amma's room as the two of them went in. She was propped up in bed wearing a clean dress. Mother had smoothed out a blanket, folded over the edge and tucked it neatly under her arms. It was encouraging that Amma recognized everyone, though the signs were slight. A blink or a sigh, the hint of a smile.

Bergthora hovered over Amma's bed, kissed her on the forehead and held her hands. She spoke clearly and directly, waiting for a response before continuing. She behaved no differently to Amma than she ever had while Magnus simply stood at the foot of the bed.

"I will leave the two of you alone," she said, patting Amma's thigh.

Our eyes met at the door. Softly squeezing my shoulder, she forced cheerfulness into her voice. "Come along," she said to me.

Magnus went to Amma's side. I paused.

As he bent in close, Amma reached up with her working hand to grasp his arm. Her body was shaking ever so slightly, face contorted. She started to cry. His rough hand held her face, wiping the tears with his thumb. He kissed her, long and full on the lips, then whispered something, words that prompted her to tremble and sigh deeply.

"Asta," Mother called out, "Bjorn is waiting outside for you."

I found him patiently sitting in the democrat. His hair was tied back and he wore one of his better shirts. It was a shade of blue that matched his eyes.

As soon as he saw me he hopped out. "I didn't want to intrude. How is she?"

"Very happy to see them."

Instead of going inside we meandered down the road.

"We heard last night," he said.

"Only a few days and it already feels like a month," I said. "I try to be hopeful, but—"

He tried to reassure me that Amma was going to be fine.

I told him about an old man I'd forgotten about until that day. He'd lived not far from us in Iceland. All the children believed he was a skrímsli, a monster, because of his grotesque, drooping head and bony legs that turned at unnatural angles. One writhen arm stuck out like an oak branch. Whenever he'd sit outside we'd run by in fear. He'd call out, begging us to stop but we never did.

"Amma will hate this," I said. There was a part of me that wished for her sake that she'd died.

We walked down the road. The only sound was the rustling of the wind in the trees, the brittle scatter of leaves. A flock of geese flew south overhead so low we heard the whir of their wings and looked up. Spread out in front of us was a remarkable autumn day.

"You didn't come to the picnic," he finally said.

I told him that I needed to spend the day alone, then blurted out what had happened.

"Bensi came here," I said. "He looked all around inside the house. I hid but didn't tell anyone."

Bjorn was shocked. "That is strange, even for him."

"I know," I said. "And then he came yesterday."

It took me a few minutes to formulate the words, to explain what I didn't fully understand myself. "Bensi came with his wife and their visit caught us all by surprise. Bensi's wife handed Mother a dish. Bensi shook Pabbi's hand. I am not sure what it was, the shock of seeing him standing in our kitchen or the look of remorse in his eyes, but every one of us was teary, except for Leifur who went upstairs."

"Bensi wanted to see her?" Bjorn asked.

"He went into Amma's room then returned to the kitchen a few minutes later. The visit lasted less than ten minutes. Has Amma said anything to Magnus about what happened in Iceland between Pabbi and Bensi before we came?"

"All I know is what J.K. told Father, that Bensi took advantage of Pjetur causing him to lose his farm," he said. "Why? Do you think there is more to it?"

"I'm not sure," I said. "It was the oddest thing."

Bjorn listened carefully as I continued.

"I think he was truly sad to see her like that," I said. All the encounters with him over the years flipped through my mind. "It doesn't make sense considering the terrible things he said about her."

"Maybe he is tired of fighting with everyone. He must have some regrets by now. Especially after snitching on Frimanns."

Bjorn picked up a handful of stones and started side-arming them up the road.

"Stefan told me he confided in you," he said. "He believes his dreams foretell the future and that his life will be short."

"Amma has similar dreams, but I doubt she saw this for herself."

Our conversation was winding its way back to the beginning. I thought of Amma. If I expected to be a competent nurse, I needed to learn how to control my emotions. I dug into my skirt pocket for a handkerchief. It was still damp but I managed to find a dry spot to dab my eyes.

"I am sorry," he said wrapping his arm around my shoulder.

I shook my head, sniffled, words stuck in my throat.

"What I am trying to say is that Stefan knows how to make the most of every day," he said. "It is a good lesson for all of us. I have decided to forget about the past and hope you can do the same."

There was still awkwardness between us. He gripped my shoulder with his hand, gave it an easy shake. He told me that he needed help in the store and that he'd offer a fair wage.

We'd strolled far enough by then so we started back. Another flock of geese flew over, honking loudly.

"I have already decided I will stay here to take care of Amma," I said. "I won't be going to Winnipeg after all."

"What do you think Finn will say?"

"What do you say?" I asked.

"Me? I would be disappointed if you went, but I would accept your decision."

Bjorn waited in the democrat and I went inside.

"I know of a place where they do rehabilitative work," Bergthora said. "A hospital in Minnesota. People with Freda's condition go there. Many regain their speech and some even learn to walk again."

Pabbi and Mother listened carefully.

"But she would have to go away," Mother said. "For how long?"

Bergthora tilted her head in thought. "Four months," she said. "The doctors would have a better idea once she is assessed."

"We will think about it. Thank you," Pabbi said.

He followed them outside where they talked for a few moments. Pabbi and Magnus went around to the back of the democrat and together they lifted a high-backed, invalid chair to the ground.

"If cost is a concern, Pjetur, I want you to know that you needn't worry. Freda has been a good friend to me and I have the means."

Pabbi reached out to shake Magnus's hand.

Magnus climbed into the democrat, took the reins, and turned the horses down the road, stirring up a cloud of dust.

Hours later I looked out the window to see Pabbi sitting on a chair under the tree. Setta's head rested on his lap. They stared off to the west, Pabbi stroking Setta's neck, running his hand down her back. He slumped forward, lay his head on Setta's back, and his shoulders started to heave.

CHAPTER THIRTY

One should not ask more than would be thought fitting.
—KRÓKA-REFS SAGA

THAT NIGHT I TOLD THORA MY DECISION TO NURSE AMMA. SHE understood and said she'd been expecting it. Finn said the same thing in his next letter. Truer friends didn't exist.

"I would like to help," Thora said. "It will be good practice for us both."

Bergthora rode up the next morning to instruct me in the proper procedures to care for a bedridden patient.

"You are fortunate to have Asta," she said to Amma before she left two days later, bolstering my confidence probably more than I deserved. "I will return to check on you both in a few days."

Each morning I went to Amma's room and pushed back the drape. "Another lovely morning," I would say, or "It is starting to snow."

I described every detail of what the day held for everyone as I wiped her face and hands with a warm cloth. Once a week I washed her hair and bathed her. Uncomfortable that her private parts needed to be dealt with in a not-so-private way, I was thankful that she still had mobility in one arm and leg, that she was able to help. I removed her undergarments if they were soiled but if they were not, quickly helped her to the toilet that Pabbi had built in the corner of her room.

"Leifur can hardly wait to start fishing. Setta misses you. I think we should go outside today." I'd help her to the edge of the bed to dress. I would place her arm over my shoulder then swing her into the wheeled chair Magnus gave us, which was a true Godsend.

"We should help Mama bake buns later, what do you think?"

Then we'd roll into the kitchen for breakfast.

"Good morning, Amma," everyone said. She'd mumble a reply. Mother permanently moved her chair so that Amma could be wheeled up to the end of the table.

"Do you want bread this morning?" I'd ask, and wait until she bowed or shook her head. I'd prepare it exactly how she liked it. "Eggs?"

Everything was minced into bite-sized pieces. She said the same word every time I tried to feed her and it sounded like "self." At first it was sad watching her shake the spoon up to her mouth, but we grew accustomed to it. Into her coffee cup I stirred a bit of sugar then after it cooled, handed it to her. She could no longer manage the saucer.

I learned quickly what not to do. The first time I tried wiping her chin at the table she hissed and thrashed her hands, so I never did it again. Instead, I gave her a cloth or washed her face in private.

Her mornings were spent in the kitchen watching Mother. This gave me time to empty the bowl under the toilet, make her bed, launder her clothes and sheets if needed.

After dinner I took her back to her room for a nap, then helped her out of bed again so she could spend the afternoon in the front room. She listened as I studied out loud, and watched Lars dart back and forth playing games. If it was warm enough, he'd help wheel her outside.

"Look, Amma," Lars would say, standing on the chair footrest with his hands in the air, showing off how well he could balance. Amma seemed to like this so he did it often.

When Freyja and Solrun returned home from school, it was mandatory they sit with Amma for at least five minutes.

"Think about what you want to say while walking home," I told them.

Freyja often protested, mostly because she was feeling sorry for herself since Pabbi had begun limiting the amount of time she spent with Stefan.

After supper I would cover Amma's lap with a blanket and everyone would listen as I read out loud. Mother blew out the lamps. I pushed Amma to her room. Another visit to the toilet, then I would call Leifur because by then Amma was wrung out so I needed his help getting her into bed. Leifur would leave, then, before putting on her nightdress, I'd rub the tender spots on her hips with a salve Bergthora gave me. Once her nightdress was on and she was comfortable, I'd pull up the covers.

"Good night."

She always tried to say it back.

All winter, every week without fail, Magnus and Bergthora visited. They came in the evening and Bjorn often tagged along. Sitting with our legs crossed on the front room floor, we'd play chess as everyone visited around us. Mostly he would win, but occasionally I would squeak out a victory. Many nights J.K. and Gudrun would show up and a game of whist would break out on the kitchen table. Leifur would sit beside the wheeled chair to play Amma's hand with her.

Spring hesitated that year. Usually the melt began in March, but temperatures remained well below freezing until the third week of April, when the temperatures soared and the wind shifted, bringing warm air from the south. Combined with the sun's heat during the day and above-freezing temperatures at night, the ice was off the lake in record time. The melt came fast and, with it, word that the north was still under deep snow.

"Asi predicts it will flood," Magnus said one evening in early May during their weekly visit. He explained that the water flowed into our lake from the Waterhen in the north and the Assiniboine in the south when it overran its banks. All the rain didn't help. A storm was brewing in the west, but we had no way of knowing this until its arrival two days later.

"A letter from Finn," Freyja interrupted, dropping an envelope on the chessboard. Bjorn and I were sitting with the game between us. We were finding it difficult to concentrate with all the talk about flooding.

"Freyja," I scolded. Not only had she knocked over my rook, but she'd picked up the mail two days ago.

"I forgot." She shrugged.

Bjorn didn't seem to mind pausing the game while I tore open the envelope.

I always scanned Finn's letters, mentally flagging the sentences to skip before reading out loud:

April 30, 1913
Dearest Ásta,

"Oooooh," Freyja teased.

"Hush," Mother said.

I hope this letter finds you well.

I imagine it must be flooding there as it is starting to here. The rivers have risen up, threatening the homes along the banks of both the Red River and the Assiniboine. Fortunately, they predict it will not rise as high as in 1861, but it makes me think twice about building along either river. So far the Burroughs house is safe. I hear the situation can become dire here in the city during wet years.

This of course delights our professor who has challenged us to present ideas how the city can plan to mitigate this in the future. I have a few theories but do not want to appear foolish so I will wait until I have thought carefully.

My professor favors the idea of re-directing water but I disagree. Father's hired man would tell the story of the beaver, and I saw for myself the problems they cause with their dams. He would say that water flows where it is meant to, and eventually it will find a way. But nobody here cares what the Indians think.

Father would enjoy it at the University where he could debate all day long. He told me that people here are well-educated but not necessarily more intelligent than us, especially when it comes to the lake. He is right.

I received a letter from Stefán. I suppose he decided to write after carrying everyone's letters to and fro. His handwriting is terrible but I have decided not to tease him. He says that he and Leifur have trapped more muskrats this year than all the other years combined. That is not something I ever cared to do. As you know, I am not much for killing. But I wish them well. Why did you not tell me that he and Leifur plan to start a fish and fur buying company?

With Helgi selling out to move up north, it is a good idea. Stefán says the new owners at The Narrows don't have nearly the stock that Helgi carried and their prices for the pelts are not nearly as good. This must bode well for Björn's store. Maybe 'Frímann and Guðmundsson Fish and Furs' can work out an arrangement with him?

How is your Amma?

We can talk about everything more when I am home in two months, less by the time you receive this letter.

Finn.

"Will you be at church on Sunday?" Bjorn asked as they were getting ready to leave. "Any chance I can persuade you to a rematch?"

I was still basking in the delight of beating him twice in a row.

"Bergthora says it is time we host all of you," he said. "As soon as it stops raining, Father and I will build a ramp. It should be done by Sunday."

That night, I lit the lamp on the night stand and took the letter from my pocket before crawling under the blanket. The wind was howling outside and the rain beat hard against the window. I thought of Bjorn riding home in the rain.

I opened the letter again, skimming until I came to the parts I'd left out:

It is admirable how you care for your Amma, but the time will come that you will need to get on with your life. From what Mother says it does not appear that Freda will get better. Thora says she has offered to help, but so far you have refused. I am asking you to not be stubborn because you are sometimes.

Please consider applying to Nurses College. Sacrificing your life for someone else, even someone you love, will only lead to regret later.

We can talk about everything when I am home in two months, less by the time you receive this letter. I can barely stand it until the day I can take you in my arms and kiss your sweet lips. I love you, Asta, more than anything.

Lovingly, Finn

Two days later I sat in the back of the wagon holding on as the wheels sloshed through four inches of water. Pabbi fervently coaxed the horses who despised stepping on soft ground. He focused on where he knew the trail was, holding the reins tight to let them know who was boss.

Everyone gasped at the sight of the lake which had risen so high it was only 50 yards from J.K.'s house.

"Has it come this high before?" Pabbi called out.

J.K. was on the verandah, staring out over the water.

"Not since we've been here," he said. "Asi says it was like this in 1882."

Pabbi led the horses up onto the yard where it was still dry, pushing down on the wheel brake. We climbed down then stood, turning in all directions, seeing for the first time what Asi had meant when he talked about the ridge. Water pooled in all the low spots making their house look like an island on the edge of a glistening sea.

"How high will it come?" Mother asked.

J.K. frowned. It was the first time since knowing him that I saw worry.

"Hopefully it will crest soon," he said. "If we expect to make our living here along the lake, we cannot fight the water. We must learn to work with it."

Gudrun greeted us at the door. Thora was standing at the counter making pönnukökur. I helped her roll the crepes and sprinkle them with sugar.

"Asi was here yesterday and told Father to prepare for the worst," Thora whispered. "Hayland is mostly underwater."

"And the mill?" I whispered.

"The house is high enough," she said. "But water is creeping in from the north so they are re-stacking the lumber on higher ground."

"The store?"

Thora shrugged. "He said Bjorn is moving everything to the highest shelves."

The whole time we sat visiting, drinking coffee and licking the melted sugar from our fingers, everyone kept glancing out the window. When it came time to leave we stood in disbelief on the verandah.

"It looks higher already," Leifur said, taking off his shoes. J.K handed him a knife and we watched as he sloshed to the fence post J.K. was notching every few hours. Leifur dug the knife into the post then hurried back.

"An inch above the last notch." He shivered.

That evening the storm arrived.

The last thing we wanted was to spin wool and knit, but once the evening chores were done and the bickering started, that is exactly what Mother made us do.

"You could go out to pick stones," Pabbi said above our complaints as rain pelted the windows. Everyone groaned. Picking stones from a freshly ploughed field was a miserable job and it seemed that every year Pabbi turned up more acres.

Leifur had started knitting after Pabbi said it would make him a better hunter.

"It improves how well your eyes and hands work together," he'd said.

Occasionally Pabbi went to the window, reporting that all he could see in the darkness were the treetops bending in the wind.

The next morning as we sat eating breakfast, a wet fist pounded on the door. We all looked at one another. Pabbi went to the door. J.K. stepped inside. He looked like someone had tried to drown him.

"The lake surged up in the storm," he gasped. "I need help."

Pabbi grabbed his coat from the lean-to hook with Leifur on his heels.

"Tell Gudrun and the children to come here," Mother shouted after them.

Freyja and I hurried to the window to watch them slosh down the trail to the lake.

"Why is the lake doing this to us?" she cried.

I tried my best to reassure her, to explain what I barely understood myself. Apparently there was a mathematical equation that estimated how much run-off it took before the rivers in Winnipeg overflowed their banks, but more important to us was the amount that came in from the north-west.

"Asi said it won't rise much higher if it stops raining," I said.

"Go upstairs for the blankets," Mother said when we saw Gudrun urging the horses through the bush trail. Mother held open the door as Gudrun helped J.K.'s mother down. Everyone ran inside. Thora looked frightened as a mouse who'd just clawed its way out of a water bucket.

"Ella, it is the most terrible thing to see," Gudrun said as she led J.K.'s mother to the front room. "Water was splashing on the verandah."

She said that fortunately J.K. had already moved the sheep and cows to higher ground, but he'd had no idea that the storm would push the water all the way to the house. They'd moved everything they could upstairs but feared if the pounding continued, the foundation might not hold.

The men returned hours later, soaked. The Kristjanssons stayed with us two nights until the storm ended. The next morning J.K. and Pabbi rode off before breakfast to assess the damage.

Leifur, Freyja, Thora and I snuck off to the west, further onto the ridge where it was high, to see for ourselves. Shielding our eyes against the reflection off the water, we saw the barn pushed off its foundation, wedged up against the bush behind the house. Most of the fence posts were beaten out of the ground and scattered like match sticks. Where the water had risen up, the ground was washed bare except for debris—sand, rocks, branches, dead fish—even a few lost, tangled nets.

We were mesmerized by the destruction. Had I not seen it firsthand, I never would have believed the lake could do so much damage.

"The house will be fine," J.K. told Gudrun when they returned. "Some water damage to the foundation but it is easily fixed. The barn was destroyed, but we expected that might happen. We will rebuild on higher ground. The lake is back to where it was before the storm, about 25 yards from the house. The low spots are full of water, but now it should dry up quick."

Relieved and thankful, we decided that since it was Sunday we would all go to church. It was a glorious morning as we piled into the wagons. The sun shone bright, sparkling in the wet grass. We pointed to every blossoming Saskatoon bush we passed, making a mental note where they were along the road. Soon the leaves would be thick and we wouldn't see them again.

"Look Amma," Solrun said, "your favorite spot."

Amma wagged her head and a few unintelligible words stammered out. When Mother wasn't looking, Leifur snuck her a pinch of snuff.

"Full moon tonight so the weather should be in our favor for a whole month," J.K. said.

As usual, he was right. As the decades passed we came to understand the weather. High water every ten years or so in the early spring left behind valuable nutrients on our wild hay fields, and when they dried up—and they always did by July—the crop had improved over the year before. We were quickly integrating ourselves with elements that had ebbed and flowed for centuries.

Neighbors were standing outside the church in three clusters, the men and women who arrived early were in two groups, while the latecomers were standing together. No one was smiling.

"I wonder how Bensi made out in the storm," Mother said, voice softening.

We all looked at Bensi who was helping his wife down from their wagon. He lived as close to the lake as Kristjanssons, and the Siglunes creek fractured his land. We hadn't seen him all winter. In fact, the last time was right after Amma's stroke. I was curious to see how he would react seeing us today.

Pabbi parked the wagon alongside the others and we jumped down. Asi was sitting—something he seldom did—with Olafur standing beside him, and Oli's hand rested sympathetically on his back. Signy looked stricken. She held the baby, and when our eyes met she looked away.

When Oli saw us he came over quickly.

"Pjetur, J.K.," he said, shaking their hands. "Glad you are here and that everyone is safe."

"What is wrong?" Pabbi asked.

Oli inhaled and his eyes went to his shoes as he struggled to find the words.

"I have terrible news to report," he said. "There has been an accident."

We waited as he steeled himself, taking a deep breath.

"Magnus's sons drowned yesterday."

CHAPTER THIRTY-ONE

If a man's time has not come, something will save him.
—FÓSTBROEÐRA SAGA

I DIDN'T LOOK BACK.

There were no thoughts, only the sound of my breath echoing in my ears. Water splashed against my legs. My feet pounded into the soft ground. Mother called my name but like a deer, I was already gone.

The heart is an amazing muscle. It works so much more efficiently than the brain. Once it receives the signal that you need to go, it takes you there, pumping blood, moving oxygen from the lungs to the legs. Set the rhythm and you can go for miles, for as long as you need.

All was quiet in the mill yard. I ran through the mud, past the barn and the cottage, to the house. I choked back a sob at the sight of the ramp that jutted off to the side of the stairs. It was nearly finished. Two hammers lay on the ground beside a pail of kicked-over nails.

I pushed open the door.

Bergthora and Magnus were sitting at the table. They looked up at me, expressionless, tired and ancient, as if nothing in their world would ever be right again.

I went over to Bergthora, who stood up and wrapped her arms around me. Over her shoulder I saw Magnus staring at his folded hands. The house was never so silent.

"I nearly lost all three," he whispered.

I pulled away to look into Bergthora's eyes. She motioned toward the front door. I ran down the hallway and flung it open, stepping out onto the verandah that overlooked the water. He stood, legs wide, arms crossed, staring defiantly at the choppy lake. There are no words to describe the tumble of emotions I felt when I saw his hair blowing back in the wind, the elation after imagining the whole way there how life might be to never see him again.

"Bjorn?"

He swiveled at the waist; it wasn't until I saw his face, older than it had been days before, that I was convinced my eyes weren't playing tricks. He didn't acknowledge me, only turned back to face the water.

My knees wobbled. I nearly collapsed against the railing but held on, catching my breath and balance. "I am so sorry," was all I could say.

We stood there in silence for the longest time, listening to the wind.

"I tried to save them," he whispered, voice broken. "They are still out there. It will take days until they come up and I cannot go inside until they do."

Bjorn tells me what he can.

Now I see the events unfold.

The storm had abated enough that Bjorn and Magnus were able to leave the house to assess damage to the mill and store. The lake was still churning but the waves were no longer splashing over the ridge where the house sat like a fortress. A wise decision it was to construct such a house.

Water lay in all the low spots and the floor of the store was wet, but everything inside was salvageable, as was most of the piled lumber. Only the planks on the ground were swollen. Relieved that the damage was minimal, they decided to finish building the ramp. Little else could be done until the lake receded, the ground dried up and the workers returned.

When they were an hour into it, Bergthora arrived with Magnus's field glasses.

"I think they have swamped the boat," she said.

Of course Bjorn was quicker than Magnus. He darted to the front of the house. He could see a speck in the choppy waves two miles out and once magnified knew it was Siggi and Arn. The wind still blew hard from the south, pushing them slowly north.

"Go get Asi," Magnus hollered.

Soon Magnus had the Lady Ellen ready to go. They accelerated, pounding through the bitterly cold waves, Magnus at the front holding the glasses, Bjorn and Asi at the stern.

The mast had snapped off the little boat and the weight of the sail was pulling it under. Arn was trying to hack it loose. Siggi lay sprawled, arms hanging over the bow. They must have set out from Ghost Island an hour or so before.

Bjorn readied the lifeboat and the anchor.

Arn gave up on the sail. He waded back to Siggi, tried to lift Siggi onto his back, but he was too weak. Arn wrapped the rope around Siggi's waist and pulled him tight against his back, tying the two of them together.

"I thought we had them saved, we were right there."

The bow of the boat sank. Arn was treading water for the both of them.

Asi cut the engine and Bjorn threw the anchor.

"Hold on," Magnus yelled.

The lifeboat dropped into the water and Asi and Bjorn scrambled down the ladder. Asi rowed. Bjorn threw a buoy which landed close, but Arn couldn't grab it. Siggi's head was dipping in and out of the water.

"I hollered at him to have faith, to keep treading."

Bjorn saw but could not admit Arn's relief as their eyes meet. He knew what was about to happen but couldn't stop it.

You cannot live on an island and not be touched by the sea. Centuries of knowledge had been passed down by his forebears who fished the waters off the coast of Iceland. Bjorn knew in his bones the critical point at which a drowning man, believing he is saved, will weaken.

“He should have conserved his strength.”

Arn began swimming toward the lifeboat but Siggi’s weight was pulling him down. A wave came up over his head. He took in a lung full of water.

Bjorn dove in but when he surfaced, Arn and Siggi were nowhere to be seen. The cold shocked the wind out of him. Asi pointed to the spot they went down. Bjorn dove again. Up and down again. The storm had churned the lake to a sickening brown. He came up and inhaled. He dove down, stayed under. He re-surfaced.

Magnus was yelling frantically. Not wanting to let his father down, Bjorn dove again.

This time when he came up, Magnus was yelling at Asi, “Save my Bjorn!”

Asi reached over the side and strong-armed him against the boat. Bjorn wanted to struggle, to dive down again but he didn’t have the strength.

“They are gone,” Asi hollered into the wind and waves. “There is nothing more you can do.”

Bjorn’s forehead rested on my shoulder.

“I felt a hand,” he whispered. “I went down as far as I could, but couldn’t find them again.”

He dropped to his knees. “It wasn’t even Arn’s fault,” he cried. “He didn’t even know what we did to Einar.” Face to the sky he let out a fierce wail.

The wagons arrived a few hours later. First the men came, marching toward the dock with their heads down, carrying nets and poles.

“The current would have taken them north,” J.K. said as they prepared to launch the skiffs.

The front door opened then Magnus came heavily down the steps. Without a word he and Bjorn joined the search.

I was inside with Bergthora when the women arrived. Mother brought Amma, Freyja, Gudrun and Thora. Oli was right behind with his wife, Signy and Bensi's wife; two wagonloads came from Hayland.

Pabbi and Oli didn't go on the lake, they stayed behind. Oli lifted his tool box from the back of the wagon. Pabbi stoked the firebox while Oli carefully chose two of the finest oaks from the pile. Soon there was enough steam, and from the kitchen we heard the whine of the saw as the oaks were sliced into six-foot lengths.

"First their Mama and now the twins." Bergthora coughed, bringing a handkerchief to her lips. Her eyes went to Amma in her chair between the kitchen and front room. "No man deserves this much heartache."

The women all shook their heads, tsking and muttering in agreement as they began making sandwiches.

Bensi's wife was the only one who had the courage to ask what we were all thinking: Why in God's name would the boys have set out from Ghost Island for home when the lake was so rough? Why not wait another day?

"They went out three days before the storm to do some work on the cabin," Bergthora said, shaking her head. "Siggi had pneumonia. I told him not to go."

And then a half hour later: "Arn wouldn't have tried to bring him back unless he needed to."

The boats rowed in at dusk.

Bjorn stayed outside with Leifur and Stefan to build a fire, so Thora and I took food out to them. We young people stayed the night, wrapped in blankets I brought down from the upper bedrooms. We were silent most of the time, staring into the flames.

"We'll find them tomorrow," Leifur said. He added another log to the fire.

"And if not," Stefan said, "we will keep looking until we do."

Their words sounded forced and hollow. Nothing we said lightened Bjorn's mood. The back door opened and slammed closed many times and we listened to quiet voices as the last wagon rolled down the lane.

Eventually, we lay on our sides listening to the coyotes yipping and howling in the distance. I fell into a restless sleep, waking a few times; at dawn, I lay there, realizing Leifur had stayed awake all night to keep the fire going for the rest of us.

They dragged the lake for three more days.

On the fourth morning when I went in to get Amma up, I opened her window to the sound of birds chattering and heard, in the distance, the faint sound of the Lady Ellen's death knell—three long pulls on the horn, a fifteen second pause, three more.

I wheeled Amma into the kitchen as Mother and Freyja came in carrying the milk.

"They are found," I said.

"Probably washed ashore during the night," Mother said. "Likely near The Narrows."

Now that there was a church at Hayland, we shared a pastor with The Narrows. The day of the funeral he stood in his black robe at the edge of the grassy knoll beside Magnus and Bergthora.

We didn't all begin crying at once.

Bjorn, Leifur, Stefan, Olafur, Asi, and J.K. emerged from the bunkhouse, eyebrows clenched and faces screwed up, carrying the first casket. Pabbi lowered his head.

I presumed it was Siggi because they laid the casket down beside Runa's grave. They went back for Arn and we created a large semi-circle around the graves. Everything was so still under the overcast sky that not a sound could be heard except for the wind on water.

The Pastor went to the head of the graves and opened his Bible. We listened, prayed and sang. A few women cried, including Amma, whose heart always opened up at the sound of a hymn.

When the Pastor closed his Bible, Bjorn stepped forward and the others followed, grasping the rope handles, carefully lowering each casket into its grave. Mother leaned on Pabbi who wrapped his arm around her shoulder as the pallbearers took turns filling in the graves. Freyja cried in her hands when Asi handed Stefan the shovel. But it was Bjorn and Leifur who finished the job—digging slow and steady, pitching in perfect unison—as the rest of us made our way to the house.

We'd been talking about the accident and grieving for a week, but the collective mood was definitely lighter now that the worst of it was done. Watching the younger children run and play was a welcome distraction.

Bjorn stayed as far away from the conversation as he could. He sat building another fire. Seeing he wanted to be alone, everyone drifted away from him. When most were gone, I went to sit beside him. It was early evening so the air was already cool.

"I cannot listen to it any longer," he said. "All of them telling Father how sorry they are when I know half of them couldn't care less."

I was stunned.

"It's true," he said. "I've seen their jealousy my whole life."

"Who?" I asked. "Asi?"

"No."

"Pabbi?"

"Of course not."

"J.K.? Oli?"

"No." Bjorn turned to face me. "Bensi and the others. They think we deserve this."

"What have they said?"

"They don't have to say a word. I can see it when they look at us. They feign sorrow, but really are quite satisfied now that Father has been knocked down a notch."

I shook my head in disagreement. All I saw from everyone was kindness and compassion.

"Father does not deserve this," he said. "It is all my fault. First, God punished Siggi by letting Runa and the baby die. Now He's punishing me for killing Einar. I knew I would have to pay for it someday. I just didn't expect that Arn and Father would suffer as well."

Had I been older, wiser, I would have known what to say, how to shake him out of it, but the truth was I understood his guilt. I felt it also. My cheeks burned with shame knowing that what they did to Einar was my fault, but I was too cowardly to say it out loud.

The next afternoon I made an arrangement with Thora. The morning after that, once Amma was settled, I went to the mill. I met Bjorn at the barn door.

"I am here for the job," I said, catching him by surprise.

"I don't need your help," he said. His eyes were red, swollen.

"Yes, you do," I said. "Amma thinks so, too."

Truthfully, it was difficult to know exactly what Amma thought when I explained my plan. It was a good sign, though, when Thora happily took the back of the chair and wheeled Amma into the kitchen without her hissing a fit.

"I am ready to get started," I said.

He seemed to lack direction, as if there was a giant fog in front of him, so I started towards the store and he followed, Bergthora watching us from the kitchen window.

"How many days will you need me?" I asked, pulling open the door. "Five days? Four? Is it normally busy on Friday? I have only been here twice. I think it will be good for me and for Amma too. Freyja is miffed that you didn't offer her the job, but nothing pleases her right now."

"What will Finn say?" he asked.

"Finn is not my husband," I said.

The door had been closed for more than a week so it smelled musty inside. I unlatched the front window then swung it open. I went to all the others and did the same, banging the stuck ones with my palm. "My life is still my own."

I sounded so cavalier. So independent. So very—Amma.

"This will not create difficulties between you and him?"

"Why should it?" I said, slapping the dust from my hands. I surveyed the floor. It was in dire need of sweeping. "Now show me what I need to do."

Finn completed his third year at the University, returning home the last weekend in May. This time he came by train (the train now ran all the way from Winnipeg) and J.K. picked him up at the station in Lundi. I found an excuse to take Amma outside that afternoon—I think Mother knew why—and we waved wildly when the democrat passed. I hadn't seen him since Christmas so I was stunned by how much older he looked and how handsome in his new suit.

I ran upstairs to change into my best dress and comb my hair. He arrived at our door an hour later, saying he couldn't stay long because Gudrun was preparing a special meal. We hugged and kissed in privacy around the corner of the house then went to sit under Amma's tree.

We'd written letters weekly so were already privy to the workings of each other's lives. I asked him what it was like riding on the train and he raved about it, saying how fast it was compared to travelling by horse.

"Are things improving at the store?" he asked, taking my hand.

By 'things' he meant Bjorn. I'd confided in my last two letters how difficult it was, having to take charge of a business I barely understood since Bjorn seemed to have lost all interest.

"I hope I didn't sound too harsh," I said, examining his elegant fingers and neatly trimmed nails. "Everything is a mess right now. Two workers quit last week so they are behind."

"Yes, but he shouldn't be taking out his frustrations on you."

"He's not," I said. "He blames himself and is not thinking clearly."

Finn thought for a moment. "I don't understand why, by what you said he did everything he could. By God, jumping into that freezing water was a feat in itself."

"I know," I said, resisting the temptation to say more, to disclose my own guilt.

"If working there makes you unhappy—"

"It doesn't," I said, forcing away unpleasant thoughts. "Let's talk about something else."

Finn smiled. "Fair enough," he said. He took my other hand in his, leaning in close. "I've been thinking a lot about our future. And Thora's. It is honorable what the two of you are doing, but this cannot go on indefinitely. Decisions need to be made."

"We still have a year."

"Yes, you do. Plenty of time to prepare your family and Bjorn for the inevitable," he said, soft gray eyes reading my expression. "Unless you have changed your mind?"

What I didn't have the courage to tell him is that I was undecided. Every time he'd written about Thora and I enrolling in the nursing program, I'd been vague in my reply.

"I'm not sure how they would manage without us," I said.

"What about Freyja?" he said. "She could take care of your Amma or work in the store."

"Freyja? She doesn't want that," I said.

He laughed. "Do you hear yourself? You are more concerned about them than yourself. What do you want?"

I pulled my hands away and stood up. "I want all of this to stop," I said. "The fear, the nightmares, the uncertainty. You have no idea how I feel, so stop acting as if you do."

I turned and ran towards the barn.

"Asta, wait."

He caught up to me by the road, grabbing my arm, spinning me around to face him. "What is wrong with you?"

In a mixture of anger and relief I told him, blurting out what Einar had done to Runa and what happened after I'd told Bjorn. I was too ashamed to disclose what Einar did to me.

"They murdered him?" he said, eyes wide.

"No," I said, hushing my voice. "Bjorn took him to Ghost Island."

"Well that's what it sounds like to me."

Frustrated, I shook my head. "They didn't actually kill him."

"Do you know that for sure?"

"He probably tried to walk across the lake after that," I said, hoping beyond reason that it was true. Not that it made much difference, but imagining that part of Einar's fate lay in his own actions made it easier to bear.

Finn looked skeptical. I could see he was calculating, and when he was done he shook his head. He pulled out his pocket watch.

"I'm sorry, I have to go."

He took my hand, tugging me in the direction of the yard. When we were at the door, he pulled me into a strong embrace.

"You can't tell anyone," I whispered.

"Don't worry," he said. "I won't."

Immediately I regretted telling Finn the secret, so the next day I could barely face Bjorn. And that evening, when Finn arrived to pick me up from the store, we discussed Einar the whole way home.

"I cannot imagine how it would feel to kill someone," he said softly.

It was remarkable how the secret that had driven a wedge between Bjorn and me now brought Finn and me closer together. We had a wonderful summer. I worked most days at the store while he helped his father on the farm. We went to picnics, community dances, played chess most evenings, and even snuck away together on Sunday afternoons, sailing out to Gull Reef which became our secret spot. Before we knew it August had arrived. Once again I waved good-bye to him from the dock. I had a year to decide.

CHAPTER THIRTY-TWO

Who can say what sorrow seemingly carefree folk bear to their life's end.
—VÖLSUNGA SAGA

I AWAKEN TO SEE SOLRUN FLIPPING THROUGH MY SCRAPBOOK THAT sits heavily on her lap.

"Amazing," she says. "I forgot what you collected over the years."

A half a lifetime of memories all saved in a box then condensed, trimmed and glued in meticulous, chronological order. The second half of my life was far less compelling, but I added everything worth remembering.

"You saved all our cut-outs," she says, lifting the book so I can see. Brittle and faded, these were the figurines we played house with, pictures of people and furniture all clipped from the Eaton's catalogue.

I want to ask if she remembers all the hours we spent at the kitchen table propping up our two-dimensional family, imagining their spectacular three-dimensional lives. I never told her that the handsome cut-out man was Bjorn. I'd not clipped the paper between his head and shoulders so that I could pencil in his long hair. The woman holding a baby was me. Sometimes, when Solrun and Lars weren't looking, those cut-outs kissed.

She continues thumbing the pages. She seems touched by it all when she looks up.

"You still have Finn's letters," she says, "after all these years."

She turns the pages, counts the letters, then flips back.

"So long ago. Would you like me to read them to you?"

Yes, I nod. *I would like that very much.*

She waves Lars in when he appears in the doorway.

"We are going through the scrapbook," she says, opening the envelope glued to the page, pulling out two yellowed sheets.

"Do you remember when we went to Winnipeg?"

"How could I forget," he says, sliding a chair up beside her. "I'd never seen so many toys."

Solrun scans the letter then begins reading out loud:

March 1, 1914

Dearest Ásta,

The day I received your letter, I immediately went to the hospital to find your Mother. She was tending to Sólrún in the children's ward. The nurse was showing her how to pummel Sólrún's chest to work the fluid out of her lungs and how to stretch her affected leg so that the joints will not become too stiff.

It was a good decision to send Freyja along as translator. The doctor reports Sólrún has infantile paralysis. She is weak but her spirits are good. The doctor called her 'plucky' which means the same as brave. I looked it up in the dictionary.

I told Stanley's parents about your Mother's situation and you will be relieved to know that they insisted your family stay with them. They even sent a car to pick them up from the hospital. At first your Mother was hesitant, but Freyja talked her into it.

Each was given their own room (even Lars) and every morning a car takes your mother to the hospital then picks her up at night. Yesterday, Stanley and I, and our chum Bjarni from the University (I have mentioned him to you before), joined them for dinner. It was a lively time and the first I am sure that the Burroughs were so outnumbered by Icelanders. We kept our manners intact, spoke mostly English, but it was difficult, especially since your Mother could not understand most of what we said.

Stanley's mother, Elizabeth, is quite taken with Lars so she insists that he stay with her during the day. They still have Stanley's wind-up toys so Lars is thrilled. Today Freyja came to the University and spent the day with us. Tomorrow Elizabeth will take her to the Hudson's Bay store on Portage Avenue. Freyja can hardly wait, but she is starting to miss Stefán. I overheard your mother and Freyja arguing but I do not know what it was about.

Rest assured, I have taken care of everything.

Love always, Finn.

"Bjarni," I say. "That bastard."

Lars chuckles but Solrun is silent for a few moments. I see that finally she understands why the scrapbook means so much to me.

"It was you I missed most while in the hospital," she says. "Because of you, nobody treated me any differently after I came home."

"You didn't feel sorry for yourself," I say. This pleases her.

"Do you remember what you told us after Amma's stroke?" she asks.

I shake my head.

Lars remembers. "You said that it was hard for Amma and that we should treat her the same as always; to look past who she'd become by remembering who she'd been."

Now I am the one who is pleased. We never know the affect our words might have, but thankfully sometimes people remember and tell us.

* * *

The months flew by and soon I'd have to make a decision.

In the meantime, I enjoyed the store immensely. It was a bit of a challenge keeping everything straight and balancing the ledgers. Mathematics had been my preferred subject in school so I took great pride in knowing exactly how much inventory we had. At any given moment Bjorn could walk in and I could tell him to the penny what had sold, who had paid, how much was owed and the value of goods on hand. He seemed pleased by my diligence.

It was surprising the number of customers who came in. When I wasn't tallying purchases in the ledger, I measured dress cloth, repackaged the flour, sugar, coffee, and salt from hundred pound bags into five, ten or twenty pound sacks. I stocked the shelves with tobacco, kerosene, matches, lye, ink, and notepaper. We carried a few canned goods, crackers, vanilla, raisins, and cheese. I placed the underwear, shirts, hats, and shoes on one shelf—the razors, pipes, harmonicas, coffee pots, and lanterns behind the counter. We sold barbed wire, chicken wire, pliers, nuts, and bolts. Pretty much whatever was needed, we stocked, and if not, I put it on a list so Bjorn could order it from a wholesaler in Portage la Prairie.

Sometimes when there was nothing to do, I sat on my stool behind the counter writing letters. I became accustomed to the squeal of the mill saw and even welcomed the industrious sound as a pleasant backdrop to my day.

May 6, 1914
Dearest Finn,

I received a letter from Mama today and the good news is that she will be bringing Sólrún home soon, though I expect you already know this.

There are seven men hired at the mill now and Ólafur is one of them. Signý was in the other day and said they need extra money, which does not surprise me. The Thorsteinssons are fencing most of their land with barbed wire (which we all know is costly) so they must pay for it somehow. Little Pétur loves coming in, so does Óli. I always give them a treat. Steini is too young for a sour ball so I give him a licorice whip instead. Signý is expecting again. She says if this one is not a girl, Ólafur is going to have to start sleeping on the sofa. I don't think I was supposed to tell you that so please keep it to yourself.

Yesterday, Ási said I am getting fat because of all the candy I eat, but this is not true at all. He is the one with the sweet tooth. I am starting to worry about him, though. I've noticed that he often smells of liquor, sometimes already by afternoon. I don't have the courage to tell his wife. Has your father said anything to you?

Amma adjusted surprisingly well to Mama being gone, but I give all the credit to Thora. She takes such good care of Amma and even gives her a daily whiff of snuff and, while it is disgusting, Amma enjoys it so much we cannot deny her that pleasure. Wait until Mama gets home, she will be livid.

I think Guðrún has the toughest job right now. Since Mama left she's been baking bread for our family as well. Have you seen how much bread Leifur eats?

When are you coming home? I can hardly wait to see you.

Tell Stanley that Leifur and I would like to meet him. Knowing he already has friends waiting here might entice him to come.

Lovingly, Ástfriður

On the day Mother and the children were scheduled to arrive home from Winnipeg, Bergthora drove me home in the democrat. She'd baked a cake that I held on my knees.

Father came in from fencing early and we checked the clock. Then he looked out the window. Checked the clock again. He startled when he saw our new democrat coming up the road, ran outside with me behind him. Leifur barely had the horses stopped and Mother was off her seat, running toward us. Pabbi braced himself as she flew into his open arms, then he swung her around.

Freyja nearly knocked me over with her hug.

"I need Amma," Lars said, darting past us to the house.

Leifur lifted Solrun out of the back seat. She was wrapped in the same blanket as the day she left. Pabbi's eyes glistened as Leifur carried her inside.

I expected Leifur would lay Solrun down on the sofa, but instead he put her feet first on the floor in front of Amma, who was sitting in the kitchen with Lars on her lap, then unwrapped the blanket.

Solrun threw her arms to the ceiling. "See my new leg?" She beamed, first at Amma then up at us, lifting her skirt to show off the brace before clanking across the floor.

"Well look at that," Pabbi said. "Good as new."

Determined to prove him right, Solrun stomped back and forth, calling each of us by name to be sure we were watching.

"It cost more than the others," Mother whispered. "It bends at the knee—"

Pabbi quickly waved off talk of money. "Then you made the only choice."

Mother explained how important it was to remove the brace twice daily and that Solrun's leg be flexed and stretched every night then again in the morning. She needed to walk each day without it to help strengthen her leg. If we were diligent, someday she might not need it at all.

"From now on everyone washes their hands, especially after visiting the outhouse," Mother said, herding us all to the wash basin.

That night, I overheard Mother and Pabbi talking.

"Uncleanliness," she whispered.

Now I see her standing in the hospital room. Freyja interprets as the doctor explains the cause of what we now call Polio. Mother's face is crimson and I feel her shame. She flinches as her eyes go to the window and she cannot face the doctor again.

Freyja had matured so much in her time away that now I barely knew her. Three months of freedom in the city had made her bold.

"I know what I want to do," she said the following morning as we walked together to the store. She was intent on seeing Stefan and knew he'd be delivering the mail. "There is a need for translators in Winnipeg. Kent says there are so few. I have already applied to study at the Academy."

"Do you like Winnipeg?" I asked.

"It is beautiful. There is so much to see and do. I would like to go this fall with you, that is if Pabbi has enough money to send me."

We knew that Mother had taken the little box that held our education fund to Winnipeg but only our parents knew how much was left.

"What will you tell Stefan?" I asked.

"I want him to come with us," she said, giddy with excitement. "You heard Gudrun. He would make an excellent lawyer. He is clever, you know. Kent says the firm needs young men like him."

I thought about what he'd said to me in the barn.

"He loves to fish," I warned. "And he shows no interest in going to school."

"Maybe so, but fishing is so difficult for him," she said. "Kent says he can begin this winter by doing research for the other lawyers, to see if he enjoys it. I hope that Kent will talk sense into him."

Mother had convinced the Burroughs to visit so they decided to come out with Finn, two days before The Narrows picnic.

"He is a very convincing man," Freyja said. "Very successful."

To be honest, I was growing tired of hearing about Stanley and his family.

Then a thought struck her. "Are you still planning to go?"

I told her I wasn't sure. I'd put off sending in my application and wasn't sure if I'd be accepted for that fall.

She rolled her eyes. "All because of Bjorn. I see the way he looks at you. Everyone does, including Finn. I think it worries him."

"Nonsense," I said. "Bjorn and I are just friends."

"Then why?"

Before I had the chance to explain, Freyja saw Stefan in the mill yard on the horse Magnus had given him, just as Stefan had predicted. She called his name and when he saw her, he jumped down, dropped the mail bag, and the two collided in an embrace. They kissed for so long that when Bjorn came out of the store, he abruptly turned around to go back inside.

Freyja and Stefan spent the whole day together and the next. Mother found out that Freyja wasn't helping in the store and said that she should stay home to care for Amma. Freyja objected, saying she could not stomach the job.

I agreed. "That would be unfair to Amma," I said.

Mother handed Freyja a stack of laundry to fold. "I do not want you there all the time," she said.

"Why?" Freyja demanded, rolling Leifur's shirt into a ball. "Because of Stefan?"

Exasperated, Mother grabbed the shirt from her grasp.

"We have discussed this many times," she said, handing it back to her. "Now fold this properly."

Freyja threw it on the floor. "No one ever listens to me." Then she stormed upstairs and slammed the bedroom door.

With the mill in full swing and the lumber orders greater than ever, Bergthora needed help in the kitchen, so I suggested that she hire Freyja for the summer. Bergthora was looking thin and her eyes had lost their sparkle, but she seemed to perk up at this idea. I was the go-between who told Mother that Freyja would be kept busy and, while I did not say it, thought to myself that with Bergthora giving orders, there would be no further opportunity for Freyja and Stefan to hide out in the barn together.

The day Finn came home finally arrived. I see my family standing at Kristjansson's door, Pabbi fidgeting with his collar, Mother nervously holding a Vínarterta made especially for Stanley's mother. Pabbi had asked on the way if Mother was sure she didn't mind taking an ox to the opera. He'd muttered it in Icelandic (we have a saying for every occasion).

"Not if he is wearing his best shirt," she'd said. "Now remember, we must speak English."

I am the last to go in. Elizabeth gets up to give Mother a hug. Kent shakes Pabbi's hand vigorously, as he tries to assess the sort of man

Pabbi is. I see the look of disappointment on Thora's face when Stanley abruptly stops talking to her the moment he sets eyes on Freyja—the girl with the God-given gift of stopping a room without even realizing it.

All I saw was Finn, heard his ever so slight gasp when he noticed me. I hung back. He pushed past everyone to take me into his arms, squeezing the breath out of me. He led me by the hand over to the bookshelf where Stanley stood. Our introduction interrupted Stanley's pleasure at seeing Freyja, and, although Finn did not notice, I saw Stanley's annoyance and surprise when, like Amma, I extended my hand. His palm was clammy, hand limp. How strange it was that Stanley's father, broad-shouldered and solid as a house, hadn't taught his son the importance of a firm greeting.

He looked like his mother, doe-eyed and angular, long-legged as a fawn. It was easy to imagine Finn and Stanley in the University lecture hall together, both knowing the answers before the others; studying quietly in their dorm room at night. Neither was in residence by choice—Finn who lived so far from home, Stanley because his father said it was bloody-well-high-time he went out into the world.

What the two also had in common were their fathers. Politically the same, J.K. and Kent held similar religious beliefs, even though they disagreed on the ideology of war. Both had the same boisterous confidence and were gregarious men who enjoyed showing off their intimidating wit.

Finn gave Stanley a wolfish poke in the side. "See," he said, glancing sideways at me.

Stanley could not resist Freyja and I sensed that he'd expected I'd look more like her. He barely acknowledged me.

"Where is Bjarni?" I asked.

"He went to Big Point to visit relatives," Finn said.

I wondered out loud if Bjarni was a relation to Arni who'd brought diphtheria to the mill. But before Finn could answer, there was a commotion in the kitchen.

"Vínarterta," J.K. announced, eyeing Mother's cake on the table. "No offence, dear wife, but Ella does make the best Vínarterta."

"None taken," Gudrun quipped as she went to the counter to fetch a knife. "So long as you are not offended if I never make you one again."

Laughter. The whole evening was filled with it.

"Veena—?" Elizabeth asked.

"Vínarterta," Mother said. Everyone stopped to watch as she sliced it first length ways in a thin strip, then into inch wide pieces that she overlapped on a plate.

"I thought you might like to try it," she said, looking pleased as she held it out. The cake had settled into perfection, the moist filling almost completely soaking through the cake layers.

"Like this," J.K. said pinching a piece lengthwise then lifting it off the plate. He raised his eyebrows as he split it in two, eating the bottom half. He rolled his eyes and looked up to the ceiling as if thanking God, chewed, then ate the other half.

Elizabeth did the same, even licking her fingers as he'd done.

"Mmmmm," she said, eyes widening as she began counting the cake layers with a well-manicured finger. "How many are there?"

"Seven," Mother said, holding the plate out to Kent as the rest of us milled around.

"Veena—"

"terta."

Because they were British, they could not manage our words no matter how many times we rolled them off our tongues. They could not hear the disciplined inflections, softened vowels, clipped consonants. It would be impolite to correct these fine people, so we all smiled, forgiving their harsh accents pounding through toothy grins with every word they said.

All of the hot issues were avoided and the few times J.K. began winding up to debate, Gudrun quietly interrupted. Mother and Pabbi stole the occasional glance across the table, waiting to discuss the contentious issues privately, which they did when we rode home at 2:00 a.m. Lars fell asleep on Mother's lap, Solrun on mine.

"I don't care that we have different opinions," Mother said into the clear, morning air. "They were so generous to us that I will remain forever in their debt."

We left early the morning of the picnic, travelling by wagon to The Narrows. The new road, which had taken the government three years to build, was an absolute blessing to us. The night before, the room had turned silent when Kent stated that building roads in the north was a waste of money. We hoped that once he saw for himself how it linked our communities, he would understand the need.

J.K. and Kent sat in the front of the democrat. Our wagon kept pace behind, and all of their children were with us. We overheard bits of their conversation and the occasional burst of laughter.

"They are still discussing whether or not to bring a rail line this way," J.K. said, opening the discussion again. He projected his words over his shoulder into the back seat where Gudrun sat with Elizabeth.

"I hope they do," Gudrun said quickly. "It will be far more cost efficient to bring goods out by rail than water."

Elizabeth nodded thoughtfully. "That drive from the train station at . . . where was it—Loon-dee? It was exhausting. I am not looking forward to leaving in the morning."

"Imagine if you could catch the train right here," Gudrun said.

"Do you play hardball?" I asked Stanley in careful English.

He shook his head no. "You must be very skilled to earn a spot on a Winnipeg team."

Finn laughed. "Not true. I have seen them play. Siglunes is as good as the University team, maybe better."

"You have so few players to choose from out here. Statistics prove your team cannot be better."

"Not so," Leifur said. "How many on the University team are bigger than your father?"

"Only one."

"Does he hit home runs?"

"He is their best player."

Leifur and Finn grinned at one another. "We have four his size."

Stanley was not convinced.

"Can their fastest runner beat Finn in a race?" Leifur asked.

Stanley looked at him sideways. "No."

We were enjoying this immensely. "Can their pitcher kill a squirrel with a stone?"

Now he looked outraged. "How should I know?"

"Well, we have the Larsons who were born with gloves on," Leifur said, puffing out his chest, "and the Sveistrup brothers."

"Now, boys," Pabbi said over his shoulder. "Save the bragging until after you win."

Knowing that Kent was watching the game seemed to drive J.K. to a higher level of competitiveness. Before the first pitch was thrown he rallied the team into a huddle, enthusiastically patted Bjorn on the back and shook Olafur's arm. As they broke apart to run onto the field, we all cheered and clapped. Everyone looked particularly focused, especially Bjorn, who set an impressive tone by striking out the first three batters on the Kinosota team.

By the fifth inning it was apparent that we would win. Mother and Pabbi enjoyed watching Kent, who hollered, clapped loudly and was thoroughly engrossed in the game.

"I must admit I did not expect to see such a thrashing," Kent said, as we sat down on the blankets to have dinner. Crouched on his knees, he bit into a sandwich.

"What a marvelous place, Elizabeth," he said, scanning the water.

We followed his gaze across the channel to watch a steamship cut its engine and approach the dock.

The next hour was spent introducing the Burroughs to our neighbors, who made their way, family by family, over to where we were sitting. Mother and Gudrun always brought extra food for the young ballplayers who did not yet have wives.

Freyja was glowing. She took Stefan by the arm and led him to where Kent was sitting.

"Mr. Burroughs," she said. "I would like to introduce my beau, Stefan."

Kent quickly stood up to shake Stefan's hand.

"You are quite the ball player," he said, unable to avoid looking at his uniform sleeve sewn shut at the shoulder. Stefan was accustomed to the curiosity by then, the shock when strangers noticed his missing arm, the admiration that followed when they saw him accomplish what so few could do.

"This is the young man you told me about," Kent said to Freyja, then turned to Stefan, a wide smile opening up his face. "Thinking of becoming a lawyer, I hear? Good for you."

Stefan's head jerked back ever so slightly. I saw it and others did too; as he mentally withdrew from the conversation. He was polite, even nodded a few times, but he was no longer listening.

"Winnipeg has a fine law school, second only to McGill, but you must speak French to enroll there and I take it you do not."

"Pardon me?"

"French, do you speak French?"

"No sir," Stefan said. "I am Icelandic."

This seemed unimportant to Kent who waved it off with a flourish.

"It takes more than stellar marks to be accepted at either school. Experience is the key. I will be glad to offer assistance in that regard. I am proud to say that we have the finest firm in the city. When you arrive in Winnipeg come by my office. Freyja knows where it is. Of course you are welcome to stay with us until you get settled."

Stefan slowly turned to look at Freyja, but he did not say a word. Her cheeks were flushed by then and those of us who saw it, who knew Stefan, felt embarrassed for both of them. Stefan made an excuse that he had to be elsewhere and left her standing in her own awkwardness. Thankfully, Kent was oblivious.

Pabbi quickly diverted the attention away from her by telling the rest of the team that Finn had graduated top of the class and that Stanley's grades were second highest. This pleased the Burroughs to no end; they did not notice Freyja looking over her shoulder then running after Stefan.

"Where is Freyja?" Mother asked as we followed the players back to the ball diamond. Two hours had passed and we hadn't seen either her or Stefan. He'd missed the tug-o-war and now the team was set to play two more games, back-to-back. They were nowhere to be seen.

"She is with Petra," Signy said.

A few minutes later Stefan re-appeared, jogging across the field toward us.

Halfway through the first game, Amma started to nod off. The sun was particularly hot that day so I wheeled her back to the water's edge so she could nap in the shade. I gave her a drink of water, slipped a pillow behind her head, telling her I would be back soon.

It was a heart-stopping final game against Big Point and everyone at the picnic was watching. Our team came from behind to win by one run and we took home our first tournament victory. The editor of *Lögberg* snapped a team photo with his big, square camera. When everyone began making their way to the hall for the dance, Finn came running over to me.

"Come, I have something to tell you," he said, dragging me by the hand away from everyone. I slowed as we reached the lake bank. Amma was jerking her arms, trying to make herself understood to Bergthora, who was leaning in, listening. She lifted a jar of water, but Amma slapped it away.

"I should go to her," I said, but Finn told me to stop worrying.

Bergthora will take care of her," he said, eyes the brightest I'd ever seen. "This is important."

He took my hand to lead me down to the water and we followed the shoreline, around a small bend, until we were out of sight.

"What is it?" I asked, but he would not tell me until we were sitting.

"Mother gave me this yesterday," he grinned, taking a folded envelope from his pocket. "I did not open it until after the game."

He waited, eyes dancing. I begged him to tell me what it said.

"I have been hired by a firm in Winnipeg. They want me to start at the beginning of August," he said.

Thrilled, I threw myself into his arms.

"There is more," he said hopefully, pushing the hair off my forehead. He hesitated, settling into the moment as he calmly formulated his words. "I will earn more salary in four months than Father makes in a whole year," he said. "I will be able to afford to hire a private nurse for your Amma so you can come to Winnipeg. That is if you will agree."

A private nurse. Someone qualified to care for Amma, who also would understand how to rehabilitate Solrun's leg. We'd never even considered such an expensive idea. But now Finn was offering it. I wondered how Pabbi would react.

"I still don't know if I've been accepted into nursing school," I said.

"You will be," he said softly. "And if not, it doesn't matter. You can still come with me."

"Well, it matters to me. What would I do?"

He shook his head, smiling. "What I am asking is, will you marry me?"

I was so surprised I could barely breathe.

I closed my eyes, feeling the heaviness of the years spent longing for Bjorn, the weight of what he'd done to Einar because of me. Then Bensi's words came: *Tragedy follows them everywhere and a young man would be wise to stay away.*

When I opened my eyes they settled on Finn. He was so bright and hopeful. Only good luck had touched him since I'd come into his life. This was my chance to prove that Bensi was wrong.

"Yes," I said. "I will be your wife."

CHAPTER THIRTY-THREE

Often it is that anger is blind to the truth.
—FÓSTBROEÐRA SAGA

As the placid waves lapped the shoreline, Finn and I sat on the rock planning our future. He assured me that I would not long for home because there was so much to do in Winnipeg. We would go to plays, picture shows and dances. Did I even realize how vibrant an Icelandic community existed there? We could join the church on Victor Street, eat dinner at Runey's café. Buy as many books as we wanted.

"They can come visit and we will take the train home for Christmas," he said. "I will buy a motor car. Father will love that."

For an hour we sat there, until the sun dipped low, turning the sky over the water a brilliant shade of pink.

"Now I must ask your Father," he said, standing up. "What do you think he will say?"

I told him not to worry, that Pabbi would be very pleased.

Finn was on edge nevertheless and, as we started back to the picnic area, I looked up to see Signy hurrying toward us, hands holding her sweater tight over her swollen belly. She looked anxious and my first thought was of Amma.

"Have you seen Freyja?" she asked. She looked out over the water. I followed her gaze along the shoreline, then up at the bush that spread out behind us for countless miles. Bewildered, she shook her head, then her eyes met mine.

"She is gone."

Pabbi stood with his hands on his hips, looking desperately alone despite the throng of neighbors who gathered around him. Mother was staring silently, wringing her hands. They startled a bit, looking hopeful as they saw Finn and me following Signy. When they realized Freyja was not with us, Mother started crying.

Gudrun had her arms wrapped around Solrun and Lars. Leifur and Bjorn stood off to the side, each with their legs wide and arms crossed. Bensi stood directly behind Pabbi.

The Burroughs appeared stunned.

"Olafur," Bjorn called, motioning for him.

Olafur strode across the grass and Bjorn turned his back to everyone as they bent their heads together.

Amma was distraught, pounding her armrest.

"Who was the last to see her?" J.K. asked.

Stefan and Petra both raised their hands.

"When?"

Stefan was in a daze and spoke so low J.K. had to ask him to repeat himself.

"During the tug-o-war," Stefan said, pointing toward the edge of the bush by the road. "We were over there."

Then J.K. turned to Petra. "When did you see her last?"

Petra always looked pale, but that evening, under the fading light, she was ghostlike.

"We talked for, I don't know, possibly an hour," she whispered.

"After she left Stefan?"

"They had a fight. She was crying."

Stefan stared at the ground, shaking his head. He either didn't agree or couldn't believe what was happening, but I couldn't tell which.

"Where did you two go?" J.K. asked Petra.

Her eyes began to well. She looked at her father then back again. “We walked around.”

“Where?”

“Over there,” she said, pointing at the hall.

“Then where?”

She shrugged. “When I came back from the outhouse she was gone. I thought she went to watch the game.”

“Where was your father?” Bjorn called out.

Eyes settled on Bensi.

It took Pabbi a moment for the thought to register, then he swung around. Before Bensi could step back, nearly two decades of resentment were concentrated in Pabbi’s fist. He caught Bensi on the chin, knocking him to the ground. The women screamed. Asi grabbed Pabbi, holding him back.

“You criminal,” Pabbi rasped. “Waiting until my guard was down to strike again.”

Amma pounded her armrest.

Bensi held his jaw, eyes panicked at all the uncertainty surrounding him. “Pjetur,” he cried as he staggered to his feet.

By then Amma was wailing.

J.K. stepped in front of Pabbi grabbing him by the shoulders. “We have to eliminate all possibilities,” he said. “Do you hear me?”

“What if it was Thora?” Pabbi choked. “Would you be so calm then?”

“I would be out of my mind. I would need you to be the one thinking straight, understand?”

Pabbi looked at Amma shaking in her chair. His eyes went to Bensi, then to his family. Pall stood red-faced beside his mother, mouth agape.

“All right,” J.K. said, clapping his hands to rally everyone the way he did the ball team. “We will start searching.”

The men broke into groups, marching off in all directions.

Olafur strode across the grass to Bensi. Bold as the devil, he thrust his chin out. “I know what you said about Freda and the girls,” he whispered through tight lips. “Watch a wolf long enough, and soon you learn his tricks. If you did anything to Freyja, I will kill you."

As I pay attention now, the one who surprises me most is Leifur. He does not utter one word. He just quietly studies Bensi and Pall.

It was so incredibly difficult to leave The Narrows that night. Mother and I almost wouldn't, but Pabbi insisted we follow Kent and Gudrun home to make sure Freyja wasn't there, while he and J.K. stayed behind with the rest of the men. As the sun set, we watched the men split up to begin combing the shoreline.

Before we left, Kent took Pabbi aside. "Edward Elliott is the police chief and a good friend of mine," he said. "I shall speak to him the moment we are in Winnipeg. I'm sure she will show up, but if not I will see to it that a constable is sent out to investigate."

"Thank you," Pabbi said.

"Send me a telegram."

"I will."

We were all in a state of disbelief. The whole way home we scanned the road, calling her name. Around every bend we expected to see her waiting.

"Look," Solrun said, "there she is!" Our hearts leapt, but as we came closer, we realized the shadow at the edge of the bush was a fallen tree. Our eyes played tricks on us the whole way.

Our last hope was that she'd boarded the steamship and got off at Kristjansson's dock. I prayed we'd find her at home. Knowing Freyja, she would be completely unaware of our worry.

"That would be just like her," I said as the house came into view, but Mother was so distraught she couldn't even reply.

I jumped off the wagon and ran to the door ahead of everyone. The house was quiet, exactly as we'd left it, except now it was stifling hot inside. I called her name, took the stairs two at a time, hoping that she was lying on the bed pouting. I pushed open the door, praying this would all be over.

CHAPTER THIRTY-FOUR

It is a long time before scorched ground grows again.
—FÓSTBROEÐRA SAGA

BULBS FLASHING. A CAMERA. I AM WIDE AWAKE.

It is so obvious now, the clue was right here all along. Solrun went home, so it is Lars who relaxes in the chair.

"Scrap . . . book," I say, startling him.

He spills coffee on his knee as he quickly stands up. I say it twice more before he hears correctly then picks it up. He opens the book. He wonders where to start.

I motion for him to crank the bed up because I cannot see lying down. I quickly grow impatient, clawing at his arm. "Please," I say, pointing at my spectacles.

He flexes them open and, careful not to poke my eyes, lets them rest on my nose. They are crooked, but I can still see the *Lögberg* masthead. July 1908. Below it is a full page of text and photos from the opening of The Narrows Hall. There is a photo of suffragist Margrét Benedictsson and a politician I no longer recognize, plus the ball team, everyone's name carefully typeset underneath.

"Later," I say, so Lars begins turning the pages, hesitating each time the paper's masthead runs across the top. Ball tournaments from July 1909. 1910. 1911. 1912. 1913. 1915. 1916. Wait. I drop my hand down to stop him. I motion to go back. The year Freyja disappeared is not here.

Now I remember. Pabbi put the unread papers straight into the stove in the months that followed. Not until the world outside his own became so large that he had no choice, did he open the papers again.

"Photo," I say. With no strength to explain, I close my eyes.

There were three grainy photos in *Lögberg,* early July 1914. I saw them, briefly, before waking up. The first is of the team cheering as they held Bjorn on their shoulders. The second shows them lined up, Asi holding the trophy, everyone grinning, unaware of the tragedy that would soon unfold. And there is a third, a little bit smaller, on an inside page, the image of an old woman sitting in a wheelchair under the shade of a tree, looking out over the water, taken from the back. Barely noticeable, off to the side stands a teenaged girl cooling her feet at the edge of the swirling water, hands delicately holding up her skirt, a man at her side.

* * *

Finn came the following evening. I should have been heartened to see him but wasn't. Amma was frustrated and bone tired from trying to make me understand something. Hours earlier, before preparing supper, I'd placed a book on her lap, laid a sheet on top, and crooked a pencil in her good hand. I was studying the paper when he came in. Solrun and Lars sat on my knees, as if holding me down so I wouldn't disappear, too.

"Can we go outside?" Finn asked.

I shook my head no and my eyes went back to the page. Of the eight scrawled images I counted, none were actual words.

I could see he felt silly right then, carrying the chessboard under his arm. He tried to hide it, setting it down behind the door.

"I would like to talk," he said. "About our future."

"Not now." I said. *Not ever,* is what I thought. What future? I could not imagine how I would get through the next day, never mind how I was going to escape from under the blanket of grief that was smothering our house.

I gave him credit for not giving up. It must have been hard to come so soon after it happened.

"Where is everybody?" he asked. He meant Pabbi and Leifur who'd arrived home late morning and were likely outside doing their best to exhaust themselves, to keep from thinking about what might have happened to her.

I shrugged.

Finn took the sheet and began trying to decipher Amma's puzzle. I left him to it, took the little ones upstairs to get them ready for bed, then did the same with Amma who was nearly asleep in her chair.

I pushed her past Mother silently rocking back and forth in the front room. She´d been sitting there since shortly after we arrived home and hadn't spoken a word.

Once Amma was comfortable in bed, head on the pillow, I gazed into her eyes.

"What is it Amma, what are you trying to tell us?"

She shook her head, tongue suffocating every word, as tears leaked down her temples.

Finn was still bent over the page when I returned.

"Do you think she saw something?" he asked.

I shrugged. Knowing Amma, anything could be written on that paper.

Finn must have reported what a sorry state we were in because the next day Gudrun arrived. She did not say a word, except "good morning," then set to work, pretending she couldn't hear Mother crying in the bedroom. Some women, when faced with crisis, dive into housework to distract themselves, but that was not Mother's way. Fortunately, it was Gudrun's. She whipped everything into shape and came back again two days later to do it all over again.

We mourned like that for a week, and while the days passed quickly, it felt like we'd been grieving for months. It is hard to say exactly when or if we ever stopped.

Losing Freyja wounded each one of us in a different way.

Pabbi felt it in his heart. It was obvious in the way he stood after that, shoulders slumped and chest caved in, a posture that became more pronounced whenever someone mentioned her name, as if by reflex his ribs were shielding his heart.

Leifur took it in the gut. You could see his instincts come alive, riling him to the point that he needed to do something—anything. He tackled next winter's wood supply all by himself. He hammered into the bush, pulling out the deadfall, then sawed each log into three foot lengths, splitting some of it, then, like a man possessed, piled it to the eaves along the lean-to wall.

Signy, well, she let her brain take care of it. She always was prone to reasoning everything out and, with the exception of letting herself fall in love with Olafur, her brain trumped her heart every time. She was the only one mad at Freyja, concluding that no matter what had happened, it was Freyja´s fault; therefore, anger was her response.

Losing Freyja was a cut to Mother's soul. Once she started speaking, I knew by the things she said that she believed fate was thrashing her again—first she'd lost her sister now her daughter.

For me, losing Freyja was hardest on my eyes. I saw everything differently after that.

One morning, as I hung out the laundry, Solrun and Lars came to ask, checking over their shoulders first, if it was possible the huldufólk had taken Freyja. I knelt down, pulling them close.

"There are no huldufólk here," I said. "But if there were, why would they take her?"

"She made Mama angry," Solrun said.

"Not everyone believes they exist," I said.

"Freyja does," Lars said. "She told us they live in the knoll by Bensi's and that we should stay away from there."

"You know Freyja has a wonderful imagination," I replied. "She wanted to tell you stories, just like Amma."

“Then where is she?” Solrun asked.

“She has gone away for a while.”

“When will she back?”

They both looked so hopeful that my eyes stung. “When she is ready.”

This seemed to satisfy them and since the rest of us never spoke our fears out loud, it didn’t occur to Solrun or Lars that Freyja might never return.

Signy arrived two days later right after dinner.

“Where are the men?” she asked.

“Out building a fence,” I said. “Between our place and Bensi’s.”

Rationally it made no sense, but none of us were thinking clearly.

She kissed Amma on the forehead then went in to see Mother. She asked how I was, but didn’t wait for the answer. I must have looked pathetic standing there with my arms wrapped around myself, hair still in the same frizzed out braid from the picnic.

“There is work to do,” she said.

That, I have to say, was the worst part. No matter what tragedy befell us, there was never time to stop, to forget about the chores and sit down to think. For some, work was like a salve; it kept a person from thinking too much. For those, like me, who could not stop the endless scenarios from rolling through my mind, the pressure of endless work had the power to drive a person crazy.

We bumped Amma outside so she could enjoy a bit of sun. Setta broke away from the children to come lie down in the grass beside her.

“What does Pabbi think happened?” Signy asked as we each picked up a scythe and began cutting the tall grass around the house. “Did he send for the police?”

“On Tuesday.”

“And Leifur?”

“Hasn’t said a word.”

“Olafur doesn’t think Bensi did anything,” she said with a sideways glance. “I agree.”

I chuckled to myself. Those two thought they knew everything.

"He didn't see deception in Bensi's eyes," she said. "Olafur understands people."

I was in no mood to quarrel. I'd regretted not telling Pabbi that Bensi had been in our house, so I'd told Leifur the day after the picnic. He hadn't replied, just continued splitting wood as if I wasn't even there.

"So what happened to her then?" I asked, taking a break to catch my breath.

Signy leaned heavy against the scythe handle. "She must have run away."

"Never," I said, swinging it again, chopping the curved knife blade through the grass. "Where would she go? She had no money. And what about Stefan? She would never leave him. Leave by boat? Someone would have seen her. No, she either got lost in the bush or . . ."

Signy turned to listen, waiting for me to finish.

When I closed my eyes, I felt the steady rhythm of my heart. The nightmare was vivid, Freyja's terror so real. That morning I'd jolted awake, heart aching. It had knocked me off balance and I still felt that way. I couldn't tell Signy what I saw every time I closed my eyes.

"Someone took her," I rasped.

"Who?" Signy was not easily deterred. She'd given this considerable thought and had come to a few conclusions I hadn't even considered. "Did she meet anyone in Winnipeg? Someone she wanted to visit?" she asked, appearing so sure of herself she looked almost satisfied.

I shook my head.

"Olafur doesn't like Stanley," she said. "Thinks he is strange."

I knew this was the reason she'd come, to tell me what the two of them had discussed long into the night.

"Too intelligent," she said. "Don't you agree?"

I did. It was hard to admit that I wasn't particularly fond of my fiancé's closest friend. The night I'd met him he'd made me uneasy; he couldn't take his eyes off Freyja; how convenient it would have been for him to slip away during the game. He'd stood so quietly after the picnic, almost invisible between his parents, watching as fearful possibilities flew all around him.

"You think Stanley?" I asked.

She shrugged.

"Leifur and I are certain," I said, swinging the scythe hard, "that Bensi or Pall . . . you know Pall, always trying to lift up the girls' skirts."

Signy thought for a few moments then shook her head. "All Freyja could talk about was living in Winnipeg," she said. "I am convinced she ran away, perhaps with Stanley, and will come home when we least expect it. You'll see."

It was difficult to get on with our lives after that.

Bergthora and Magnus hugged me hard that first day back to work. Bjorn hung around the store all day, asking what I needed, rushing ahead to lift anything that had a bit of weight to it. He hovered near the counter, waiting to talk, but I had nothing to say. Before I left, he put his hand on my shoulder.

"I know how you feel," he said.

"Nobody knows how I feel," I said.

The memory of Pabbi sitting under the tree the night before was still fresh. I'd gone to sit with him. An hour passed before he turned to me. He looked like a man defeated.

"I would rather have found her dead that first night," he said.

It was a painfully selfish thing to admit.

Then I wondered: What is worse? To watch your brothers drown in front of you, helpless to save them; or to have a loved one disappear, to live with gut-wrenching uncertainty?

Bjorn was trying to offer solace. I shouldn't have reacted the way I did. We could debate whose suffering was worse for years, but all it would do was rip our hearts open time and again.

He easily forgave me, even apologized. He said that I was right. He didn't know how I felt.

Two weeks after Freyja disappeared, Mother decided that we should go to church. To pray. None of us felt ready to leave the cloister of home, but it was such a relief to hear her finally speak, that we agreed.

Everyone except Leifur. There was a ball tournament in Kinosota. “The team needs me,” he said.

Normally, Mother would have argued that we needed him too, but there was no fight left in her. “Be careful,” was all she said.

We rode by wagon to Hayland while he caught Lady Ellen across the lake to Kinosota. We arrived at the church the same time as Bensi and his family.

“Why do they even come here?” I asked. “He does not share our beliefs.”

Mother sighed as Pabbi pushed on the wagon brake. Olafur was waiting outside and waved us over. Pabbi told us to go inside so he could speak to Olafur alone.

It was obvious that Gudrun had told everyone that Freyja was not yet found since no one asked. Likely they all had opinions but thankfully kept their thoughts to themselves. Pabbi and Olafur came in and sat at the end of our pew. Whatever it was Olafur had said had Pabbi thinking hard.

Not long after the service began, there was faint whispering and mumbling at the back of the church. We all turned in our seats. Olafur’s father Oli got up from the last pew and went to open the door.

“Fire,” he said, eyes wide.

Instantly we all smelled the heavy, acrid smoke that blew in from across the prairie. Miles away, in the direction of home, smoke billowed up over the trees. The men scattered, quickly hitching the teams, as their wives gathered up the children. Forming a long line, we raced across the prairie toward the smoke, which now looked like it was coming from our farm. It’s so difficult to judge fire from a distance, it never ends up being where you think.

A mile from home it became clear that the fire was either at J.K.’s or Bensi’s. Petra and Pall held on for dear life as Bensi drove his horses like a wild man across the hayfield.

Somehow his sheep had managed to escape and were snaking along the creek in a long line, their walnut brains fixed on reaching the road. Pabbi slowed so Solrun and Lars could jump down to herd the sheep while we carried on. When we caught up to J.K. and Gudrun, tears of relief were streaming down her cheeks.

This was one of the few blessings God gave us that year.

The Thorsteinsson brothers all yelled wildly, the two oldest spurring their horses ahead. Olafur drove his team beside us, pointing and hollering, "We will start a burn."

The neighbors crossed the bridge over the creek, then turned onto Magnus's land. Likely the fire wouldn't jump the creek but they would stand guard, just in case.

"I will get shovels," J.K. said as he drove his team home.

The men jumped from the wagons while the women continued on, taking the children away from the smoke. Bensi drove his family as close as he dared. He jumped down but stood paralyzed on the lane. The fire burned furiously in the center of the bush, licking its way steadily away from the lake, toward the hayfield.

Mother turned our wagon and drove to Bensi's family. They were watching helplessly as their home burned.

"Petra," I hollered, coughing through the smoke. For a moment it looked like she might stay with her parents and brother, but then turned and ran to our wagon. My heart softened as I reached down and took her trembling hand, pulling her up.

Pabbi and Leifur had spent years clearing bush, turning up ground. At least two hundred feet of black dirt sat between our bush and the fire, and Pabbi's new fence—the symbolic line in the sand that he had finally drawn— needed saving.

To keep the fire from spreading, Olafur and his brothers lit the brush bordering J.K.'s land, letting it burn in a six-foot swath, stomping it out as it crept along. They also set another fire ten feet wide on Bensi's hay land, to keep the fire from building momentum as it burned to the north. J.K. brought shovels, buckets and grain sacks to pound out the flames.

Years later, when we recalled that awful, fateful day, Olafur always concluded that luck had been on our side. It was a cool, overcast day and soon after the controlled burn was out, the breeze shifted and came from the northwest. Billowing gray clouds materialized, darkening as they came toward us. It started to rain. Lightly at first, then torrentially, lasting an hour.

But before the rain, as the fire grew, preventing Bensi from getting close enough to salvage anything from his farm, he came raging across his hayfield at Pabbi who was pounding out sparks threatening his fence.

"How could you do this to me?" he screamed. "You of all people."

Pabbi paused, his face black with soot and sweat. He was not a hard-hearted man, but on that day he looked satisfied. He lifted the shovel and pointed it at Bensi.

"You did this to yourself."

CHAPTER THIRTY-FIVE

One evil is mended by a worse one.
—GRETTIR'S SAGA

PABBI STAYED UP THAT NIGHT WAITING FOR LEIFUR, ONCE AGAIN worried about rough weather on the lake. I awoke to Setta's bark and heard the lean-to door close. I went quietly downstairs to find Pabbi and Leifur sitting at the table.

"The barn *and* the house?" Leifur said.

Pabbi studied him carefully.

They each waited for the other to say something, but neither did.

When it came time for me to leave for the store the next morning, Pabbi handed me a piece of paper. It was another telegram to Kent. This time I opened it and read it out loud:

"My son-in-law changed my mind. No point sending the police. Thank you. Pjetur Guðmundsson."

"But why, Pabbi?" I asked.

"Because," he said. "Bensi has finally received his just desserts."

At night, my thoughts wouldn't leave me alone.

Even worse than lying awake, keeping the nightmares at bay, were times during the day that I momentarily forgot Freyja was missing. I'd almost call out to her, turn, but she was never there. I couldn't laugh without feeling guilt, could barely smile. Finn saw all of this and, after a month had passed, said quietly that I needed to snap out of it. He wasn't trying to be cruel, but his words felt like a knife to the heart.

Every day I walked to the store, unaware of what went on around me. I did not know how long the days were, what the weather had been yesterday or even what day it was. I walked ghost-like through the whole month of July.

"Hello," I'd say to customers and they would reply, but our conversation ended there. Nothing mattered anymore. Bjorn would come in, stand for a while, but then leave when I didn't look up from the ledger. Sometimes I'd stare out the window for hours on end.

Three days before Finn was to leave to begin his new job in Winnipeg, he picked me up at the store.

"Congratulations," Bjorn said, shaking Finn's hand. "Asta tells me your job is with a top firm in the city. Your father must be proud."

Finn was in an incredibly good mood. "I am anxious to get started," he said. "Have you decided what you are going to do?"

Puzzled, Bjorn looked at Finn then at me. He shrugged and waited for one of us to explain.

"When Asta leaves," Finn said. "Once I am settled in the city we are going to get married."

Bjorn blinked quickly but didn't look away, though his cheeks began to flush. I could feel his hurt as he cleared his throat, pretending that he'd known, even though I hadn't told him or anyone else about our engagement.

"I suppose I will have to find someone else," he said.

Finn was sincere when he said: "It shouldn't be too difficult finding someone to work in a store."

Bjorn saw me flinch and we both narrowed our eyes.

"You are right," he said. "But finding someone as competent as Asta . . . I hate to see her go."

Without a word I followed Finn to the democrat. The longer I thought about what he'd said, the harder my blood boiled. We were halfway home and I couldn't stand his cheerful chatter any longer.

"How could you say that?" I asked.

"What?" he asked, looking across the seat at me.

"To Bjorn," I said. "Do you really think that my work is unimportant?"

"I didn't say that," he said.

"That is how it sounded," I said. "I happen to find it very satisfying work, but you wouldn't know because you've never asked me."

Finn was incredulous. "I am not asking you? I have nothing to say? It is you who refuses to talk to me."

"That's not true."

"It is. You are right, but I will not apologize for my belief that clerking is beneath you. Truth be told, you should be at the University, training to be a doctor."

More silence.

"You didn't tell him, did you?" he said, and when I didn't reply, "I have always thought there was something between the two of you."

"This has nothing to do with Bjorn," I said.

"Then what is it?" he asked, pulling the horses to a stop. "Every time I try to discuss our future, you refuse. I am beginning to think we don't have one."

I covered my face with my hands.

"Asta, what is it?" he said softly, reaching across to rest his hand on my knee.

"I cannot bear the thought of telling Mama and Pabbi that I am leaving," I said. "How can I go now?"

"They will manage."

"They are devastated. Can't you see that?"

He sighed. "Father says—"

"I don't care what your father says," I hissed. "I care about how mine *feels*. First Amma, then Solrun—Freyja—and now me?"

He withdrew his hand and began rubbing his face. "But I said I would pay for a nurse."

"I appreciate that, I really do. But they need me right now."

"More than I do?"

I couldn't answer.

"It's been four long years," he said, slapping the reins. The horses jolted forward. "I have been patient but can't wait much longer."

I rolled the conversation over in my mind and imagined he was doing the same. Gudrun had invited my family for supper so I wasn't surprised to see all was quiet at home as we rode by. Finn seemed lighter having voiced his thoughts, but I wasn't sure if what he'd said was an ultimatum. Mind still churning, I followed him up onto the verandah. We could see through the front window everyone sitting in the front room. It struck me as odd. They were all huddled around J.K.'s crystal set.

"Shhh," they chorused over their shoulders as we came in.

J.K. sat closest to it, leaning forward with his elbows resting on his knees, ear attached to a wire headphone. I'll never forget his expression as he turned and his eyes met Pabbi's. The creases in his forehead were pronounced, his eyebrows furrowed. His hair stuck straight up the same as it did when he coached hardball.

Gudrun motioned for us to sit down.

"What is it?" Finn asked.

"Shhhh." J.K. held up his finger for us to wait, then began translating what Sir Wilfred Laurier, leader of the Liberal party, was saying over the airwaves into his ear:

"It is our duty . . . to let Great Britain know . . . and to let the friends and foes . . . of Great Britain know . . . that there is in Canada but one mind . . . and one heart . . . and that all Canadians are behind the Mother Country."

When J.K. removed the earpiece his hand ran from his forehead all the way back to his neck.

"My God," Pabbi said. "We are at war."

Finn left as planned two days later. I told him that I would follow soon, but we both knew I wasn't ready to leave.

For the rest of my life, whenever I've thought of Finn I've remembered him that day, how he stood waving from the back of the democrat as his father took him down the road to the train. It was the wistful hopefulness in his expression that I'll never forget; his youth and naiveté.

And in the moment that he and J.K. faded from sight, I was overcome by the all too familiar feeling that my heart would be broken all over again.

Three weeks later, I received a letter:

August 15, 1914
Dearest Ásta,

I am so excited I do not even know how to begin.

The job did not turn out as planned. The war announcement halted everything and plans to construct the new store for the Hudson's Bay Company were put on hold, so I was terminated before I even began.

The Burroughs were generous enough to allow me stay with them. Stanley was in the same predicament as I. We were job searching and found ourselves in the middle of a rally. It was a most incredible thing to witness. People marching in the streets, cheering, and so many speeches. The 90th Winnipeg Rifles were in full uniform and hundreds of civilians (that is what they call anyone not in the military) joined in behind. Stanley and I followed the march that ended at City Hall. A recruitment officer offered us a fair wage. We decided we had nothing to lose so I am proud to say we are now members of the 90th Winnipeg Rifles.

Kent is thrilled. He said it is our duty to fight for our country. He has rejoined as well and will resume his duties as a Captain. Elizabeth sent a telegram to her brother asking he watch out for us. I hope that he does not find us desk jobs because that doesn't sound very exciting.

So now I must ask you once again - will you wait for me?

Kent believes the war will be short. I expect to be back by springtime. Once the war is over, life will return to normal in Winnipeg. Everyone says so. I will contact the firm again or find a job elsewhere.

By then, I hope you will be ready to move to Winnipeg and we can begin our lives together. If you would rather work in a store than be a nurse, tell me so. I will not think less of you; in fact, I now realize that being a merchant takes considerable skill. All I want is what is best for you.

I apologize for not being more understanding about Freyja. I honestly cannot imagine how you feel, only know that it is my love that clouds my thinking. Please forgive me and remember that no one will ever love you the way I do.

Forever in my heart, Finn

Oh what a foolish girl I was! So relieved that Finn's love for me was still strong, I burst into joyous laughter. I read the letter out loud to everyone the moment I arrived home. When I looked up from the page, Mother and Pabbi's jaws were slack.

"You," Mother said, pointing a finger immediately at Leifur, "will not even consider it."

Leifur opened his mouth, but before even one word escaped, Pabbi stood up. "Under no circumstances."

"But—"

"Not another word," Pabbi said. "My son will not go off to war and get himself killed."

Mother's voice started to shake. "How could Finn make such a foolish decision? He is such a bright, promising young man."

It took a few moments for me to recover from the shock of their reaction.

Mother began pacing. "Poor Gudrun. What will J.K. think?"

"The same as I do," Pabbi growled. "That this is Kent's doing."

Up until that point in our lives, Leifur and I had found little reason to disagree with our parents, but on this issue, I believe, he and I were of the same mind. Later that evening, after Lars and Solrun were asleep, I tiptoed to his room. He was sitting up in bed reading by lamplight.

"I wish now that I had kept it to myself," I whispered.

Leifur shrugged. “They would have found out soon enough.”

“What do you think about Finn enlisting?”

Leifur flinched as he closed the book. I wanted desperately for him to say that he believed Finn would return home safely, but he seemed as apprehensive as Pabbi.

“Why does everyone believe he is incompetent?” I asked.

Leifur sighed. “Finn belongs behind a desk,” he said, adding it felt wrong that he should stay home while others went off to fight. There were other young men from the community who were going to enlist and Leifur wanted to go with them.

“Do you think Olafur will sign up?” he asked.

“He would never leave Signy.”

“Finn left you,” he said.

His words stung. “They are married and have children,” I said, but I knew deep inside that Signy was more to Olafur than just his wife, she was his whole life.

Believing Finn wouldn’t have enlisted had I promised to go to Winnipeg, I came to blame myself for everything that happened afterwards. But that night, while standing in Leifur’s bedroom I said something I’d never regret.

“You can’t go,” I said. “Pabbi needs you.”

As far removed as we were from the battlefields in Europe, the war wrapped itself around us, doing its best to weigh down every thought and conversation. It took great discipline for Pabbi to not go to J.K.’s daily to listen to the crystal set. Instead, he waited until Thora arrived every morning to care for Amma, then grilled her about what they’d heard the night before.

He waited impatiently for *Lögberg* to arrive and, even though the news was dated, the editor was thorough, providing tremendous insight into the war. This prompted Pabbi to write letters to the editor; and to renew Amma’s subscription to *Heimskringla* so that he could also read an opposing view.

Bjorn was behind the counter one morning when I pushed open the door, the bell quietly jingling behind me. He was fiddling with the cash register he'd bought second-hand the week before and had it over on its side with the back plate off.

"Can you sort the mail today?" he asked. "Bergthora is not well."

"Of course," I said. She could no longer keep up with the daily chores. They'd hired the Sveistrup girl to replace Freyja, but she only worked three days a week. Not a day went by that I wasn't reminded Freyja was gone, even though nobody ever mentioned her name.

"All they talk about is the war," I said. "It is like she never even existed."

By then Bjorn had grown accustomed to my outbursts.

"I know, it is the same with Siggi and Arn." He sighed, pressing the cash drawer button. It was sticking, no doubt the reason the previous owner had decided to sell it. Like Magnus, Bjorn believed that everything could be fixed.

"The way they were found, with Siggi tied to Arn's back, that is all people remember about them," he said, jimmying the workings with thin-nosed pliers. "At least you still have hope. Have you heard from Finn again?"

"You know I haven't," I said.

He shrugged. "I spoke to J.K. the other day. He is more worried than he lets on."

I recalled the first time I saw him after receiving the letter, his pained expression and the forced optimism in his voice. He said he was confident Finn would return home safely, but his words after that were less so. Gudrun finally asked him to discuss something else, so we did for a while, but the conversation always wound back to where it started.

"Of course there is hope," I said, glancing out the window. Stefan was in the yard with the mail bag slung over his shoulder. I reached for the door handle. "Finn is brave and resourceful."

"Asta," Bjorn said, looking up from the cash register. "I wasn't talking about Finn. Freyja must have ran away, and once she realizes her mistake, she will come home."

The sun shone in through the window brightening his face. He looked hopeful, eyes warm. Seeing him like that jarred my insides, tugging at that place in my heart where I'd tucked all those old feelings. I'd made my choice. But when it came to Freyja, Bjorn understood me in a way Finn never could.

In the kitchen Stefan slipped the bag off his shoulder. He seemed surprised, almost embarrassed, to see me. One would think our common love for Freyja would have united us, but it didn't. I had a fleeting thought that Stefan may not have loved Freyja as much as we believed.

When he turned to leave I told him what Bjorn had said. He froze on the spot, not daring to look up from the floor.

"Do you think she ran away?" I asked.

He told me again about their argument, his refusal to go to Winnipeg and Freyja's humiliation. She'd run off crying when he'd said he no longer wanted to be her beau.

"This is all my fault, I never should have pushed her away," he said. "But if she is still . . . alive . . . then why hasn't she contacted anyone?"

I could see something inside him was broken. None of it, I told him, made any sense.

"At night do you dream?" I asked.

"Always."

The kitchen fell silent.

"The dreams are all similar," he whispered. "She is trying to tell me something important. She wants to come home but cannot get here."

"Then she is still alive?" I said.

"I'm not sure. My sister is always with her and that doesn't give me much hope."

September arrived, my second favorite month of the year. Outside, the oak leaves had faded to orange and brown—last to bud in the spring, first to fall in autumn. The post office smelled of stale paper and ink while outside the sharp tang of wood smoke was everywhere, so clear it bit the inside of your nose. You could feel winter coming as the days grew short. The sky was pale blue, interrupted by the good-byes of the geese as they skimmed overhead. The midday sun still had some heat to it, but as soon as it dropped behind the trees the warmth fell out of the air.

I was busy sorting mail one morning when a voice caused me to look up. Petra was standing in the doorway looking sad as ever. She apologized for interrupting.

"We are leaving today," she said.

This came as no surprise since they'd been living in a tent since the fire. Rumors had been circulating for weeks.

"I'm sorry to hear that," I lied, relief washing over me. It would be nice to live without the shadow of Bensi's loathing hanging over us. She studied me for a few moments.

"Where are you going?" I asked.

"Papa wants to return to North Dakota," she said. "He does not agree with Canada's decision to support Britain. He thinks the Americans have their heads screwed on straight, at least when it comes to the war."

I chuckled to myself. On that point he and Pabbi agreed.

"Do we have any mail?" she asked.

I pulled a letter from their box, wrapping it into the fold of *Heimskringla*. "Something to read along the way."

She sighed as she took it. "Papa is paying his bill. He did not want anyone to say he left behind a debt," she said, catching herself. "But I mean no offence."

Pabbi's secret was long forgotten by then. Petra seemed relieved that my expression did not change, but then she scrunched her eyes. "My papa believes your father lit the fire."

Her honesty caught me off guard. "He is wrong," I said.

"I know," she added quickly. "He can be—"

"Difficult?"

She sighed.

"Well my brother is convinced your brother or father is responsible for Freyja's disappearance," I said. "And I believe this too."

"You're all wrong," she said as she looked around the kitchen to be sure no one was listening. Her mood shifted and she leaned over the counter, lowering her voice.

"There is something I've been meaning to tell you," she said. "It is about Freyja."

My heart skipped, then rose up into my throat, and my first impulse was to lunge forward, grab her by the shoulders and shake her, but I held back and waited.

"I overheard Papa telling Pall that he saw Freyja on the steamer," she said.

"He saw Freyja leave?"

Petra nodded.

"Why didn't he say something that night?"

"He was afraid."

"Of what?"

Petra hesitated. "That Mother would find out he was on the steamer, too."

My mind was reeling by then. "Are you sure?"

Petra nodded. "I saw him. He snuck away with a woman from across the lake," she said. Her words came out fast as they do when a person makes a confession. "He was gone for hours . . . but couldn't tell anyone."

I was so shocked I could barely think.

"Was Freyja alone?"

"He didn't say."

Petra stared off, losing herself, then her eyes became soft, full of sadness. "Freyja was my only friend. I really wish I knew what happened to her."

It all began knitting together; Petra's silence that night, Bensi's pleas, Olafur's gut feeling.

"I have to go," she said.

"One more thing," I asked. "What happened to your step-sisters?"

She laughed under her breath. "They hated him because he wasn't their father. One day they ran off. They write to Mother. A letter came last week."

She backed away then hurried through the kitchen, pausing as she grasped the door knob. She looked back at me, wanting to say something else.

"What is it?" I asked.

"You don't know, do you?"

I could not even guess what she might say next.

"My papa was two years old when his mother left," she said. "Your Amma married his father, Soli, and raised him until she kicked Soli out. Papa never forgave her, not until the stroke."

I was flabbergasted.

"Our fathers are half brothers?"

She nodded, expression softening.

"We are cousins," she said. "When you find Freyja, tell her I say hello."

That was the last time I ever saw Petra Solmundsson.

CHAPTER THIRTY-SIX

Better to fight and fall than live without hope.
—VÖLSUNGA SAGA

CONFIDENTLY, I TOOK THORA'S HAND, LEADING HER THROUGH THE throng, pretending to be brave. Instinct told me to follow the jostling people away from the trains rattling the tracks, far from the sound of steam whistles and porters yelling over the noise on the platform.

By then I was exhausted, having played over and over again the tears and good-byes. It was the first time either of us had ridden a train so we were excited. We felt like sophisticates. But the farther it snaked south, the quieter we became. Thora and I stared wordlessly out the window that last hour, thinking about home.

A little more than a week had passed since Petra's revelation that Pabbi and Bensi were half-brothers. That day it had taken me a long while to reign in my thoughts enough to finish sorting the mail. One of the last letters I'd pulled from the bag was from the Winnipeg General Hospital addressed to me.

I'd watched for Bjorn through the post office window then called him to the little room when he came in for dinner. Petra's words came tumbling out of me in an excited, harsh whisper. He'd asked me to slow down, to explain it all again.

"How can you be sure she isn't lying?" he whispered back.

We could hear Magnus banging around in the kitchen and Bergthora croaking from her room for him to stop—that she was coming.

After I told him about Bensi's woman from across the lake, he pieced it all together the same way I had. I waited. Then I showed my acceptance letter. I knew in my heart what I needed to do.

"You have to go find her," he said. "I will come with you."

It was knee-jerk and noble, but we both knew it was impossible for him to get away. Instead, we hatched a plan over dinner.

That evening at home, after Thora left, I wheeled Amma into the front room and looked deep into her eyes.

"Did Freyja get on the steamer?" I whispered.

I was certain her good eye widened, grew brighter.

"I am going to find her," I said, bringing my finger to my lips.

Amma clutched my arm, digging her fingernails deep. I think she may have even said "yes."

Initially I told no one except Bjorn that my plan would include a search for Freyja. When I sat my parents down to tell them I'd been accepted and had decided to take my nurse training after all, both looked disheartened.

"I have it all arranged," I said. "Magnus has hired a private nurse for Bergthora and has offered for Amma to go live there. "She will receive better care than we can give."

We all looked at Amma, who rocked back and forth, a signal that she agreed.

According to the letter, in exchange for on-the-job training, I'd receive room and board. My only expense would be books, the required uniform and sundry items.

"It is not the expense that concerns us," Pabbi said.

Mother looked as though she might cry. The image of Freyja's surprised smiling face on the day I'd find her helped steady my resolve. I told them I'd made up my mind.

On the day before I left, I was upstairs packing my freshly laundered clothes in the same duffel Amma had carried from Iceland, when I turned to see Mother standing in the doorway.

"Please stay," she said.

We'd moved Amma to Magnus's house the prior morning. Solrun and Lars were at school. Pabbi and Leifur were doing chores. Everything was quiet and I felt the loneliness floating through the house.

"I am going to find Freyja," I said.

Mother brought a hand to her mouth; her head tilted ever so slightly. She listened in rapt silence, nods barely perceptible, as I told her about the conversation with Petra.

"Bjorn and Amma are the only ones who know my plan," I said.

She didn't reply right away as she weighed the possibility.

"It makes sense," she finally said, looking around the room, a renewed brightness springing to her eyes. She sighed, heavy with relief, bent forward; then she slapped her knees and laughed a little bit.

"Petra told me something I find hard to believe," I said.

Mother became alert, waiting for me to say more. When I didn't she sighed. "Your Pabbi didn't want you children to know."

"Why not?"

"As a youngster he idolized Bensi," she explained. "Bensi was four years older. Pabbi missed him terribly after Soli left. They didn't see each other after that, until they were grown."

She went on to say that Pabbi had trusted Bensi until he'd been deceived by him in the lumber deal. Pabbi was devastated and it took years for him to get over it. He was so humiliated that he declared Bensi no longer his brother.

"Pabbi believed when we moved here that he'd never see him again," she said. "They hadn't spoken in years."

Not wanting to raise everyone's hopes, we decided it best not to tell anyone else my plan to find Freyja. Knowing I had her blessing and that she'd find the words to soothe Pabbi, it was easier to look him in the eye when it came time to say good-bye.

"You will make a fine nurse," he said, lifting the duffel from the wagon, carrying it to the platform. "Take care, elskan."

Mother stood in silence and I knew her sentiments were the same, but also that her hopes hung on me for a different reason.

Thora and I had boarded the train. I pressed my forehead against the window, looking back to see Mother's palms together in prayer. Pabbi waved, his expression the same as that morning I'd ridden away with Bergthora to Siglunes.

Now here we were, following closely behind a stranger wearing a long overcoat, along a plank walkway away from the station onto the street. It was nearly dark and snow fell frivolously, dusting the hard-packed ground.

"Father said we need to hire someone to take us," Thora said nervously.

Bjorn, too, had offered plenty of advice. He'd told me about the many ways we could travel the city; warned me about strangers, to beware of pickpockets and thieves. Look confident, he'd said.

I patted my breast pocket. The money I'd need to carry me through the year was still there. A small democrat and horse was parked on the street. I threw up my hand to catch the attention of the driver who sat hunched, waiting, with his collar up, newspaper on his lap.

"How much to the General Hospital Nursing residence?" I asked.

"Nurses, aye?" he said with a heavy accent. He motioned over his shoulder for us to climb in.

I waited for him to name a price, asked him to repeat it, then nervously counted out the coins jangling in my mitten.

"Should be a Scot by the way you're handlin' those coins," he chuckled, dropping them in his hip pocket. "But I can tell ya ain't."

As the carriage traversed the mud-packed streets, Thora and I broke our rule to speak only English while in Winnipeg. We couldn't find the words fast enough to describe everything in this foreign place. Motorized cars sped by and trollies scuttled down the street like giant centipedes. Buildings loomed overhead, each one so tall it was impossible to imagine what sort of businesses might be housed there. Had you told me that, by the time my training was done, I'd know all of those corners by both sight and name, I would never have believed it.

"Goolies?" the driver asked, glancing over his shoulder.

Neither of us answered. He looked back raising his eyebrows.

"Not surprised, aye." He chuckled again as he turned onto McDermot Avenue. "Ya can smell each other from a mile away."

Thora and I were stunned. I'd double wrapped the harðfiskur before putting it in my bag.

Seeing my embarrassment—and Thora's fear—he laughed. "Nay, ladies, I meant to say that where yar goin', 'tis where all yar kin live. 'Tis like that here, ya know. The frogs 'cross the river, the chinks over there," he said pointing. "My kin, we lives on the other side of the tracks, with the Scots. Ya think there ain't no difference between the Irish and the Scots but there is."

It wasn't until the hospital came into view that either of us relaxed. It is a shame we were so unhinged. I remember little else of that first ride, as pleasant or terrifying as it may have been.

"'Tis Emily Street," he said as he halted the horse. "Here's a little tip. If ever ya need help, just say yar a nurse. Everybody loves the nurses. Blokes will double over backwards to help ya, 'specially now with the war."

Three young women stood on the sidewalk shivering in the cold, sharing a cigarette. They snickered as we climbed out of the democrat. We stood for a moment unsure where to go.

"The Superintendent's office is inside to the right," one of the girls said, taking pity on us. Then a car carrying two young men pulled up. The girl holding the cigarette flicked it to the ground then stomped on it. They hurried past us, giggling, climbed in then sped away.

The moment we stepped inside, Thora pulled on my jacket sleeve.

"Look at this place," she whispered. "It's beautiful."

We took in the ornate wood trim, glass-paned interior doors, brocade carpet, stuffed chairs, and side tables. A piano sat in the corner back-dropped by a wall of windows.

A door opened and a woman came out. She smiled, but only for a moment, then her eyes ran the full length of us, settling back on our faces. She introduced herself as the Superintendent of Nursing, Miss Mabel Gray.

"Come in," she said, turning back into the office.

She asked our names then thumbed through a stack of folders on her desk. She opened one and I recognized Thora's handwriting on the application form. Pabbi's letter of recommendation was peeking out from underneath.

"Thora Krist-jans-son?"

Thora timidly raised her hand.

Then eyeing the other folder. "And Ast—?"

"Ástfriður," I said. "In English they say 'Asta.'"

"Ow-sta?"

I nodded.

"Why did neither of you send a letter from your clergy?"

This surprised both of us. Being of sound character was something we took for granted.

"Our Pastor arrived only recently," I said. "It would have been misleading to send a recommendation from someone who does not know us well."

She tilted her head and raised one eyebrow ever so slightly.

"The results of your provincial exams show outstanding scores," she said. "Especially you, Ow-sta."

"We have exceptional teachers at Siglunes."

This answer seemed to please her. "Your English is better than I had expected. Foreign girls often grow so homesick they quit. Any chance of that happening with either of you?"

"No, ma'am," I said.

She turned to Thora, who looked like a surprised deer. She quickly shook her head.

"Good," Miss Gray said. "I expect from you both the same level of achievement here as you accomplished at home, understand?"

"Of course," I said.

"Come with me."

We followed her out of the office, up the oak staircase.

"No young men allowed. No smoking or horseplay. Temperance and discipline is a nurse's life and anyone who breaks those rules will be immediately dismissed."

Our room was on the third floor at the end of a hallway lined with doors. Some were propped open with a wedge, letting out the quiet conversations of the girls inside.

"There are no locks," she said, turning the knob then pushing it open. "Thievery is not tolerated."

She flipped a switch and the room lit up.

The room was long and narrow, with white plastered walls. It contained a desk, two chairs, closet space and two steel-framed beds side by side under a small window.

"You will share the water closet and bathing facilities down the hall with a dozen other first year students," she said. "Cleanliness is of utmost importance. That and punctuality. Breakfast is at 6:00 a.m. Classes begin at 7:00 a.m. Do not be late."

"Thank you," we chorused, still holding our duffels.

"I assume you are both Lutheran?" She did not wait for a reply. "Your church is a few blocks from here. Tomorrow is Sunday, your only free day. I expect you will make good use of your spare time. We have a list of volunteer work and I am confident you will find something to your liking. Any questions?"

We shook our heads.

"You know where to find me if you do," she said. "Good night."

We stood in silence, listening to her heavy heels marching down the hall, thinking exactly the same thing. When our eyes met, I reached out to turn the light off, plunging the room in darkness. Then I turned it on again.

Electric power. Mother had described the wonder of it after her stay with the Burroughs, but this was so magical it was beyond imagination.

I awoke early the next morning and, while Thora slept, finished writing the letter I'd started the day before Petra came into the post office:

September 22, 1914

Dearest Finn,

It has been just over month and already I miss you terribly. I am so very proud of you even though I understand little about this war.

Have you seen Jack? And the Larson boys? They enlisted days after you. I hope that the army is sensible enough to put the four of you in the same unit. You can look out for one another that way. From what I hear, the Germans are heartless. Do your best to stay away from them. Do not be afraid to use your gun and run if you have to.

The store is busy today, but I've stolen a few minutes to write. Björn thinks that Bensi will leave Siglunes since he has not yet ordered lumber to rebuild.

October 3, 1914

I am sorry it has taken me so long to finish this letter. Once I explain, I think you will understand why. I have news that I believe will please you. Thora and I are in Winnipeg, about to start our training. It was a last minute decision. We arrived in the city last night and it is everything you described. I am especially thrilled with the electric power. I am writing from my bed as there is a lamp over it that turns on and off with a switch. What a luxury.

Today we will explore the city. It is a good thing I am here. Thora would not have managed very well on her own.

That is all for now. I will write again once classes have started. Make note of the hospital's address as I have written it on the envelope.

Lovingly yours, Ástfriður.

P.S. Did you know that they call us 'Goolies' here in Winnipeg? What in God's name does it mean?

The niggling feeling that I was about to embark on the impossible crept in that morning. Thora and I stood on the street corner after breakfast, deciding which way to go. She had no idea what I was looking for and I was at a loss where to find it.

"We should go to the church," I said.

A nurse came down the steps and pointed us in the direction. "At the corner, on Victor Street."

It was a beautiful, crisp morning. Everything was covered in frost, already melting in places where the sun shone brightly. I was excited by the possibility that Freyja was somewhere here. It was a reflex to search every face that passed, peer around every corner and look through every door.

We spent the entire day walking. We stopped briefly at the church, made mental notes of the landmarks, street names, and even handed the streetcar driver a few coins, then rode it as far as it would take us and back again. The smell of fried meat and onions lured us into a little café on Main Street, and we nervously ordered from a printed menu for the first time.

"It's so noisy," Thora said, over the sound of dishes being stacked in the kitchen. The roar of passing motorcars rushed in every time the door opened. And voices, so many voices, as pedestrians greeted one another on the street. Trains whistled, and each time one passed, the café floor rumbled.

What I also noticed were the smells. Coal and oil, damp dirt, the faint whiff of sewage—all layered to create a scent so different than home. In the years to come, that is what I would miss most about Siglunes, the pure air and, of course, the water—both would remain untouched by civilization for the rest of our lives.

"We should go visit Elizabeth," I said, grabbing Thora by the hand. Mother had told me the address and how to get there. We hurried across the street between passing motorcars. A man waved at us cheerily, as did a fellow driving a democrat. We followed the streets that wound along the river, then paused for a few moments to regain our bearings.

"Armstrong's Point?" I asked a man who came toward us. "Can you tell us where it is?"

He pointed and we hurried in that direction, passing by homes that became increasingly stately the farther we walked down a street called Middle Gate. It was unbelievable to see so many homes that were more beautiful than the castle at Siglunes. These mansions were numbered sequentially and after only a few blocks we were there.

We hesitated at the end of the long drive, a lovely elm blocking our view of the brick house set a distance away from the street, backing quietly, as Mother had described, onto the river. It had a most unusual roof.

"What should we say?" Thora asked.

Now was the time to be bold. I took the lead up the verandah steps. A woman wearing a crisp white apron answered the door. She invited us in. Off to the left, women's voices could be heard. Elizabeth appeared a few moments later holding a note pad and pen. She caught her breath at the sight of us.

"Thora . . . Ass-ta," she said, perplexed. Then she relaxed and hurried over to where we stood, embracing us. "It is so nice to see you again. What a pleasant surprise."

I explained that we were there to take our nurses' training.

"You are most welcome to join us," she said, inviting us into the parlor.

It wasn't until years later that I realized some of the city's most influential women were gathered there that afternoon—all members of the International Order of Daughters of the Empire. The women paused as we came in.

"Everyone, let me introduce Ass-ta Good-munds-son and Thora Krist-jans-son," she said, mispronouncing badly. "They are from Sigloons way up north in the wilderness."

As she began introducing each woman, I tried my best to meet their gaze while Thora tucked herself behind my shoulder. The only name I recognized was Joanna Skaptasson, an Icelander to whom I felt an instant connection. My cheeks burned when Elizabeth told them about

Freyja's disappearance.

"Has she been found yet?" she asked.

"No, ma'am," I said, wishing I had the courage to look somewhere other than the floor.

"Pity." She tutted. "A delightful girl she was."

Elizabeth invited us to sit down. The maid offered cups of strong tea and tiny sandwiches arranged neatly on china plates.

"Jo-anna has agreed to lead an IODE chapter for the Icelandic women in Manitoba," Elizabeth said proudly. "Perhaps you might like to join?"

We agreed immediately though we had little understanding of what the IODE did or what would be expected of us. Joanna was between Mother and Amma in age. She listened patiently like Gudrun and had Bergthora's fiery efficiency. As the room buzzed around her, she committed to memory her assigned duties. Then she looked across the room at me. Not a word was said, but I sensed I'd found my first ally.

The meeting continued and, by the time it was done, I knew that the women were mobilizing volunteers to knit sweaters, socks and mittens, gather newspapers and periodicals, request donations of cigarettes and other comfort items, that all would be packaged then sent to our troops overseas. They also discussed efforts to provide financial relief to the soldiers' wives and children here at home.

Elizabeth's enthusiasm grew along with her list. She was IODE President so it was her duty to motivate these women and motivate them she would.

"Did you enjoy that as much as I?" Thora asked, breathless, as we ran up the dormitory steps. We watched as the jitney carrying Joanna—a private car that darted passengers through the city for a small fee—zoomed out of sight. She had offered us a ride saying it wasn't far out of her way.

"I sure did," I said. "Leifur would have loved it."

Monday morning the Superintendent stood watching as Thora and I, in a long line of girls, filed into the dining room. Fifty of us would start training but only three quarters would finish.

The cook spooned food onto our plates as we 'queued up.' Such a novel thing it was for Thora and I to eat somewhere other than home. The eggs, cured pork, boiled oats, and toasted bread were very good. It was so long since I had tasted an apple that I risked a slap on the hand by taking two.

The Superintendent spoke as we ate, explaining the routine: Twelve hour days in the hospital, evening lectures, rotational cleaning duties, laundry. She circled the room, placing a handbook on the table beside each of us. We were told to have it memorized by the end of the day.

We stood in another queue after that, to a room filled with supplies that smelled of used books and starched cotton. The prospect of all the learning I was about to experience was intoxicating.

"You take after your father's side of the family," the matron stated, sizing me up. "The taller girls often do. You may need to let down the hem." I took the stack of folded uniforms, aprons, sleeves, caps, collars, and underclothes up to my room. We would return later for our textbooks and a pair each of high-backed shoes.

We assembled again and were told that our probationary period would last two months. If we performed satisfactorily we would become Junior nurses. It was at that point, and not before, we'd be allowed to start wearing our caps and sleeves.

Everyone listened quietly. Even the girls who giggled in small clannish groups flinched at Miss Gray's words. If she noticed she did not let on. Then we were dismissed.

"And—" she called out, over the scraping of fifty chairs all pushing back across the floor at once, "first year nursing students may not leave the hospital grounds without permission. Doing so will result in disciplinary action or immediate expulsion."

October 5, 1914
Dear Björn,

We arrived in Winnipeg safely. I am thrilled to say we have electric power in our rooms so I can write and study into the night as long as I want.

We received our uniforms and books this morning but were warned this is not a profession for the faint of heart. I fear nursing school will be more difficult than I expected. Many nurses left for overseas, so there is a shortage at the hospital. I worry the next two months will leave me little time to find Freyja. But I have good news to report. I met a woman who has offered help. Her name is Jóanna Skaptasson. I confided in her about my search for Freyja and she will ask if anyone in the Icelandic community here has seen her. At least it is a start. Otherwise I am at a loss where to begin.

How is Amma? I hope that she does not drive the nurse mad with her screeching. I hope Bergthora is feeling better and that your father is well.

Any letters that come to the post office for me should be re-directed here.

When you see Mother will you tell her about Jóanna? Hopefully soon I will find Freyja and everyone will rejoice.

Wish me good luck, Ástfriður

CHAPTER THIRTY-SEVEN

Many a trifle happens at eve.
—GRETTIR'S SAGA

THE NEXT TWO MONTHS WERE A COMPLETE BLUR.

Nurses were expected to keep a frantic pace. It reminded me of farming. The girls unaccustomed to physical work struggled. Since Thora and I had never experienced an active social life we didn't miss dating and going to picture shows. Some of the second and third year nurses knew how to sneak out at night to see their beaus. Under no circumstances were any of us to say a word. Those experienced students could make our lives miserable if they chose.

Our day looked something like this:

After breakfast, we spent the morning on the wards following graduate nurses who taught us general patient care. After dinner, two hours were spent in the classroom learning bacteriology, sterilization, microscopy, hygiene, anatomy, and dietetics. Then we returned to the wards until 7:00 p.m., at which time the daytime nurses were replaced by the evening shift while we ate supper. Three times a week we attended evening lectures by staff doctors that lasted until 10:00 p.m.

On alternate nights it was mandatory that we read and study. Once that was done, we had to fulfill our volunteer obligations. Those in their second and third years spent evenings at a nearby nursing mission or with the social services department. Everyone was expected to contribute to the war effort, so Thora and I chose to knit. We even taught other girls how to make socks and mitts. This pleased Superintendent Gray, since she was a woman whose hands were never idle.

Often our schedule would change without warning. The hospital would suddenly overflow with new patients, victims of the latest outbreak or epidemic, and our classes were abruptly postponed. We would work late into the night, with barely the chance to wolf down a sandwich, grabbed while hurrying from one ward to the next.

Every young woman caused me to look twice. I am sure the patients thought me strange, especially the pale ones with their blankets pulled up. More than once my heart nearly stopped when I saw a girl I thought was Freyja, only to be disappointed when she turned to face me.

It felt like years since I'd seen her. At night I was gripped with a terrible fear that someday I might pass her on the street or that she might be sitting at the back of a trolley but I wouldn't see her. Had she stood in that same spot I was standing? Was she around the next corner? What if too many years passed and we would not recognize each other at all?

That fear gripped me more than anything, more than contracting consumption from a patient or failing my exams. Not finding Freyja worried me even more than Finn not coming home. Freyja was alive and it was my responsibility to find her.

"She is here somewhere, I can feel it," I said boldly to Joanna as we sat together at church. Six weeks had passed and so far nothing indicated I might be correct.

Finally, I received two letters from Finn. The first must have been lost for a while:

September 15, 1914
My dearest Ásta,

I miss you terribly but if I am to function properly as a soldier I must put my longing for you aside to concentrate on my training.

I haven't yet received a letter from you and this concerns me greatly. I can only hope that you still care for me, so I shall continue writing until I hear otherwise. They warned me that the mail is slow.

Our regiment left Winnipeg and now we are in a training camp in Valcartier, Quebec. We came by train, thousands of us, and it was confusing. The army has reinstated many officers who served in the Boer War so it didn't take long and we were organized. I am now acquainted with a fellow named George McDonald, a Mohawk from Quebec whose demeanor is much like the Indians at home. I wish that I had received French language training while at the University as there is much I want to say to him. I have taught him some Icelandic and he is teaching me French. I had to show him Iceland on a map. Most men here have never heard of our homeland.

Many carry pictures of their wives and sweethearts over their hearts and I so badly wish I had one of you.

I hope all is well in Siglunes. I miss everyone but there is much here to keep my mind occupied.

Lovingly yours, Finn

October 25, 1914
Dearest Ásta,

I received your letter today and cannot describe how thrilled I am to hear from you. We have arrived in Britain. Surprising as this may sound, growing up in Siglunes has well prepared me for this experience. Stanley is having a difficult time. He was naive to think that he and his father would be serving together. For their sakes, I hope Kent can arrange it, but this war is a much larger undertaking than I originally imagined.

That you decided to take your training pleases me greatly. We can marry as soon as you graduate. Just think how wonderful it will be when I am home. Marrying you is my only wish in life.

Au revoir, mon amour. I will write again as soon as I can.

Lovingly, Finn.

One day in early December I hurried down the staircase to find Thora waiting for me by the piano. Clearly she was upset. She held two letters in her hand. It was dinner time but if we didn't hurry, we'd be late.

"What is wrong?" I asked.

One letter was from her father, the other from mine. Both were posted from Siglunes on the same day. "What do you suppose this means?" she asked.

We both feared the same thing. Together we each slipped a finger under the flap, ripping the envelopes open. I finished reading before she did and turned away, to look out the window at the gray skies.

At the time I could only imagine what it must have been like for them when they heard of the tragedy. Now I see it unfold:

Bjorn arrives in the early morning by horse.

He dismounts then walks to our house staring at the ground.

Pabbi opens the door.

Mother hushes Solrun and Lars as Bjorn follows Pabbi to the kitchen where Leifur is eating breakfast.

"I have terrible news to report. Stefan fell through the ice yesterday morning. He took the dog team to The Narrows to get the mail. The Postmaster said that he'd been in, filled his satchel then started south. Asi found the hole. The dogs were still harnessed to the sleigh floating under the ice."

Mother gasps. Pabbi closes his eyes and turns to the window. "Poor Asi," he says.

Leifur looks as if Bjorn has hit him with a hammer. He begins pacing between the kitchen and front room, tiny groans escaping his lips as he repeats Stefan's name over and over, then grabs his jacket and runs outside, through the snow, across the road to the barn.

Mother starts to cry.

"They are already searching," Bjorn says. "I am going to tell J.K. now."

Pabbi takes a deep breath. "We will come with you."

Our beloved lake, once again.

In the tradition of our forefathers, every fisherman pulled up his nets. Pabbi and Leifur went every day onto the lake to help search.

Thinking back on it, Lars changed that year. Maybe it was Freyja's disappearance or our sadness, or maybe imagining the dark mass under the ice, hearing the men chiseling holes with a needle bar. They used a large hook to snag and pull the waterlogged one-armed body out of the hole. They laid Stefan gently on his side so that those who could not bear it didn't have to see his slack jaw and fear-frozen eyes. Pabbi tried to shield Leifur, but he was too late. Perhaps it was witnessing our brother's pain that turned Lars quiet and solemn.

December 13, 1914
Dearest Finn,

I am sure by now you have received a letter from your father about Stefán. Leifur is taking it particularly hard. Losing Freyja first and now her beau. Both have been erased from his life in less than a year.

I hope this letter finds you well and you are not as overwhelmed as I. Training is far more demanding than I expected. That is why it has taken me so long to write.

Do they have water closets there? Not using an outhouse was a difficult thing to imagine. It is convenient, especially this time of year. There is no odor, which surprised me, but now I understand why. It is essential that everything here at the hospital be kept clean and sterilized.

Did you know that many substances transmit molecules into the air and that's why we smell them? Some are harmful, such as bacteria. That is why the Tuberculosis patients are housed in a separate wing. The bacteria from their lungs is exhaled into the air and that is how others catch the disease. We always must be careful of what we inhale. What a learning experience this is.

Tell me what it is like there.

Lovingly, Ástfriður

Christmas that year was spent in the pediatrics ward with at least thirty ailing children, some two to a bed. They looked so pathetic I couldn't help but think of poor little Solrun being here. I spent every waking hour with them, reading aloud from the Sagas. I saw how comforting this was, especially to the Icelandic children, and was able to hold the wide-eyed attention of the others, who of course, had never heard the stories before. It was a challenge at first, reading in Icelandic then translating to English, but I am proud to say I did an adequate job.

A letter from Mother arrived early in the New Year:

December 26, 1914
Dear Ásta,

We received your photograph on Friday. What a smart looking uniform, and you look so grown up wearing that cap. I hope the workload has eased a bit, you sounded tired last time you wrote. I hope you are getting enough rest.

Björn is spending more time in the store, especially in the evenings. We see him sometimes going through the accounts under lamplight. He hasn't said, but I think he misses having you there. The Sveistrup girl is doing a satisfactory job but she is young and no doubt misses her beau. You will have to ask Finn if he has seen him yet.

Signý and the boys are all fine and Ólafur is cheerful as ever. Thankfully, baby Jón can sleep through all the noise. They were here yesterday. Pétur has grown nearly as tall as Sólrún. He constantly wants to try her brace.

Amma was here for Christmas. I trust you find the time to attend church. Our congregation has reduced by a third with so many young men, you, and Thora away.

Leifur seems much happier these days with Bensi gone. Sigrid Gunnarsson is the new teacher. They have been spending a lot of time together and it would not surprise me if they marry.

Leifur has moved into Amma's house and is hoping to buy Bensi's land which would be a great addition to our farm.

And then in Pabbi's handwriting:

I will try not to repeat what your Mama has already written. Unfortunately fishing is poor this year which I am attributing to the slow freeze up. It started out quite promising but those two weeks of warm temperatures at the end of November (when Stefán drowned), accompanied by a strong wind from the west, broke up the ice and we lost a dozen nets. We were able to replace them, but as with everything else, there is always a cost. The weather is cold now. I measured over a foot of snow on the ice, and the wind is howling again. I think the winter will be long.

I'd hoped that you would write more about what it is like living in Winnipeg. Do find time to go by the Lögberg office to meet the editor. Tell him that I think he is doing a fine job and that I particularly enjoy his perspective on the war. We are very proud of you. I am confident you will do well.

Pabbi

The months flew by. I barely saw Thora as we were placed in different classes. The workload was exhausting. I arrived to our room one evening to find a note, written in Superintendent Gray's strict hand, tacked to the door. A note usually meant something was wrong. I quickly tore it down hoping no one else had seen it. I was to meet in her office the next day. I lay awake half the night worrying. I already knew the reason.

As I lowered myself into the chair across the desk from her, Miss Gray opened the file folder with my name on it.

"Thora tells me that you are engaged to her brother," she said, not looking up as she flipped through the pages. "He is overseas?"

She leaned back in the chair removing her spectacles. She read my expression for a few moments. I tried to hide my embarrassment but wasn't doing a good job of it.

"Your marks," she said, "are not what I expected."

Unable to meet her gaze I agreed, a huge lump rising in my throat. I'd never received anything but perfect grades. She waited for me to say something but I couldn't speak.

"He is the reason?"

"No, ma'am."

"You are not worried about him?" she asked, surprised.

"Finn is resourceful. He is capable of taking care of himself."

Her eyebrows went up. "Then what is wrong?"

I shook my head. I could not lie but I also couldn't tell the truth. She waited for my response. When none came, she looked at the folder again and sighed.

"The head nurses say that during class your thoughts are elsewhere and the results of your latest tests reflect that."

"Yes, ma'am."

"I have seen many girls pass through these doors and few are as capable as you. Have you given up?"

"No, Ma'am, I never give up."

She looked skeptical. "Beginning in March there will be a series of preparatory tests and then first year exams at the end of April. If you fail—"

I didn't hear what she said after that. I held back the tears until I was through the front door and into the crisp, February air. The hospital front entrance was only a few blocks away. I kept my head down, holding my hat to keep it from blowing off as I ran, Amma's words from years ago rolling through my mind: *We came to America for the girls so they can achieve their heart's desire.*

CHAPTER THIRTY-EIGHT

Do not expect to make headway with a frail sailcloth
—EYRBYGGJA SAGA

HOW MANY HOURS HAVE PASSED THIS TIME?

"Amma," I whisper, feeling her presence. Slowly she comes into focus, standing beside life-sized Jesus. My Amma, in her prime. Beautiful, strong, erect. So much younger than I am now.

"Freyja," I whisper, "where did she go?"

Amma looks serene, more so than she ever did in life. So calm, so full of love.

The answer you want, she says as the vision fades, *is right here in this room.*

I barely have time to say: "I will see you again soon," then Amma is gone.

Thora is alarmed. She raises a hand to her chest and looks over her shoulder at the wall. It takes a few moments for her to recover. "Did you see her?" she asks.

I point to the scrapbook on the side table and she shakily rounds the bed to pick it up, opening to a random page. She keeps turning until I motion for her to stop.

"There," I say. The years we spent in Winnipeg. That photo from the *Winnipeg Free Press* of the 1915 war rally. Pabbi's editorials. And the faraway photo of Thora and me with the rest of our graduating class taken two years later.

"What is it?" she asks, her expression a curious mixture of fear and hope. "Are you remembering something?"

All at once I understand what Amma meant. Thora knows more than she is letting on. I see in her expression that she has known all along.

* * *

NORMALLY I REJOICED AT THE ONSET OF SPRING. I'D TURN MY FACE up to the sky, drink in the warmth of the sun, listen to everything at the farm come to life. Here in Winnipeg though, there was none of that. I became so focused on my studies and absorbed in the life of a student nurse, there was no time to enjoy the change of seasons, or even to consider if this was the life I wanted.

At the end of March, I received this letter from Finn:

February 7, 1915
Dearest Ásta,

Who would have guessed a year ago that I'd be writing to you from France? We landed at Calais then travelled by train to Hazebrouck which I am told is near the Belgium border. Our squadron is part of the reserve right now. Apparently the allied forces are fighting nearby, but aside from aeroplanes overhead and the sound of explosions in the distance, I have not seen much of the war. As you can imagine everyone is growing restless since we've done nothing but training exercises. Only a few brought books so I trade with them. Thankfully there is much gained from reading a book twice.

A package arrived from the Red Cross. I received a pair of wool socks, mitts, cigarettes (which I gave away). I am convinced the mitts were made by you as they have two thumbs, but how is this possible? They say the IODE in Winnipeg sent the box. If you can, please pass on our thanks. It is cold and rainy here so these items will bring us much comfort.

The men accustomed to physical work are faring much better than those who held office jobs. Stanley now wishes that he'd spent his summers at the farm. The people in the nearby towns hold us in high regard, especially George because he is an Indian, which is opposite to what we see at home. He is as proficient with a gun as I, and equally surefooted in the drills.

There is a fellow in our unit who reminds me so much of Olafur it is staggering. He is a wonderful inspiration to everyone. Stanley has changed his tune about farmers. Yesterday he said that he wishes there were more 'Thorsteinsson boys' enlisted and now compares everyone to them.

I have to say that I don't mind this life of strict discipline. Colonel Lipsett reminds me of Father. I expect once this idleness ends everyone will be in a much better state of mind.

I received the photo of you in your uniform and you look quite beautiful. I am sure the sight of you is comforting to the sick and weary, I know it certainly heartens me.

Reading back over my letter I see that I am beginning to speak more like an Englishman. It is difficult not to whilst being surrounded by so many. Do not let this trouble you. I will always be an Icelander at heart.

Lovingly, Finn

Years later, I would re-read this letter and it would always take me back to our week of exams and I'd wonder how Thora and I struggled through it.

The morning after our first exam the dining room was abuzz with an unusual amount of chatter. The students were huddled over a table reading the *Winnipeg Free Press.*

"Have you heard the news?" a second year student asked.

Until that point the war hadn't touched us, the details scant. But there on the front page was a photograph from the trenches in Ypres,

Belgium. The scene was horrendous. Dead soldiers lying in the deep, mud-packed crevice, while others carried the injured away on stretchers. The room grew silent as a nurse began reading out loud:

" . . . the 1st Canadian Division was hit particularly hard in the brutal and unethical attack by the Germans who have employed the use of chlorine gas against our troops. Ninety men died immediately in the trenches and of the 207 brought to the nearest dressing stations, 46 died almost immediately and a dozen after long suffering . . . many men from our own 8th battalion are still unaccounted for . . . "

I closed my eyes. Thora grew tense beside me. Another girl ran from the room. Three students quit that day to go home.

Thora and I did not speak to anyone for the rest of the day. We crawled silently into bed that night after writing our second exam. As we lay in the darkness, she began crying.

"I cannot imagine life without my brother," she sobbed.

Reality struck me for the first time. I whispered, barely recognizing my own voice, "Neither can I."

Every morning after that, I rose a half hour earlier. I went out into the cool spring air to buy a paper from the boy yelling headlines from the corner.

Somehow we managed to get through the weeks. We held our breath every morning as we took turns running a finger down the daily list of fatalities, thankful when we did not see his name. I read every word concerning the war, clipped the pages, bundled them and mailed the packages home.

May 7, 1915
Dear Pabbi,

Here is the latest package regarding the war.

It saddens me to say that in today's paper there is a story about Kent and Stanley (page 3, Prominent City Lawyer and Son Killed). As soon as we can, Thora and I will visit Elizabeth to offer condolences.

With classes done and exams written, we should have more free time now. It would be impossible to have any less.

The entire average is down from last year as the war is on everyone's mind. The Superintendent will take this into consideration so anyone with a failing grade can re-write the test this summer. Fortunately, I am not one of them.

I did not have to go by the Lögberg office as the editor is a member of our church. I found the courage to introduce myself and he remembers your letters to him on education reform and the war. Apparently you are a celebrity in the Icelandic community here as many share your views. He would like to meet you one day.

I have not yet heard from Finn.

Ástfriður

Two days later, on Sunday morning, there was a knock on our door. Thora and I'd finished breakfast and were getting ready for church. I was surprised to see Joanna standing in the hallway.

"Today is the Decoration Day parade," she said. "Would you like to join me and other members of the IODE?"

She explained that there would be no church service as everyone was encouraged to attend the memorial at the University of Manitoba grounds instead. She told us to put on our uniforms and meet her downstairs.

The parade was like nothing we'd ever witnessed. I counted eleven cars filled with IODE members and we were only a small part of the parade. Veterans from earlier wars, all dressed in khaki, carried flags as they strode uniformly ahead of the cadets, boy scouts and a marching band.

The streets were lined with waving, cheering people. As we rolled by I was overcome with pride. The little bit of volunteering we did and the fact we were nurses somehow linked us to the suffering that was going on overseas. It was impossible to come away from it unchanged.

We stopped briefly in front of City Hall where a wreath was placed at the foot of the 90th Regiment Memorial, honoring Winnipeg's deceased from earlier wars. I caught a glimpse of Elizabeth standing with other mourners. She was dressed sharply, in solid black, a sheer veil covering her face. She did not cry, not even once, and in later years when I'd hear reference to the British 'stiff upper lip,' I always thought of her in that moment. It was such a grave contrast to the memory of her throwing back her head in laughter and trying to pronounce Vínarterta in Gudrun's kitchen.

When the parade was over, Joanna's husband drove us back to the dormitory. Before I got out of the car, Joanna touched my hand.

"A woman from our church thinks she may have seen Freyja," she whispered. "I will find out more."

A month later I received this letter from Bjorn:

June 16, 1915
Dear Ásta,

I hope this letter finds you well. Any progress on the search for Freyja? You sounded so discouraged the last time you wrote that I dared not say anything to your mother.

I have cleared a spot on the wall by the post office so your father can post your clippings. Our kitchen is the place where everyone stops to read, drink coffee, and discuss the war. I am not sure if the nurse who takes care of Bergthora and your Amma enjoys making coffee for so many, but so far she has not complained. I suggested we charge one cent a cup to cover our costs, but Father will not hear of it.

I think the nurse has a soft spot for Father who constantly charms her. The nurse believes Freda is his wife but he has not corrected her, even though it makes your Amma furious. It is most humorous to watch.

We decided to forego the picnic at The Narrows. With Stefán drowned and so many of our players at war, we can't muster the excitement needed to play ball decently. Life is not the same around here.

Ási brings the mail now since nobody wanted Stefán's job. He is taking Stefán's death hard and drinking far too much. Father has tried talking to him but to no avail.

Have you heard from Finn? Guðrún comes in every mail day looking for a letter. The last one came three months ago, in March.

Everyone misses seeing you here, including me. I honestly never realized how much you did around this place.

Fondly, Björn

P.S. Father insisted on sending enough to pay for the newspapers. Now you are obliged to keep sending them, a strategy he enjoys. I hope that you will use your allowance to buy something for yourself. Have you been to the Hudson's Bay Company store yet?

I wrote back, telling him that a girl who matched Freyja's description had been seen, but I was feeling discouraged again since a month had passed and I'd heard nothing more. I also had not yet heard from Finn. But then, two days after posting the letter to Bjorn, one arrived. I shook with excitement and thanked God.

May 5, 1915
Dear Ásta,

By now I am sure word has reached home about the many men who died in Ypres. I am alive and recovering in hospital from acute bronchitis, a result of the gas attack. I will convalesce here for a month then be re-assigned. I have written the same to Father. I have told him not to worry and I ask that you do the same.

I will write again soon.

Finn

Summer passed before I had time to realize it. I kept expecting another letter from Finn but none came, only twice-monthly letters from Bjorn, lengthy ones that kept me current on the goings on at home.

One Saturday evening in late September, two weeks before our second year of training would begin, Joanna surprised me once again by coming to our dorm room. This time she looked delighted.

"I have an address," she said, holding up a paper. "I think we may have found her."

She explained that a girl named Freyja, who matched the description I'd given, had applied at the Jón Bjarnason Academy in April, hoping to study art.

I was so shocked I barely knew what to say.

"Can we go now?" I asked.

"Tomorrow," she said. "After church. My husband and I will take you there."

After she left Thora turned to me, perplexed. "What was that about?"

It came as a relief to finally tell her what I'd kept hidden the past year. As the words spilled out, I realized how unfair I had been, all those times I'd dragged her to places and had secret conversations; sometimes I ignored her, so lost was I in my own thoughts.

"Why didn't you tell me?" she asked, clearly hurt.

"Bjorn and I decided it would be best—"

"Bjorn knows?"

"Yes, I thou—"

"You told him but not me?" she cried. "Why him?"

"Because," I said, thinking back, trying to remember exactly why I'd taken him into my confidence, "of Amma. You and I could not both leave without hiring a nurse. He spoke to Magnus."

"So is that the only reason you came?" she asked. "To find Freyja?"

"No," I said quickly, explaining everything, including the conversation with Petra. "I want to be a nurse. It was the possibility of finding her that gave me the courage to leave Mama and Pabbi."

Thora was still frowning, but slowly she softened. "Joanna knows where she is?"

I grabbed her hands and started shaking them, giddy at the prospect of seeing Freyja tomorrow—*tomorrow!*

Before we fell asleep, Thora asked what had made me trust Petra's word after everything her father had done to my family.

"Every night after Freyja disappeared I prayed for an answer," I said into the darkness. "God would never be so cruel to send Petra to me if it wasn't true."

Joanna's husband easily found the address and parked in front of a three-storey, brick apartment building on Richot Street in the French part of town. It was no wonder I hadn't found her, I was looking in the wrong place.

Joanna pulled open the door and we followed her up the creaking stairs to the second floor. As our hushed voices echoed down the hall, it suddenly occurred to me that I didn't know what to say when Freyja opened the door. Would she be glad to see us? Until then it hadn't once occurred to me that she might slam the door.

"What's wrong?" Thora asked when she looked back to see me lagging behind. By then I was feeling dizzy and had stopped, heart pounding in my chest.

"What if—?" I whispered, realizing with tremendous clarity why everyone else was so quick to believe that Freyja was dead. It hurt far less than the other possibility.

"What if she does not want to see you?" Joanna asked softly.

I nodded sheepishly. Why else would Freyja be living right here in Winnipeg but not contacting home?

"A misunderstanding," Joanna said. "It happens often. You will see."

Joanna paused until all three of us were in front of the door. She checked the address on the sheet of paper again then rapped hard. We waited. She knocked again. When no answer came, she pressed an ear to the door.

"Nobody is home," she said.

No. No. No.

"This is most unfortunate."

Please, please, please open the door.

Joanna sighed. "We will have to return tomorrow."

Desperate, I glanced back toward the stairway hoping beyond reason that Freyja might come through the front door.

"I am sorry," Joanna said. "We tried."

I shook my head. "I cannot leave. Not when we are this close."

Joanna lifted her wrist to check the time.

"You can go," I said quickly. "We will find our way back."

"I do not like the idea of leaving you here," she said with a sideways glance.

We reassured her that it would be fine. Reluctantly, she looked back at us twice as she went to the front door. "There is a café on the corner of Richot and Taché," she said, voice echoing loudly. "We passed it coming here. You will be able to catch a streetcar there."

CHAPTER THIRTY-NINE

Stubbornness brings either great humiliation or greater honour.
—THE SAGA OF HRAFNKELS FREYSGOÐA

WITHOUT A POCKET WATCH IT WAS IMPOSSIBLE TO KNOW HOW long we waited. I knocked on the door again. When we grew too tired to stand, we sat with our backs against the wall. Bored, Thora began humming. I sang along as we stretched our legs, glanced toward the front door, picked up the song again, laughing and reminiscing about home. Most of the stories involved Freyja—bold, naive, impetuous, sweetly infuriating Freyja.

"Do you think less of her now?" I asked.

It took Thora a few moments to know exactly what I meant. "In what way?"

"That she ran away. For worrying us so."

Thora thought for a moment. "It will depend on the reason."

Hours passed. The front door opened and a man came up the stairs. Key in hand, he opened the door to his apartment then went inside. A few moments later he stuck his head out.

"Are you waiting for someone?" he asked with a heavy French accent.

We quickly stood up. "Yes, my sister. She lives in this apartment. Do you know her?"

"What does she look like?"

"Seventeen. Very pretty, with white hair."

He thought for a moment. "I saw her only once or twice," he said. "Spoke with an accent. Said she came from a farm on Lake Winnipeg."

"Lake Manitoba?" I asked. "Siglunes?"

He smiled. "That could be where they went."

"They?" I asked, glancing at Thora.

"Her husband, but he did not seem like the farming type." He shrugged. "He works for the Grain Exchange. That is like farming, I suppose, so he must know a bit about it."

"You said they moved somewhere?"

"Yes. In May. He moved all their belongings out. Left."

I looked at the door then back at him. "Are you sure?"

"Quite," he said. "People move in and out all the time. Nobody lives there right now."

He shrugged in apology then stepped back, closing the door behind him. Reluctantly, we left.

Thankfully it was not dark yet, but it would be soon. Neither one of us was in the mood to eat so we stood outside the café waiting for a streetcar.

"Freyja would not get married," I said. "That cannot be right."

"He didn't seem reliable."

"He said he spoke to her once or twice. That is ridiculous. I can see him not knowing if it were 10 or 15 times, but once *or* twice?"

"An idiot," Thora agreed.

"Freyja married?"

"Seems unlikely to me. She was in love with Stefan."

"He did not even know the difference between the lakes. How foolish. He must be wrong about her moving as well. We should go back tomorrow and see."

"We should," she said.

But we both knew we wouldn't. Telling me what I needed to hear was Thora's way of softening my disappointment. Through the streetcar window I peered down Richot Street. While I never went to that apartment again, the building haunted my dreams for years.

The next morning it felt good to walk with solid purpose into the warm sun, already blinking up over the river as the city was coming alive. Despite not knowing the man's name, I was determined to find him and would start at the Grain Exchange. Most people I passed took notice of my uniform, offering a gracious 'good morning.'

An hour earlier I'd lied to Superintendent Gray, feigning illness, so that I might sneak away. Tinged with guilt, I looked up at the building towering overhead. I hadn't yet formulated how I was going to find the man who was supposedly Freyja's husband.

Once inside, I couldn't help but admire the marble floors and beautiful fixtures. Men dressed in suits streamed in, all wearing hats, and carrying leather valises. They greeted one another, then took the stairs or elevator. I decided to follow one of them.

"Good morning," the young man said to the elevator operator as we stepped on.

"How are you today?" the operator asked as the cage door closed. He pulled a lever on the wall and the elevator jolted, taking us up four floors, jolted again when it stopped and the young man stepped out.

"Where to, Miss Nurse?" the operator asked.

I said that I needed to find someone who worked there.

"Do you know which floor?"

I told him no.

"Do you know his name?"

I was starting to feel a bit foolish. "No."

He chuckled. "Well that is like finding a needle in a haystack."

I'd never heard the expression before but committed it to memory so that I might use it again. I told him the man was a former patient who was looking to hire a private nurse for his ailing grandmother, but I'd misplaced his name.

"He works in this building," I said. It was alarming how proficient I'd become at lying since the saga with Freyja began. I silently vowed that once I found her, I would never lie again.

"Try this office," he said taking me up another floor, then pointing to a door at the end of the hall.

"May I help you?" the clerk asked, looking up from her desk.

I told the story again, this time adding that the man I was looking for lived in an apartment on Richot Street.

"How old is he?"

"Late 20s? I am not good at estimating age."

"Can you tell me anything else about him?"

I said he had a young wife with lovely white hair, blue eyes. Beautiful and petite. Icelandic. She enjoyed music and art. "If you met her you would never forget her."

Stepping away from her desk, she called out to a dignified-looking man with a moustache that curled up at the ends. He was annoyed until he saw my uniform.

She repeated my lie.

"I went to his apartment but he was not there," I added.

"Icelandic, you say? Sounds like Barney Thordarson. He works as an intern on the fifth floor, but his grandmother died—I believe it was last year."

"Then I will offer my condolences," I said without missing a beat, turned, clicking exactly like Miss Gray, and marched out the door.

Bjarni Thordarson, I remembered the name. He was Finn's acquaintance, who'd been there the day they took Freyja sightseeing and to the University. He had relatives at Big Point, across the lake. Perhaps he was a relation to poor Arni from who'd died in the bunkhouse.

This time when I stepped off the elevator, I turned to my left.

"I am here to see Bjarni Thordarson," I said to the receptionist, looking past her at the rows of desks where men sat with their heads down, some writing, others reading. Two stood talking by a window that overlooked the city.

She called out his name and a handsome young man, only a few years older than me, pushed back his chair and stood up. I saw a brief hint of recognition and, dare I suggest, panic?

"Yes?" he asked, straining a smile.

When I did not reply, he was forced to come reluctantly from behind the safety of his desk. He resembled Arni enough that I was convinced the two were related, though his hair was more the shade of sand. He held his chin high in the air, looking down on me as he spoke, different from Arni in that way, too.

"What is this about?" he asked. There was a tint to his cheeks and he refused to look me in the eye. I knew what I would say to him and would do so in Icelandic.

"My name is Asta Gudmundsson and I am here looking for my sister Freyja. I understand that you know her whereabouts."

Self-consciously he shot a glance at the receptionist, who didn't understand one word.

"I don't know who you are talking about," he replied, equally quick.

"I have been told that you do. By my fiancé, Finn Kristjansson."

He looked surprised, but it was not genuine. "Freyja—who?"

"Gudmundsson. From Siglunes."

He shook his head, turning his palms to the ceiling. "I don't know where that is."

"Surely you do, it is across the lake from Big Point. You have relatives there."

Another blank stare.

"Stanley Burroughs. Do you know him?"

Still nothing.

"All I want is to find my sister," I said. "There was a girl who fit her description that lived in your apartment on Richot Street."

He rolled his eyes and smirked. "That explains it," he said. "I've never lived there. You mistake me for someone else."

By then most of the men in the office were snickering, believing they were witnessing a lover's quarrel. My mind was spinning.

"I am sorry," he said, taking a few steps back to his desk. "I have a lot to do."

I could think of nothing else to say, but didn't believe one word he said.

"Good luck finding her." He offered a sympathetic wave as I left.

A shadow darkened the front window of the little yellow house on Simcoe Street. It was shockingly easy to find. I simply asked the Pastor if he knew where Bjarni Thordarson lived. He pointed me to it, only three blocks from the church.

"You must have the wrong house," an old man said when he answered the door. He was fat and leaned heavily on a cane. "I did not call for a nurse."

"Does Bjarni Thordarson live here?" I asked in Icelandic.

His eyebrows lifted. "My grandson. He is at work. Did he arrange to have you come see me?"

"I am here to see his wife."

"Nei," he said shaking his head. "He does not have one. Poor boy. No girl wants him."

He saw my disappointment as he shuffled back from the door, inviting me in.

"I have made a pot of coffee."

"I should get back to the hospital," I said.

Seeing my hesitation, he offered a bit of hangikjöt as well.

"Do you have time to check my feet?" he asked.

It occurred to me that all was not lost as I followed him to the front room. Befriending the old man could lead to information about Bjarni.

Once he'd struggled himself into a chair, he lifted his feet onto the footstool. I pulled off his heavy wool socks. It was clear by the swelling that his condition was serious. As I began massaging his calves and ankles, I suggested that he come by the hospital to see a doctor.

"How will I get there?"

"Hire a car," I said, squeezing his instep.

He groaned with delight, telling me to continue.

"Nei, I have always walked. When I was a boy, I was a shepherd. I walked many miles every day through the mountains," he said. "Here I walked to my job, where I walked some more, and then back home again to this little house."

"Then walk to the hospital," I said. "It is not far."

"I am too old." He laughed.

"Then I will carry you," I said, "on my back."

"Nei." He laughed again. "I am too fat. You are just a little girl."

I helped him pull up his socks. Not wanting the 'ad kvedast a'—silly rhymes we invent to show our wit—to end, he thought hard what to say next.

"I know," he said, reaching for his cane. "I will hire a car to take me."

I took him by the arm to help him stand up. "A car?" I said. "Would you not rather walk?"

"I would," he said, eyes twinkling. "But I am too old. And fat. And I cannot get my shoes over my swollen feet."

"You can wear these socks."

"It is what I wore in Iceland in the mountains."

"Surely you can wear them here."

"But how will the driver know I wish to hire him?"

I brought my finger up to my chin, pretending to think hard. "I will flag him down and send him here. I will say there is an old fat man living in a yellow house who longs for the mountains in Iceland but must go to the hospital here instead."

He laughed hard, pounding his thigh.

"I saw you sneak away this morning," Thora said that night in the dorm. She did not ask for details, so I offered none and we went to bed without saying another word.

The following afternoon we strolled back after our shift, taking the long way around so that we might stop at the confectionery. We'd discovered it earlier that summer and now couldn't resist the ice cream. The door tinkled as it opened and the clerk, wearing a tidy white uniform, standing behind the soda fountain, greeted us when we came in.

Cakes, biscuits, pies, and every sweet imaginable was right there on display. This time Thora chose strawberry with chocolate sauce. I always ordered vanilla. We took the bowls to a small table in the corner.

I told her everything that had happened the day before.

"If it is the same Bjarni," she said, turning the spoon over, licking it, "why would he lie to you?"

"He is hiding something," I said, adding that I planned to go back in two days to question the old man. I sensed by the way she stared at her spoon she thought it a bad idea.

"What if you get caught?"

I told her the house was so close I could easily sneak away during dinner.

"It seems to me," she began, but stopped to stare out the window, then looked back at her bowl. "All you think about is Freyja. You are risking everything for her. What if she does not want to be found and that is what Bjarni is hiding?"

The anger rose in me and we barely spoke after that, avoiding each other for the rest of the evening. In the morning, she came late to breakfast then found an excuse to take a sandwich back to the ward. I chatted with another nurse when I saw her come into the dining room for dinner. I snuck out and ran to the little house as planned.

This time the drapes were open. The old man was sitting in his chair. He hollered for me to come in.

"Elskan, nice to see you again," he said.

I asked how he was feeling. He held up a small jar of ointment prescribed by the doctor the day before. There was another bottle of medication sitting on the end table. I slipped off his socks, gave his feet another quick massage, then wiggled his socks back on.

"Can you walk better now?"

"I think I can," he said. "Thanks to you."

It was easy to ask about his home in Iceland. He sat back comfortably and told me a story encased in hardship, that ended with the decision to come here with his wife, daughter, son-in-law and their two boys.

"Bjarni's father, where was he from?" I asked.

"Hofsós," he said. "So many came here I am not sure there is anyone left."

"Where is his mother now?

"With her new husband in Vancouver," he said, adding that he and his wife hadn't followed because they enjoyed the community here.

The door opened, surprising us both.

"Bjarni," the old man said, sitting up straight in the chair. "You remember Ástfriður, she is the nurse I told you about."

I thought it curious that Bjarni's expression did not change; it was almost as if he expected to see me there.

"Come sit with us," the old man called.

"I came to check on you," Bjarni said. "The doctor thinks you should be in the hospital."

"Nei," the old man said, waving it off. "If I am going to die, I'd like to do it right here."

Bjarni and I both looked at the clock. Half past one.

"I must get back to work," I said, realizing that I was already late. Bjarni seemed anxious as well.

"I would like to apologize for interrupting your work the other day," I said, watching his reaction. Somehow Bjarni had mastered the ability to keep every thought and emotion from showing on his face. It was something I needed to learn.

"I understand," he finally said. "You mistook me for someone else."

"You see," I said, turning back to the grandfather, watching Bjarni from the corner of my eye, "I have a sister, Freyja. She is somewhere in the city and I am trying to find her. That is how I met your grandson."

This seemed to please the old man. "He should help you."

A heavy silence filled the room, interrupted by the sound of a car horn in the street.

"Our parents' hearts are broken and I fear Amma will never be the same. Freyja was her favorite."

"Já." He nodded in understanding.

"My beau will return from the war soon and he will help me," I said. "In the meantime, I will contact the police. Do you think that is a good idea?"

The grandfather shrugged, while Bjarni fidgeted, glancing at the clock again.

"I am sorry to take so much of your time," I gushed, making my way to the door. The old man brightened when I said that I would return. I told him to keep his feet up and to take his medication as prescribed.

As Bjarni moved to let me by, I whispered: "I was at the mill when Arni died. That must have been hard for you, to lose your only brother." Then I smiled at him sweetly.

The cracks in the wall he hid behind were beginning to show.

Later that week I was assisting in obstetrics—one of the most exciting rotations in the hospital—when the head nurse tapped me on the shoulder to say that the superintendent wanted to see me in her office.

Usually when Miss Gray looked up from her desk at me her expression was pleasant, but not this time.

"Come in," she said. "Please close the door."

I was barely in the chair and she began.

"I will get straight to the point." She looked me square in the eye. "Yesterday I received a complaint from a Mr. B-jar-ni Thor-dar-son that you have been harassing him."

She held up a letter. "He claims that you are a stranger who turned up at his office and began questioning him about God knows what. Then you went to his home, have involved his grandfather, who is ill, and now are harassing them both."

"That is not true," I said.

"He claims that you," reading directly from the page, "are obsessed, delusional, unstable; and that you are using your vocation as a nurse to gain access to their home."

She looked over her glasses at me. "Please tell me these accusations are false."

"They are," I said. "His grandfather invited me in. I checked his feet and it was obvious something was wrong so I recommended he see the doctor. I went back to check on him. We had coffee and a visit."

"So you admit being there, in your uniform?"

"Yes, but I am not delusional."

"Why did you go in the first place?" she asked.

"Because I am looking for someone," I said.

She sat for a long while thinking while I waited with my heart in my throat.

"You lied to me about being ill," she said. "And you were nearly an hour late for your shift. You do realize that such conduct warrants suspension? This letter is a serious complaint and I have no choice but to report to the Board of Directors."

CHAPTER FORTY

Let another's wounds be your warning.
—NJÁL'S SAGA

THE BOARD CONVENED THE DAY BEFORE CLASSES BEGAN.

Five people sat behind a long table. I was told to sit on a chair in front of them. Worried that I'd be unable to express myself clearly, I had a written apology folded in my hand that was growing sweatier by the minute. When I allowed my mind to wander, all I saw was Pabbi's disappointment.

The chairman was a rotund, older man who spoke with a wheeze, likely from an underlying condition made worse by the extra weight he carried on his chest. The man beside him was opposite in the extreme. He looked malnourished and possibly anemic. I recognized him as the hospital administrator, the man to whom Superintendent Gray reported. Unlike everyone else at the table, he appeared quite bored by the proceedings. Superintendent Gray, along with the supervisors of each department, was healthy and robust, and not bored at all.

How embarrassing it was to face Dr. Oli Bjornsson, the Head of Obstetrics. He was thick-boned and carried that same loose-knit frame and washed-out hair that made him instantly recognizable as one of us. Through overheard snippets of conversation, I knew that his mother was a midwife in New Iceland. I saw her accomplishments shine through his eyes when he spoke of her. He was genuinely shocked to see me.

"Miss Gudmundsson," the Chairman began, "do you understand why you have been asked to come here today?"

I nodded.

"Are these allegations that you have behaved in a manner unbefitting a nursing student of this hospital true?"

I nodded again.

"What do you say for yourself?"

I cleared my throat as I unfolded the paper. Then I read from it, apologizing for the embarrassment I caused, promising that if allowed to stay, I would never allow anything personal or otherwise to interfere with my studies again. I was wholly committed to a lifetime of nursing and asked that they forgive my poor judgment.

"I have been preoccupied with a personal matter," I said.

He waited, expecting me to elaborate. "Miss Gudmundsson?"

I could not bear witness to my family's pain, at least not to so many people. It rankled me that he would expect an explanation after I'd told him it was personal.

"Nursing is my calling," I said.

"But why did you go to this young man's house?" he asked.

When I refused to answer, Doctor Bjornsson intervened.

"Do you understand the question?" he asked me in Icelandic.

"Yes, but I cannot tell everyone," I replied quickly, seeing their bewilderment.

Turning to them, Doctor Bjornsson said, "She cannot explain it in English. If the Chairman will allow it—"

"This is highly unusual," he grunted.

"What harm is there in it? You said yourself that she will make a fine nurse."

He shrugged, waving his hand. "Go ahead. Chirp if you must."

I told him in Icelandic about Freyja and everything that had happened since. That I was the only one in the family who could find her, that Mother knew but Pabbi didn't, and that he blamed himself for

Freyja's disappearance. I told him about my prayers and dreams, that all of it led to Bjarni Thordarson.

"My kindness towards the old man was sincere," I said. "Bjarni lied about me harassing his Afi. Why would he do that unless he was hiding something?"

The doctor listened thoughtfully. I saw in his expression understanding; it was not our way to lay bare family troubles.

"I will help locate your sister," he said. "But from today forward, you must leave it to me, understand?"

I solemnly agreed.

"That is all. You may go now."

Whatever he said to the others after the door had closed behind me must have been convincing as I was allowed to continue my training, and Superintendent Gray became far more understanding.

As promised, I began focusing on my studies, so that in two year's time the 'Miss' would be dropped and I'd be Nurse Gudmundsson. Doctor Bjornsson kept his word as well. One evening he took me aside to ask for Freyja's particulars and wrote it all on a piece of paper.

"I'm not convinced Bjarni is involved," he said. "I know the family and have never seen her with them. None of it makes sense."

I resigned myself to the possibility that the path leading to Bjarni was a dead end. Thora was relieved when I told her I had no plans to return to the little yellow house. Doctor Bjornsson suggested I check a home for wayward girls in the north end of the city.

"I need you to come with me," I said to Thora who hated the thought that I might ask someone else to join in the adventure. With address in hand, one Sunday after church, we took the streetcar to Main Street then transferred onto another. I so wished that I had a photograph of Freyja.

The house resembled all the others that lined the street, mostly two-storey, and so close you couldn't walk between them with outstretched arms. You never would guess that this particular address was filled to the rafters with homeless girls.

The retired nurse who ran the house invited us in.

"Doris Armstrong," she said, introducing herself.

I was soon impressed by how firmly she ran the place, though it must have been challenging to keep a shipload of troubled girls on an even keel.

"She was never here," Doris said; her words had a Scottish bite.

Two girls were in the kitchen at the end of the hall wiping dishes, while a third was sitting at a massive table polishing silverware. Doris called them over, saying they were "more reliable than the others." She asked if either had seen Freyja. Two shook their heads, but the third, a girl of about nineteen named Clara, grinned. Though it was impolite to stare, my eyes kept returning to the tender red scar that ran from just under her left ear up across to her nose.

Everything about her begged annoyance, from the meanness in her eyes to her swagger. She stood with her hip thrust out, chin high in the air. She looked down her nose at Thora and me, huffing at our decentness, thinking less of us because of it.

"She is at Minnie's place," Clara said.

"Is Minnie your friend?" I asked.

Clara laughed, throaty and disgusting. "Minnie ain't got no friends. She only has girls. And lots of mans who come to visit."

Doris frowned, clicking her tongue in disapproval. It took a few moments before I understood the sort of house Minnie ran.

"Yep, tiny blonde thing. Cried all the time," she said. "It ain't too bad though. She will be used to it by now. Some of the mans are nice."

Thora blanched and this delighted Clara who leaned in close to us, pointed to her scar with a bitten down fingernail. "But some of them ain't."

"Where is this place?" I asked Doris.

"Not too far from here," she said. "I will take you."

Clara called out a warning as she trotted upstairs. "Minnie ain't going to let her go, she's an earner."

We climbed into a little cart that Doris hitched to a horse kept in a lean-to outside the back door. She snapped a little whip in the air and off we went down the back lane onto the street.

As she drove, Doris explained that she and Minnie had an agreement. The girls who wanted to reform were allowed to move into the halfway house. In exchange, Doris "took care of things" when the girls who worked for Minnie found themselves in trouble. It would be days before I fully understood what she meant. Doris spoke delicately, easing her way into the details that she knew were difficult for us to hear or comprehend.

"It is surprising how many girls choose this life," she said. "It is safer than living on the street. A roof over their heads, regular meals."

Nothing she said convinced me that Freyja would want that over coming home.

"Young girls can be so foolish," she added. "Think they know everything. They run away and end up with no place to go. The ones from good families sometimes find their way home. The others, well, they flee one bad situation straight into another."

"Someone should tell the police," I said.

Doris laughed. "Who do you think encouraged all the brothels to congregate in one part of the city? The mayor and police chief. All they care about is keeping them out of the respectable neighborhoods."

I was too dumfounded to reply.

We followed Main Street through the hotel district, past the rail yards, then turned onto a street towards the Red River.

The street looked even worse than I'd imagined. When I voiced surprise at seeing children out playing, Doris explained the foreigners and "DPs" had begun moving in the year before because the rent was low.

"Now, this might be difficult," she said, pulling the horse to a stop in front of a two-storey pink house. "Best you leave the talking to me."

We followed her up the front steps. She knocked as if she meant it, and a few moments later a girl our age wearing a colorful, silk dress opened the door. My revulsion did not bother her in the least as I looked away from her painted face and naked legs.

The girl alerted Minnie then stepped aside to allow us in. The house was luxuriously warm, filled to the brim with ornate overstuffed chairs, tables, tinkling chandeliers and Persian carpets. A wide, polished staircase wound to the second floor. A most pleasing mixture of spicy and floral scents filled the air and electric power cast a warm glow from the lamps that hung throughout the house.

Minnie sat relaxing in the parlor, basking in the sunlight that came in through the large front window. She did not stand to greet us, but was quick to invite us to sit down. She looked like a calico cat allowed to eat whenever it wanted.

"Doris," she purred, "how are you this fine afternoon?"

"I am well, and you?"

Minnie smiled pleasantly, her cat eyes settling on Thora and me. "What brings you here today?"

Doris hesitated, glancing up the staircase. "Do you have any . . . guests?"

"Not right now," Minnie said, raising one eyebrow. "I expect they are all at church. Business should pick up later. We serve a lovely Sunday dinner, as you know. Would you like to join us?"

"No thank you," Doris said carefully.

Two girls lounged on the sofa opposite her with their legs up. They immediately obeyed when Minnie shooed them into the other room. They stood giggling on the other side of glass-paned doors, watching us through the little windows.

"Doctor Bjornsson sent us," said Doris. "These young ladies are relatives."

"Ahhh, how is he?" Minnie asked sweetly. "I have not needed his services in a while."

"He is fine."

"An uncle?"

"On their Mother's side and you know how clannish the Icelanders are," Doris said, equally sweet. "These girls are looking for their sister. Clara believes she may be here."

"Clara? How is she? Still making trouble for herself?"

Doris laughed. "Certainly a challenge to have around."

"Not back on the street yet?"

"Not so far."

"Time will tell." Minnie tilted her head at Thora and me. "What is your sister's name?" she asked.

A feeling of utter dread came over me, escalating to the point I could barely speak.

"Freyja."

"Why did she run away?"

Her question took me aback.

"Come now, you must know," she asked. "How do you expect me to help if you keep secrets?"

Thankfully, Doris interjected. "She is young, petite. White curly hair. Timid."

"There is no one here by that name," Minnie said.

"But there is a girl here who fits that description," Doris pressed. "Might we talk to her? To find out if she is Doctor Bjornsson's niece?"

"Why did he not come here himself?" she asked.

Doris was crafty indeed. "Surely he would be seen," she said. "How would he explain it to the Board? We both could lose our only ally at the hospital."

Minnie thought for a few minutes then she let out a powerful sigh. She called for the girl who'd answered the door.

"Go get Anna," she said. "She has visitors."

A jarring silence fell over the room as the girl hurried up the stairs. Doris made small talk but all I heard were footsteps on the floor above us. I could not take my eyes off the staircase and held my breath as a pair of legs wearing a short dress started slowly down the stairs. The girl hesitated, then she appeared around the corner.

She looked so much like Freyja that, had I seen her at a distance, I would have easily believed she was my sister. I saw relief as her eyes settled on us, likely that we were not men.

Minnie measured all our reactions. Mine was sheer delight. Never have I been so glad to be disappointed. I would have wished dear sweet Freyja dead rather than live through what this poor girl must endure.

The girl stood with her mouth open ever so slightly, staring across the room at Thora and me. She looked beaten down and I thought of Einar. Anger flared and for a moment I imagined what Amma would do if she stood in my spot. Decisions are often made in an instant.

I spoke quietly in Icelandic. "I came looking for my sister. Do you want to leave this place? You can pretend to be her and we will take you with us."

She tilted her head with a look of utter disbelief.

"My sister's name is Freyja Gudmundsson. I am Asta. This is Thora. Come across the floor and hug us so she believes we are sisters."

Anja looked at Minnie whose eyes already showed suspicion. The girl was terrified and uncertain.

"Anna, what is she saying?" Minnie asked.

"You have been praying to God, haven't you?" I said, grabbing the girl's attention again. "Who do you think sent us here?"

Anja inhaled sharply. Her eyes turned inward. She found the strength to look at Minnie, but only for a moment. She whispered that she was sorry, then came across the floor. I took her in my arms and, closing my eyes, imagined for a moment. We both laughed and wiped away the tears.

Minnie clearly trusted none of this, but dared not risk getting on the wrong side of Doctor Bjornsson. Doris thanked her as we hurried to the door.

Anja hesitated. "My things."

"Leave them," I said, my hand grasping hers tightly. "You want no reminder of this place."

We climbed into the cart. I turned back, waving wildly at Minnie standing in the doorway, wickedly pleased with myself. I relished the moment she realized she'd been duped; it was too late, Doris had already snapped the whip and we were away.

Doctor Bjornsson contacted Anja's parents and she returned to New Iceland within the week, and Doris promised to watch for Freyja. It was reassuring to know that the circle of people looking for her was widening.

January 28, 1916
Dear Pabbi and Mama,

I hope this letter finds everyone in good health.

Normally the hospital is filled to capacity this time of year but patient numbers are down. Superintendent Gray warns this respite will be brief.

I find working the night shift agrees with me. I have no trouble sleeping during the day and wake refreshed. This is opposite to most, however the superintendent says she is much the same as I, and does her best work at night.

As a reward for achieving the highest marks last term, the superintendent invited me to attend the third reading of the Bill, asking that women in Manitoba be granted the vote. There was not one seat in the gallery. Being I am so tall, I stood near the back.

Tómas Jónsson did not let us down! I am sure you've heard by now that he was Acting Premier and he moved the Bill. Some say that Premier Norris wanted to save face with people on both sides of the debate, so he was purposely absent that day. Even though all women are not yet allowed to vote, at least this is a start. I was disappointed that Margrét Benedictsson was not there to witness it. Apparently the worst possible fate has befallen her—failing eyesight. Margrét now lives in Washington State.

As you will see in the clippings I've enclosed, there is much talk about conscription and the government is trying to determine how many men live in Manitoba.

Have you received a ballot in the mail? Tell Leifur to ignore it. That is what many men in the city are doing.

I received a letter from Finn a few days ago. The gas crippled his lungs but not enough that they will send him home. Tell J.K. and Gudrún that he is doing fine and is too busy to write.

Love, Ástfriður

I unfolded Finn's letter to re-read it:

December 24, 1915

Ásta,

Forgive me for not writing sooner. Every time I sit down to it I am forced to recall the last weeks and must decide what to include about life here on the front line. In all honesty, the terror leaves me without words.

My lungs have healed but I can no longer run like before. They sent me from the hospital to Linghem (in France) then back to Ypres where I am now. Both George and I have been outfitted with sniper's capes and rifles that have a telescopic sight. I prefer the intense nature of sharp shooting to fieldwork despite its dangers, because there is no room to allow my mind to wander. That gets many men killed.

Initially I was ashamed to say that this Battalion from Winnipeg was nicknamed the 'Little Black Devils,' but now I say it with pride. When entering the gates of hell, it does a man no good to have angels by his side if he has any hope of surviving this God-forsaken place. Had I known war would be like this, I never would have enlisted. Cowardice is the worst crime, so I admit this to no one. Instead, I put on a brave face and pretend I am not here.

Now I understand Stefán's pain the day he shot his arm. Seeing others die with similar injuries speaks to his strong constitution. It is too bad that he drowned, but there are much worse ways to die. At least he lies at home, in peace.

All that keeps me alive are thoughts of you and beautiful Siglunes. I miss the lake desperately. I no longer desire a life in Winnipeg. All I want is to come home.

Finn

Oh, how my life could have turned out differently. Take Finn's letter for example. It is obvious now what I should have seen when I read it. Had I examined it critically, instead of lying to myself and everyone else, I would have been better prepared when the final blow came. I was also blind in my search for Freyja. Every path led to the same conclusion, but I refused to accept it.

Amma had read from the Sagas: 'Nothing good can happen to people who break their solemn vows.' Noble, but not easy to live up to. Just try making a promise then watch how fate turns on its head, rejoicing at your sorrow as it throws daggers in your path.

That is exactly what happened that year to me. It began one day in the second week of June.

CHAPTER FORTY-ONE

Nothing good can happen to people who break their solemn vows.
—THE SAGA OF HRAFNKELS FREYSGOÐA

THERE WERE A HALF DOZEN STUDENTS STANDING IN THE RECEPtion room whispering as I pulled open the door after a harried day. A summer flu was making its rounds.

They tittered when they saw me. Superintendent Gray's office door was ajar and she was watching.

He was standing with his back to the room, arms folded across his chest, admiring a painting by the staircase. A duffel sat on the floor at his feet. The moment our eyes met, a wide smile opened across his face.

He was still the finest man this earth had ever seen.

"Bjorn," I sang.

"Asta, it is so good to see you." His eyes settled first on my cap then moved quickly over my uniform. "Look at you."

I blushed, feeling proud.

He came across the floor, taking me into his arms, hugging me hard. By then, Superintendent Gray stood in her doorway. The girls were swooning as I took him over to meet her. Once we'd dispensed with the pleasantries, she reminded me that men were not allowed beyond the reception area.

"He is not my beau," I said, feeling my cheeks warm again. "Just a friend from home."

"Hmmm," she said, lips tight. "You know the rules. Change before going out. Report to me when you return."

I left a note for Thora telling her Bjorn was in town, that we were going for supper, then hurried back to find him standing on the sidewalk.

"Thought I should wait out here," he said. "Miss Gray makes me nervous."

"She is like that to everyone." I laughed, trotting down the steps. "How long are you here for?"

"A few days."

"Hungry?" I asked. "I know a place."

"So this is where you work." He tilted his head back to see the hospital towering overhead.

"Mostly we go in this door. Patients through the front."

"Far more impressive than my store at Siglunes." He chuckled. "It embarrasses me now to think I tried to talk you into staying."

I groaned, swinging his hand. "Sometimes I long for those days again."

"But you enjoy nursing?"

"I do. And I don't despise the city."

"How can you enjoy this?" he asked. I knew he meant the buildings, people and noise.

"I love the motorcars," I said, giving him a sly look. "You chose a good time to come."

"Why is that?"

"It's the most beautiful month of the year," I said. "Look how green it is, not as beautiful as Siglunes, but the city is never so fresh as this."

The café was dwarfed by two large buildings, Lögberg headquarters on one side, a bookstore on the other.

"This is Runey's," I said. "We have to eat here. They will let us sit and talk for as long as we want."

Doctor Bjornsson was getting up to leave as we came in. With the exception of Sunday at church, it wasn't often we saw each other outside of the hospital. I introduced the two of them; it was the first time they'd met, though each knew of the other, his profession, and efforts in the search for Freyja.

"In the city for a few days?" the doctor asked, paying his chit. "You should try to take in a few sights."

"I am, and I will," he said.

"I am off to Winnipeg Beach. We have a summer cottage there. My wife has been expecting me for a few days now, but you know how it is at the hospital."

He took from his pocket a folded piece of paper and handed it to me.

"I was going to leave this for you with Superintendent Gray," he said. "Enjoy your dinner."

We found a quiet table along the window. I anxiously read the note.

"He has done further investigating. Apparently last winter Bjarni was seen with a girl matching Freyja's description. He will ask Bjarni himself, but he wants to wait a few days. Bjarni's Afi died and the funeral is tomorrow."

"We should go," Bjorn said. "I would like to meet this scoundrel and ask him a few questions."

"I can't risk it," I said. "If Bjarni writes another letter—"

"After I finish with him he won't be writing to anyone," Bjorn said.

The waitress came to our table but we hadn't yet opened the menu. Bjorn quickly looked it over. I ordered the same as always—lamb chops with potatoes and peas. Bjorn ordered the beef kidney pie.

The café was quickly filling up.

"So what has brought you to the city?" I asked, shaking away thoughts of Bjarni.

His eyes lingered for a moment on the young couple seated at the table next to us. "You."

My stomach lurched. "Nothing bad has happened?"

"No, nothing like that," he said, eyes meeting mine. "But your letters do leave me wondering. They are . . . vague."

I apologized, saying there was so little to report. "I've had to put

Freyja out of my mind to get through my studies. The work is very demanding."

He let me go on and on about the schedule, the patients, other nurses and the staff. I must have talked without interruption for a half hour until I finally caught myself, seeing he was listening but focused on his plate, looking up from it to watch the goings on out the window.

"What is it?"

His eyes slowly met mine. "I wonder why it is you never mention Finn."

"There is nothing to say," I said, pushing my empty plate away. "He seldom writes because he finds it too difficult."

Bjorn's voice softened. "Do you write to him?"

"Of course."

We spent the next hour catching up. He described Stefan's funeral, saying that he was buried in a spot overlooking the lake. I'd already written about visiting the brothel, but he wanted me to tell him the part about spiriting Anja away firsthand.

"That was very brave of you," he said. "I will tell your Amma the story when I get home."

We each ordered a piece of pie. I told him everything I'd done to find Freyja, including putting notices up in places I thought she might frequent. I'd visited another halfway house, and even one for unwed mothers, but had come away with nothing.

"I am beginning to think—" but I could not say the words out loud. Tears blurred everything and I pushed the pie aside. "Please don't tell Mama, not yet."

We left the café and walked together for hours, so absorbed in conversation we saw nothing around us. Finally we settled on a bench in front of the hospital.

"Father has decided to sell Asi the mill," he said. "His wife will take over the store."

I'd been so preoccupied with my own worries that I hadn't even seen that there was something he'd been waiting to tell me.

"Sell the store? What are you going to do?" For a brief moment I thought he might say he had no plans of going home, that he was in the city for good. The notion was so appealing it excited me more than I dared admit.

He must have read my mind because he looked pleased. "I am going back to Swan River," he said softly. "I have decided to buy the store from Sifton." He waited for my reaction but I was so surprised by the news I didn't know what to say.

"It is a beautiful place and business is booming. I already have a spot picked out right along the river to build a house, not far from the school. I think it will be a wonderful place to raise a family." He took my hand. "The town has even built a new hospital and they are looking for qualified nurses."

The feeling that came over me compares to nothing else I have ever experienced; it was utter joy and grief all rolled into one. I knew what he was hinting at without him having to say it. The emotion began rising in my throat. Swan River. With Bjorn.

"Happy Birthday," he said.

"You remembered?"

"Of course," he said, taking a small box from his pocket. Inside was a gold locket dangling from a bronze bow studded with diamonds and tiny ceramic flowers. It was the most beautiful piece of jewelry I'd ever seen.

"I can't accept it," I whispered, but could barely take my eyes off the necklace.

"Because you are still engaged to Finn," he said, watching my reaction carefully.

"Yes."

"But it must be hard for you," he said, softly. "Not knowing if he is coming home."

"He will."

Bjorn studied me as I blinked back tears.

"I cannot give up on him," I said. "Finn has been so patient and now he needs me more than ever."

"But do you love him?"

I hesitated. Closed my eyes so that everything I was feeling would slide into focus. "Enough that I will not hurt him," I finally said. "What sort of man would even want a woman so callous?"

Surprised, but pleased by my answer, the corner of his mouth turned up ever so slightly. "An imperfect man. One who has made mistakes of his own," he said, closing the box and returning it to is pocket. "I was once loved by a young girl, but was too preoccupied to see it. I'd do anything to have that love again."

I had not expected our evening to turn out this way, him baring his soul. I wished that I could rewind, not just that day, but my whole life since meeting him, to start over again.

He wrapped his arm around my shoulder, pulling me in tight. We sat like that for a long while in silence as the light around us faded and the air grew damp. Finally, it was time for me to go in.

"Where will you stay tonight?" I asked as we drifted toward the residence door.

"The Leland Hotel. I've been there before."

We stood awkwardly knowing we needed to say good-bye. A motorcar rounded the corner. Four young recruits in uniform hung over the side, tight on booze, hooting as they sped by.

"Get a haircut," one of them yelled as they passed us.

I burst into laughter seeing Bjorn's shocked face. He growled, grabbed me by the waist and began tickling, then pulled me close. His warmth was intoxicating; our faces inches apart. Another car was coming, this one for hire. He stuck out his arm to flag it down.

"I love you, Asta," he said, kissing me on the cheek. "And I promise I will never let anyone hurt you ever again."

"I need time to think," I whispered.

"I will wait," he said.

He climbed into the car and I went inside and stuck my head into Superintendent Gray's office. She looked up at the clock then back at her paperwork.

"Did you have a pleasant evening?" she asked.

"Yes I did," I said.

"Asta." She did not look up from the desk. "If he is the one you discarded, I am anxious to see who you kept."

Thora was still awake. She looked terribly angry. And hurt. As I climbed into bed, she closed her book loudly, let it drop to the floor, switched off the light and turned away from me.

"How could you do this to Finn?"

Already exhausted and frustrated and excited and anxious, it took every ounce of energy I had left to formulate a civil reply.

"He came to ask about Freyja," I said into the darkness. "That is all."

"I saw you hugging him on the street."

"I was happy to see an old friend from home." Hearing the words out loud helped solidify my feelings. "I promised your brother I'd wait for him and nothing has changed."

The next day Thora and I stood together on either side of a microscope, taking turns peering through the lens.

"I am sorry," she said quietly, one eye focused on the germs wiggling on the glass.

"I understand," I said, writing notes in the tablet. "Had I been you, I probably would have thought the same thing."

Now I see Bjorn, across town, at the edge of the cemetery, waiting for the service to end. Bjarni makes his way across the grass, frowning at the stranger standing with his arms crossed.

"Bjarni Thordarson?" Bjorn says.

"Yes?"

"I am Bjorn Magnusson from Siglunes. Your brother died at our mill. He was a good worker and well-liked."

"Thank you." Bjarni is cautious.

"I am looking for Freyja Gudmundsson. Numerous people have

seen her with you and I want to know where she is."

"Freyja who?"

"Stop pretending. Why does her name make you so nervous? You have fooled no one, least of all me."

Bjarni laughs. "Her sister sent you, didn't she?"

"Asta knows nothing about this. Lodge another complaint against her and you will deal with me, understand?"

"No girl is worth this much trouble," Bjarni says.

"This one is."

"If this harassment continues, I will notify the police."

"Why don't we go to the police station right now?" Bjorn says.

Bjarni turns and marches to a motor car. He slams it into reverse then jolts onto the road.

Bjorn flags down a jitney and climbs in. "Follow him," he says, pointing at Bjarni's car speeding down the street, turning at the first intersection. He reaches into his pocket and pulls out a large bill. "Don't lose him."

They round corners, quick turns left and right, then onto a side street.

"Enjoy driving motorcars?" Bjorn asks.

"Today I do." The driver laughs.

"A pleasant way to see the sights."

"Why are we following him?"

"He needs to know I am serious."

"I don't want any trouble."

"Neither does he."

They settle into the rhythm of the traffic, skirting trolleys and carriages, keeping Bjarni in their sights as he crosses the river.

"What did the bloke do?" the driver asks. "About a woman, isn't it? I see a lot of jilted lovers, especially now with the war on."

"Well they are not lovers, at least I don't think so. And nobody has been jilted. But the woman I love has been hurt twice and I'm sure as hell not going to let it happen a third time."

"How long do you want me to keep following him?"

"Until he out-maneuvers you."

"All afternoon, then?"

Two weeks later a letter from Bjorn arrived. I did not want to read it. I didn't want to know. I took it upstairs and, after staring at my name written in his hand, carefully tracing it with my finger, tucked it unopened in the bureau drawer.

As the Great War raged in Europe, I thought carefully about everything Bjorn had said during our visit. The promise I'd made to Finn weighed heavily on me. Living with Thora was a constant reminder that hurting him would also mean losing my only true friend. I believed as so often young people do that I didn't have a choice.

One afternoon a few weeks later I returned briefly to my room to find a note slipped under the door. The envelope was addressed to me in handwriting I didn't recognize. I opened it and went straight to the bottom of the page. It was from Bjarni.

July 13, 1916

To Ástfriður Guðmundsson:

I am writing to inform you that I have departed for Iceland. My Afi died last month so there is nothing left for me here in Canada.

By the time you read this, I will be at sea. This is a tremendous relief for me unless you decide to pursue me across the ocean.

Freyja came to my apartment one evening so I took her in. She was broken-hearted and said she never wanted to see her beau again. She begged me to keep her presence a secret, fearing that one of you might come looking for her. Doing so caused me a great inconvenience as I was forced to lie to everyone—my friends, co-workers, the Pastor and even my Afi.

After I fell in love with her I continued with the lie. Freyja feared that your father would never accept me, and if he found her would force her to go home and I would lose her forever.

You are probably wondering why I have decided to confess. It is time I unburden myself and, considering the lengths you went to, you deserve to know the truth . . .

I skipped to the final paragraph, and ran downstairs. I caught Superintendent Gray outside her office.

"What is it?" she asked, seeing immediately that something was wrong.

I held up the letter.

"Is this regarding your sister?"

I was shaking violently. "I need to go right now."

"Very well," she said. "Be careful."

CHAPTER FORTY-TWO

Ill it is to sit lamenting for what cannot be had
—VÖLSUNGA SAGA

All the way there I prayed. The driver stopped at the main entrance then asked if he should wait. I told him no, this would take a while. Clutching the letter, I stepped out of the car. I consulted the small map Bjarni had sketched at the bottom of the page.

Following the path, I wondered how I was going to find her amongst so many, and then, without warning, with so little time to work out how to react, there she was under a beautiful elm tree.

Whenever I'd imagined finding Freyja it always was the same. I would see her, call her name, and she would turn. Her mouth would open and delight would spread across her face. She would cry out my name and come running into my arms. All I'd thought about for years was how pleased Mother and Pabbi would be, that Leifur would stop blaming Bensi, the little ones would dance, and Amma might die in peace.

Now, with the moment in front of me, I resigned myself to the truth that the quest was over. I read the final paragraph again.

Freyja died on May 12, 1915. Pneumonia. You can check the hospital records at St. Boniface if you like. I arranged to have her buried in the Brookside Cemetery. I am sure you will have no trouble locating her grave. Losing your sister broke my heart.

Since I have given you what you wanted, I will leave you to grieve in peace and ask that you allow me to do the same.

Bjarni Thordarson

Two graves lay side by side. The one piled with fresh dirt I knew was Bjarni's grandfather's. The other to the left of it was sun-bleached and ever so slightly sunken. A wooden cross with 'Freyja Guðmundsson' carved into it was pressed into the ground.

The only comfort I felt as I walked the four miles back to the residence was that all of the headstones surrounding Freyja bore Icelandic names.

I handed Superintendent Gray the letter. "Please give this to Doctor Bjornsson."

Days passed. I remember nothing from that time except lying in bed sobbing. I slept fitfully and finally, on what I believe was the third morning, awoke with an empty mind. I simply couldn't cry anymore.

Thora was sitting beside my bed wearing nothing but her underclothes, fanning herself in the July heat. A book rested on her lap and an English dictionary on the bed behind her.

"How do you feel?" she asked.

"Hot." I exhaled, pushing the hair back from my sweaty forehead. "And miserable."

"I'm so sorry," she said.

I couldn't stand lying down anymore so I pushed myself up, swinging my legs over so I could sit with my feet touching the cool floor.

It was so hard to admit what I'd refused to consider for so long.

"Well at least now we know," she said calmly, pouring me a glass of water from the pitcher on our night table.

I was so thirsty I drank every ounce despite the muddy taste.

Thora delighted in my screwed up face. The book slid from her lap onto the floor.

"What are you reading?" I asked.

"*The Wanderer* by Frances Burney," she said, picking it up. "The clerk at the bookstore said it was poorly reviewed but I am enjoying it. The heroine finds herself in countless predicaments. She reminds me a bit of you."

We both chuckled at that.

"What have I missed?" I asked, still in a daze from too much sleep.

"Not much," she said. "I was worried about you so I asked Miss Gray if I might stay here. She was kind enough to allow it."

"You are such a good friend."

"No," she said wistfully, "I am your sister. That is, if you will have me. I know that I will never replace Freyja, but would like to try."

The sun rose the next morning then set that evening, just as it had at the farm after Freyja's disappearance. The world felt different, even though nothing had changed, except now the quest to find Freyja was over. Looking for her had become such a habit it would take a while for me to stop. The worst part, the hardest to get over, was knowing that I'd been right there—*right there*—on the other side of the river the day she died.

I decided not to tell anyone just yet and swore Thora to secrecy. I would find a way to tell Bjorn and my family once I'd worked through my own grief.

I never did ask for the letter back. Probably a wise decision. Without it, I could let go of the obsession and instead of pouring over it endlessly, dredging up the pain time and again, I'd simply remember how brightly the sun shone the day I found her resting peacefully.

When September arrived I threw myself into my final year of studies, determined that if I couldn't bring Freyja home, I could at least make my parents proud.

November 27, 1916
Ásta,

I cannot remember the last time I wrote.

With winter nearing, we have nothing to look forward to except depressing skies and wet, shivering cold. I have been careful not to ruin my feet, a soldier is useless otherwise. They do their best to feed us, but it is impossible to quell our hunger. And the noise! The dog-fights overhead and shell-fire are relentless.

My God how I miss the solitude at home.

We are finally gaining ground but I overheard the Colonel say we've lost thousands of men trying to capture the Regina trench at the Somme. Heat stroke killed some of us. The temperatures are unbearable. Worst 'tho are the rats, they are huge and come when we are sleeping. We take turns staying awake and one night me and a chum killed 32 of the bastards.

Colonel Lipsett was so impressed that I was able to pick off a German operating a machine gun, and on the second shot, pierce the casing of the breech-block, that he called me a genius. The strategy seemed obvious to me.

Did I mention that I took sharpshooter's training? The Commander assessed the trenches when he arrived here and ours were healthier than most. Lipsett did not want to give me up, but the Major insisted that I go with him.

A month later I returned to my battalion to find my chum George dead. This saddens me greatly because had I been here, George would still be alive. He was my partner but when I left they replaced me with an idiot who cost them both their lives.

Now I'm the sharpshooter who travels with the Colonel. It is my responsibility to kill the Germans who so desperately want to kill him.

Finn

A letter from Mother arrived the following spring:

April 17, 1917
Dear Ásta,

By the time you receive this you will be studying for your final exams. Good luck dear, I am sure you will do well.

I considered holding off telling you the following news, but it is inevitable that you find out, so your father and I decided it best you hear it from us.

Your beloved Amma has died. She was found one morning last week, with a most peaceful look on her face. Her suffering is over. She died knowing that her final act of belligerence kept Leifur from going to war.

A military man intent on enforcing conscription came to the farm. We decided against your advice and filled out the ballots honestly. I didn't think it possible that they would find us, but alas, they are desperate for young men.

It was plain for him to see that Lars is not much use to Pabbi on the farm and while we have grown accustomed to Sólrún stomping around in the brace, to a stranger we must be a sorrowful sight. But I believe it was Amma who forced him take pity on us. By the grace of God, she was home that week while the nurse was away on leave in Brandon.

The moment Amma saw his uniform she began raving and there was nothing any of us could do to quieten her. Amma overheard many discussions about the war and knew that only weeks ago the Larsons found out that Jon was killed. She grabbed onto Leifur's arm and would not let go.

The officer was disappointed but granted Pabbi's request that Leifur be allowed to stay on the farm. Your brother has grown into an impressive young man, level-headed and strong as the oxen.

I am distressed to say that conscription has divided our community. J.K. is of the same mind as us - that everyone should do their part, but that unfair hardship should not be placed on any one family. Leifur leaving would certainly have done that to us.

Which brings me to the next piece of news.

J.K. received a telegram yesterday. As I understand it, Finn took a bullet to the leg and is recovering in a hospital in England. When he is strong enough, likely by the end of the month, he will be sent home. You have not said what your plans are after graduation so I thought knowing this may help.

After Amma's funeral, Magnús handed us her sack of money. Who would have guessed that she had it after all? She gave it to him for safekeeping prior to her stroke with the instruction that half of it be given to Leifur to establish his farm and the other half to our family's education fund. You will find in the bottom of this parcel an envelope. Leifur insisted that a portion of Amma's money bequeathed to him be donated to the war effort, so please give it to the IODE on his behalf. He says that the donation makes it easier for him to sleep at night.

Ási is coping much better. He was a sorry sight when he came to visit your father and they talked long into the night. Whatever Pabbi said to him must have worked because he stopped drinking spirits. The mill is thriving now as is the store.

Magnús and Bergthora are still in the big house but it saddens me to report that she took to her bed and we do not expect she will live much longer.

We buried Amma at the edge of the yard not far from the oak. Setta has taken to lying on her grave and it brings a tear to my eye every time I see this.

Take care my daughter, Mama

Every out-of-town nurse had the same dream: that one day she would return to the residence after her shift at the hospital to find a loved one waiting.

I cried nearly as hard as Thora at the sight of J.K. and Gudrun—J.K. absorbing everything he could about hospital administration from

Superintendent Gray; Gudrun seeing us first, smiling wide. Thora flew into her outstretched arms.

"Asta, you come here this instant," Gudrun said, waving me into her generous fold.

Superintendent Gray's expression held a touch of admiration. "Two of the finest students I have ever taught," she said. "You should be very proud." Then she slipped quietly away to leave us to it.

"Good news," J.K. said, but he did not reveal it right away. He stood there brimming, waiting for us to plead. We turned to Gudrun but all she did was smile.

"Telegraph from Finn," he said, holding up a piece of paper. "He arrives on the train late tonight, so tomorrow we can take him home."

They followed us up to our room where it was quiet so we could speak privately. They were as impressed by the electric lighting as we had been. Although our room was a little too warm, and with the window open the noise from the street below was loud, they thought it a pleasant enough place to have spent three years.

"You have another exam tomorrow?" Gudrun asked.

The reminder sent a quiver through my stomach.

They invited us to join them for supper at the café; hard as it was, I declined. Nothing, not even excitement over seeing Finn again, would get in the way of my studying that night.

"I will come," said Thora.

As they stood up to leave, J.K.'s eyes met mine.

"Thank you for believing in him," he said quietly, squeezing my shoulder. "It is no secret that I had a difficult time keeping faith, but you never wavered."

"She never did, not once," Thora said proudly.

"And now he is coming home," Gudrun said.

"I could not ask for a finer daughter-in-law than you," J.K. said, pulling me close. Then he laughed, pushing me back so he could see my face. "That is presuming the two of you still intend to marry."

I nodded in agreement.

"I know it will be three weeks until you are home," he said. "We will bring him by to see the two of you tomorrow, around dinner time?"

"That sounds wonderful," I said.

When the door closed behind them I stood in the middle of the floor listening to their footsteps and laughter down the hall. Once all was silent, except for the sound of the occasional car passing on the street, I pulled open the top drawer of my bureau. Fishing underneath my stockings and undergarments I found Bjorn's letter from the year before, still unopened. Was it time?

I closed my eyes to take in the silence. I could feel my heart beating quick and solid in my chest. I could see J.K. and Gudrun's smiling faces. My thoughts rewound and, in perfect sequence, I remembered all the times Finn and I had spent together; sun on our faces as we sailed the bay, his frustration and my laughter every time I beat him at chess, the quickening deep inside me when he took me in his arms and kissed my lips and neck. Then I allowed myself to feel again the heartbreak over losing Bjorn to Steina, my initial apprehension towards Finn, and then, finally, the love that blossomed between us.

I was consumed by guilt. A lie by omission was still a lie and I'd been deceiving everyone, including myself, these past three years. The truth was, deep inside where we hide our worst fears, I'd had no more faith than anyone else that Finn would survive. I simply pretended for his sake and mine.

And now he was back so I could allow myself to feel again. I laughed out loud and cried, still holding the envelope. Taking a deep breath, I went to the window and pushed it open wide.

It was time I let go of Bjorn once and for all.

I held the letter up then, difficult as it was, ripped it in half, then three times again, until his words were broken into tiny pieces. I threw them out into the wind.

Thora floated in hours later, humming to herself. We agreed this was the happiest day we'd experienced since coming to Winnipeg. We decided that, next morning, whoever was finished the exam first would wait in the lobby for the other.

"Are you excited?" she asked.

Finn had been absent so long, I was still finding it difficult to believe he was on his way back to me.

"I am," I said, reaffirming the vow I'd made seven years earlier.

Nursing school taught us many lessons, but none more useful than discipline and focus. I put Finn out of my mind and methodically answered every question on the exam, finishing shortly after Thora. I went to the lobby but she wasn't there. I paced until I could stand it no longer then asked a classmate if she'd seen her.

"Thora left. With her mother."

I went to the window but saw nothing, so I hurried down the steps, expecting to see them waiting for me around the corner in the shade, or on the bench in the hospital garden. I circled the hospital and the residence, realizing that somehow I'd missed them.

Dread grew in my stomach as I waited in the stuffy room, preparing to begin the next exam. I watched the door until Thora hurried in, barely in time, red-cheeked and breathless. Our eyes met and she waved, taking the last seat left at the back of the room.

Focus, I told myself. There was a reasonable explanation. Thora would tell me once the exam was written. The instructor closed the door, set the timer, then told us to begin.

When we were finished, I met Thora at the door.

"I'm sorry I couldn't wait for you," she said. "Finn couldn't make it up the steps. He was late getting in, not until this morning. They needed to hurry or they'd miss the train."

"How is he?" I asked.

"Tired, and his leg is sore. All he wanted was to go home."

"Did he ask about me?" I said, feeling silly.

She hesitated, but only for a moment. "Yes, he can hardly wait to see you. Everything will be better once he is settled."

Miss Gray called it 'an unfortunate blessing.'

With so many injured men returning to Manitoba, it was easy to find a job nursing. Thora and I were each offered a position at the IODE Convalescent Soldiers Home beginning in July and we both accepted.

On May 23, 1917 our graduating class gathered to receive diplomas and school medals. A photo was taken in front of the residence.

"Well done, good and faithful servant," Superintendent Gray said as she pinned the school medal on each of our chests. The Lieutenant-Governor, J.S. Hough, and the Chairman of the Hospital Board, handed us our diplomas.

"Impressive," the chairman said when it was my turn. "I dare say, if I ever end up in hospital it is you I will request as my nurse."

The following day we bid our good-byes, but it took longer than expected. Our intention had been to visit Freyja's grave before we left, but time was running short.

"We will be back soon enough," I said to Thora. We told the driver to take us directly to the station.

We boarded the train. It chugged its way through the north end of the city. I craned my neck as we crossed Brookside Boulevard, looking for the cemetery. Brimming with melancholy, I promised Freyja in a prayer that I would replace the wooden marker with a proper stone once I'd saved enough money.

CHAPTER FORTY-THREE

Varied will be his fortunes who fares far.
—THE SAGA OF FRIÐÞJÓF THE BOLD

LEIFUR LEAPT ABOARD THE TRAIN TO HUG ME AND THEN THORA. Marriage must have softened him. He introduced us to Sigrid after loading our duffels into the back of the democrat. We chatted the whole way home.

"Have you seen Finn?" I asked.

"A few times," he said. "Still recovering. You heard Bergthora died?"

I told him yes, that during their visit J.K. and Gudrun had delivered the news.

As the horses fell into rhythm, their shoes clopping down the road, it felt as if we'd never left.

"Tell me about the motorized cars," he said. "Is there much work for men in the city?"

"Did you go to a picture show?" Sigrid asked.

"Does anyone talk about the price of grain?" he asked.

Merriment carried us the whole way home.

"Everyone from the community is invited to your homecoming tomorrow afternoon," Sigrid said. "Gudrun is throwing it."

I'd bought a dress at the Hudson's Bay store and silent pleasure swirled inside me as I imagined the look on Finn's face when he saw me in it.

As we turned the final mile, I was amazed by how alive everything looked. Leifur said the leaves had been out for two weeks already and that he'd never seen so many Saskatoon blossoms.

Someone must have been waiting by the window because as soon as the road opened up into the yard, they all came out at once. Mother and Pabbi stood beaming beside the oak, while Lars ran onto the road with Solrun limping behind him.

They looked at me, mouths wide in astonishment. Pabbi held his tears, face beaming with pride, while Mother allowed hers to flow. She told me later that she'd hoped I'd surprise them all by bringing Freyja with me. That disappointment was the only thing that tarnished the sweet reunion for her. I climbed out of the democrat. Leifur and Sigridur carried on down the road, taking Thora home.

"Asta, you cut your hair," Mother exclaimed. It had been a year since I'd done it, so I'd forgotten. I was proud of it. With the weight gone, it bounced in a mass of chin-length curls.

"You look marvelous," Pabbi said.

Polio had stunted Solrun's growth a bit so she was small for a ten-year-old.

"Where is your brace?" I asked her.

"I barely need it anymore," she said, chin turned up with delight.

Lars hugged me quietly. He came nearly to my shoulders.

"Where is Finn?" I asked.

Then I saw Setta, tail wagging from where she sat under the tree. "Come on girl," I called, and she heaved herself up, wagging over. She'd turned gray around the muzzle but, except for a hint of sadness, nothing had changed her eyes. Leifur had warned me that she'd aged a lot the past few years and that sometimes her hips were so stiff she couldn't stand.

"Finn sent word he is too tired," Mother said, motioning that we follow her into the house. "I held supper for you."

"How is he?" I linked my arm in hers.

"We are just thankful he is alive."

The next morning when I came down for breakfast it felt strange to not have Amma and Leifur there. Mother already had a batch of buns in the oven for the party. Pabbi squeezed my shoulder gently before hurrying out to do chores.

"This came for you yesterday." Mother handed me a small package from Bjorn. She waited, studying my reaction. "I think you should open it."

"I will," I said, tucking it in my dress pocket then sat down at the table.

Solrun pulled her chair close to mine while Lars sat in Mother's chair. Both were curious about the hospital, having only faint memories of it.

"Is my friend Betsy still there?" Solrun asked.

"No, Betsy went home."

"Did you make her better?"

"She was a good patient," I fibbed, glancing up at Mother who was slicing rúllupylsa onto a plate. "When you are grown up you can come visit Finn and me in the city and I will take you to see her."

Mother turned her head slightly, a dove-like smile parting her lips.

"Did you go see Elizabeth?" Solrun asked.

"Only once. She has moved back to England to be near her family."

Solrun looked across the table at Lars who was waiting patiently for his turn. They shared a silent moment of understanding, then she nudged him with her eyes.

He hesitated. "Did you find Freyja?"

They waited, wide-eyed with anticipation. I was surprised, but thinking back, I suppose it is logical that children so young would draw such a conclusion. Freyja and I both went away, now I was back.

"Yes, I found her."

Mother's hands became still. The children beamed.

"Where is she?" Solrun asked.

"She was living in Winnipeg for a while but now she's gone," I said.

"Where did she go?"

"Home."

Mother inhaled sharply and our eyes met across the kitchen.

"Back to Iceland?" asked Solrun.

I hesitated. "It is very beautiful there and she loves it very much."

"But why did she go, is she angry with us?" Lars asked.

"Of course not." I said. "Freyja is not mad at anyone. She is very happy."

"I miss her," Solrun said.

"So do I, but when I am feeling lonely I talk to her," I said. "Always remember that once a person has lived in a place, a part of them remains there forever."

Solrun's eyes went to the spot on the bench where Freyja once sat.

"Will I ever see her again?" she asked.

"You will, someday."

"That is what Amma told me, in the dream," Lars said. "I will find her living in a castle in the mountains by the ocean."

A calm warmth settled over me as I went upstairs to get ready to see Finn. So much in my life had changed and yet here at Eikheimar everything was much the same. I took the package from my pocket and placed it on the night stand.

A person would have to be deaf not to hear Signy and her family arrive. I ran downstairs the moment I heard the commotion in the kitchen, and she met me at the bottom of the stairs.

"That," she squealed, pointing at my dress, "is beautiful."

I spun around to show off the feathery hem. The dress was sailor-inspired—all the rage—cream-colored with a V-neck, fitted with a wide waistband. It sported navy blue embellishments on the cuff and a cord that crisscrossed down the front. I wore a matching hat. It is the only dress I've ever owned worth describing.

"Do you think Finn will like it?"

"Of course he will," she said.

I blushed. “Do you think this time you will have a girl?” I lay a hand on her bulge before hugging her tight.

“No, I have given up,” she said, rolling her eyes.

As we came into the kitchen, Olafur let out a long, slow whistle then pulled his arms up to protect himself when Signy darted over to poke him.

“She is spoken for, and so are you.”

“Now, now, dear wife,” he said, lifting back the cloth on the counter to sneak a piece of rúllupylsa, “you are just as beautiful.”

“Ha.” She rolled her eyes again. “I look worse than a sack of flour compared to her. Look at her, look at her!”

Olafur grinned, eyes focused on the plate as he took another slice of meat, folding it in half into his mouth. “Not falling for that again. No sirree.”

We laughed and chatted our way out to the wagon. I rode beside Signy so she could fill me in on all the local gossip, but I barely heard any of it. My heart was racing wildly as we came through the bush trail. What an incredible feeling it was—seeing the lake spread out like a magnificent sheet of glass, even more mesmerizing than I remembered. Neighbors were milling around J.K.’s house while children of all ages and sizes ran along the beach and through the yard.

Finn was standing under a tree in the front yard with the men gathered around. He and one of the Larson boys were the only two in uniform. They were looking at something that lay at Finn’s feet as he leaned against his gun, grinning wildly.

Someone called out, “Asta’s here,” and my cheeks warmed. Finn looked up in our direction as Olafur circled the drive and stopped the wagon. This was the moment I’d waited on for three long years.

Finn handed Asi his gun and came across the yard, favoring his left leg. I jumped down and ran to him. I’d seen many soldiers on Winnipeg streets so it had been easy to imagine what he might look like in uniform, but he was even more handsome than I’d expected. His eyes shone more fiercely than I remembered. He hesitated, like me, as if he could hardly believe the moment was real.

"Asta," he said warmly, opening his arms. I flung mine around him hard, burying my face in the crook of his neck.

The men hooted and the women clapped as we kissed. For a fleeting moment it felt different, he felt different, but I brushed the notion aside and it vanished as quick as it had come.

"Come see what I shot," he said, taking my hand. The circle of men opened to let us in and there, lying on the ground with a bullet in its heart, was the fiercest looking wolf I'd ever imagined. It was nearly black with a gray underbelly. Its yellow eyes were shocked open in death and it bled from the mouth, tongue pinched between jagged teeth.

"How much do you think it weighs?" someone asked.

"Let's find out," Olafur said, pushing past. He bent over and tried picking it up by the hind legs, but it was so heavy he was forced to kneel then wrestle it into a bear hug to get it off the ground.

"Hundred and sixty?" he guessed.

"At least," someone said.

Finn's youngest brother ran to us from the barn holding a rope. He handed it to Finn, who knotted it tight around the wolf's back legs; he threw the loose end over a branch and, with Olafur's help, hoisted it off the ground. It was then I noticed the three medals pinned to Finn's chest.

Leifur stood watching with no expression at all. He caught my eye then turned, walking back toward the house. Anxious to get away from the gruesome sight, I followed.

"Has he talked to you yet?" he asked quietly.

"We haven't had the chance," I said.

He issued a warning: "Prepare yourself. So far I have not liked what I've heard."

Caught in the web of women, all anxious to admire my dress, I found myself migrating farther and farther away from Finn, who was surrounded by the men desperate to hear a firsthand account of the war. We stole smiles at each other, before patiently returning to the conversations at hand.

Mid-afternoon, J.K. stood on the third verandah step and tinkled his fork against his glass so that everyone would gather around. No event at Siglunes was considered a true success unless someone made a speech, and usually it was J.K.

He began by welcoming everyone. Since it was time to eat, he promised to make it quick. Asi stood off to J.K.'s right and rolled his eyes at the crowd in disbelief. He brought his hand up to his mouth, pretending to yawn, and we all laughed.

J.K. ignored him, saying that he was pleased to have Finn, Thora and me home.

"Here, here." Everyone clapped.

I caught Magnus's eye and he bowed his head. I guessed life must be lonely for him now with Bjorn moved away, Amma and Bergthora both gone.

"Before I speak to each of our honored guest's accomplishments, I would like ask that we stand in silence, to acknowledge all the young men who have given their lives, including our own Jon Larson and, though he did not die on the battlefield, Stefan Frimann. Both will always be remembered as brave, courageous young men."

Asi sniffled loudly as we bowed our heads. The air was clear and silent; the only sounds were the waves gently lapping against shore. When J.K. prayed, his deep voice resonated out over the water.

J.K. described the day he found out that Finn had enlisted and the three years of uncertainty that followed; the time Thora spent caring for Amma while I assisted in the store after the Magnusson's devastating loss, and how it felt to send us to the city, how badly we were all missed.

"God went with them," J.K. said, sending shivers up our spines, "and now God has brought them home."

Thora reached out to grab my hand. We both looked at Finn who flinched ever so slightly. To everyone else it appeared he was listening, but I knew his mind was elsewhere.

J.K. congratulated Thora first, saying that she had graduated at the top of our class.

"I am proud to say that she was awarded a prize at graduation, having achieved top marks in the area of infectious disease."

Thora giggled, did a little curtsey, then covered her face as we all clapped.

"I am told that Asta also earned a prize," J.K. said. "And I cannot say it surprises me. In fact, I predicted it long ago when she sat at my table doing sums." Like every great orator, J.K. waited to let the tension build. When everyone's eyes were on me, he said: "Asta was awarded the Royal Household Prize for the Highest Overall Proficiency. The Superintendent told me that her third year grades were the highest the school has ever seen."

"What about the first year?" Asi called out.

"Missing Finn too much," someone else said, and they all laughed.

I beamed at Finn who looked as though he hadn't heard one word.

As J.K. began again, I slipped by all the neighbors so that I might stand by Finn. He noticed me coming and snapped back to the present. I took his hand. It felt cold; it hung there with no life at all.

"What's wrong?" I whispered, giving his hand a little shake.

He forced a smile.

" . . . took awhile for me to get it out of him," J.K. said to the crowd. "Finally he relented since I had him trapped on the train."

More laughter.

Finn's muscles tensed. His eyes went to the ground.

"The first medal he was awarded is for heroism at Ypres, after the gas attacks. Countless men were saved because of him."

A murmur floated through the crowd. Jon Larson's brother stood on the other side of Finn. He patted him on the back.

"The second one because last year, during fighting at the Somme, he took out more German machine gunners than any other sharpshooter."

All eyes turned to Finn. Many shook their heads in amazement. J.K. waited until Finn looked up.

"And the third," he said proudly, "was for bravery while in the battle at Vimy in Nord-Pas-de-Calais where he saved Colonel Lipsett's life. In doing so, he was shot in the thigh."

I thought my heart might burst with pride and could not resist the temptation to kiss him on the cheek. The yard erupted in cheers. If ever there was a moment that Finn Kristjansson was vindicated, it was right then.

"Thank you, everyone," he said, then turned away from us all and hobbled toward the lake.

CHAPTER FORTY-FOUR

The one you trust most can disappoint you most.
—FLJÓTSDÆLA SAGA

CARRYING TWO PLATES OF FOOD, I SLIPPED AWAY TO WHERE HE SAT on a makeshift bench—a fallen tree across two rocks in the sand. I heard Mother in the distance calling Lars back as he tried to follow. A faint haze hung over the lake, but we could still see Gull Reef. The mosquitoes were biting as always.

Finn was leaning forward, elbow on knee, watching tiny insects burrowing in the sand. He batted away a swarm of sandflies as I sat down. It was such a relief to get away from everyone, to sit in silence.

"I want to show you something," he said, reaching into his coat pocket. He pulled out a bent and tattered eagle's feather, stared at it solemnly. "Father shouldn't have bragged like that." He carefully placed the feather on the log between us.

"He is very proud of you," I said, handing him a plate. "So am I."

I was concerned, though, about the wheeze, a whistling deep in his lungs that came between words with every breath.

Finn scoffed. "I didn't want to embarrass him in front of everyone, but it wasn't God who brought me home."

"Of course it was," I said.

He poked a piece of meat then scraped it off the fork with his teeth.

He chewed violently, swallowing hard.

"Do you like my dress?" I said, lowering my eyes. "I bought it especially for today."

He glanced at me and softened a bit. "You always look beautiful. It doesn't matter what you wear."

"Why thank you," I said, giggling as I struck a pose. "So tell me, are you glad to be home?"

"I thought I'd be thrilled," he said. "It is all we ever thought about. Now that I'm here, I can hardly believe how empty I feel."

His words were so shocking I didn't know what to say. He looked at me, shaking his head in disbelief that I couldn't read his thoughts.

"God brought me home," he said, "and left my only friends there?" He took another forkful of food and looked out over the water as he chewed, swallowing hard. "It makes no sense. Why would God allow Stanley and George to die but spare me?"

"Maybe they didn't pray." I realized the words sounded mean once said out loud.

There was no joy in his laughter. "They prayed alright. We all did." He took the bun from his plate and bit into it. "Prayer had nothing to do with it. God has nothing to do with it. The ruthless and the lucky, those are the ones who survive."

"Which are you?" I asked, taken aback.

"Both," he said, tapping the medals with his fork. "That is why I have these."

I grasped for something to say but nothing came. We finished eating in silence, then he lit a cigarette.

"How is your leg?" I asked.

"It will heal."

"And your lungs?"

"Cannot run worth a goddamn, but I fared better than most."

"Tell me about the hospital," I said. "Was it well equipped?"

"The nurses were nice. One brought me books so it wasn't a total waste of time."

That was all he would say about the hospital, even when I asked about supplies, treatment methods, if the nurses spoke English.

"What was the main cause of death?" I asked.

"Being blown to bits," he said, puffing smoke in the air, chuckling and coughing a bit.

I felt my cheeks grow warm. "That is not what I meant. Sepsis or inadequate medication, a shortage of doctors—" But my words lost their steam.

"You don't understand," he said under his breath. "You weren't there. Neither was Leifur."

"I know. That is why I am asking."

"The design of war," he began, "is to create a common enemy so that we believe they are evil. It is all nonsense. The Germans are no worse than us."

"Of course they are."

Finn shook his head. "Not the boys in the trenches. Not the men I killed. But do you want to know the worst of it?" He took a deep breath and shook his head at the memory. "I knew," he said, digging the toe of his boot into the sand. "I knew but I did it anyway."

Then he told me a story.

After the battle at Ypres, his unit finally began to advance and a group of them surprised three Germans separated from their unit. The Germans immediately laid down their guns to raise their hands in surrender. One of the Canadian soldiers fired anyway.

"One German, damn him, he looked me in the eye. He was younger than me, for Chris' sakes. A nice lad, I could tell. Scared to die. As he lay there pleading for his life, the soldier beside me shot him again. In the face."

Finn hung his head at the memory, then he whispered: "That moment I knew. I saw war for what it is."

He startled me when he raised his hands and shouted up at the sky, "Father, forgive them; for they know not what they do." And then he laughed, throaty and sarcastic.

I gasped. Finn thought me naive. We all were I suppose, those of us who did not go off to war. It took months before I fully understood that what had kept him alive on the battlefield was now destroying him at home.

"I knew in the eyes of God killing was wrong, but still, after seeing that act of brutality, I made the conscious choice to kill again. That is why I say it was not God who brought me home."

His words sent a chill through me. I reached out to take his hand but he pulled away.

"And to think how harshly I'd judged Bjorn," he said, stabbing the cigarette butt into the sand. "How much better I thought I was than him because he'd killed a man. At least Bjorn felt regret. All I feel is a haunting."

I suggested we go back to join the festivities.

He refused. His voice grew soft when he asked, "What do you think happens to us after we die?" He lit another cigarette while waiting for my answer, drawing hard on it, then let the smoke out of his lungs, watching the wind take it away.

"I wish I knew," I said. That same question had been lurking in me since seeing Runa take her last breath.

"Everything can be proven with science," he said, "except the existence of God, heaven, hell … the devil. We are expected to have faith, to believe." He shook his head, disgusted. "What is all this, then?" He waved his arm out over the water.

I understood he meant more than the lake. He was talking about everyone, everything. The profound question of life's purpose.

"I don't know," I said, stifling the urge to tell him about Freyja, fearing her death might somehow prove correct the theory he was formulating. That there was no purpose. That after we die we turn to dust and our souls do not reunite in heaven. The thought settled in my stomach like a stone.

"I think all God wants is for us to do our best," I said.

He took another desperate pull on the cigarette.

"What exactly is that?" he asked, turning to face me. "To fulfill our solemn vows? We promised to defend our country, to not let each other down. But at what price?"

He had not an inkling how his words mocked me, that soldiers weren't the only ones who made promises. I shook it off, telling him he should feel blessed to be alive; that we had so much to look forward to once the war ended. We could live in Winnipeg, build our house along the river as planned.

"Life will be normal again," I said.

But he wasn't listening. His thoughts had moved across the ocean to the battlefield; the memory of all he'd seen was trapped inside his head. A simpler man might have known how to release it. "Life will never be normal again, not for you and me," he said. "I am not the man you fell in love with."

His words exploded inside me, shattering my dreams like glass.

"You go back to the party," he said. "I want to stay here. Alone."

Dumbstruck, I stood up and started toward the house, tripping across the uneven ground. Anger caused me to stop, to turn around. "How long have you known?"

"Since the Somme," he said.

"Last fall?"

He nodded.

"Why didn't you tell me?"

In my rush to leave I'd knocked the feather to the ground. Finn stooped to pick it up and went to the water's edge. He examined it carefully one last time then flicked his wrist, spinning it out onto the water. It bobbed in the peaceful waves and slowly moved towards Gull Reef as he said good-bye to me.

"I only want what is best for you, Asta," he said. "And it isn't me."

The hardest part after that was facing everyone, forced to pretend that everything was fine, hiding my humiliation. I could not talk to the women, who would no doubt ask about wedding plans, so I went to stand by Pabbi and J.K. They were so absorbed they didn't see me behind them.

"Been hunting that wolf the better part of five years," J.K. said quietly, one eye on Pabbi the other on the wolf still hanging from the tree. "I didn't see it once. Only its tracks. Finn slipped out last night and stalked it for miles, fired only one shot."

Pabbi looked out to where Finn sat.

"I blame myself, Pjetur."

"There is nothing you—"

J.K. shook his head. "He knew that none of us thought he had what it takes," he said sadly. "Turns out he had more than we ever realized."

I held my tears until the walk home, alone, while everyone stayed at the party. Laughter and music echoed into the cool evening air as I made my way along the bush trail. Night sounds and being amongst the trees no longer frightened me. Exhausted and still in a state of disbelief, I slipped out of the dress and hung it over a chair before putting on my nightgown and lighting the lamp.

Bjorn had told me he would wait and that sparked an inkling of hope. Pushing away the image of Finn's enraged face and his words that kept rolling through my mind, I pulled the covers up and carefully opened Bjorn's package. In it was the jewelry box and a letter.

May 16, 1917
Dear Ásta,

It is with a heavy heart I sit down to write to you.

You did not reply to my last letter. I feel like a fool now, professing my undying love for you. I prayed that you would change your mind about waiting for Finn, but alas it appears that you have not.

Father tells me that Finn is home now so this leaves me no choice but to give up on the chance that we may someday be together.

It has been nearly a year since I last saw you and our time apart has been lonely for me. Business at the store is excellent and I enjoy it immensely. I built a house as planned along the river, but it feels empty living here alone. I desperately want a wife and family and I have decided it is time to get on with my life.

I met a young woman named Katherine a few months ago. She is not Icelandic but I am pleased to say she is intelligent and kind nonetheless so I have asked her to marry me. I, too, need to follow my heart even if it takes me away from you.

I have no use for the locket as I cannot imagine ever giving it to anyone else. Please accept it as a symbol of our friendship.

My sincerest hope is that you and Finn have a life filled with love and peace. Letting go of the past is the only way you will find happiness. I know because that is what I have done.

I have concluded that this is God's plan for us. Sometimes we are not meant to know why things happen as they do. All we can do is trust.

Good bye, Ásta. Best of luck.

Your friend, Björn

CHAPTER FORTY-FIVE

Long is it remembered what youth has gained.
—THE TALE OF GUNNLAUG THE WORM-TONGUE AND RAVEN THE SKALD

I CONVINCED MYSELF THAT FINN WOULD REGRET EVERYTHING HE'D said then come ask for forgiveness. I waited by the window for him to show up at the house with the chessboard and, as it always had been between us, all would be forgotten. But he didn't come. Not that day or the next.

Thora and I discussed his decision when she came to see me. We sat in the front room, talking about nothing until I couldn't stand it any longer.

"How is Finn?" I asked, still hoping he'd changed his mind.

"Quiet," she said, unable to meet my gaze. "Mostly he reads. Father says we need to be patient, that he will come around."

There was nothing more to say, really, and it was terribly disheartening that I couldn't confide in my closest friend about the inner turmoil I'd kept secret for years.

"I still hope the two of you will marry," she said, but the words sounded hollow. I think deep down we both knew.

"Pabbi?" I whispered.

A week had passed since the homecoming. It was late evening and

Pabbi was sitting in the front room reading. The house was quiet except for Mother working in the kitchen.

"Yes, Asta?"

I studied my fingernails for a while then turned my hands over, seeing for the first time how similar mine were to his, to Amma's.

"I have made a terrible mistake," I said.

He closed the book to wait.

I sat down on the sofa. "It is about Finn," I said.

"I have noticed."

"He no longer wants to marry me."

He sighed. "I thought as much."

There it was, out in the open. Seven years, wasted.

"You are not the only one concerned about him." He lay the book on the side table. "But I don't understand. How is this your mistake?"

"I made the wrong choice."

He nodded, and while he probably knew, waited for me to explain.

"I saw a glimpse of it in his letters, that war had changed him, but I refused to believe it, thinking everything would be fine once he came home."

"You cannot be faulted for that," he said.

"After I saw Bjorn last summer I had to make a choice."

Pabbi's face softened. "I always thought you were in love with both of them."

"But I'd made a promise to Finn and it would have been heartless to leave him when he was at war," I said. "Why did he let me believe we still had a future?"

"Because the truth shamed him," Pabbi said.

I thought back to that conversation in the garden with Amma. She had been standing with her fingers raised, unable to think of the fifth reason men don't tell us what is on their minds.

Mother came in holding three cups. She handed one to each of us, then sat down beside me. She gently patted my knee.

Pabbi took a sip. "Now it is time to do what you should have in the first place," he said. "You must follow your heart."

"I can't," I sobbed. "Bjorn plans to marry someone else."

Three weeks later, Thora returned to Winnipeg. It surprised everyone that she would go without me, evidence that the years away from Siglunes had changed not only Finn.

Mother and Pabbi were thrilled by my decision to stay. I was content for the time being to help Lars with his homework and exercise Solrun's legs. I spent time with Signy and the boys. It is true with sisters that time away brings them closer together; it certainly did with us.

I came to know Leifur better and liked his wife Sigrid. It turned out she'd been raised in Swan River, a revelation that caused me to listen carefully whenever she talked about the place. I overheard her mention Bjorn's Katherine once; that must have been August, after word had filtered back to Siglunes that they'd married in July.

Winter would blow in on us soon and a few decisions loomed, but we skirted around them, hoping they would miraculously resolve.

There was a position opening in Lundi at the doctor's office. The doctor's wife, also his nurse, was expecting her first child. If I wanted the job, I needed to act quickly.

The second decision concerned Setta, and that was the more difficult of the two, having already been put off by a year. I came outside one afternoon to see Leifur and J.K. standing on the road in conversation.

"I don't have the courage to do it," Leifur said.

J.K. wrapped his arm around my brother's shoulder. "There are worse things to be ashamed of, my boy. I have a horse who is too old to be useful anymore. I feed him the best oats, and brush him most days. Someday I will have to call on you, but neither he nor I are ready yet."

J.K. took the gun from him and gently patted Setta, long strokes across her back. Leifur's head dropped and he turned away. The sight of his broad shoulders heaving pierced my heart. In all the years I've known Leifur this was the only time I ever saw him cry.

"Come on, girl," J.K. said softly, coaxing Setta up.

Her tail drooped as she slowly stood, obediently following him towards the bush, looking back to see if we were coming.

I couldn't watch any longer. I ran to the house, flung open the door and took the stairs to my bedroom two at a time, falling heavily on the bed, covering my ears. I didn't hold back the tears; in fact I cried as loud as I could, needing to drown out the sound that I knew would come, but couldn't bear to hear.

CHAPTER FORTY-SIX

All should be told to a friend.
—EGIL'S SAGA

ELEVEN YEARS IS A LONG TIME IN A WOMAN'S LIFE.

It is a long time to be in the same job, in the same town. It is a long time to live alone. Had I not been kept incredibly busy, I may have been unhappy. With all the traumas, disease, and sickness sandwiched between birth on one end and death on the other, few people escaped their lives without coming through our door.

The office took up two back bedrooms in the doctor's rambling two-storey house that backed onto the river that meandered through town. To find it was simple enough: cross the bridge on Main Street, turn right at the grocery store, four houses down on the right. A young elm tree grew tall where the doctor's wife had planted it along the driveway.

Sometimes, patients made the mistake of knocking on the front door, but most knew to follow the path the length of the house to the back. The doctor owned a Model T that he'd purchased shortly after the war ended, but, due to the road conditions around Lundi, he still kept his horse, buggy, and sleigh for those times of just-in-case.

Me? I walked pretty much everywhere. For five years I boarded at the doctor's house, until his wife gave birth to their third child and my room was no longer considered spare. I moved in with an elderly couple across the street. The old woman died first, then the man, highly irregular in those days. If a woman survived her childbearing years, the dubious reward was usually outliving her husband.

I turned thirty-four that year and decided that, rather than move, I'd buy the house. What I liked most about it was the front verandah. In the evenings I'd sit out there and read, covered with a blanket, spring and fall. Later on, I hired a local carpenter to screen it in to keep out the mosquitoes. The house was boxed in on three sides by lilac and caragana bushes, a lovely mix of soothing lavender and sweet yellow in springtime. I kept six hens and grew a large garden out back.

Buying when I did was a fortuitous decision as the Great Depression lurked right around the corner, though none of us could anticipate the coming hardships. After it hit, I worked for the next ten years with little pay since our patients could barely afford shoes for their children. Mostly the doctor was paid in kind—wood for the stove, fresh milk, meat, and fish. My house was a blessing that I believed was God's way of rewarding me for promises kept. That house enabled me to keep right on doing His work.

Thora and I corresponded by letter regularly. I knew immediately by the change in her tone when she'd met the man she was destined to marry. He was a soldier who spent a month at the convalescent home. They married shortly after that and bought a little house on Pine Street. She mothered five children and occasionally, when they came out to visit, she would take me with them to Siglunes.

It was on one of those car rides, as I sat in the back seat with her second born on my lap, that she told me Finn had moved to England. After the war ended he'd spent a year in France as a volunteer who moved the bodies of fallen soldiers into the cemetery at Flanders.

"He is married now," she said, over her shoulder. "To the British nurse. The one he met while in hospital there."

I never forgot how she said it, offhandedly, as if the revelation would mean nothing to me.

I sensed she thought it romantic that Finn and his British wife had met under the same circumstances as she and her husband. She told me that only a woman who'd witnessed what the soldiers endured could ever truly understand how war changed them.

Now I am flown back to the battlefield: Ypres, April 1915, minutes after the gas attack.

Finn immediately recognizes the smell of the gas and, since his mind always processes faster than everyone else's, scrambles up out of the trench, hollers to the men around him to do the same, and then unfastens his pants, urinates on a rag and holds it up to his face. Simple chemistry. Uric acid neutralizes chlorine gas. He waves his arms like a man possessed. The ones who understand his brilliance follow his lead, climb out of the trenches where the heavy gas is settling and are saved.

He searches frantically for Stanley, finds him lying in the mud at the bottom of the trench, gasping for air, drawing the deadly gas into his lungs with every breath, and pulls him up over the top then falls to his knees, covering Stanley's mouth with his rag; he can do nothing but hold Stanley in his arms and watch him die. It is an agonizing death that Finn will spend the rest of his life reliving.

One afternoon, as I was arranging the adoption of a baby born in Winnipeg to a childless Lundi couple—our office did such work for Dr. Bjornsson—the door opened and Pabbi came in with Magnus on his arm.

"In here," I said, pushing open the examining room door.

"Elskan? Is that you?" Magnus rasped as Pabbi helped him into a chair.

"How are you?" I asked, feeling like a girl again, as if none of the years since I'd met him were spent.

"Not good," he said, coughing a bit. He reached out his crooked old hand to grasp mine. "Asta, my favorite. How have you been?"

The doctor understood my request. He and his wife said they would manage without me for however long it took. I was granted a leave of absence and returned to the castle to care for my dear old friend.

Pabbi and I helped him into Amma's wheeled chair then pushed him up the ramp. The smell of stale fish greeted us inside the door where his thick coat hung on a hook, boots directly underneath a high-backed chair. I imagined Bergthora's voice welcoming us from somewhere in the magnificent old house.

"Your Mother and I will come by for a visit tomorrow," Pabbi said to me once we had Magnus settled in his bed, which had been moved into the front room so he could rest by the fire.

I walked outside with Pabbi and stood squinting into the bright sun. The image of him standing beside the car he'd bought a few years earlier is one that comes to mind every time I think of him. The way he savored the moment, eyes filled with love.

"I don't think I ever thanked you for finding Freyja," he said. "Because of you, your Mother and I know the truth."

That night, when Magnus was comfortable, feet facing the fire, I helped him sip medicinal tea from a cup and eased his strained breathing with a hot plaster.

"Bjorn and the boys were here," he rasped with a hint of sadness. "Last week. I do not imagine they will come again. Swan River is so far."

I coaxed him to eat a bit then pulled one of the heavy chairs to the side of his bed so I could read to him from the book of John. That seemed to bring him comfort.

The next afternoon he asked that I take him outside.

"What if you slip?" I asked when he refused to get into the wheeled chair.

He took my arm. "You will not let that happen, já?"

We shuffled down the long hall, through the door onto the verandah. He sat down heavily on a thick wooden chair and I covered his lap with an old wool blanket and we looked out over the water. Flocks of noisy geese traveled towards their winter home. Soft gusts of wind rose up like a song, rolling the amber fallen leaves across the grass. The air was crisp with still a bit of warmth to it.

We sat listening to the silence until finally I summoned enough courage to ask something I'd always wondered.

"Do you believe that I brought a curse to Siglunes?"

I'd expected he might be either embarrassed or insulted, but he was neither.

"Some of the old ways I still believe, but no, I never thought that." He saw my relief. "Bjorn told me what happened when you stayed here and I am sorry," he said. "Shortly after moving to Swan. A way to relieve his guilt, I suppose."

"He told you everything?"

Magnus nodded slowly, eyes fixed on the lake. "Young men make mistakes." He reached across to take my hand. "Mistakes they have to live with for the rest of their lives. What Einar did I could never forgive. As for my son, God wasn't punishing him. Bjorn punished himself. And now it is time you let go of it as well."

So there it was. Our secret finally out in the open.

"I was in love with him," I said.

He showed no surprise, just let his mind drift back to those days, eyes smiling in remembrance. "Your Amma told me. She was a fine woman, so full of life I hardly knew what to expect from her," he said. "She challenged me in ways I've never properly understood."

"Was it you who bought her that stove?" I asked.

He chuckled softly to himself. "Já, and the house. It was the only thing she asked of me in exchange for the nights we spent together."

My suspicions, confirmed. The keeping of these secrets, so important then, now was irrelevant.

"I asked her to marry me, but she refused." He laughed. "Said I was only after her money. She told me that Leifur needed it more. She'd made a promise to him that she planned to keep."

The irony in the moment was more than I could stand. I went to the kitchen, returning a few minutes later with a cup of coffee. His hand wavered as he took it.

"Did you ever regret coming here?" I asked, settling into the chair beside him.

"Never," he said. "This lake is much like a love affair. It took from me, that is true, but it gave so much more in return. I cannot imagine my life without it."

"Did you ever blame yourself for what happened?"

"At first. But not for the reason you may imagine."

I waited for him to continue.

"It is said that God does not give us more heartbreak than we can endure," he said, blowing into the cup before taking a sip. "I felt responsible in a way. It took a few years, but eventually I was able to forgive myself. The son who survived is the one I could not bear to lose."

"Why do we love some more than others?" I asked, thinking of Freyja.

"Bjorn reminded me so much of his Mama that it was like having her around," he said as we watched a family of ducks paddle close to shore. "First love is like that. It tarnishes all love that comes later."

That I believed was true. That I still believe.

"Nei, we cannot blame the lake for what happened," he said, resting the cup on his lap. "My sons grew complacent. So did Stefan. It is the way of young men. Fortunately, Bjorn's luck held out, somehow he learned a man cannot just take. Something is always expected in return."

I asked him to explain.

"I see my life's events reflected in the lake. Never take the still water for granted. Storms come without warning, ice thaws unevenly. At times there is too much water, and at other times too little. It births life then steals it away. The lake teaches us to appreciate when times are good, and that carries us through the stormy weather."

A long silence followed as I thought about my own life. I had loved Finn, but our love had been like ice in the springtime, whereas my love for Bjorn was solid as the bay in the dead of winter.

"It takes a special kind of woman to forget herself and think only of others," he said, taking a sip. "You and Bergthora are the same that way."

My heart swelled at the compliment.

"She is still here you know," he said, eyes twinkling. "Sometimes I hear her footsteps in the kitchen. Waiting on me I suppose."

His last days began as so many final days do. One morning, following a period of semi-consciousness, his body came alive again and he spoke as if his soul knew time was short. His eyes took on an especially beautiful quality and, like others I'd seen, his body woke with an energy that tricked loved ones into thinking that the dying were not dying at all.

That is how it was for Asi who visited that afternoon.

"You are a remarkable nurse." He grinned. "I hope someday you will do the same for me."

He understood the truth only after I took him aside to ask that he send for Bjorn.

Asi ran home the moment the door closed behind him, then rode hard to The Narrows to place a telephone call to Swan River.

The next morning a car sped up the drive.

I felt a shiver as I realized that I was standing in the exact same spot as when I'd first seen him. Except this time he wasn't a carefree teenager but a middle-aged man, although he looked as he always had—as pleased to see me as I was to see him.

"Asta, thank goodness you are here."

"Of course," I whispered.

His expression held tremendous hope. "How is he?"

"Waiting for you."

He softened with relief, touching my shoulder as he hurried past, stepping into the front room. I rounded the corner after him to watch them from the doorway. Magnus was on the bed propped up with two pillows. He faced the window, big hands folded across his chest. A beam of sunlight filtered in through the branches of an oak with such intensity it looked as if it was coming straight from God to illuminate his weathered face.

"How are you feeling?" Bjorn said softly as he inched around the bed.

I adored the simplicity of it, thinking how everyone said pretty much the same thing to their dying loved ones. A whole life of love, anger, expectation, disappointment and pride summed up in four words.

Magnus croaked a reply I couldn't hear; Bjorn followed his father's line of sight out the window.

It was a glorious morning, one of those perfect fall days those who live by the lake spend their entire lives anticipating, remembering. Wishing for.

The window was open an inch, letting in the cool air, and a magpie squawked, dancing across the ground. It picked up an acorn with its beak then flew into the tree, calling for its mate who suddenly appeared. They bent their necks, looking in the window, but it was unclear if they could see us or merely their own reflections.

Bjorn pulled a chair in front of the window and sat in the Godly light. He talked about everything Magnus wanted to hear again; how the boys were enjoying school, profit margins at the store, fishing. I interrupted, coaxing Magnus to take a few sips of water, then brought Bjorn a plate of food that he balanced on his knee.

"Elskan, come eat," Magnus said.

Sympathy pains wracked my chest when he started to cough, a raspy, suffocating ordeal that went on far too long.

I sat opposite Bjorn, watching the rhythmic rise and fall of Magnus's chest as Bjorn described with pride how a team of Icelandic boys from Winnipeg had won Canada's first Olympic Gold medal in hockey. It was an eight-year-old story by then—the rest of their recollections even older than that—but Magnus reveled in it as if hearing it all for the first time. There was no future left, only memories.

Magnus reached out over the edge of the bed. I took one hand, Bjorn the other. Bjorn's eyes met mine.

Magnus sighed. "Why do women always want to cover up the windows?" he rasped, and we laughed.

He fell asleep shortly after that. Too nice a day to be cooped up, so Bjorn and I went out onto the verandah. We didn't sit right away but walked across the yard to the water's edge. He stood there with his hands on his hips, breathing in the lake air, as much for his dying father as for himself.

"He looks better than I'd expected," he said. "By the way Asi spoke . . ."

"Magnus is not getting better," I said gently. "He is getting ready to say good-bye." My voice caught on the last few words. "It is good that you came." I took my own deep breath, holding it until I was forced to let go.

"Thank you for letting me know," he said.

I pretended not to notice his lip quivering. We both shook off the tension, laughing a little as we strolled along the uneven shore.

"You cut your hair," he said. "I think those soldiers in the car—remember in Winnipeg? 'Get a haircut'—they meant me."

I laughed. "Will you ever?"

"Everyone keeps telling me to, that this is out of style, but I am so used to it."

"I like it long," I said. "It suits you."

"Yours looks better short."

We laughed at that, then an awkward silence wedged itself between us. We slipped across the pebbles and sand, mowed through the lake grass where it grew high, skipped around the waves that grasped for our shoes.

I'd heard snippets about his life from family and friends but had dared not ask for details, fearing they might sense how badly I wanted to know.

"You came alone," I said.

"It is too long a drive for the boys, and we were just here," he said. "Katherine is looking after the store until I return."

Hearing him say her name didn't hurt as much as I'd anticipated.

"Have you been back to Winnipeg?" he asked.

"A few times. But I haven't visited Freyja's grave. It feels rather pointless now."

He didn't seem surprised. "How did your family take the news?" He picked up a handful of stones.

"Solrun and Lars might still believe she is living happily in Iceland," I said. "Mama knows. Pabbi, too, but it pains him to talk about it, so I leave it alone."

Bjorn smoothed his thumb across one of the stones. We stopped for him to skim it out over the water. It skipped only once. He tried again, this time it jumped twice.

He laughed. "Out of practice."

I picked up a stone, tossing it out. "You are the only one to ask about her," I said. "All of the neighbors have forgotten."

"Do you think about her much?"

It was the common bond we shared. Losing a sibling evoked emotions few understood.

"All the time," I said. "I still can't believe in my heart that she's dead."

"Do you dream?" he asked, saying that after the twins drowned they came to him in a dream. So did Stefan. Those dreams felt different from ordinary dreams, he said, hard to describe. He held his palm up in front of his face. "They were right here. Their faces glowed peacefully. They told me they weren't really gone."

"Amma came to me the same way," I said.

"I wish I understood what it meant."

We walked for a little while longer then turned back.

"So you enjoy nursing?"

"I do."

"You are at Lundi?"

"I am."

"Happy?"

"Yes."

I sensed there was more he wanted to say, that he was edging toward it, trying to find a way without shattering the pleasant feelings between us.

"Remember Steina, the teacher? I told her about Einar. Not what he did to you, but what I did to him. She didn't look at me the same after that, especially when I got angry. I believe that is why she left me."

"Oh, Bjorn," I said.

"When you didn't reply to my letter I was certain you felt the same way."

I thought back to the day I'd torn up the envelope and cast it into the wind.

"Nothing turned out as I expected," I said.

His lips tightened; he leaned in ever so slightly, away from the wind.

"Finn decided he didn't want to marry me after all." It hurt saying it out loud, especially to him, to admit that my loyalty had been misplaced. It was humbling. And terribly sad. "Everyone thought that Finn would die. And I suppose you could say he did. In order to make it home alive, he became someone else."

"I heard," he said. "How could he do that to you?"

I shrugged. "The war changed us both."

Bjorn thought for a moment. "Maybe him, but not you."

CHAPTER FORTY-SEVEN

Few things are more powerful than fate.
—VATNSDÆLA SAGA

MAGNUS SLEPT FOR THE REST OF THE AFTERNOON. BJORN SAT ON the chair, attention divided between a book and his father, looking up every time Magnus moved or took a labored breath.

I busied myself in the kitchen, preparing a meal that neither Bjorn nor I were hungry enough to eat. He came so quietly into the kitchen he startled me as I stood staring out the window, lost in thoughts of years ago.

"Asta," he whispered, motioning for me to come. "He is talking to someone."

I followed him silently to the side of the bed. Magnus was completely unaware of us as he muttered cheerfully, eyes fixed on the wall.

"Your Mama," I whispered, our faces just inches apart.

"He is imagining it?"

"Nobody knows, but I have seen how it brings the dying a sense of peace."

He seemed fascinated looking into the empty corner. "I wish I could see her too."

That evening, Bjorn brought in an armful of wood for a fire. I moved a table between our two chairs and set up the chessboard. I brewed a fresh pot of coffee and lit the lamps, casting the room in a golden hue.

"Over the past few days his organs have started shutting down," I explained as we sat across from each other.

Bjorn made a move then looked at his father. Magnus's breathing was shallow. "Is he in pain?" he asked.

Moving my rook, I told him no.

Bjorn matched my move.

"The most difficult part will be letting him go," I said, not looking up from the board.

"How will we know?" he asked.

I peeked at my wristwatch. So many I'd seen, if not waiting for someone, would let go at the beginning of a new day.

"Hear how his breathing stops and starts? Gradually the breaths grow farther apart."

Bjorn listened as he concentrated on the board, elbow resting on his knee, chin in the palm of his hand.

"Do you think he knows we are still here?" he whispered.

"I am sure of it."

Hours passed. We began another game.

"What I have always admired most about your father is his kindness," I said, loud enough for Magnus to hear. "No matter whom he speaks to he always makes them feel like the most important person in the room."

Bjorn agreed.

This was the most satisfying part of my job. It was exhilarating to save someone, but deeply gratifying to help the dying let go.

"Tell me," I asked, "what is your fondest memory of life with your father?"

Bjorn's eyes grew distant and soft. "Fishing. Being out there on the lake with him, working side by side. We talked about everything. I learned so much from him just being out there. It is the reason I love fishing so much."

"Do you take the boys?"

"I do," he said. "The fishing is pretty good there. They get so excited. You should see them pulling the fish box up the bank. You'd think it was filled with gold."

Minutes later, Magnus stirred. We stood beside him. I gently lifted his hand into mine. It had lost all its warmth and strength.

"It is all right," I whispered. "Everything is going to be fine."

His body quivered. He opened his eyes. He smiled straight up at us.

"Father?" Bjorn whispered.

There was nothing in his eyes but pure joy, the full glory of his soul shining through. He stayed like that for a minute or so, then slowly his lids closed, but the smile remained. He took a deep breath, then stopped. Another breath and then a long pause.

"Father?" Bjorn said again, a hint of panic in his voice.

I squeezed Bjorn's arm with one hand and pushed Magnus's hair back with the other. It always amazes me how my senses come alive while watching someone die. That is how it feels to be totally present, when everything else simply falls away.

"We are here, Magnus."

Minutes later his body shook and he was gone.

Magnus lay in state in the front room for two days, in a beautiful oak casket he'd crafted for himself. People came from all around and shook hands with Bjorn, offered their condolences, stayed well into the night. There was reminiscing and sympathetic hugs, spirits, laughter, and food. Always there was plenty of food.

The next afternoon we buried him alongside Bergthora. After everyone left I went out to see Bjorn. He was standing at the foot of the grave, leaning on the shovel, his thoughts far away.

He heard the rustle of the leaves and turned. "I am the only one left," he said.

I almost corrected him, he had his sons. But he wasn't thinking about the fruit that grew on his family tree, his mind was on the roots. All that remained from his youth was the house, and that now belonged to Asi.

"A toast," I said, holding up a glass of Magnus's finest whiskey.

Our glasses clinked.

"To Magnus," he said.

We sat in front of the fire which burned too hot. Practical matters needed to be dealt with, but all of it could wait until tomorrow.

"There is no reason to mourn," he said, more to himself than me. "He had a long life. He died content. I should be happy about that."

"Yes, you should."

He took a sip from the glass while staring into the fire. "So why do I feel so bad?"

It wasn't so much a question as a statement. I told him we all felt the same when someone died. But he knew that, too. We were simply filling the air with conversation, allowing the whiskey to warm our throats, make us brave enough to say everything that up until that point had been left unsaid.

"Do you like it?" he asked, clinking my glass again.

"Not much, but I enjoy how it makes me feel."

He laughed. "Bergthora sipped sometimes but would never admit to it."

"Oh, how Magnus would have teased her—"

We laughed together at the memory of them. I expect, in the quiet moments that followed, he was recalling their smiling faces the same way I was.

Setting his glass down, he got up to put a record on the phonograph. I joined him in the middle of the floor and we waltzed, remembering together every humorous moment, until the sad ones started creeping in. The music stopped, but we continued dancing, his firm, gentle hand on my lower back.

"Why?" he whispered into my ear. "Why did it turn out this way?"

"It was my fault," I said, close to his cheek. "After you said you loved me, I knew how impossible it would be to stay true to Finn if I opened your letter and read those words again."

He kept moving us in a circle. Our hug began with a sob. I felt him release all the emotion built up over the last few days and I held him, feeling his tears soak my neck.

"Father saw my regret," he finally said.

I closed my eyes as a warm shudder settled deep inside.

"He asked if I was happy," he said.

"Are you?"

"I love Katherine," he said. "But I often wonder . . . "

"So do I."

His face moved level to mine and our lips touched, tentatively at first, then I fell into his fierce rhythm; his fingers ran through my hair; my body relaxed into warm butter; Bjorn's arms were taut, his feet planted firmly on the floor. It was a sin to kiss another woman's husband, but it was impossible for me to think of him belonging to anyone but me.

"I have always wanted you," he whispered, pulling my body close.

I felt his kiss go all through me. It had been so long since I'd felt a man's body against mine, I grew dizzy. "This is wrong," I whispered.

He sighed, letting his lips rest on my cheek. "Oh Asta, mínn, how I've missed you."

Morning came and I awoke alone.

I'd lain awake most of the night in Bergthora's former room, staring up at the ceiling, willing the darkness to put me to sleep. A part of me regretted turning him down and wondered if he felt regret that we'd not followed our bodies, our hearts. He must have known that I would have welcomed him, had he knocked on my door.

He was leaning on the verandah railing with a cup of coffee in hand, looking out over the water, the wind blowing the hair back from his face.

"I'm sorry," he said, without looking away from the lake.

"No harm done." I waved it off. "Come inside. I will make you breakfast."

Once everything was settled, I stood at the door waiting with my packed bag as he started the car. I mouthed a silent good-bye to the house, not knowing if fate would arrange a return visit.

He drove me home to Lundi and we chatted the whole way. I invited him to stay the night since it was a long drive back to Siglunes in the dark, but he refused, saying he wanted to get an early start back to Swan River the next morning. We stood on the stoop, sharing another, much softer, kiss.

He walked backwards slowly to the sidewalk. This was a wrenching good-bye.

"Asta," he said into the darkness.

"Yes?"

"Why do I feel it will never be finished between us?"

"Because it never will," I said softly. "I will wait for you, Bjorn Magnusson, for as long it takes."

I saw Bjorn again, two years later, at Oli Thorsteinsson's funeral. He introduced me to Katherine as a family friend.

She shook my hand warmly. By then you would think I was too old for such pettiness, but I noticed immediately that she was much prettier than I'd ever been. Fine-boned, short, blonde, with a young, sweet voice. My fantasy that she was an unbearable shrew came to an abrupt end.

She beamed as she watched him move through the crowd. No harm done, really. It would never occur to her that Bjorn might desire someone like me.

What hurt most was seeing the boy. Their second born looked so much like him.

"Like my father, I will be an old man with young sons," I overheard him say.

I avoided their family after that, walking home alone after the lunch, holding on to nothing but the memory of the only man I've ever truly loved.

CHAPTER FORTY-EIGHT

Great deeds and ill deeds often fall within each other's shadow.
—GÍSLI SÚRSSON'S SAGA

It is night again. I wonder how they do it, decide which of them will sleep on the hard chair. I imagine they stand outside where I can't see them, flipping a coin or drawing straws. Thora has plucked the short one again.

I feel annoyed but have forgotten why. There is a part of me that wants to die alone. But my heart cannot tell her to go.

"Leifur . . . Signy," I say.

Her smile is angelic as she wipes sleep from her eyes.

"I have called them. They will be here soon."

Good, I nod. *There is not much time left.*

Only one question left to answer, the one she asked earlier.

I came to terms with my regrets long ago. I believe that, given the chance, Bjorn would have kept his promise to come looking for me. There has been solace in knowing that, because we never married, there was no opportunity for day-to-day disappointments, no arguments that ended in frustration and tears. We didn't lose respect for each other and my love for him remains strong to this day. The vision of what I believed we could have had together remains untarnished. There is some joy in that.

"I have . . . no regrets," I whisper.

Thora seems relieved. She pats my hand. There are tears when our eyes meet.

"Except," I manage to say, "Freyja."

* * *

ONE MORNING, LEIFUR AND PABBI WERE OUT ON THE LAKE FISHING. Pabbi filled the fish box as Leifur took the line over his shoulder and began pulling the net back under the ice. When he turned to shield his face from the bitter wind, he caught a glimpse of Pabbi lying on his back, holding a fish in one hand.

I was in the examination room assisting the doctor, who was draining infection from an old woman's leg, when Mother came rushing into the waiting area. I recognized her voice calling my name.

"It's your Pabbi," she said.

Leifur and Olafur carried him inside. The diagnosis: heart attack. Severe. Fortunately, he hadn't lost consciousness, but his heart muscle was severely damaged. The tincture Mother had forced him to sip along the way may have helped.

They stayed with me in Lundi for three days, then we brought him home.

By then Lars was studying history and literature at the University of Manitoba and Solrun was newly married. Signy and Olafur had six boys. Everyone arrived. The older ones stayed outside to make a castle in the snow while the two youngest entertained Leifur and Sigrid's twins in the front room.

"Girls," Signy exclaimed. "What I would give for a daughter."

Mother was nearly sixty-years-old by then. I sensed it was her experience with Solrun, who now walked with only a slight limp, that gave her hope. The doctor said Pabbi had many years left if he stopped working so hard and she was determined that was exactly what he would do.

"I will come help every day once my chores are done," Olafur said, thick forearms folded on the table. Signy reached out to touch his big, calloused hand. It was an admirable offer but his eternal optimism meant he'd already taken on too much.

"No need," Leifur said. "I will handle it."

"You'll need help," Olafur said.

Mother and I set supper on the table.

Until then, Lars's eyes had been downcast, but now he looked up. It is remarkable how calculated he was, that he so easily could conceal his disappointment from us all.

"I will come home," he said. "When Pabbi is better I will enroll again."

Pabbi lay sleeping with a soft, faded quilt pulled up to his chin. Had he been awake he wouldn't have allowed it. Though the newspaper headlines screamed Depression, we were only two years into it and they'd barely felt the affects yet. He would have hired a man from Dog Creek to do his share of the chores. But the decision was made without him and, by the time he realized that Lars had withdrawn from the University, it was too late.

I always thought that I knew Lars. Now I see I barely understood him at all. It may have been the age difference, sixteen years. I was long finished school before he even started. I also question his memories of Freyja: were they genuine, or a compilation of frozen images in his mind of everything we'd said about her?

Had I paid closer attention, I would have noticed the shelves in his attic bedroom were lined with twice as many books as the rest of us owned. Living in Lundi, I did not see how he spent every spare moment cloistered upstairs, door closed, bent over notebooks, writing the stories that swirled in his head. He had aspirations he told no one, dreams of a life different than any we'd imagined.

Now I feel clearly his resignation. That evening he said good-night to everyone, but none of us noticed that his feet were heavier than usual on the stairs. Once in his bedroom, he stands in front of the bookcase, removes two notebooks from the shelf, then sits down at the tiny desk. He lifts his pen but lays it back down. Instead, he begins to read a short story written in his own hand. His face relaxes as he soaks in every word, lingering for a moment, staring off. He carefully closes the notebook, opens another and does the same thing. Heaving a sigh, he stands up, stares at the battered covers for a few moments before placing them in the trunk at the foot of his bed.

They would remain there untouched for the next twenty years.

By the time the effects of the Great Depression were lessening, we'd lived in the aftermath of Pabbi's heart attack for the better part of a decade. As his heart congested, his overall health began a slow decline. Every morning after waking he shuffled to the chair by the window to sit with the radio. Sometimes Mother grew impatient and intervened when he faltered.

"Ella, I can do it myself," he'd say.

Strangely, Pabbi looked almost satisfied as he wore down the radio battery, listening as grain prices fell, businesses closed and unemployment lines lengthened. Perhaps he felt vindicated: his predictions had come true. Some immigrants who'd settled the same time as us became discouraged, sold out, packed up and returned to Iceland. He often speculated what it must have been like upon their return; would they be called traitors, weaklings, and cowards for leaving in the first place?

"I am not sure which is worse, to be deemed a traitor once or twice," he said to J.K. one evening as they sat in our kitchen discussing the Depression.

"Twice," J.K. said. "We are far better off here in Siglunes than anywhere else. We own our land, have plenty to eat, and there will always be fish."

That night, when Leifur walked him to the door, J.K. gripped his shoulder, lowered his voice. "Everything will turn out, you will see."

Leifur never once told Pabbi how incredibly lean those years were. He and Lars simply put their heads down and cleared more land, set more nets, bred more heifers and milked a few extra cows. They were so determined that they didn't even see the turn-around coming. They simply looked up one day to find that J.K. had been right.

When the Second World War began, the Depression ended. Soon after that, the need for health care became so great that a small hospital was built in Lundi. The doctor moved his office there and I followed.

I still took part in many community events, riding with Solrun's family to the Hayland hall.

One evening, the band was already set up by the time we arrived. Everyone was there, visiting and dancing as the children ran back and forth across the floor. Once again the war in Europe was on everyone's mind.

A discussion began at Pabbi's table so of course J.K. was in the middle of it. I sat directly behind them with Solrun. As usual, J.K. and Asi believed one line of reasoning while a handful of men from the community, including Pabbi, took the opposite view.

Midway through the evening three men we did not recognize came in. "Do you remember me?" one asked Pabbi. Clearly he'd been drinking.

Mother tilted her head for a moment. "Pall, how are you?"

"You," he said, pointing at Pabbi, "killed my father."

Pabbi's expression did not change. "I always tried to get along with your father," he said.

"Like hell you did. You hated him and everyone knew it."

"Pall," Mother said. "Their differences began long before you were born. You remember Pall," she said to J.K. and Gudrun as they returned to the table, breathless from dancing.

Pabbi pushed himself to his feet. Mother stood as well, taking his arm. Everyone had heard the news years earlier of Bensi's suicide in the Dakotas.

I waved my hand, trying to get Leifur's attention, but he was at the far end of the hall, leaning into a conversation, and the music was loud.

Pabbi turned slowly, a wobbly arm reaching for his cane as he began shuffling toward the door.

Amusement spread across Pall's face.

"Not so fast now," he snorted. The friends with him laughed.

"There, there," J.K. said. "No need to—"

"And you, look at you sitting there in your fancy suit," he said. "Thinking you are smarter than everyone else."

By then everyone at my table had turned around in their chairs.

"Those sonsabitches burned down our place," he hollered, pointing at Pabbi. "Do you know what happens to a man after he loses everything? He kills himself, that's what."

"We were sorry to hear about your father," J.K. said. "You know that fire was an—"

"Bullshit," Pall said, pounding his fist on the table. "They had it in for us from the day they moved here." Then he swiped his hand across, knocking over J.K.'s drink.

Pabbi and Mother stopped.

J.K. was silent for a few moments, then, to everyone's surprise, he began chuckling. He leaned back in his chair, placing one foot casually across his knee, and pulled a cotton handkerchief out of his breast pocket, dabbed it in the spilled whiskey and began to wipe the dirt from his shoe.

"What are you laughing at, old man?" Pall spat.

J.K.'s grin grew wider.

Gudrun quickly stood and backed away from the table as a thick hand grasped Pall's shoulder.

"We are going to finish this little talk outside," said Olafur.

Pall and his buddies leapt up, knocking their chairs back, ready to fight, but their energy quickly drained when they saw Olafur's brothers coming across the floor.

"I think you should apologize," Olafur said quietly.

"Now, now, it was just a friendly discussion, right boys?" J.K.'s merry eyes were taking it all in. He placed his foot on the floor and, dabbing the handkerchief again, began polishing the other shoe.

Olafur's focus never left Pall, whose confidence by then had withered like a week-old balloon. Olafur grabbed him by the shirt and shoved him towards the door. Pall stumbled backwards and the Thorsteinsson brothers escorted him and his friends outside.

"Thank you," Pabbi said quietly to Olafur at the door. "But please, Pall has suffered enough."

"Pall Solmundsson," J.K. said when Leifur returned. "He is as ridiculous as Bensi. Accused your father of burning down their place."

Leifur's lips pressed together and his cheeks flushed. His eyes went to Pabbi. He said very little the rest of the night.

CHAPTER FORTY-NINE

There is a time for everything.
—GRETTIR'S SAGA

ONE MORNING, TWO YEARS AFTER THE INCIDENT AT THE HALL, Mother woke up and knew immediately by the stillness in the room that Pabbi was gone. She didn't fling off the blanket, check to see if he was breathing then run to Leifur for help, even though there was no help to give. Instead, she stayed in bed with Pabbi until she was ready to let him go.

Five years later she sold the farm to Lars and came to live with me. Mother was frail by then and had lost her gleam, and her eyesight was failing, a punishment she didn't deserve.

"Your Amma would be very proud of your independence," she said one day.

It was a Saturday afternoon in mid-July. We sat together on the verandah tailing and snapping beans. The heat came from all directions, radiating in through the screens that kept most of the bugs out. This is where we'd grown accustomed to preparing our garden bounty, listening to the birds, flanked by potted tomatoes and geraniums you could smell growing in the heat.

The pail of beans was on the floor between us. She reached down for a handful, dropping them in her lap.

"I always hoped that you would marry Bjorn," she said. "It was not my intention when I gave you Amma's name that you would spend your life alone."

"She was content with her choices in the end," I said.

"Maybe so," she said, tossing beans in the bowl. "Are you?"

I still speculated. I still thought about Einar now and again. At least I wasn't angry anymore. For years a notion had nagged at me, crept in during moments of regret. I wondered if I'd clung to Bjorn, never ready to give myself fully to another man, because of what Einar did to me.

"You knew I wouldn't marry Finn?"

Mother smiled. "It was so obvious you loved Bjorn. Amma said she spoke to you, but you were stubborn, just like her." Across the table came a playful, sideways glance.

"Sometimes I blamed her," I said.

"You were different than our other girls," she said. "You were suspicious of men. That changed with Finn and we were grateful." A murmur caught in her throat. She picked up the swatter when a fly landed on the wall and, despite her trembling hand, killed it. "Hold nothing against your Amma. She so desperately wanted you girls to have a better life. The stories were her way of lighting a candle along your path to keep you from making the same mistakes she did."

I waited while she collected her thoughts.

"Freda ran away to escape her father's tyranny when she was just 14 years old. She lied, stole, and manipulated to stay alive; destroyed a few marriages in her early 20s, then finally settled down with Soli and your father was born. Soli beat her only once, then she kicked him out. He wouldn't let her keep Bensi."

"How did she earn a living?" I asked.

"Freda was a kept woman after that," she said. "Men loved her. She used the only thing she had."

"The house in Reykjavik?"

"It belonged to a wealthy man who took care of her after your father and I married. He died and she somehow got the title plus his money."

I went to the kitchen to make a fresh pot of coffee. As the water began to bubble up into the glass perk, I wondered what other questions to ask. I'd never experienced Mother in such a talkative mood.

"We all expect hardship but none of us heartbreak," Mother said as I handed her a cup.

"Tell me, what did the letter say?" I asked.

"Which letter?"

"From Iceland. When we were children."

She was still puzzled, thinking back. "From Uncle Ásgeir?"

"Yes. The one you threw in the stove."

She explained that Ásgeir offered to watch over her sister. He'd arranged for Aunt Freyja to work as a domestic on a farm halfway across Iceland. By the time Pabbi sent the money, Freyja was dead from influenza.

"At least that is what he told me," she said. "I never believed him."

"Do you think naming a child after someone dooms them to a similar fate?"

"No harm came to Lars." She smiled. "I knew it wouldn't."

And we relaxed, listening to the buzz of mosquitoes, watching iridescent dragonflies whirr into the yard. Mother said she wanted my sister's body moved to the cemetery here. She asked if Leifur and I would take care of the arrangements. We'd already moved Amma and baby Lars's remains to the plots beside Pabbi.

"I always blamed myself for losing both of them," she said.

Believing this was likely her deathbed confession, I told her that none of us blamed her, hoping it might ease her conscience.

"That piece of lemon pie," she said. "Is it still in the refrigerator? I would like it right about now."

Back then, women never spoke about it, not even to their daughters. It began in the breast, spread steadily as the months marched on while the pain kept pace. Eventually, we all knew she didn't have much time. My sisters and brothers came to see her every week.

What happened in mid-April of 1950 can only be described as an extreme coincidence, or if you believe in the divine, a knowing wink from God.

Mother was sitting on a chair pulled up to the wall directly under the telephone, waiting anxiously, when I arrived home.

"I would have dialed you, but that would have tied up the line," she said, words spilling out. "A woman called. The connection was bad. I did not get to the phone in time so I missed the first call. I was taking a nap—"

"Slow down," I said. "Start from the beginning."

Mother took a deep breath. The brightness that hadn't been there since Pabbi died had returned to her eyes.

"It was a long distance call," she said. "The voice sounded familiar."

I knew that she still hoped for a miracle.

"It was likely Thora," I said softly. "Calling to say they've arrived safely in B.C."

Thora and her husband had decided to retire in British Columbia and had left a month earlier.

Mother thought hard. When she answered, her tone was resigned. "You are probably right."

She should have gone to the hospital days earlier, but determination had kept her at home. When she could no longer sleep for more than two hours at a time, she agreed to go. I helped her into the wheeled chair and we bumped down the sidewalk.

"It is a beautiful day," she said. "Must be near 20 degrees. Spring has definitely arrived. I wonder how life is at Eikheimar." She turned her face to the sun.

I pulled open the door, wheeling her up to the admitting desk.

"Where did you get that old thing?" the nurse on duty asked.

"Me?" Mother quipped. "Or the chair?"

The nurse laughed.

"It was my Amma's," I said, the words catching in my throat. First

Amma, then Magnus, Pabbi and now . . .

Being a nurse has been a blessing. As you can probably imagine it is most satisfying to be the person everyone turns to when they need reassurance and comfort. Working at the hospital meant I didn't have to leave Mother. In fact, I spent all my time there, either on duty or at her bedside. She preferred it to be me to swab her sores. She welcomed the sting of an antiseptic that neutralized the odor of decaying flesh and, so worried she might offend the grandchildren, she insisted on more than a few dabs of perfume. She saved her energy for those visits.

Because I was there daily I didn't see her decline, only read the looks of shock as they all rotated through, one family at a time.

"Will you have enough hay until pasture?"

Yes.

"How was fishing?"

Not bad.

"Those two March storms, how many calves did you lose?"

Only a few.

"Come closer so I can see you."

Yes, Amma.

"How is school?"

Good.

"What did you learn yesterday?"

Nothing.

And so it went. I wet her lips with a bit of water. She pretended she wasn't dying. Everyone acted as though they believed it.

"Be careful with that," she whispered, eyeing the morphine. "I do not want to die any sooner than God intends."

I slept most nights on the chair beside her bed, emptied the commode, fed her when she grew too weak, held the straw to her lips.

"Remember when they all came?" she whispered, eyes watery. Her voice had the soft, dreamy quality that comes when death is near. At first I thought she was talking about two days before, when Signy's tribe all marched in—big, fresh-faced boys, each one reminding me of their father.

"Your pabbi was so relieved that day. What a community it was. Building our house, the way they did."

I took Mother's hand and squeezed. What a privilege it was to offer comfort to the woman who gave me life, through the most difficult transition of all. In that moment, it wasn't my mother lying there, but a woman no different than myself. One day this would be me.

"I never regretted leaving Iceland," she said. "Not once."

Signy arrived late that afternoon.

"I will sit with her now," she said. She took Mother's hand in hers. She turned to face me. "You go home and take a bath. Have something to eat. Get a good night's sleep."

Had it been anyone else but my sister, I would have declined the offer.

I pulled on my coat, waved good-bye to my work mates, pushed open the door and stepped outside. It already felt late. A storm was blowing in, the temperature had dropped and the skies were swirling blue-black. Buttoning my coat all the way up, I hurried the few blocks home. The house was cool and the dull ache in my stomach reminded me I hadn't eaten since morning. I lit the coal boiler and it wasn't long before the radiators started to clang and warm air filled the room. Electricity could be unreliable, so I kept oil lamps on hand just in case. I flipped the switches and the lights came on. The refrigerator hummed quietly beside the stove, a beautiful appliance that Mother had insisted we purchase because it heated with both electricity and coal. Oh how our world had changed.

I ran water in the bathtub, then stripped off my rumpled clothes, slid into it. Sometimes I felt guilty knowing that none of these conveniences had made their way to Eikheimar yet, a scant 30 miles away.

The only sound was the train whistle in the distance. The quiet that consumed the house was not as lonesome as one might imagine. Having something then losing it is much harder than never having had it at all.

I enjoyed my work and volunteer activities with the Lundi Ladies Aid. I walked to church every Sunday and visited regularly with Solrun. There was always a store-bought treat hidden somewhere for her daughters when they came to visit and together we'd go to the Fair. It was something we all looked forward to, the day the Fair came to town.

Mine was a good life.

A sandwich for supper followed by a bit of reading to clear my thoughts. I fought that bone-tired feeling that kept me in my chair some nights, and slowly pushed myself up, went to my room. As I passed by Mother's door, I half expected to see her there. But I'd stopped being disappointed about being alone years ago.

That evening hard rain splattered the windows from the west, running through the drain spouts with such force a little river ran alongside the house into the back yard. The next morning, I put on rubber boots, opened my umbrella and stepped outside, lowering it to block the wind and sleet.

The nurse on duty at the front desk looked up when I came in. She informed me that Signy had left a few hours ago, that Mother was resting comfortably but didn't have much time left.

"Signy seemed upset," the nurse said quietly.

We both knew how difficult it was for those not accustomed to sitting with a dying loved one.

"Freyja? Where is Freyja?" Mother asked dreamy-eyed. "She was here."

Though her body lacked strength, her eyes were bright.

"It's all right, Mama, you will see her again," I said. "How is the pain?"

"It is gone." She sounded surprised, relieved.

"Then you should rest," I said, checking her chart. When her eyes closed I slipped away to make the necessary phone calls.

We were all there when she died, early that evening, looking wistfully happy and at peace. Reunited, I suppose, with those who had gone before her, all the questions finally answered about her sister, and mine, too.

We buried Mother three days later beside Pabbi. J.K. and Gudrun's headstones lined the next row. Still neighbors. She would be pleased.

My mind went back to the incident with Pall at the dance. J.K. waving good night to Pabbi then taking Gudrun by the hand, hollering out to the band it was time for a Red River Jig, how the hall erupted in cheers as the music flared up again. The incredible lightness to J.K.'s step, his confident cheer, as he spun Gudrun around the dance floor.

Gudrun had died at home a few years later and shortly afterwards J.K. moved to Winnipeg where Thora cared for him until his death in 1945.

We stood in the rain, listening to the Pastor reflect on Mother's life, none of us needing to say anything out loud.

As the church basement began filling up after the service, we were heartened to see our elderly neighbors from Siglunes and Hayland, and their children who now owned the farms and fished the lake. Three generations were there to pay their respects.

Everyone handles the loss of a parent differently. Our brothers said very little. Solrun and I were serene and reflective. But Signy was struggling and we all saw it. She looked lost in the church kitchen, opening cupboard doors but not seeing anything inside. Two women from the Ladies Aid tried to usher her out but she refused. For a reason none of us understood, Signy became bitter after the funeral and stayed that way for months.

Leifur and I took charge. He made all of the arrangements, ordering modest, matching headstones for all the graves, including one for Freyja. The funeral director said he would have her remains moved once the situation in Winnipeg was resolved. He meant the impending flood. Not since 1861 had the Red River risen up as much as it did that spring.

Two weeks after Mother's funeral, the city of Winnipeg was devastated by water. The conditions that foretold the coming flood—a wet autumn, above-normal amounts of snow, below-normal temperatures and a late thaw, all combined with heavy rainfall—saw the Red and Assiniboine rivers overflow their banks. Our beloved lake was spared that spring but four wet years loomed on the horizon.

CHAPTER FIFTY

Beware of those who speak fairly but think falsely.
—THE SAGA OF BJARN OF THE HITDOELA CHAMPIONS

I WAS CHARGED WITH THE TASK OF SETTLING MOTHER'S ESTATE. After the funeral expenses were paid, the remainder was divided among the five of us. Mother had suggested in her will that those of us with children establish an education fund. We gathered on Thanksgiving at Eikheimar for an early afternoon meal. It was strange to see a new, one-and-a-half-storey home with a cement foundation where our house had once stood. I was pleased that the kitchen window still faced east. From it we could look out over Amma's meadow and, as before, see the bay in the distance.

Once dinner was done, and everyone was sitting with their coffee and dessert, I laid out the ledger book with all the expenses and Mother's bank account, then handed each of my brothers and sisters an envelope. Nobody bothered to check my figures so I didn't have to explain why I'd divided the balance by four. They were all farming so they needed money more than I.

"You paid for the headstones?" Leifur asked. He'd met with the funeral director the month before and had been present when the stones were put in place. He seemed troubled.

"Yes, two days after they were delivered," I said. "Is something wrong?"

Leifur sighed, setting his plate down. He picked up his coffee and winced. "I'm not sure exactly how to say this." The room grew quiet. "But it appears whoever told you Freyja was buried in the Brookside Cemetery was wrong."

"There must be a mistake," I said. "I saw the marker. It was her grave."

Leifur shook his head. "There is no record of Freyja being buried there."

Signy went to the kitchen. She returned carrying the coffee pot and refilled everyone's cup. "So we paid for a headstone and plot for nothing?" she said, annoyed.

"Mama did," I snapped back.

She flung daggers at me, the first time in many years.

"It was her dying request," I said, "to have Freyja home."

Leifur handed me a copy of the Brookside Cemetery map.

I looked at it, my mind reeling. "If Freyja isn't here then where is she?"

"I tried warning you all," Signy said, but her words were directed at me. "All we ever talked about was Freyja, how sweet and wonderful she was, how perfect our lives would be if you found her."

"You'd left home already," I said. "You didn't know what it was like for us, how we suffered."

"Yes, I did," she said, bottom lip quivering. "And that is why I cannot forgive her."

"Forgive her? For what?" I said.

Signy pointed to the map I still held. "You wasted your whole life looking for someone who doesn't want to be found."

I was so flabbergasted I barely took in what was said after that. I stared at the map again. Signy believed I had wasted my life.

"Freyja knows where we are," she said, planting one hand on her hip; the other still held the coffee pot. She offered nothing more, just spun around and stomped back to the kitchen.

I turned the map. Finding the entrance, I used my finger to retrace my steps. Someone had scratched two crosses with a pen on the plot that

I believed belonged to Freyja. Handwritten beside the crosses were the names Borga and Mundi Solmundsson with the dates of their deaths. Bjarni's grandmother had died a year before his grandfather. I'd known that and yet . . .

"My God," I said. "That bastard tricked me."

CHAPTER FIFTY-ONE

Pride and wrong often end badly.
—VÍGA GLÚM'S SAGA

DO YOU KNOW THE DYING CAN HEAR EVERYTHING THAT GOES ON around them?

A person's sense of hearing and touch are the last to go. Remember this. It is why the infirm shouldn't be discarded like old pieces of furniture, but treated with reverence like the antiques they are. A bit of polishing and admiring never hurts.

Freyja didn't die. Deep inside my heart I've known it all along.

I feel a warm wind trying to lift me off the bed, a whispering of encouraging voices. I follow.

A chair is pushed abruptly back and heels run toward the hospital room door. This flurry of activity pulls me back. Once again I am confronted with light and noise.

"Solrun, please hurry," I hear Thora call out.

Both of them are beside me now. They've summoned Doctor Steen. Minutes later I recognize his footfalls. His voice is calm and reassuring. Even though I cannot hear their whispers, I know what he is saying. There is no way to predict how long it will take now my breathing has begun to stop and start. Some die within hours, others linger for days.

* * *

My soul has been brought to the edge of the west hayfield, to where Leifur stands facing the Siglunes Creek, watching as it overflows its banks. Pelicans and seagulls paddle lazily where hay should be growing.

It is May, 1955—five years since Mother died and I found out that Bjarni had deceived me. The lake flooded last year so not enough hay was made. Another wet spring, more flooding and it is still raining.

Signy sloshes from the house wearing rubber boots. Leifur sees her coming but turns back to face the water.

"Sigrid said I'd find you here," she says. "She tells me you've been out here for hours. She is worried you will catch your death, standing in the rain like this."

I can feel the heaviness in his heart. Poor Leifur can barely remember back to those years when he believed all it took was hard work to be successful. The past few years have deepened the lines on his face, put sadness in his eyes. He is thankful that Pabbi and J.K. aren't alive to witness the devastation. I want to reach out to comfort him, but all I can do in this ghostly state is watch.

"I never should have bought that place," he says, pointing at Bensi's bush. "Amma was right. That land is cursed."

Truth be told, Bensi's bush is still a solemn and dark place, despite its beauty. Even the cattle won't graze there.

"I should have listened when you said Freyja ran away," Leifur says.

Signy tilts her head in curiosity. "What does she have to do with this?"

He looks at the drowning grass. "This is all my fault." His shoulders droop under the weight of his soaked jacket.

"Now you are being silly," she says,

They both hear the uncertainty in her voice.

"Pabbi always said an eye-for-an-eye is wrong," he says. "I punished Bensi years ago and now it is my turn. Like him, I may lose my farm."

They stand for a few minutes staring at the raindrops pooling in the low spots on the land.

"I hid in the bush that morning," he says. "When the family rode away to church I let the sheep go and lit the barn on fire, then ran to J.K.'s dock to catch the Lady Ellen across the lake to the ball tournament. I didn't intend to burn the whole place."

Signy gently shakes her head. "Did you tell Pabbi you were the one?"

"I think he knew. That is why he told the police not to come. We never spoke about it."

"Who else have you told?"

"No one."

Signy reaches out to pat his back, high up between the shoulder blades. "We are all worried about you."

He takes another deep breath as he looks out over the waterlogged field.

They start walking back toward the house.

"I have a confession as well," she says. "Freyja is very much alive."

Leifur stops and turns to face her. "Are you sure?"

"I know it for a fact." Signy looks away then defiantly crosses her arms. "I saw her."

"You saw her? When?"

"At the hospital, the night before Mama died."

He is speechless.

"After Asta went home from the hospital, I sat with Mama. Freyja arrived that evening on the train."

"She came to Lundi?" he asks in disbelief.

Signy nods. "Thora found her. They bumped into each other in Vancouver. Thora told her that Mama was dying, so Freyja came home."

Leifur brings his hands up to his face and rubs hard.

Signy's eyes are brimming with tears. "I was so furious, I told her to leave."

"Signy—"

"I didn't think she'd go," she says defensively. "But maybe it is for the best, after everything she put us through."

"Did Mama see her?"

"Yes, and she forgave her. She didn't even ask where Freyja had been all those years. She just said that she was thankful to have her home."

It starts raining harder as they turn back toward the house and begin sloshing through the field, past the cattle huddled with their heads down under a bluff of trees, their young calves pressing in close for warmth. A cow coughs and I know Leifur thinks immediately of pneumonia and foot rot, that he will need to check them as soon as it stops raining. He is a farmer through and through. He pushes the barbed wire down and swings his legs over, holding it for Signy who does the same. As the house comes into view, he looks up at the roof. I can see the spot where the shingles have blown off in the wind. Hopefully his patch will hold and it won't start leaking again.

"Why didn't you tell us?" he asks.

"It wasn't up to me," she says. "If Freyja wanted us to know her whereabouts, she could have easily told us. Or written. But she hasn't, has she?"

"We have to tell them," he says.

"Why? So that we can invite her back into our lives as if nothing has happened?"

"They need to know the truth."

"Solrun and Lars barely remember her. And you know how the story will be twisted. It will be all my fault."

He stops at the foot of the verandah. "You should have told Asta right away, at Thanksgiving."

"You think I don't know that?" she cries, voice breaking. "I thought Asta would talk to Thora and find out on her own. How was I supposed to know she'd nearly get herself killed?"

"Are you afraid we'll blame you for Asta's accident?" he asks.

"Do you?"

He inhales slowly and sighs. "No, you are right. Freyja knows where we are."

Leifur turns away from her to look out over the gray, dimpled lake drinking in every drop of rain. The beach is almost entirely under water.

"I do have a bit of good news," she says brightening. "Bjorn Magnusson decided to sell the store in Swan River and has retired in Lundi."

"Really?"

"You heard his wife died last fall?"

"No, I hadn't."

"We should pay him a visit. Take Asta along and talk about old times. I think it will be good for her."

Leifur nods. "How is she doing?"

"Settling in at the care home, but it is painful to see her like this."

They slowly climb the verandah steps.

"You should go visit her," Signy says. She reaches out to pat his shoulder again.

"I will," he says. "There is nothing more I can do here until it stops raining."

CHAPTER FIFTY-TWO

A tale is but half told, when only one person tells it.
—THE SAGA OF GRETTIR THE STRONG

SO MUCH TO TAKE IN.

How could Signy have kept this from me?

There was an accident . . . yes, I vaguely remember. As soon as I realized Bjarni had deceived me, I went to Winnipeg to hire a private investigator to find Freyja. Something happened. My memories are vacant shadows after that.

Solrun sniffles and I hear her pull a tissue from the box. She sighs into it, stifling a sob.

Dr. Steen tries to explain to her and Thora that my soul is holding on longer than it should. They understand better when he says that my body will only live for so long.

They settle into the chairs beside my bed, determined I won't take my final breaths alone.

My mind drifts in and out of the room. I am brought back by the sound of a nurse at my side. Another needle of morphine in the hip.

Do you know that men have a decidedly different sound to their footfalls than women do? When I was with a patient I often guessed correctly by the echo coming down the hallway if the visitor was a man or woman. Generally speaking, women walk quicker than men, though not necessarily lighter.

The footsteps I hear now remind me of Pabbi. Lars, it must be. I hope he brought Leifur and Signy. It has been such a long time since I've seen them.

I am able to creak open my eyes a sliver and there in front of me are two wisps of glowing light.

Mama?

Although she doesn't speak, there is a sweet understanding between us, one brimming with love. She senses my confusion.

Who is that with you? But already I know, even though the truth takes a few moments to register. It is Thora's spirit. And while I do not remember ever knowing this, I realize that she died ten years ago.

Then who has been sitting at my bedside?

Mother smiles softly and I remember the morning she died, how she'd said Freyja came for a visit. Now everything makes sense.

Freyja is here at the hospital, beside Solrun. She has been sitting with me all along.

* * *

One last visit to the past and all my questions will be answered.

Solrun's kitchen. Fifteen years since Mother died. It is October, 1965. Solrun is waiting impatiently by the sink, watching through the window that looks out onto the farmyard. I can feel her anticipation, read her thoughts as she glances at the clock over the kitchen table. Her husband and Olafur should be back from Winnipeg soon with Lars and Freyja, that is if the plane from Vancouver was on time. She has never been on one herself, but Lars has told her it is a wonderful way to travel.

Solrun wonders if she will still recognize our sister after all these years. The only photo of Freyja was taken when she was seven-years-old—two years before she was born. The family portrait that Mother treasured so much now hangs in her living room, over the end table beside the sofa. She doesn't look at it often, but when she does it tugs sadly at her heart now that Amma, Pabbi, Mother and Signy are all gone.

Signy has died? Why didn't anyone tell me?

Finally, a car comes up the drive. Solrun hurries out to stand on the stoop, wrapping her sweater tight to keep out the wind. Leaves swirl at her feet, break loose, and then dance across the walkway onto the grass.

Solrun's husband and Olafur get out and stretch their backs. Olafur went along because he was curious to see Freyja again—the ghost who so many of our family's stories were built around. None of us except him saw it, her disappearance the dividing mark: before or after; just as everything later was remembered as prior to or following my accident.

The passenger doors open. Lars and Freyja step out.

Solrun's eyes dance, filled with tears, as she brings her fingers to her chin. Freyja's poise. Fine-boned and slim as ever, her platinum hair perfectly coifed in solid, wide curls away from her face. She is wearing a fine suit, silk blouse with matching shoes and handbag.

Now I recognize her, this is my sister—the same woman who has been sitting diligently at my bedside. How many times has she come back to see us since this first visit years ago? Why don't I remember?

"Solrun," Freyja sings over the car roof.

The two meet on the grass, wrapping their arms around each other.

"It's so good to see you," they both chime.

Freyja pulls back, grabbing Solrun's hands and they start laughing. Digging her heels into the grass, Freyja spins them around. Laughter fills the air as the men watch.

"Oh, how I've missed you," Freyja cries.

I can't stand it any longer and will my soul toward them and slip into their embrace. What an incredible sensation to feel their hearts beating on either side of mine.

"Supper will be ready in an hour," Solrun calls after the men, who are on their way to the barn to do the evening chores before dark.

Still holding hands, my sisters walk quickly to the house to escape the wind that is starting to feel cool.

I watch from the corner of the kitchen as they discuss pleasantries—

the flight, weather and the farm—as Solrun darts from the cupboard to the table and stove, preparing the meal. Now an awkwardness that shouldn't exist has developed between them. They are like two old friends trying to reconcile after a falling out, the reason long forgotten.

The men come into the kitchen, pull out the chairs and sit down just like old times.

Lars looks pleased with himself, that he has arranged this reunion.

"You will stay the night," Solrun says to Olafur. "Both the girls' rooms are empty."

"No reason for me to go home now," he says, a hint of sadness in his voice.

"Dibs on who has to share a room with him," Lars says. "I've done it before. He snores."

"I do not," Olafur says.

Freyja laughs.

Lars points a thumb at Olafur. "Whoever snores the loudest has to milk the cow in the morning."

"What? You've forgotten how to already?"

"Snore?"

"No, milk the cow!"

My heart sings to hear their banter. *Where is Leifur,* I wonder. He should be here for this.

When supper is done, Solrun and Freyja leave the men in the kitchen to discuss farming and, with coffee in hand, move to the living room.

"This is a lovely home," Freyja says.

"Lars tells me you live in a mansion."

"It's just a house." Freyja looks bright and happy. "I am fortunate," she says. She stops in front of the family portrait, examines it for a long time. "Wonderful to see this again. Did my hair always look like that?"

Solrun laughs. "Everybody said so."

Freyja resists the impulse to touch her curls. "Hair rollers, what a marvelous invention."

They sit on the couch and sip from their mugs. Freyja runs a well-manicured finger down the crease in her pants.

"I never intended to stay away so long," she says. "As soon as I realized running away was a mistake, I wrote a letter to Mama but she didn't reply. So I wrote another."

For a moment I'm back in those hot, summer days. Solrun is only seven-years-old when Freyja disappears. The days following were sad, confusing.

"When did you mail them?" says Solrun.

"I sent the first at the end of June. The second in early August, right after the war started."

"Were you with Bjarni?"

"I gave him the letters to mail," she says. "I only realized later that was a mistake."

Freyja takes a mouthful of coffee and swallows hard. "Remember, Finn invited Bjarni to the ball tournament? Well, he came on the steamer that afternoon. He saw my argument with Stefan and was very sympathetic. He convinced me to go with him back to Winnipeg."

"But Freyja, why?"

"I was embarrassed. Stefan had ended our relationship. Bensi saw me on the steamer, so I knew Pabbi would find out. I assumed that Stefan would be jealous and come looking for me."

Solrun is shocked. "Bensi didn't tell us."

"In late July I realized I was expecting Stefan's child and that Bjarni was in love with me," she said. "He must have thrown out the letters. I wrote two more that fall, one to Stefan and one to Mother, telling them everything and asking for forgiveness. I wanted to come home to have the baby. I mailed those letters myself."

Solrun shakes her head sadly. "Mama didn't receive a letter. I would have remembered that."

"Was Stefan carrying the mail then?" she says.

"Stefan would never have kept you from us," Solrun says.

"You don't know that for sure," Freyja says. "I believed he didn't want me or the baby so I never wrote again."

Freyja looks deep into her sister's eyes. "After the baby was born I was so sad I didn't go outside for months. It was the loneliest time of my life. I was glad to leave Winnipeg. British Columbia reminded Bjarni so much of Iceland, he said we should go there. Eventually I fell in love with him."

Solrun sighs. "If only you'd known how much you were missed," she says. And then hesitating, "Asta nearly found you, but Bjarni said that you had died . . . you would never purposely deceive us like that, would you?"

Freyja is adamant. "I had no idea until Lars told me."

They sit for a few moments, letting the details settle.

"Tell me about the day Thora found you," Solrun says.

Freyja tilts her head and her eyes go to the ceiling. "Fifteen years ago, right before Mama died, I was in a restaurant in Vancouver. Thora recognized me. She said I should call Asta and handed me the phone number. When I called a few days later, the connection was very poor but I recognized Mother's voice and I knew I needed to come home. I went straight to the hospital. Signy was so hostile, I caught the train home the next morning."

"I wished you'd waited for Asta," Solrun says. "You knew how hasty Signy could be."

Freyja looks away and closes her eyes. She takes a deep breath. "I wasn't ready to face any of you anyway, especially Asta. Thora told me all the pain I'd caused."

They sit quietly for a few moments. Solrun takes a sip from her mug. Freyja sets her cup down on the end table.

"Lars tells us you have a family," Solrun says.

"We had a son together, and when he was five, Bjarni died from an aneurysm. I live in White Rock now and have four daughters with my husband Sigmar."

"Did you know that Asta went to Winnipeg and hired a private investigator to find you?"

"Lars didn't mention that," she says, perplexed, then slowly nods. "Bjarni feared conscription so he changed his name after we moved. Finding us would have been impossible."

"It was. We told him to stop searching after Asta's accident," Solrun says. "She stepped right in front of a car and spent months in hospital."

Freyja closes her eyes. "How is she?"

"Asta lives at the care home now and may outlive us all."

"And Leifur?"

"The doctor says his heart is enlarged, his lungs are filling with fluid. He doesn't have much time."

CHAPTER FIFTY-THREE

It is an old custom for the wisest to give way.
—THE SAGA OF HARALD HARDRADA

THE NEXT MORNING AFTER BREAKFAST, WHILE THE MEN ARE DOING chores, Freyja takes an envelope from her purse and places it on the table.

"Olafur seems to be doing well," she says. "Optimistic as ever."

Solrun hands her a towel. They stand at the sink wiping dishes. "It is hard for him now that Signy is gone."

"What was it?"

"Cancer," Solrun says. "Just like Mama. She was sick for five years."

They stare out the window over the sink at the grass covered in morning frost.

"Signy told me I broke Pabbi's heart," Freyja says.

Solrun continues washing, placing plates in the drainer.

"Do you think Pabbi would have accepted the baby?" Freyja asks.

Solrun thinks for a moment. "Of course he would have. But you had no way of knowing it then. I understand why you were afraid."

"I always believed Stefan loved me. That he didn't write back . . . it changed the way I felt about everything."

When the dishes are done, they sit together at the table. Freyja's hands are trembling as she opens the envelope and pulls out the first photo.

Solrun takes it.

It isn't a snapshot of a little boy, but of a family standing in the driveway alongside a Buick. The man is smiling at the camera, a cigarette in the corner of his mouth. His wife is admiring him, while two adolescent girls squint into the sun. A boy about five-years-old stands on the trunk, one hand resting on his hip, the other on top of his father's head.

"Oh my goodness." Solrun laughs. "He looks so much like Leifur."

Freyja beams. "That is his name. He owns a fleet of trawlers and a fish packing plant along the coast." She admires the photo for a few moments after Solrun hands it back to her.

"Why did he keep you away from us?" Solrun asks, leaning forward. "How could you fall in love with someone who'd do that to you? Why didn't you come home after he died, or at least write?"

Freyja shrinks a bit in the chair. "I was angry and hurt. And ashamed, I suppose. I felt like an outcast so all I could do was put my family first and the past out of my mind."

She hands Solrun the next photo. "This is Ella. Of all the girls, she looks most like my husband."

"A handsome man."

The next is of a middle-aged couple surrounded by young adults and two babies. Freyja points to each of her children and grandchildren, stating their names and occupations. Then she hands Solrun the next photo. "This is Asta."

"Asta," Solrun repeats.

"I didn't name her right away. I waited to see if she had Amma's eyes."

This photo has been professionally taken, in a studio. It's the sort that would be enlarged and mounted on an office wall. The woman is wearing a dark gray suit jacket and the ruffle on her blouse delicately touches the bottom of her chin. She stares seriously into the camera, lips parted ever so slightly. She has deep blue eyes and thick eyebrows.

Even though my namesake isn't smiling, there is the trace of a dimple on her left cheek.

"Asta is a partner in my husband's firm. One of the first women to practice law in B.C. She is married, has two teenaged sons. Smart as a whip. Takes on all the firm's hard luck cases and wins most of them."

Solrun chuckles as she sets the photo off to the side. She gets up to put a pan of cinnamon buns in the oven. When she sits back down, Freyja hands her another photo.

"Solrun Elizabeth," she says proudly. "A little you. She and her husband have a fruit farm in the Okanagan Valley. Three sons, two daughters."

"If you were so angry with us—"

"Why did I name them after you? I didn't stop loving you all."

Freyja pulls out the last photo but holds it to her chest for a few moments, eyes sparkling with pride. "This is my baby, Bjorg."

This photo was taken in an art gallery. There are large windows in the background, paintings on the wall. Bjorg is standing in front of a pottery display. The room is filled with light and it shines on her smiling face. She has the same delicate features and white hair as her mother.

"Bjorg was a surprise," Freyja says. "I was forty-nine when she was born. Didn't think I'd get my little artist, but along she came."

Stefan's child is missing from the story and the photos but Solrun does not ask.

Leifur is already dressed and sitting on a chair in his room at the Lundi hospital. His elbows rest on the arms, knarled fingers entwine above his lap. He is freshly shaved and his hair is combed neatly in place. The years have stamped a permanent sadness on his face that pains me to see, but there is still fire in his eyes. He has exasperated the nurse by getting out of bed, but doesn't care. Sigrid is beside him reading aloud from *Lögberg-Heimskringla*.

"Hi, big brother, how are you?" Lars says as he steps in the room. "I brought someone to see you."

"Good," Leifur says. "I would be disappointed if it was only you."

His eyes are on the door. Freyja and Solrun are giggling out of sight.

I can hardly wait to see the look on his face.

But Olafur comes in next.

“Not you again,” Leifur says.

“What? And miss the family reunion? Not a chance.”

Sigrid folds the paper.

Solrun steps inside with a pan concealed behind her back.

“I smell cinnamon buns,” Leifur says.

She slowly reveals what she’s brought and pulls back the cloth. “Only if you’ve been good. I will have to ask the nurse first.”

“You’d better ask Sigrid instead,” he says, bringing a fist up to muffle the cough that erupts into a fit of slow, heavy barks. He shakes his head, disgusted with himself.

Solrun waits, pretending not to notice any of it. “What have you done to annoy her now?”

“Drum roll, please.” Olafur bangs his hands on the table top.

With that, Freyja steps in, eyes glistening.

“Come here you,” Leifur says softly, pushing himself up to his full height.

Freyja moves across the room in an instant, tears running loose now. She falls into his open arms. She closes her eyes.

And it seems as if time has stopped. The moment is so tender, so anticipated.

“Oh Leifur, it is so good to see you.”

“You too,” he whispers.

She releases her hold on him and backs up, wiping tears quickly away. “You always were the handsome one.”

“I wish everyone would stop reminding me,” Lars says.

“How do you think I feel?” Olafur chimes. “Even you are better looking than me.”

Everyone laughs.

“Who wants a cinnamon bun?”

Mother and Pabbi would be so happy to see them all right now.

Olafur clears his throat. “I only wish Signy were here. Don’t anyone be angry with her. She cried as hard as you all when Freyja disappeared. The only way she could stop herself was to get mad. She died regretting what she'd done."

"He is right," Solrun says softly. "Signy told me, too."

"Actually I am the one to blame for this reunion taking so long," Leifur says, slowly lowering himself into the chair, setting the napkin on the table beside him. "I wasn't thinking clearly. All those wet years, I feared we'd lose the farm, and the turmoil with Asta—to start looking for you again, well—"

"No," Freyja says. "This is my fault. I am so very sorry."

Silence washes into the room and Freyja whispers to Solrun, "These are delicious." She turns back to Leifur. "I hear you ran a successful fish buying company before you sold out."

"For about twenty years." Leifur is wheezing now. "I would have lost the farm without it."

"Where is Asta?" Freyja asks, licking her fingers. She finishes the last of the bun. "I was expecting her to be here."

I am thinking the same thing. *Where am I? Why aren't I with my family?*

Solrun turns her wrist to look at her watch. "She is in the care home," she says. "Let's you and I go see."

CHAPTER FIFTY-FOUR

The fire seems hottest to a burned man.
—GRETTIR'S SAGA

I WISH I COULD REACH OUT TO TOUCH THEM, BUT ALL I CAN DO IN this place between worlds is follow curiously as Solrun and Freyja leave the hospital wing, stopping briefly at the nurse's station.

"We are going to visit Asta," Solrun says to the nurse on duty. She pushes open the steel door that separates the hospital from the care home. She says in a low voice to Freyja, "The staff are very good to her."

They follow the hallway, passing rooms on both sides. All is quiet except for the click of their heels on the polished tile floor and the rumble of a voice at the end of the hall that becomes louder at they approach. Turning into the large common room, they pause at the entrance.

There are white-haired women and baldheaded men wearing robes crumpled in wheelchairs, staring into their laps around the tables. Others not as infirm watch attentively. A few visitors sit on leather chairs against the wall. They are all listening to me. I stand in the middle of the floor, holding my scrapbook, my reading glasses halfway down my nose. My voice is strong and heavy with emphasis.

Freyja inhales sharply. "She reads just like Amma."

The audience is listening raptly; many are nodding their heads. I am reading in English, then translating each paragraph seamlessly to

Icelandic.

" . . . dismantle the barge and get the lumber to a safe place. The following night brought on the worst weather I think anyone remembers up in that country. By about ten o'clock that night the wind became southwesterly with the heaviest driving rain that anyone remembered seeing and the wind velocity had reached 50 to 60 miles an hour. It raised the lake that night close to eight feet. This heavy wind and high rain kept up all night and the following day until about five o'clock."

"She is reading from Geirfinnur Peterson," Solrun whispers. "He wrote about the flood, remember? It was published in *Lögberg*."

My voice echoes across the room.

"When we awoke in the morning, I looked out across meadows and sloughs for two and a half miles. There wasn't a thing sticking out of the water anywhere, not even willow bushes, and the waves from the south lake ploughed inland as far north as we could see."

Solrun looks at Freyja who is biting her lip hard.

"We saw eight of our horses that had been on a high knoll about a quarter mile south. The water kept rising and one small pony started to get restless and then finally, when he could no longer reach bottom, he started swimming toward the bush and the others followed.

"By now there was more than two-and-a-half feet of water in the kitchen and one foot in the sleeping quarters. By the second night the wind began to subside and the following morning the rain had let up. We managed to row down to the Matthews place to see what had happened. The first thing we noticed was their big boat sitting in the garden. The weather had driven it over the beach and the willow bushes, past the big pile of flour and feed, past the house and into the garden. No one will ever know, except the people who lived along the lake, the terrible hardships imposed by flooding."

"Já, já." An old man sitting at the table croaks, banging his big fist on the table. It is Asi Frimann, the oldest resident at the home. "Now the government wants to build a diversion and send us water from the south. How will we manage during wet years then?"

The residents begin clapping in support of Asi.

He shakes his head in frustration. "Nobody understands. Not like we do."

I close the book. "Have you told the government?" I ask.

"They already know everything," Asi says, shaking his fist in frustration.

"Keep speaking until they listen," I say, patting the worn scrapbook. "The men and women in here would have made them understand."

Raspy cheers and a few names are mentioned. A voice calls out from the back of the room: "What we need, Asta, are more Icelanders in government."

The statement comes from an elderly gentleman I vaguely recognize. He is sitting alone along the wall with one leg casually crossed over the other.

"He visits her every day," Solrun whispers, "Do you remember him?"

Freyja cocks her head. "Finn?"

"I'll re-introduce you," she says.

Seeing their approach, the man stands up.

"Bjorn Magnusson," Freyja says.

"Freyja. My goodness, what a surprise. It is so nice to see you."

What am I witnessing? Travelling to the past has never been so confusing. Bjorn lives in Lundi? He visits me every day and I cannot remember? *How can I not recognize my Bjorn?*

I see myself in the distance, talking to Asi. My hand rests on his shoulder. Then I help him to his feet and, with an arm around his back, lead him to his room.

"After his wife passed away, Bjorn moved here from Swan River to be near Asta," Solrun explains to Freyja. "What has it been now, eight years?"

"Ten," Bjorn says, looking to the ceiling as he thinks back. "My son took over the store in . . . 1955."

Then Solrun asks if he will join them for supper that night and to bring me along. They want to tell me that Freyja has come home.

"He volunteers here," Solrun says. "Asta does not recognize him, she believes he is the handyman."

They stop to watch Freyja's reaction, until she begins to understand.

"She senses the bond between us, I can tell," he says slowly. "Sometimes I'm able to sneak a kiss, but she has told me nothing more can happen between us because she has promised herself to Bjorn Magnusson."

Freyja is stunned. "It can't be that bad." She looks between the two of them, but neither reacts.

"Anterograde Amnesia," Bjorn says. "Caused by a brain injury. She was hit by a car in Winnipeg—she was looking for you."

The meaning takes a few moments to sink in.

"Her recollections of the past are stellar, better than any of ours," Solrun says, "but she has difficulty remembering what happened yesterday."

"She recalls everything up until the accident," Bjorn adds. "We took her to the funeral, but she does not remember that Signy died. Every time we tell her, she grieves as if hearing of it for the first time."

"No—," Freyja says.

"So it is easier if her life remains in a state of suspension," Solrun says. "Stuck in 1950."

"You lie to her?"

"Sometimes."

"But she must remember you," she says to Bjorn.

He shakes his head.

"How is it possible? You were such an important part of her life."

Bjorn sighs. "The only explanation I can think of is that she didn't see me for over twenty years." He pats his rounded mid-section. "Age, I suppose . . . and I cut my hair."

"You do look very different," Freyja says.

"So do you."

CHAPTER FIFTY-FIVE

Many are wise after the event.
—FLJÓTSDÆLA SAGA

AMNESIA. MY LIFE HAS NEVER BEEN SO CLEAR.

I am dumbstruck. And thankful. So very thankful that the brain injury did not leave me a rambling fool. And to see the things I've done, conversations I had that I don't remember, is fascinating. There is no need to feel sadness that I cannot remember, only joy that both Bjorn and Freyja came back to me, that even though I lost my twilight years, they are worth remembering.

The snow begins falling lightly and I watch Bjorn and I leave the care home together. He has just introduced himself again, told me that Katherine has died and that he has moved to Lundi so we can be together. My step is lighter than it has been in years, I look thrilled. We hurry to the truck idling in the parking lot. Olafur is in the driver's seat.

"Where is Signy?" I ask, climbing in beside him.

"At home," he says. "She has the flu."

A look of uncertainty passes quickly across my face. Then: "You remember Bjorn?" I say cheerily. "He has moved to Lundi now that the boys are grown."

We ride in silence for a few bumpy miles, snowflakes melting on the windshield, whisked back by the beat of the wipers, the lights illuminating the snow-covered road ahead.

"Did Bjorn tell you that we have a visitor?" Olafur asks as we turn up the driveway.

A big dog stands under the yard light, barking.

"Yes, from B.C.," I say. "I shouldn't ruin Solrun's surprise, but I already know it's Thora. Who else could it be?"

Olafur parks the truck and we hurry through the swirling snow. We leave our coats in the porch and step into the kitchen. Everyone is relaxing in the living room. Solrun waves us in.

"I hope it is OK that we brought Bjorn," I say, cheeks flushed. "You all remember him? But I don't think you two have met." I step aside so Bjorn and Solrun's husband can shake hands. The men smile at each other and I blurt out, "Bjorn is the new handyman at the hospital."

"Is that so?" Solrun's husband twinkles.

"Well, it does makes sense," I say. "He did own a hardware store."

Everyone chuckles. They look at one another while Solrun fidgets. She points at the family portrait on the wall.

"Asta, do you remember when that photo was taken?"

"Of course. We were living in Lundi with Mama's cousin, not too far from here on the Mary Hill road. A notice was put up that a photographer was coming to town. Mama said we could not afford such an extravagance, but Pabbi insisted."

"Where was it taken?"

"At the school. Everything back then was done at the school or church," I say, pausing for a few moments to think. "We moved to Eikheimar and I cannot remember if a hall was built at Mary Hill by then."

I take a few steps closer to the photograph and my face softens.

"Nobody smiled in those days. Leifur was trying to figure out how the photographer would fit us all in the box. Signy was talking of course, see her mouth is open."

Olafur laughs, clapping his knee.

"I was told to keep Freyja still. What a job that was. And look at her hair. Amma tried putting the brush through it but she screamed so hard Amma gave up. She said: 'It will serve you right. When your children ask what you were like as I child, I will point to the photograph and say, look at her hair.'"

"Wilful," Solrun says.

"And stubborn." Olafur grins, eyes on the staircase leading to the upstairs bedrooms.

I reach out and gently wipe a whisper of dust from the frame.

"I thought that by now the private investigator would have found something," I say. "I let everyone down."

"Well, Asta," Solrun says, smoothing her skirt. "We have some very good news."

I turn from the photo to face her. "Is that why we are here?"

"Yes, and you will be very pleased," she says, pausing for a moment. "We found Freyja. Would you like to see her?"

I look stunned, apprehensive. "How can you be sure it is her?"

Solrun is beaming. "It was Thora who found her."

Footsteps cause me to look up at the ceiling and the staircase. I see feet and then legs coming down the stairs.

I am instantly confused, propelled into the brothel.

"It is not Freyja," I whisper as the woman comes around the corner. Her eyes are the same shocking blue and her hair is white, but this is an old woman. Anja?

How surprised and frightened she is.

"Anja," I say, quickly reverting to Icelandic. "Do you want to leave here?"

Anja is shocked speechless. Solrun quickly stands up.

I ignore her. "Anja," I say again. "Pretend you are my sister. Come here and hug me now."

Anja walks slowly across the floor. We embrace.

I whisper: "I will protect you from these men."

"Asta," Bjorn says, "This is Freyja."

I refuse to look at him. Linking arms with the woman, I lead her to the front door. Solrun tries to intercept us and I turn instead toward the kitchen. Solrun steps in front of us and blocks the doorway with her arms. "Asta," she says.

"Einar will not do to her what he did to me," I say through clenched teeth.

"Asta! It's me, Solrun."

My eyes move around the room, back to the sofa. "Olafur," I whisper. "What are you doing here?"

"And Bjorn," Solrun says. "Remember?"

I release the woman's arm and step back to stare at her long and hard, squinting as I search for something, anything, familiar.

"Thora?"

"No, it is me, Freyja."

"Freyja? You are home? But you look so old."

Freyja throws her head back in laughter. Then she takes both my hands. "My God, how I have missed you."

We both grin in disbelief to finally be together again. "Thora found you? How? Where in God's name have you been?"

I am sitting between Solrun and Freyja, smiling. Bjorn is talking with the men. I can hardly believe my good luck—both Freyja and Bjorn have come back to me.

Freyja is handing me photos, one by one. She is explaining who the people in them are. The names are confusing and these faces mean nothing.

That is not Leifur. Solrun does not have a son.

"Who are these people again?" I ask.

"My children."

"With Bjarni?"

She hesitates, seems unsure how to answer.

"Was Bjarni mean to you?" I ask.

Freyja's expression softens. "Not really."

"He is dead now?"

"Yes."

"Good."

"We always thought the grass in Siglunes was good, but now I know it is the best in the country," Lars says. "Seen it with my own eyes. Ranch land in B.C. may be pretty, but you have to cover a lot more ground with fewer animals than we do here."

"Do you ever regret selling Eikheimar?" Bjorn asks quietly.

"Of course he does," Olafur says.

Lars pauses. "Sometimes. I miss haying. It would have been impossible to retire if I didn't like the young man who bought the farm so much. How is Asi doing?"

"He just turned 91," Bjorn says. "He gets confused sometimes, but Asta is there to help him sort out his memories."

Everyone finds that amusing.

"I hear the government plans to divert water from the Assiniboine into our lake," Lars says. "Where are they building the channel?"

"Portage la Prairie," Bjorn says.

"That can't be good for the lake. It's not natural. Surely fishing will suffer."

"They have widened the outlet at Fairford, saying it will flow out as fast as it comes in."

Lars thinks for a moment. "What about the farms there? And all the Indians? They will be flooded out."

Olafur laughs. "They don't care about them any more than they care about us. All they want is to get rid of the water in Winnipeg."

"Sounds pretty shortsighted to me."

"Wait and see," Olafur says, "When the whole thing backfires, they'll find a way to blame us. Say we shouldn't have built along the lake in the first place."

Solrun goes to the kitchen to finish making supper. It is a special occasion so she has prepared a beef roast. Freyja starts setting the table.

"So you say the same thing every time?" Freyja whispers.

"It isn't easy." Solrun sighs, "She retains an inkling of some things, especially if repeated many times."

"She mentioned her house?"

"We were forced to sell it to pay the medical bills," says Solrun. "Once Asta was nursed back to health, she moved in with us, but she hated not being a nurse." She takes the roast from the oven. "Asta was so intent on returning to work. That's why we moved her to the care home. I think she understands she is retired now, but some days she believes she is still working."

"Who covers the cost?"

"She receives two small pensions and we take care of the rest."

"You do?" Freyja spreads the plates across the table.

"No, all of us."

Freyja counts out the cutlery and says that from now on she will pay all my living expenses.

"That's not necessary—"

"It most certainly is," she says. "You think I can't see this is all my fault?"

"Nobody thinks that."

"Well it is. Everything that went wrong . . ." She begins putting bowls of food on the table. "Since I cannot be here to help you with Asta, I can do at least that. My husband will make the arrangements."

The evening comes full circle as everyone takes a seat in the kitchen.

"Where is Signy?" I ask.

Solrun's husband slices the meat and Solrun passes around a bowl of potatoes. I take a bun then hand the plate to Freyja.

"She is sick so she stayed home," Olafur says, pouring gravy over his meat and potatoes.

"And Leifur? I thought he'd be here by now."

"He has the same flu. Doesn't want the rest of us to catch it." Solrun passes Bjorn the carrots.

I accept their explanations and my expression turns giddy as I rub shoulders with Freyja. What a joyous feeling it is to finally have her home.

After supper we enjoy coffee and chocolate cake.

"Did Lars tell you the news?" Freyja asks, looking at each one of us in turn. "He has written a novel and I'm going to help him get it published."

Lars blushes. I see how the room silently divides between the ones who have moved away and the ones who stayed.

"Isn't it a bit late to begin a new career?" Olafur asks.

"Not at all, he is a tremendous writer," Freyja says, "It really is too bad he wasted all those years on the farm."

Lars quickly tells us that he has no regrets.

"My early writing lacked depth," he says. "Age is a writer's friend. If you believe that a part of every writer is in his books, then Eikheimar will be on every page of mine."

Lars has written a book. That is wonderful news. I can see in his satisfied expression it means everything to him. Pabbi would be proud.

"If I have learned anything," I say, "it is to follow your heart."

The kitchen turns quiet as we think back on our lives.

"Don't let others make your decisions," Freyja says.

"Live and let live," Solrun says cheerfully.

"I should have gone first and stolen Asta's thought," Lars says. He is thinking hard. "My advice would have to be stop worrying, because things always work out in the end."

Everyone turns to Bjorn. He is sitting directly across from me, deep in thought. He watches my every move.

"I agree with Lars," he says. "And since I've been put on the spot, I'd have to say, do what is right. That way your conscience will always be clear."

There are smiles and satisfied nods in agreement.

"Olafur?" Solrun says.

"My turn? Well that's easy," he says. "Don't be hasty."

CHAPTER FIFTY-SIX

Kinsmen to kinsmen should be true.
—THE SAGA OF ÓLAF HARALDSSON

THE NEXT MORNING I AM DOZING ON A RECLINER IN MY ROOM when Solrun knocks quietly and pushes open the door.

"This is nice," Freyja whispers as they come inside.

There is a neatly made bed, a set of drawers, a small couch, little tables, and lamps. The space along the wall is filled with bookshelves, all the volumes neatly arranged, alphabetical, by author. Photographs of people are taped on the bathroom door.

I open my eyes and lift the blanket covering my lap over the armrest and rock back and forth. I close the footrest and hoist myself forward and up.

"You caught me napping." I rub my eyes and shake off the grogginess. "Night shift is harder than it used to be."

"Don't worry," Solrun says. "We won't tell anyone."

"Good. We all nap sometimes when we've done a double-shift."

Freyja watches me. Her unease is the one thing I do recognize, the look of apprehension that people try to hide as they wait to see if they are remembered.

"How are you today?" I ask cheerfully.

It is always a good start. Often if people are led in the right direction they are so anxious to avoid embarrassment, they give away clues to their identity.

Freyja says that she is fine, then waits, watching my expression.

"Are you having a good day?" I ask, smoothing out the front of my uniform. I hardly recognize myself. Uniforms have changed so much over the years.

"Wonderful," Freyja says.

"What are your plans for later?"

Freyja starts to say something but then abruptly stops.

"It was so nice to see everyone again," she says. "Solrun is such a good cook. She reminds me of Mama that way."

Now I look confused.

"Do you remember who this is?" Solrun asks.

"Of course," I say. "We have known each other our whole lives."

"Do you know her name?"

"Thora, my closest friend," I say, turning to her. "But you are thinner than I remember."

Freyja forces a smile.

Solrun takes a piece of paper from her purse and hands it to me along with a photo. "You can put it on the door with the others."

This is Freyja. You can stop searching for her. She is living happily in British Columbia and will come to visit you often.

I study the photo and the writing. It takes a few moments for the words to register.

"Freyja? You are home?" I look thrilled, confused, embarrassed.

"She came home yesterday," Solrun says. "We were all together."

Yesterday means nothing to this Asta. All her days are the same. I rush forward to hug her and cry with joy: "Where in God's name have you been?"

"I live in B.C. now," she says.

"Where is Bjarni?" I growl.

"He is dead."

"Good."

Similar scenarios continued for a week, varying slightly as I remembered snippets of information one day, forgot most of it the next.

"You are not leaving again?" I say.

We stand together in the common room. I glance over my shoulder at the residents starting to shuffle in.

"It is time for Freyja to go home," Solrun says.

"Back to Eikheimar?"

"No, to White Rock. She lives there now."

"Why?" I say, turning to Freyja. "You don't belong there."

"It has been a week," Freyja says cautiously. "I have to go home, my family is there."

"We are your family, your home is here with us."

"I can't."

"Why not? I spent my whole life looking for you."

Freyja turns away and brings her hands up to cover her face.

"Asta," Solrun says, "Freyja will come back."

"When?"

"Soon," she says. "And she will visit more often."

I start to cry. Sometimes they treat me like a child. Everyone makes decisions without me and that is frustrating.

"Now give me a hug," Freyja says, wiping her eyes.

"You will come back this time?"

"In a month," she says. She breaks the hold, gently.

I do not move, simply watch Freyja follow Solrun down the hallway out of sight.

"Hey, big brother." Freyja walks into Leifur's room, goes straight to the window to pull open the drapes. She turns the butterfly latch, pushing it open a sliver.

"You are a good woman," he says turning to face her. He is in bed with a sheet covering his naked legs. "It's too damn hot in here."

She takes his hand in hers and they talk for a while. Solrun is in the hallway, speaking with a nurse while her husband sits waiting in the car.

“Thanks for coming,” he says weakly.

“Of course.”

Everything has been hashed out, explained, debated and reckoned with, but Leifur never did confess to anyone else that it was he who lit the fire. Vengeance is wrong, we all knew that, but perhaps Leifur believed that a man reaps what he sows and that Bensi planted nothing but hostility between our families. He had already bankrupted Pabbi once. Only a fool would expect to get away with it twice.

“I was just a boy,” Leifur says. “You were just a girl. We both made mistakes and suffered because of them.”

Freyja cocks her head but doesn’t ask. “I’ll stay if you want me to,” she says.

Leifur shakes his head no. “One thing I need to know before you leave—”

Freyja is nodding slowly. “I have already decided. I need to be buried here. My husband was born and raised in Gimli and when the time comes, he wants his body flown home. He will understand.”

Leifur relaxes. “Lawyers,” he says. “They plan everything.”

Freyja throws her head back and with the laughter comes tears.

So strong. Leifur was always so strong.

“Well you’d better go.”

She bends down and kisses his forehead. “I love you, Leifur.”

He watches her turn, her face knotted in sadness, to sneak one final goodbye, then closes his eyes.

“Ready?” Solrun asks.

Freyja raises her finger, then hurries back down the hallway. She peeks in the common room where Bjorn and I are at the table playing chess. She watches us for a few moments, catches his eye and waves, then slips away.

Solrun and Freyja stand on the platform at the airport, her suitcase on the ground between them.

Solrun smiles softly. “Are you ready to tell me now?”

Freyja stares at nothing, lowering her eyes as if she’s just been caught in a lie.

“You remember how it was.” She bites her bottom lip. “Unmarried girls didn’t keep their babies. Men didn’t want to raise another man’s child. I have regretted it my whole life.”

“That was not Bjarni’s decision to make.”

“I know,” she says. “The hospital staff were not very sympathetic, either. I carried the baby to term. When I was in labor, the nurse convinced me it was the right thing to do. She knew of an Icelandic doctor in the city who arranged adoptions. She assured me the child would go to an Icelandic home.”

“A boy or girl?”

“I don’t know. They said it was for the best. All I remember is how the baby cried when they took it out of the room.”

“Oh Freyja.”

Freyja clenches her lips together. “It was not for the best,” she whispers, picking up her bag and backing away.

CHAPTER FIFTY-SEVEN

Good it is to end a stout life with a stout death.
—THE SAGA OF MAGNÚS BAREFOOT

FIFTEEN YEARS LATER
JUNE 17, 1980

"ASTA, YOU HAVE OPENED YOUR EYES," SOLRUN SAYS.

I know exactly how they must look, glassy and dark, with no remnant of the ego left to question or mislead. These bottomless pools she peers into, searching for some semblance of me, are now the space between this world and the next.

She leans in. "You are trying to tell us something, what is it?"

There is still an inkling of life left in me.

Solrun stares hard and listens close, watching my lips.

I want to tell them how to find Freyja's firstborn child, but the only sound that escapes is a tiny sigh.

"It is all right, dear sister," she whispers. "You can go now. Everyone is waiting for you."

She lovingly strokes my hair.

Another face comes into view and I recognize Freyja. The sister whose absence I mourned my entire life.

"It is time to go in peace," she whispers. "I am so sorry, Asta, so very sorry."

They begin to sing, high and sweet, the Icelandic hymns I loved so much as a child. Their voices fill the room.

Lars sings beside them, staring at his folded hands.

Now, I am ready to die.

The last breaths come.

Forty, then sixty, and finally ninety seconds apart, until . . .

No longer trapped within the confines of my faulty brain I see everything clearly and now I am looking down on the aged body that served me well for so many years. A light above the bed transforms the warm flesh tones to a rigid gray and the body left is shockingly inanimate and I no longer care what happens to it.

My sisters stand by the bed. Solrun. Freyja.

My brother Lars. He can see my spirit hovering. Amma's gift?

I want to tell my sisters to stop crying, to feel the message I am sending to their hearts, that I am elated to be on my way home.

Lars can feel it and nods in understanding.

Everything I came here to do is accomplished.

I must leave.

What lies waiting at the end of the light? So powerful. Its warmth pulls me out of the room towards the heavens. This is different than travelling to the past. Nothing grounds me, there is no pulling me back, not now.

Mama is the first to greet me. Pabbi next. Amma, Signy, Leifur, and all the rest. How I always remembered them, in their prime. Being together again fills me with unspeakable joy. There is so much love I can't even begin to describe it.

Pabbi's spirit speaks without words and I understand we will have much time together, but there is something I must do. He takes my hand and places it in another.

He is smiling, just like on that day we met. We are young again. It is time for us to go back to Siglunes. How light we feel. The air smells of coffee and kleinur. Though we shared much sadness on earth, we are elated, travelling like one soul back to the land where we feel the life in everything that grows.

Up the road to Eikheimar, dust swirling behind us. Life has changed here but it still feels like home. Amma's tree has thickened, grown taller. A man jumps down from the tractor and hurries to the house where his wife is baking buns for their son's wedding.

We travel to Vinðheimar, where all that is left are the remnants of a foundation where the majestic house once stood. It is called Skuli's Bay now, after J.K. and Gudrun's youngest son: the place where fishermen still set nets in November. A restless spirit is pacing along the water's edge and it is Finn.

Come with us.

Finn hesitates, but the moment he relents I feel his relief and he lets us pull him along, past Bensi's bush, along the shoreline.

I am anxious to see the castle. The mill is long gone and, as Asi predicted, the land is filled with grazing cattle. Inside, the house has been modernized. The little room where I once stayed is now filled with shelves and a filing cabinet. A heavy desk sits under the window.

One last look at the kitchen. Though the faces have changed, life here is much the same. A woman is making dinner for the men who are on the lake barging cattle to Ghost Island. She feels a cool draft when we pass and shudders.

Outside, the island appears. Stefan's spirit waits where the lighthouse once stood and I implore him to come with us, but he refuses. He is waiting for Freyja, for the chance to explain.

It is November, 1914. Stefan is mushing his dogs toward us across the ice, not far from shore. He is smiling, heart pounding with love and happiness. He has already read his letter from Freyja and has Mother's in the satchel. He can hardly wait to tell everyone the news about Freyja and his unborn child.

Tomorrow he will find a way to bring her home.

But then the heavy sleigh breaks through the ice and it drops like a stone, dragging the string of dogs backwards into the water. He must fight his way to the surface, but the dogs are desperate and he can only hold his breath for so long.

Stefan surrenders, his body floating gently to the lake bottom, and is taken with the current. The satchel slips off his shoulder and all that is left now are memories; and a few rusted buckles buried in the silt off Ghost island.

ACKNOWLEDGEMENTS

I OWE A DEBT TO MY PASSIONATE EARLY READERS: DAWN MACFARlane, Mickey Reid, Dianne Johnson, Dayna Emilson and the late Claire De'Athe who each pointed out flaws in the early story and offered encouragement. Special gratitude to Ólöf Baldwinson-Hardy and Debra Walger who met with me more than once, read the manuscript twice and offered many valuable insights and gentle suggestions.

To the pros: Jóhanna Gunnlaugsdóttir for her advice on Icelandic word usage and spelling; to Sabrina Parys and Editor Michael Kenyon whose fine hand and keen eye cleaned up my mess. W.D. Valgardson for jumping in early to write a review and to Lisa Friesen, designer extraordinaire, for presenting this book in such beautiful form to the world.

The story I tell in these pages—though a work of fiction—was inspired by real events experienced over the years by the early settlers at Siglunes. I want to thank Baldrun Paetkau for a most precious gift: the idea for my story. Gratitude to Lorna Tergesen, Nelson Gerrard, and W. John Johnson, who assisted in my research. Posthumous thanks go to Oli Johnson who wrote extensively about early life along the lake in *Taming the Wilderness*; and to the late Geirfinnur Peterson whose text, *The History of the Icelandic Settlements at the Narrows, Manitoba,* published in *Lögberg-Heimskringla - 1969-70*, gave me insight into life in those early days. Thank you to his descendants for granting me permission to re-print a portion of his writing in this book.

Gratitude to Scott Forbes for his continued efforts toward raising awareness about the hardships imposed on the farmers, fishermen and cottage owners along Lake Manitoba and for graciously reading the manuscript and agreeing to write an essay on flooding printed in the end pages of the book.

I am forever thankful to friends and readers who haven't lost faith in me during this inexcusable dry spell. Friends and readers are a blessing, names too numerous to mention—but you all know who you are. Your unwavering support reminds me of Amma's oak.

Warm thanks to the wonderful tribe that is my family—Snivelys, Unraus and Emilsons—all those related by blood, marriage or circumstance who have offered unfailing support and encouragement over the years.

And finally to my husband, Harold Unrau, a man who doesn't mind eating nachos or hot wings in front of the television while I fight my way through one final scene before calling it a night.

Love to you all.

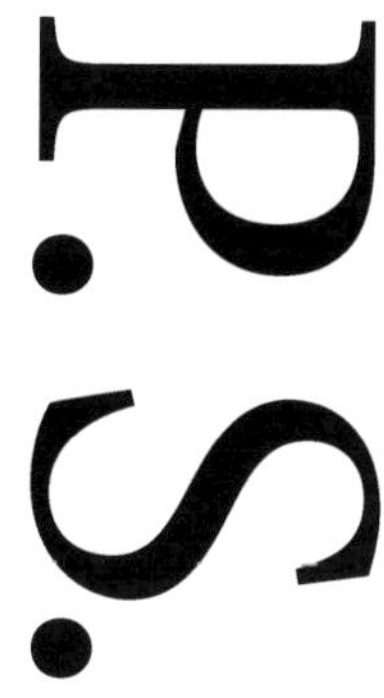

Insights,
Interviews,
and more...

ABOUT THE AUTHOR

ABOUT THE BOOK

ABOUT THE AUTHOR

Meet Karen Emilson

Karen Emilson was born and raised in southern Ontario, the daughter of Irish immigrants on her mother's side; and an eclectic mix of Swiss, German and English on her father's side. She spent all her free time as a child reading books and writing stories, dreaming of one day becoming a writer.

In 1982 she came to Manitoba as a young bride, settling at the Nordheim farm in Siglunes. Karen spent little time in the hayfield or on the lake, but instead worked as a rural newspaper reporter and wrote feature articles. Inspired by David and Dennis Pischke's story, she wrote and published the Canadian bestsellers, *Where Children Run,* in 1996 and its sequel *When Memories Remain* in 2001. For years after that she worked for the Manitoba Beef Producers Association, typeset the Icelandic Connection Magazine, and spent time as a consultant with Lögberg-Heimskringla.

When Lake Manitoba overflowed its banks in 2011—flooding out the farmland at Siglunes—she was inspired to finish a story started 10 years earlier about the immigrants who carved out a living there. *Be Still the Water* is her first novel.

Now she lives in Grunthal, Manitoba with her husband, Harold Unrau, and little dog, Scooter. She writes full time.

You can find her online at:
www.karenemilsonwrites.com
www.facebook/karenemilsonwrites/

Q & A with the author

It states in 'About the Author' that you started this book 15 years ago. What prompted the story idea and why did it take so long to write?

I always knew that someday I would write about Lake Manitoba and the immigrants who settled there. One day we had a visitor from B.C. who grew up in the area. She asked if we'd take her to visit an old grave site. Her mother lost four younger siblings during the Diphtheria outbreak in 1905 and had spoke often of the heartbreak. Standing out on the natural prairie looking at the stone memorial erected under an oak, facing the water and seeing those four young names, stirred something in me. I started visiting old grave yards after that, wondering about the immigrants who were buried there.

I sat down and wrote a 5,000 word outline but set it aside to finish the sequel to my first book. I'd also been working on my first fiction attempt, an epic tale that quite frankly, I was ill equipped to write. I must have written a million words, then finally set it aside. I wrote a non-fiction book about the Canadian cattle industry and when I was done that, started another novel, this one set in rural Saskatchewan, inspired during the time I spent at the Wallace Stegner House in Eastend.

By 2011, I was no longer living at Siglunes but I witnessed the devastation of the flood via my computer. Seeing that beautiful land completely submerged, neighbors, loved ones and friends fighting to save their homes and scrambling to relocate their cattle was heart-wrenching. On June 11th I finished reading a friend's Facebook post and instead of going back to the third draft of my Saskatchewan story, I opened the outline from 2001 and started writing.

We understand the story is based loosely on real events. Can you tell us which events in the book actually occurred and what is fiction?

In the initial draft I tried to honour the actual dates of events, but then the question arose: how close to the truth do I keep? I did not want to cause confusion and appear to be re-writing history, so I scrapped the original and started over, adhering only to major historical dates.

I wanted to give a broader audience to some of the hardships experienced by those early settlers, so I worked in the story of a young man who shot off his arm and was saved quite heroically, only to drown later; and how two of the mill owner's sons drowned.

I changed the date of the Diphtheria outbreak and the first high water event to suit the time line of my story (the real events were in 1905 and 1902 respectively).

The Siglunes School *was* built in 1907, but the Post Office was already there in 1900. The mill which employed many new settlers burned in 1912. The 'Castle on the Lake' did exist—I was in it a few times during the 1980s—but I can't remember what details are correct and which are products of my imagination. The magnificent home, owned by Jim and Lucille Freeman, burned in November 1991.

The Siglunes ball team was formed in 1913 but didn't play competitively until 1916. The team continued to be a force well into the 1990s and was inducted into the Manitoba Baseball Hall of Fame in 2005.

Siglunes is a real community and men from there did participate in the formation of the municipality that now bears its name.

The exact meaning of 'Siglunes' eludes me, though. I've seen a few translations in print, settling on the interpretation written on the Manitoba Historical Society website. Ghost Island does exist but I was never able to pinpoint its location on the map. The island you can see from shore at the former mill site is named Ducharme.

The Lake Manitoba Narrows had a store owned by Helgi Einarsson, who moved to Fairford in 1911. I apologize to his descendants for portraying Helgi in such a hard-nosed way. I am sure the real Helgi was a far more understanding man.

Other historical figures, Margrét Benedictsson and Tómas Jónsson I kept true as possible. Lundi is the fictional town of Eriksdale and Lundar combined. Eriksdale has a hospital and care home while Lundar hosts a lovely agricultural Fair every June.

As for the characters, they are all fictional. The only characters who closely resemble real people would be Dr. Steen and J.K. Kristjansson. I needed to create an optimistic, successful, community leader. In the late 1800s, there was such a man who settled along the Siglunes bay and his name was Jónas Kristján Jónasson. I never met the real J.K., but people spoke very highly of him. Some may see a resemblance but the dramas that unfold in my character's lives are products of my imagination.

What part of writing this novel did you find most challenging?

Deciding on the character names, and whether or not to include the accents and Icelandic letters. I will start with the names.

Since I knew I'd be writing for a largely non-Icelandic audience, I wanted to choose names that were fairly easy to read, and ones that people may have heard before. Shortening 'Astfridur' and 'Asmundur' was easy. Using the initials 'J.K.,' gave his character a bit of distinction from the others. With a cast of so many, I chose to not name them all, including Bensi's wife. And Einar was not given a surname.

In Icelandic communities, there are/were numerous people with the same first name, surname or both. *Be Still the Water* is not authentic in the sense that only a few names are repeated. Also, I did the unthinkable—there is only one Jon in the story.

The fact that all Icelandic couples when they immigrated did not have the same surname posed a bit of a problem as the way Icelanders name their children is not easily explained in a novel (see the explanation at the beginning of the book). I decided to refer to the families by the husband's last name.

To complicate matters, Pjetur's surname would have been Solmundsson, since Soli was his father. I wanted to keep the relationship between Pjetur and Bensi a secret, so sharing the same last name would have sent up a red flag. I decided to have Freda—the independent woman that she was—change Pjetur's name to Gudmundsson to hide the fact Soli was his father. Not too far a stretch since Amma did pretty much whatever she wanted.

The accents and a Icelandic characters posed a challenge since most names had them. I worried that adding the accents to my character names would make the text too heavy, especially during dialogue—so I adopted the 1980s spelling to the whole story.

Written correspondence had to be considered since letters to and from Asta would have been in Icelandic. I decided to add the accents and characters to names in the letters for that reason.

What is next? You mention that you've shelved a few manuscripts, is there any chance you'll be working on one of those for publication soon?

Part of the reason it took five years to write this book is that all the while I've been outlining ideas for future novels. I won't promise what is coming out next—because that would be tempting fate—but I will say it won't take me long to publish again. I'm also in discussions with someone about writing another true story—something I thought I'd never do.

I have the first draft of another novel finished. It is set in 1980, in Lundi so you'll be seeing a few of these characters again. In the final chapter Asta says she knows how to find Freyja's first born child. Well, unbeknownst to her, she had already set the wheels in motion months earlier.

I've concluded that I like writing a two-book series. So that's what you can expect from my fiction in the future.

Essay by Scott Forbes

"Trees do not grow on wet land," Asi Frimann said: "Find yourself a hundred-year-old oak to build beside and you will never be flooded out."

These are wise words for Lake Manitobans. Floods on this lake define the landscape.

The berm that rings Lake Manitoba today is the residue of a flood that occurred seven decades ago. High waters pushed sand and gravel to the lake margins, creating a new shoreline. Between 1954 and 1957 the lake rose more than four feet above its average level, flooding, farms, pastures, ranches and homes along the lake, and killing the riparian forest.

Natural floods on Lake Manitoba are slow moving events, resulting from a series of wet years that cause the lake directly upstream—Lake Winnipegosis—to rise. Lake Winnipegosis feeds the Waterhen River that in turn feeds Lake Manitoba. The Waterhen is the primary natural inflow for Lake Manitoba.

The flood of the 1950s was due to high Waterhen flows. By June of 1855, the lake had reached over 816 feet, its highest level since 1882. It was a level that would not be seen again until 2011.

In 1882 something quite extraordinary happened. A connection that had not existed for 3,000 years was re-established.

Manitoba's great lakes, including Lake Manitoba, are remnants of glacial Lake Agassiz. When the glaciers retreated the Assiniboine River flowed directly into Lake Manitoba. That changed about

3,000 years ago when the Assiniboine channel shifted, draining eastward toward its confluence with the Red River.

In the flood of 1882 the Assiniboine overflowed its banks. Floodwaters made their way north through the old channels of the Assiniboine to Lake Manitoba causing the. Lake to rise to 818 feet above sea level, about six feet above normal and its highest ever recorded level.

In 1922 and 1923, the Assiniboine overflowed again and flood water again made its way to Lake Manitoba. But by 1936 this path was closed. Human constructed dikes prevented Assiniboine floodwaters from reaching Lake Manitoba. This was not the first human alteration to natural water flows to and from Lake Manitoba nor was it the last.

Upstream drainage of wetlands by farmers in the upper Assiniboine basin had begun. Natural wetlands hold back snowmelt and reduce the rate of run-off. Without the natural wetlands, water leaves the landscape quicker and downstream flooding becomes more likely.

In the aftermath of the great Winnipeg flood of 1950, engineers and hydrologists began planning a system of flood protection for the city. From a flood management perspective the location of Winnipeg, at the confluence of two large rivers, is unfortunate. It sits on not one floodplain but two.

Two elements of Winnipeg's flood protection system are attached to Lake Manitoba. Following the flood on Lake Manitoba in the 1950's, the Fairford Water Control structure was built. It deepened the outlet to Lake Manitoba and allowed for more outflow. It was built as part of a larger plan that included the construction of a channel at Portage la Prairie. What is now known as the Portage Diversion re-establishes the connection between the Assiniboine River and Lake Manitoba. During Assiniboine floods, some or all of its flow can be diverted north to Lake Manitoba. This protects Winnipeg and others living on the Assiniboine floodplain.

Hydrologists at the time calculated that the expanded Fairford Water Control Structure could handle the extra inflow from the Portage Diversion on Lake Manitoba. But solving one problem often creates another somewhere else. Such is the case with the Portage Diversion.

The engineers of the 1950s and 1960s did not foresee the long-term changes in hydrology that were to come. The Portage Diversion opened in 1970 and for the next two decades, worked as planned. It opened infrequently, only when Assiniboine River flows were high. This was a relatively dry period and the extra inflow to Lake Manitoba had little effect on its levels. The extra water was drained through the expanded Fairford Water Control Structure.

But in the early 1990s all that began to change.

Spring flows on the Assiniboine began rising, in part due to long-term climate changes. It was also in part due to upstream drainage of wetlands, causing more rapid rises in river levels and higher peak flows.

Since the early 1990s the Portage Diversion has opened in most years, for longer periods, and at higher flows. The wet cycle that started in the 1990s affected not just the Assiniboine but the Waterhen River as well. Beginning in 2006, flow on the Waterhen River rose to above average levels and remained above average for the next decade. This raised the level of Lake Manitoba.

By the fall of 2010, Lake Manitoba had reached its highest level since the Fairford Water Control Structure opened in 1961. And events upstream in the Assiniboine basin were about to take a bad turn. Heavy fall rain left rivers, lakes and reservoirs overflowing, and soil moisture high. Heavy winter snowfall made matters worse.

The stage was now set.

The coup de grace came in the form of heavy spring rains in southern Manitoba and eastern Saskatchewan. Flows on the Assiniboine and Waterhen Rivers reached record levels. Assiniboine flows were ten times normal and the Portage Diversion opened in early April to protect people on the floodplain downstream. At that point the lake level of Lake Manitoba rose dramatically.

What took nearly three years in the 1950s, a rise in lake level of about 4.5 feet, took just three months in 2011. That couldn't have happened without the artificial inflow from the Portage Diversion.

On the 31st of May 2011 a party at The Forks in Winnipeg celebrated the return of the Winnipeg Jets to the city. At exactly the same time, 100 km to the northwest, people on Lake Manitoba were running for their lives.

The lake was already well above flood level when strong winds -- averaging more than 70 kph—made matters much, much worse. The lake rose five feet along its eastern shore in just a few hours, blocking exit routes for some who had not yet escaped. Quick action by municipal officials completed the evacuation of those stranded. People were rescued by boat, helicopter, and in one case, carried out in the bucket of a front-end loader over the surging floodwaters.

Remarkably, no one perished during this inland tsunami.

No one was really prepared for these events. Flood defenses consisted of sandbag dikes that work for river floods. But on Lake Manitoba these melted away in the driving wind and rising waters.

When people re-entered the flood zone two weeks later, they were greeted with damage unprecedented in Manitoba's history. It looked as though a tornado had travelled along the lakeshore destroying everything in its path. Homes and cottages were flattened; the land underneath was scraped clean; seawalls collapsed into the lake. Giant cottonwoods had toppled into the water.

It was the most expensive flood disaster in Manitoba's history. As bad as it was on Lake Manitoba, it was as bad or worse downstream on Lake St. Martin. Lake St. Martin is fed by the Fairford River which has risen during the flood on Lake Manitoba. Whole communities were evacuated in May 2011. The Lake St. Martin First Nation, nearly 2000 people, has yet to return home in the summer of 2016.

For the First Nations on Lake St. Martin and downstream on the Dauphin River, their troubles began not in 2011 but in 1961 with the opening of the Fairford Water Control Structure. Flooding became much more common and the problem grew worse after the Portage Diversion opened in 1970.

Engineers have now drawn plans for new outlets from Lake Manitoba and Lake St. Martin to prevent future floods. The cost is steep with a price tag of a half billion dollars. The First Nations who were not consulted when the Fairford Water Control Structure and Portage Diversion were built are wary of new channels that will run through the heart of their traditional lands.

If built and operated correctly, the proposed flood control structures could avert future flooding on both Lake St. Martin and Lake Manitoba. But they would also create new problems, disrupting fish, wildlife and lands important to local people.

What is the long-term solution? There is no simple answer. The landscape has been forever altered by human activity. In the short term new water control structures will help. In the longer term, restoration of wetlands upstream holds the most promise, reducing Assiniboine River floods and the need to open the Portage Diversion.

The wild card is our changing climate. Forecasts for the middle of the 21st century are for increased spring run-off in the Assiniboine basin, increasing the risk of flooding. If this comes to pass, we may need to change the rule of thumb for choosing where to build on Lake Manitoba.

Find a 300 year old oak and build beside that.

Scott Forbes is an ecologist and Professor of Biology at the University of Winnipeg where he has been since 1992. He has owned property on Lake Manitoba since 2000.

Reading Group Guide

1. In the opening chapter Stefan saves Freyja's life but he was forced to push her away to do so. How does this foreshadowing play out later in the book?

2. Finn said in the first chapter that he didn't believe in legends and yet near the end he pulled an eagle feather from his pocket. What do you suppose influenced his decision to take the feather with him to Winnipeg?

3. Early on Asta says: "If it wasn't for boys, girls would seldom get themselves into trouble." How true is this statement in the story?

4. Amma and Bergthora were strong, independent women. How did each influence Asta's life?

5. Do you think that Pjetur, Leifur and Asta believed that Bensi was responsible for Freyja's disappearance or do you think that in their grief he simply became a target? How many of you hoped, like Signy, that Freyja ran away?

6. Bensi's early actions toward Pjetur resulted in eventual ruin for him. Which decision sealed his fate with the family?

7. Who did you think Asta would marry—Bjorn or Finn? Or do you believe Asta was destined to never marry and devote her life to her profession?

8. *Be Still the Water* is a story about promises kept and broken. Who kept their promises and who didn't? Were these conscious decisions or were most of the disappointments in the novel a result of fate?

9. Bjorn, Leifur and Finn made choices that ultimately ended in death. Each man believed he was being punished. How do you as a reader feel about each of them?

10. Setta was an important character in the story. What parallels did you draw between her life and Asta's?

11. Before his death, Magnus reflects on his life along the lake. How did his experiences relate to the book's title?

12. What are your thoughts on Signy's reaction toward Freyja when she came home for that brief visit. She said to Leifur: "If Freyja wanted us to know her whereabouts, she could have easily told us. Or written." Should she be blamed for Asta's accident?

13. Thinking back on Amma's premonitions, how many came true?

14. In the end, when Freyja comes home, Solrun and Lars forgive her despite the fact she stayed away so long. Why do you suppose that is?

15. If Freyja had married Stefan, do you think she would have been content?

16. *Be Still the Water* takes place in rural Canada during the early 1900s. In what way is this setting important to how the story unfolds? How might the story be different if it had happened fifty years later?

Made in the USA
Middletown, DE
08 December 2019

80224244R00328